How to Seduce a Spy

Potions and Passions
Book 1

CATHERINE STEIN

ISBN: 978-1-949862-00-3

Book cover and interior design by E. McAuley:
www.impluviumstudios.com

To Daniel, who one day when I was babbling about the story in my head said, "You should write it down." So I did.

Prologue

Paris, France
January, 1880

*T*WO MEN HAD PROPOSITIONED ELLE on her way into the music hall, and it hadn't even opened yet. Was this to be her new life? Dodging groping hands and enduring lecherous stares? The indignities suffered as a shop girl would be a nightly ritual at the Folies Bergère.

She pushed the negative thought away. The pay was better here. That was all that mattered. The extra coin would put more food on the table, and would pay a nurse to visit Aunt Madeline every other week.

Elle fingered the loose bit of lace along her neckline, evidence of her poor mending skills. Aunt Madeline would have made the repairs, once, but her rheumatism had grown worse and delicate movements pained her once-nimble hands. She made sparing use of the potion Elle had created to ease her aunt's symptoms. They both knew they couldn't afford more serum if Elle's cherished supply ran out.

Elle followed her guide through the empty theater, her eyes drinking in the sights, learning this place where she would now spend most of her waking hours. The light of the potion-fueled chandeliers glinted in the polished mirrors and the gilded walls sparkled, screaming of decadence in eerie silence. Half an hour more and patrons would flood in, filling the seats, roaming the halls, eager for entertainment, drink, and potions to take their minds off life outside the walls.

"This is where you'll be." Marie, the petite barmaid assigned to mentor Elle on her new position, waved a hand at a marble-topped counter. "You performed so well at your interview that you've been assigned to a high-traffic area. Keep the pretty bottles and a few ingredients on display, but anything valuable stays under the bar. If you come around back, you can see the drawer where the serum jars are stored. Keep it locked unless you are standing here. One girl had a bottle stolen, and not only did she lose her job, but she had to pay to replace the serum."

"I won't lose anything," Elle promised, speaking as much to herself as to Marie. This job meant too much. It was the first step up. Maybe the last step she would ever take, but enough to fuel the hope that had never died inside her. The hope of enough coins to begin saving. The dream of security and independence.

A bit of the lace snapped off in her hands. Work would calm this unease in her fingers. With the tools and ingredients of her trade at her fingertips, her new situation would transform into something familiar. While she mixed she could take her mind off the rude customers and low pay and focus on the craft she loved. Keeping busy would keep her sane.

"Are you removing that trim from your dress?" Marie asked. "Good idea. It will display your figure better. Lean over the counter while you work to give the men a good look. They buy more when they are distracted."

Elle glanced down at her dress. She loved the style and thought the low, square neckline flattered her. She wore it for herself, though, not to lure men.

"I wish I had your shape," Marie continued. "You are small, but round in all the right places, while I am tiny everywhere."

"You are lovely. I'm certain you catch the eye of many men."

Marie shrugged. "I try. But beware the upper-class men. These Italian *contes* and English earls come to spend their money and fall in love with pretty French girls. They will shower you with gifts and declare their undying affection."

The passion in her voice caused Elle's brow to furrow. "Does this happen often?"

"Only once to me. He did love me, I believe, but not enough. The world is not kind to those who move outside their own social sphere. His family, his friends, his job all pulled him away from me, as mine pulled me from him. I warn all the girls. I wouldn't give up Luc for the world, but he is forever without a father, and our life is hard."

Elle recognized the grim look in Marie's blue eyes. One of wisdom beyond her years, forged from pain and adversity. The expression of a woman getting by with what little she had. Elle dared a glimpse in the mirror behind the bar. Were her own struggles reflected there in her light brown eyes?

"You needn't worry about me," she said. "I can't spare time in my life for romance."

"Good. Don't forget. My other warning is to protect yourself when coming and going. The drunks can be belligerent, and there are men who prey on working girls. I take this when I walk at night." Marie withdrew a small pistol from her skirts.

A childhood memory shuddered through Elle's mind—blood running between the cobblestones, screams echoing through the street, the sightless eyes staring up at her, a six-year-old girl who had borne witness to murder. Elle recoiled in terror.

Marie quickly hid the gun in her clothing. "I am sorry, *chérie*. I didn't mean to frighten you."

Elle steadied herself with a deep breath, willing the memory away. "Don't blame yourself. It's an old childhood fear.

I will never use firearms as you do, but I have other defenses. I will not walk unprotected."

She knew recipes for defensive potions. Making them would require several precious drops from her dwindling serum supply, but her life and safety were worth the price.

Marie smiled. "I like you. You are smart and capable. You will do well here."

"I like you too. Thank you for your advice and your kindness. My work will be less arduous with a friend nearby."

"I'm glad. I will be just over there if you have any questions, and I will bring you a list of the most requested potions. It's good to have a few on hand when the customers first arrive."

"Thank you." Elle took up her place behind the counter, running her hand over the smooth marble. "Someday this will be my counter," she whispered. "My shop."

Marie stopped in her tracks and spun around. "You hold on to that dream, Elle Deschamps. Hold it tight. For all of us."

"I will," Elle vowed.

I

A Peculiar Proposition

April, 1882

"$\mathcal{A}$ND MAKE IT LAST all night long." The customer leered.

"*Oui, monsieur.*"

Elle's fingers flew from one ingredient to the next, tossing and mixing by feel the potion she'd made hundreds of times before. She could do it with her eyes closed, but looking at her work was the best way to hide the flashes of anger certain patrons provoked.

"Last bitch who made it did a shit job. They tell me you're the best. It had better work, or I'll see you out on the street."

Her eyes rose to meet his as she offered the glass.

"My potions never fail."

The man chuckled and slapped a coin down on the bar. "A brash assertion, missy. I like you. Maybe I'll stop by later." His eyes roved across her décolletage. "Test it out." He turned away, still laughing at his own boorish comments.

Elle stashed the coin with the others and wiped down the bar. Chances were, he would forget all about her. The follies house offered a multitude of diversions for his sort. If not, well, she had ways of dealing with unwanted advances.

A tall, middle-aged gentleman approached, taking advantage of the rare lull to peruse the selection of beer and wine. His graying hair and moustache were neatly trimmed, and his clothing had been selected with an eye for both fashion and durability. He was a man who smiled often, judging by the wrinkles at the sides of his mouth and corners of his eyes. Elle's preferred sort of customer. Wealthy. Confident. Not to be rushed.

The gentleman picked up a bottle and made a pretense of examining the label. Elle watched his eyes sweep past her, using the mirror behind the bar to survey the room. Curious.

A lady stood a short distance past the end of the bar, the only other customer in earshot. She wore a pale, floral-patterned dress and a wide-brimmed hat that shadowed most of her face. The man waited until she had moved on before turning his gaze on Elle.

"Good evening." He spoke with a distinct British accent.

Elle gave a nod and forced a polite smile. "Good evening to you, monsieur. How may I help you?"

"You mix potions, I understand?"

"Oui, monsieur."

"And you are known here as the most skilled in this area?"

"So they say."

"You are too modest, Miss Deschamps. Your reputation has preceded you."

Elle stiffened. He knew her name. Who was this man, and what did he want from her? She had created specialized potions in the past, but those requests had come through her supervisor and the work had been done in a back room. Try as she might, she could think of no other reason to single her out.

The pause had grown awkward. "You are very kind," she replied. "Please, let me mix you something. Is there a particular potion that interests you?"

"I do not require a potion at this moment. I have a request of a different sort for you this evening."

A line she had heard all too often. Her cheeks burned with indignation. "I apologize, monsieur. I don't provide the nighttime services some other ladies may. You will need to take your proposition elsewhere."

Elle found no fault with the women who chose such a career, but she would sooner scrub floors or shovel shit than take up such an offer. Her body was hers and hers alone, and her favors were not for sale.

His smile dissolved into a frown. "You mistake me, *mademoiselle*. I am not in search of a paramour for the night. I have need of a partner in a very important venture—a partner with an affinity for the magical arts. I have been led to believe you have the qualities I seek. Would you be so good as to discuss the matter with me?"

A surge of hope stronger than any she'd felt in months welled inside her. A new job? Perhaps one that paid well enough to begin saving toward her dream shop?

Ne sois pas idiot, she chided herself.

Strange men with job offers didn't simply appear at random, and too often villains looked harmless. She couldn't afford to let fantasies of a better life tempt her into a foolish decision.

"I'm sorry, but I cannot leave my job, either tonight or on another day. I'm certain your proposal is a worthwhile one, but I don't believe I am a suitable choice for an assistant."

He pursed his lips. "I understand your desire to remain steadily employed and financially solvent. You will, of course, be compensated for any work you undertake." He glanced over his shoulder at the growing line of customers behind him and lowered his voice. "May I seek you out later this evening when your work is complete? I promise I will take up no more than five minutes of your time."

Her inquisitive nature got the better of her. "You may. I'm afraid, however, that I don't finish here until two o'clock."

He withdrew a gold pocket watch and flipped open the cover. "It is quarter past eleven now. I will meet you at the door just shy of three hours from now. Thank you, mademoiselle."

He replaced the watch, gave a polite nod, and hurried off, leaving Elle to the crowd of eager potion seekers. She had three hours to speculate and imagine herself in a new situation before reality would inevitably cause her to decline his offer. She would make the most of the fantasy.

Shortly after two, Elle stepped through the back door of the follies house, eager to learn if the mysterious gentleman was a man of his word. He had seemed anxious to acquire her help, though it puzzled her why he had such need of the services of a barmaid.

Squinting in the flickering light of the gas lamps, she spied him several yards down the alley, gazing at his pocket watch. Elle hung by the door, waiting for the other employees to be on their way. Marie lingered, casting a questioning glance at her friend. Elle waved her on, but she ignored the gesture and paused to talk.

"You are waiting for something." Marie scooted closer, excitement sparking in her eyes. "Have you taken my advice? Have you found yourself a lover? He is the man I recommended, no?"

Elle shook her head, a smile touching her lips. "I told you, he smells of fish and doesn't interest me."

"Doesn't interest you? How is that possible? He has very fine… assets."

"That may be, but the man cannot hold two minutes' conversation on any topic of significance."

"*Chérie*, you will not be conversing with him."

Elle answered with a stern look.

"You are so picky." Marie sighed. "I don't like to see you lonely."

"It's impossible to be lonely with a friend as attentive as you are. I will tell you all tomorrow."

"Very well." Marie gave Elle a peck on the cheek and bid her good night. Elle watched her disappear around the corner, then approached her mystery gentleman.

"I hope you haven't been waiting long, monsieur?"

"Not at all, my dear. Please, allow me to properly introduce myself. I am Edwin Millard, Lord Westfield."

Her eyes widened. An English lord? His station in life was higher than she had guessed. Yet he would meet a barmaid in a dirty alley in the middle of the night?

"Please, don't let the title trouble you. You may feel free to call me Mr. Millard, or even Edwin, if that is more comfortable for you."

Elle gaped at him before remembering her manners. "I must beg your pardon, my lord, it would be quite inappropriate to be so familiar with a man of significance such as yourself."

Most men of rank would have been pleased with her response, but he harrumphed. "My significance, I assure you, is wholly manufactured. There is no reason a woman of sound mind such as yourself shouldn't consider herself worthy of intimacy with anyone of my station."

Elle's muscles clenched. What was this, some clever means of seduction? This Lord Westfield seemed too avuncular for that sort of underhandedness, but she slipped a hand into her pocket and let her fingers curl around the spray potion. Whatever his intentions, she would reach her home unscathed.

"You may address me as you wish, for now," Westfield said. "I do hope that in time you will grow more comfortable and formalities can be dispensed with." He folded his hands behind his back. "Now, you must be quite eager to return to your home, so I will present my plan to you in brief. As you may be aware, the magic serum that gives our potions their potency is in short supply of late. I mean to discover why. I also wish to seek out new sources of serum, to replace or augment our current source. I have some background in the magical arts, but my skill is limited. I need a true expert, one I can trust not only to possess the necessary knowledge, but also to undertake this task for the good of humanity rather than self-gain. You are the most talented mixer in all the city, and everyone I have spoken with has given excellent report of your character."

Elle's heart hammered. She'd known for months that the supply of serum was dwindling. New shipments arrived ever further apart, and her employers paid more for each one. She and Marie were skilled enough to keep their potions potent using ever-smaller doses of serum, but some of the girls were struggling.

Westfield's request quashed her hope that the trouble might prove temporary. For an English lord to seek help from Parisian potions masters, the shortage must be widespread and dire, indeed. Businesses would suffer as they ran low on the potions necessary to move their carriages, light their lamps, and power their machines. Jobs would be lost. Those with the least means would be hit first and hardest. Her heart ached to think she couldn't join him in combating such a future.

"I wish I could be of help. I do appreciate your praise of my skills, and your task is of great importance, but you had best look to another expert. I have obligations that keep me here in the city and require me to continue my work at the Folies."

"You speak of an elderly relation, yes?"

Lord, but this man had been thorough in his research. How long had he been spying on her?

"Oui, monsieur. My great-aunt. My wages cover her care and our food and rent. We have no other family, so I can't leave her. I'm very sorry."

"Hmm." Westfield chewed his lower lip as he thought. "You work every day, mademoiselle?"

"Six days out of every week."

"Six days, then," Westfield acknowledged. "And your pay is four francs per day?"

"Five, monsieur. That is why so many girls with potions knowledge seek employment here."

"Of course. Well, given your financial needs, your annual salary, the particular skills required, the long periods of travel, and the uncertain duration of this project, I am prepared to offer you ten thousand francs, half in advance and half upon completion of our mission. I trust that amount is sufficient to pay a quality nurse to attend your aunt during your absence? Travel expenses, will, of course, be covered as well."

Elle gaped at the gentleman. "Ten thousand francs, monsieur? Surely you jest."

"You feel that a higher sum is deserved? I am prepared to bargain if necessary."

"*Non*, monsieur. It's too much. I couldn't possibly accept such a sum."

"Nonsense. I'm certain you will earn every cent." Westfield checked his watch again. "It's time to turn in for the night, I believe. I will take my leave of you, unless you need an escort home?"

She shook her head.

"Very well. Please think on my offer overnight. I will send a carriage for you, and your aunt, if she is up to the journey, at ten o'clock. We will have a late breakfast and you may give me your final decision then. Is that agreeable to you?"

Elle could only nod.

"Excellent. I will see you again at the prescribed time. A very good evening to you, mademoiselle."

He tipped his hat to her and walked off into the darkness. Elle took herself in the other direction, her mind in a whirl, uncertain if she would wake the next morning to find this evening was only part of a strange dream.

Ten thousand francs. A new burst of hope blossomed inside her. Another step up. Arrangements would need to be made, but Elle knew what Aunt Madeleine would say about the offer. The Folies Bergère could find itself a new barmaid.

II

Well Met

$\mathcal{E}$LLE STEPPED DOWN FROM THE CARRIAGE, gaping at the massive villa spread wide in front of her. Her eyes traveled up the facade, taking in the stuccoed walls, the tall, arched windows, and the red-tiled roof. Westfield's friend lived *here?* In this Italian palace?

She turned a slow circle. Expansive gardens gleamed lush and green beneath the blazing Italian sun. Vineyards covered the rolling hills beyond. She breathed in, inhaling the sweet, fresh scent of clean air. Beautiful.

And not a little intimidating.

"Come, my dear," Westfield urged. "The marquess will be waiting for us."

A marquess? Goodness.

Elle's hand drifted to the purse concealed beneath her skirt. The "pocket money" Westfield had given her could feed her for months. Several thousand francs sat in a bank back home, providing for Aunt Madeline's medical expenses—or whatever she chose to spend it on. The journey to a new country was nothing compared to this bizarre foray into a new social class.

A smiling butler in clothes finer than any Elle had ever worn met them at the door. He greeted her and took her cloak, not the least troubled by its faded colors and frayed hem.

"If you would follow me, please, sir and miss. His lordship will see you in the library."

Elle trailed after the butler, peeking into every room they passed, marveling at the ornate furniture and lush upholstery. Art, photos, and bric-a-brac covered every flat surface. In the distance, she could hear the tinkle of a piano and the shouts of children at play.

What would it be like to grow up in such a place? She could scarcely imagine it.

The library made a stark contrast to the rest of the house. Functional and uncluttered, it contained a neat row of bookcases, several large chairs for reading, and a pair of sturdy desks. A tall, powerfully-built man with gray-brown hair strode toward them, clasping Westfield's hand.

"Millard. Good to see you."

"A pleasure, George, always a pleasure. Please, allow me to introduce our guest." He motioned Elle forward. "This is Miss Elle Deschamps of Paris, master potion mixer. Miss Deschamps, this is my great friend George Ainsworth, Marchese di Murlo."

The marquess inclined his head. "I'm happy to make your acquaintance, mademoiselle."

Elle responded with a curtsey, but her gaze drifted past him to a younger man who stood in the background, watching her in stoic silence.

At first glance he seemed unremarkable, but the moment their eyes met the room seemed to spin and realign to center on him. Elle had never seen such a pair of eyes. Sapphire blue and clear as a cloudless sky, they bore into her with such intensity she thought he might be able to see down to her very bones.

She stared back at him, transfixed. He was neither tall nor classically handsome, but striking, with an aquiline nose and a strong, clean-shaven jaw. A spray of freckles dotted his nose and cheeks. His blond hair had been cut short and he wore a severe black suit, tailored perfectly to fit his broad shoulders.

"That would be my youngest boy, Henry," Murlo said.

Elle's head jerked. Halfway through introductions and she had been caught staring at a mysterious gentleman. This wasn't the way to earn her ten thousand francs.

"Henry, stop skulking in the shadows and introduce yourself," his father said.

Henry didn't move, but he gave her a nod. "Mademoiselle."

"A pleasure, Lord Henry," she replied, hoping she had gotten the form of address correct. Westfield had filled the journey from Paris with lessons on etiquette. Elle didn't know which was worse, the confusion of titles or the need for six different forks at dinner.

Murlo waved a hand at his luxurious armchairs. "Let's sit and talk."

The gentlemen waited for Elle to take her seat before pulling up their own chairs to sit across from her. Henry remained standing in the background. He leaned against a bookcase, one arm resting atop it, his legs crossed at the ankles. The casual stance masked his underlying tension, but his eyes and the hard set of his mouth revealed the coiled energy within. A predator, lying in wait. Elle tore her eyes away, knowing he would continue to watch her.

"I see no reason not to cut straight to the heart of the matter," Murlo continued. "Westfield and I, along with other friends across Europe, have determined the trouble with potion supplies is grave enough to warrant investigation. He has sought out the finest expert in France, while I have compiled a list of places worth visiting." His mouth curved into a smile, creating little dimples in his cheeks. "Don't look so skeptical, young lady, your reputation is deserved. Westfield has regaled me with praise of your work from employers and customers alike. I'm confident you can begin in any location and follow the potions supply chain to its source."

"Thank you," Elle replied, flattening her hands against her

skirts to stop herself from fidgeting. Compliments were a rarity in her life and made her feel a fraud.

"The plan, as we have agreed upon, is this: you and Westfield will travel to various of the locations on my list, assess the local potions trade, and seek out the source of serum. You will travel as Westfield's niece. No one will question a man and his ward seeing the world. I have acquired travel papers for you that will confirm this identity."

Henry coughed, and his father cast a frown at him.

"You will need a new wardrobe," he continued. "My wife and my daughter, Lucy, will assist you with that over the next few days. You are scheduled to depart at the end of the week. Do you have any questions or concerns with the assignment?"

"Will we be traveling to India, to study our current sources and determine the reason for the shortage?"

"No. There is some concern with heightened criminal activity in that region. Related, we believe, to the shortage. I consider it too dangerous for investigation." Murlo glanced over his shoulder at his son, who quirked a single blond eyebrow. "Instead, we will attempt to find new sources to replace or augment those we have. It is both a safer and more permanent solution."

Elle nodded. "That seems entirely sensible."

"Any other questions?"

Who are you and why are you doing this? Are you agents of the British government? Some organization of your own? And most of all, why me?

"I would like to see your list of locations. That is all. For now."

Elle trusted that Westfield's motives were honorable—he had been a man of his word thus far. Still, she would keep her eyes and ears open.

Murlo grinned. "Excellent. Westfield and I will keep in touch during your journey, and I will relay anything you learn to our contacts across Europe. Henry will accompany you, in the guise of your manservant. If, God forbid, you do run into any trouble, he has served in the army these past years and will know how to defend you. I'm sorry I can't accompany you, myself, but I suffered a bout of pneumonia this past winter and haven't yet recovered my stamina."

Henry made a noise that may have been another cough. Or a snort of disbelief.

Murlo scowled. "Isn't that right, Henry?"

"Absolutely, sir. You were at the brink of death's door. I feared to leave the house."

Elle swallowed a laugh. At the same time, a sense of doubt crept over her. This impertinent, standoffish son of a marquess was going to play a servant? That was almost as absurd as a barmaid masquerading as nobility. It would never work.

···○···

The clothes needed to play a wealthy lady were enough to drive Elle mad—multiple styles for different times of day, unwieldy bustles, corsets without front openings. As the week wore on, she did her best to choose garments that were as practical as possible, given the circumstances. She ignored the jewelry entirely. Why draw the attention of would-be-thieves and risk losing something of value?

Westfield and Murlo urged her to take whatever clothing and accessories she wished, telling her to, "have fun." Fun? Living a life she knew little about and was entirely unsuited to? Impossible. It would be a race to see who would blow their cover first: herself or Henry Ainsworth. Assuming he even came along. Elle never saw him for more than a few moments at a time.

Much to her surprise, on the day of their departure she found him beside the carriage, tossing their heavy trunks about with ease. She stumbled to a halt and stood gaping at him. Gentlemen didn't do manual labor. Yet here he was, attending to the task with a smile of genuine pleasure dimpling his cheeks. His servant's clothes, while of rougher materials than his austere suits, were equally well-tailored. The shirtsleeves were rolled up to his elbows and the thin cotton stretched taut across his shoulders and arms, revealing the flex of his muscles as he picked up her things. He was every bit as virile as the dock-workers along the Seine that Marie liked to ogle, but without the smell of fish and dirty water. Elle considered adding one last item to her trunk, just for the pleasure of watching him unload and reload it.

His piercing gaze turned on her. "Is there something I can do for you, Miss Deschamps?"

It was the first thing she'd heard him say since the day they had met in the library. His words carried a slight lilt she couldn't place. A bit of something coloring his upper-class English. It gave his accent an appealing musicality.

"I'm merely supervising. I understand that is what fine ladies do?"

Of course, fine ladies didn't stand about admiring their manservant, no matter how pleasant his physique. Not openly, at least. Elle assumed plenty of wealthy ladies used the handsome men in their employ much the way the men used the women.

Henry's eyes gleamed. "It's good to see you applying yourself to your role with such enthusiasm."

Elle couldn't decipher whether the comment was meant as a joke, an insult, or a compliment. She bobbed her head and said, "And you, as well," then ducked into the carriage.

She watched him surreptitiously from the window, puzzling over his words and behavior. Was he simply another bored, young aristocrat, happy for any entertainment? Was he the serious soldier, silent and sharp-eyed? The sarcastic rogue?

Whatever the case, the mystery of Lord Henry Ainsworth seemed every bit as challenging as the potions shortage.

III

A Market for Potions

$\mathcal{H}$ENRY LIKENED FREEDOM FROM Westfield's scrutiny to an escape from prison. Three days aboard a ship listening to lectures about protecting Miss Deschamps had been almost as tedious as his six months of so-called retirement. Westfield thought he was in charge, which was probably for the best. His plan to seek serum sources was a perfect starting point for the mission, though his hope of opening such sources to the world market was idealistic. Westfield was like that. His life's goal was to promote peace and cooperation between peoples and nations across the globe. Henry had seen too much of war to believe such a thing more than a fantasy.

Henry's own directive from Parliament was simple. End the potions crisis. By any means necessary.

Today that meant shopping. Not something he would usually consider fun, but he took to the streets of Alexandria with a spring in his step and a smile on his face. Boredom had fled. He was where he belonged, back in action, and the work was all the more interesting for the addition of an unusual—and unusually pretty—potions expert.

He watched Elle as they walked, noting how she stepped, when her head turned, where her gaze lingered. He'd already memorized her. Small and slender, but not exceptionally so, with lively, light-brown eyes, and soft pink lips. Hers was a subtle beauty, most apparent in the brightness of her eyes and the curve of her mouth. People would overlook her when passing by on the street. For the perceptive, she was worth a second glance. Most importantly, she carried herself with assurance. She could pass for a lady. She wanted only for a few pointers.

"You ought to purchase something, mademoiselle."

Elle stumbled to a halt and turned to gawk at him. "Pardon?"

Ainsworth, you imbecile.

Of course he had confused her. It was literally the only thing he had said to her today. He'd sunk too far into his unobtrusive servant role. It saved him the conundrum of what to say to her.

"Even the most discerning of ladies do eventually find something to purchase," he explained. "We will appear less conspicuous if you make a few small purchases and give me something to carry about for you."

"Ah."

The skepticism in her voice amused him. She would never take to life among the nobility. Her appearance and manners were perfect, but she showed no enthusiasm for finery, jewels, or even money. Westfield had placed no limit on the funds at her disposal, yet she had spent not one penny. Her behavior tended toward the eccentric, and eccentricity drew attention. In Henry's line of work, attention was the enemy.

"Don't fret about the cost. Westfield can afford it. I noticed your eye lingered on the cloth just across the way."

Her eyes narrowed, assessing him. He liked her sharp, inquisitive mind. "You are most observant, monsieur. It's very fine, and the one scarf in particular is of a color I admire."

"Excellent! Here's your purse, Miss Deschamps. I'm prepared to assist you in haggling over the price if you wish."

"You mistake me. I don't intend to purchase the piece."

He wasn't going to let her off so easily. She feared waste, and was too proud to accept charity. On a mission such as this, however, money wasn't a means of survival. It was a tool, and she needed to learn to spend it.

"Of course you do. You, there!" he called out to the vendor. "This fine lady is interested in one of your scarves."

The vendor's face lit up, and he named a price. Elle shook her head and turned away.

"Far too much. I told you, I don't wish to buy."

The vendor slashed the price in half. "I cannot go any lower. My cloth is much finer quality than others in the marketplace."

"No, I'm sorry. My companion has mistaken my interest. We must be on our way."

The vendor approached her, carrying the scarf she admired, and lowered his voice. "My lady, if you can keep this between us, I can take the price even lower, but just this once, and only because you have such fine tastes."

She couldn't have haggled better had she been a professional. Her genuine refusals and the wistful look in her eye were a lethal combination. She shook her head again, and he named a new price, one far below what such an item would have cost her anywhere in Europe. Henry fingered the coins in his own pocket. He would pay for the damned thing himself, if necessary.

"Very well," Elle acquiesced. She withdrew some money from her purse, and the vendor, wearing a grin, folded the scarf neatly and passed it to her.

"Thank you, my lady. You have chosen well. You won't be sorry."

She smiled and thanked him, then passed the scarf to Henry.

"Do take care with this. It is by far the nicest thing I have ever purchased for myself. I will ask Westfield to take the cost out of my pay."

Henry couldn't help but chuckle. Her tenacity was charming. "He will refuse. Expenses are covered. If my lady needs to shop as part of our research, purchases will be expected."

"I won't take advantage of his generosity," she replied

curtly. "Let's carry on. I see small bottles up ahead. A purchase of one of those might satisfy you and will actually help in this investigation. Come."

She strode off, her head held high, looking every bit the niece of a lord. Henry jogged to catch up with her.

Elle gave the bottles a cursory examination, then shook her head and moved on. She lingered longer at the next stall. After she rejected one vial, the vendor offered her a similar bottle with a liquid a shade darker than that of the first. She held it up to the light and examined it, then swirled it around and looked again. She removed the stopper and gave it a cautious sniff.

"Hmm," she murmured. "*Non. Pardon, madame*, but I'm afraid it doesn't suit me. Thank you for your time."

She handed back the bottle and walked away. Henry trailed behind, watching her work. In her role as potions expert, she possessed an air of authority that had him feeling quite subservient to her, without the need to playact.

They toured every potions stall they could find, and in most cases Elle dismissed the goods and continued on her way. When she did purchase, she haggled like a master. Her grasp of the quality of the concoctions was so great she could detect even the cleverest attempt to overvalue the product. Her tone, her body posture, and her expressions all said this was a woman accustomed to getting her own way. No one would suspect her of being anyone other than who she purported to be.

When they had perused every corner of the tourist areas, she pressed on and spent the better part of an hour shopping among the locals. Here, few of the vendors spoke English or French, and their demeanor upon seeing foreigners ranged from perplexed to hostile. Elle continued her work, no less determined than before. Henry scrutinized every man, woman, and child, prepared to whisk her away if anything should go awry.

She paused before a stall where an older man and a teenaged girl plied an assortment of dried herbs and flowers. A few charms or amulets hung from a hook, and three tiny jars sat on the counter below. Elle picked one up, as the vendors watched her with slight frowns on their faces. The girl said something to the man in Arabic and he shook his head.

Elle examined the contents of each of the three jars before deciding on one of them. "Did she make this?" she asked, pointing at the girl. The vendors looked puzzled, but when Elle mimed mixing a potion, the man's face lit up.

He put his hands on his daughter's shoulders. "Nenet," he presented her. "Yes!"

"It's exceptional. Henry, the purse, if you please."

He handed it to her, and she selected a coin and laid it on the counter. The girl's eyes widened in shock, and her father rushed to pick it up and give it back.

"No, no!" he cried, followed by some words in Arabic that Henry interpreted as, "This is far too much."

"Yes," Elle insisted, placing the coin down. She stepped back from the stall, taking the potion jar with her to make her words unmistakeable.

The man bowed, as did his daughter when he gave her a nudge.

Elle smiled at them. "Thank you, Nenet."

The girl blushed and returned the smile.

Elle gave her a final nod and then turned away. "We are done for the day. Let's return to the hotel. I'm ready to give my report to Lord Westfield."

"Yes, ma'am."

She spun to look at him, a frown lining her face. "I'm sorry. I didn't mean to order you about so."

Henry grinned. "Yes, you did. That's your role, and you performed it wonderfully."

"I don't wish to be rude. This reversal in our situations is... confusing."

"Don't concern yourself over it. I'm a soldier and accustomed to taking orders." His grin broadened. "Whether I'm capable of obeying them is another question, entirely."

IV

The Taste of Magic

$\mathcal{T}$HE AFTERNOON LIGHT FILTERED through the hotel window, casting a pool of light upon the table where Elle had laid out an array of glassware and a few simple tools. The three potions she had purchased that morning sat off to one side. She measured out a dram of water into each of three glasses, leaving the fourth empty. Her fingers had just curled around the brandy decanter when Henry entered the suite with a fully laden tray. Excellent. She was famished. She set her arrangements aside. The demonstration could wait until after tea.

Henry began to pour, and she snatched up a teacup before he could fill more than just the one.

"I can pour my own, thank you."

He set the teapot down, the corners of his mouth quirking upward. Those dimples. Lord, but he was handsome when he smiled.

"Please, feel free. I wouldn't wish to make you uncomfortable."

She almost laughed. Being near him was enough to make her uncomfortable. In the rare moments when he spoke to her, it was as an equal, though he was by far her social superior and playacting as her employee. Otherwise he remained stubbornly silent. At times he seemed deadly serious. The flashes of humor were equally confounding. She couldn't tell whether or not he was making sport of her.

She chewed her sandwich slowly, watching the sparkle in his blue eyes as he sipped his tea with obvious pleasure.

Westfield joined them at the table. "Did you have a productive day?"

"Miss Deschamps was brilliant," Henry replied.

Elle shifted in her chair, not meeting his eyes. Why couldn't she accept praise without embarrassment?

"I'm very glad to hear it. I, myself, had several lovely conversations with scholars today, but I'm afraid I did not get a great deal out of it beyond my own enjoyment. The general consensus is that potions use is most prevalent among European expatriates and visiting tourists. In these cases, the source of the serum is the same eastern trade routes that bring it to us at home. For locals, use of herbs, charms, amulets, and similar mystical items is more in keeping with their historical traditions."

Henry folded his arms across his chest and frowned. "You think this location shows little promise, then? Miss Deschamps, what have you to say? I'm curious to hear about the potions you purchased."

"Lord Westfield's information is correct."

Elle set down her teacup and turned to the items she had prepared earlier. She poured a small amount of brandy into the empty glass and unstoppered one bottle she had purchased this morning.

"The marketplace where the tourists shop was like any in Paris—a few nice things among many junk souvenirs."

She picked up a needle, dipped it into the potion bottle, and used it to drip several drops into the first glass of water.

"I found two stalls selling genuine potions. This first is a standard love potion. Not the dangerous sort that might trick someone into thinking they are in love, but the sort people drink themselves, to make them feel more friendly and amorous. No different than those I have made myself. The dose of serum is small, and it was hastily mixed."

She picked up the glass and took a small sip of the water.

"The taste, too, is weak. It will work, but not well and not for long."

Elle rinsed her needle in the brandy and moved on to the next potion, diluting a few drops of it in the next glass and tasting it.

"This potion is medicinal. Used to promote or restore health. Similar to the other in quality and amount of serum. These both looked to be sold only to tourists—Europeans, in particular. In the locals' market I found only one potion seller. There were many perfumes and oils for sale, but none of those used serum. The only true potions were at a single stall in one far corner of the market. They were not the vendor's specialty."

Elle opened the tiny ceramic jar she had purchased from the girl Nenet. She cleaned her needle once more, dipped it for a second into the jar, and then just as briefly into the remaining glass of water. She swished the water in the glass a moment and took a tiny sip. Tastes flooded her mouth, giving her a sense of the potion's makeup. It had the cool, minty bite familiar to many medicinal potions, with the warm aftertaste of quality liquor. The spice of serum lingered on her tongue, familiar, but different. She sipped again, focusing on the unusual tang. It matched the scent that had caught her notice at the market.

"Another health potion, of a sort," she said. "The recipe is unfamiliar to me. A proper potion, made by an expert. Extremely potent."

She set the glass down beside the others and waved a hand over them.

"Would you like to try for yourselves? Even diluted, you should be able to taste a difference."

Henry shook his head. "No, thank you, Miss Deschamps. I have no talent for potions, and I'm not known to have a discerning palate in any respect. I fear I can't tell the difference between a French wine and an Italian one, even though my family sells the drink for a living."

Westfield picked up a glass. "I will try it, thank you."

He sipped, thought a moment, then moved to the next glass and did the same. When he sipped from the third glass, his brows rose in surprise.

"I see what you mean. It's quite strong. The others had but a whiff of magic. This has much more, and you only just dipped the needle into this glass. Is it safe to take another sip?"

"Oui. Of course."

"Hmm. There is something unusual in this, also. A spice, perhaps, that I am unfamiliar with."

"That spiciness is the serum itself. There is a unique flavor to it. I don't believe it comes from our sources in the East. I think we have located your new source already."

Westfield clapped his hands in delight. "Very well done, Miss Deschamps! I knew you were the right woman for this task. The next step will be to ask the creator where the serum comes from."

"We will need a translator. It was made by a girl. She doesn't speak English, nor does her father."

"Damn," Henry muttered. "I knew I should have studied Arabic. I had three whole days to get started on that bloody boat."

Westfield paled. "Captain Ainsworth, you are in the presence of a lady! Kindly watch your tongue."

Henry blinked, looking flustered for the briefest instant. "My apologies, Miss Deschamps, for my inappropriate language."

"Oh, I've heard much worse, believe me." She'd *said* much worse. Certain vulgarities had a cathartic freedom that she needed sometimes after a long night at the bar.

"That does not excuse the behavior," Westfield insisted. He shook his head. "No matter. I will find a translator at the university. We will speak to this family about their potions, and that should lead us in the right direction. Wonderful! I'm well pleased. Now, tell me, my dear, did you enjoy your day?

I do hope you purchased something for yourself during your outing."

Elle cast a look at Henry. He said nothing, lounging in his chair and pouring himself another cup of tea, but a smug grin tugged at the corner of his mouth. She wasn't certain whether she wanted to thank him or slap him.

"As a matter of fact, I did."

V

An Approximation of
a Conversation

SHE WAS STARING AT HIM AGAIN. Why the devil was she always staring at him? Nobody stared at him. Until Elle Deschamps, Henry had been the most overlooked person in the whole bloody empire. And he'd liked it that way.

He forced his eyes down to his book, willing himself to study. God, but it had been painful, standing in silence while someone else translated for her. That should have been his job.

At least they'd learned what they needed to know. Nenet's serum came from upriver. Westfield had whisked them off to Cairo to gape at the pyramids like true tourists, then bundled them all aboard a sightseeing steamship.

Not that Henry could enjoy the beauty of the Nile while Elle Deschamps stared at him.

Attention is the enemy.

The dictum echoed in his mind. His body told him he was being hunted. His muscles were so tense his chair vibrated.

He snapped the book closed. Enough. He was going to march right over there and demand to know what she wanted.

Why the hell are you staring at me?

No. He couldn't say that. That's what he would say to

a man, but she was a lady, and he'd already given her one unsolicited demonstration of his cursing habit. Damn.

She looked down at her journal as he approached, her shoulders hunching slightly. She knew she'd been caught.

"You've been watching me," Henry said. Civil enough, if rather blunt.

Elle kept her eyes glued to her journal, scribbling. "Oui. *Pardon.*"

"Is there something you want from me?"

"No."

He heaved a sigh. "Miss Deschamps, if we can't hold a conversation, I don't see how we will be able to work together for the remainder of this expedition."

She did look up now, her soft brown eyes searching his face.

"Hold a conversation?" She huffed a short laugh. "You have hardly spoken two words to me our entire journey. In any event, we have very little in common. I don't know that we have anything to converse about."

"You have a keen mind and, I believe, some strong opinions. I don't doubt you could converse on any number of topics." He cast about for an example. "We had something near to a discussion about novels on the train to Cairo."

Rather, she had asked him what he was reading, and he'd given her a five-minute lecture on the literary genius of Charles Dickens. His tendency to ramble was a prime motivation for keeping his damned mouth shut.

She smiled. "I have nearly finished *A Tale of Two Cities.*"

"Already?"

"The potion-fueled lights are too much temptation. I stayed up reading. You did likewise, if that bookmark is any indication." Her smile was both guilt and defiance. His breath hitched.

"Work. I'm learning Arabic. Or attempting to. You ought to know, since you have been looking at me so often, I can hardly be considered to be studying this morning."

Her mouth twitched again. Henry vowed to stop staring at her lips.

"Do you speak many languages?"

"English, Italian, French, German, Spanish, Hindi, and Marathi. I know a smattering of words and phrases in most other European languages and a few more from India. I also read and write ancient Greek and Latin, but those are not especially useful."

"That is… impressive."

He shrugged. "I studied little else at University. Or ever."

They lapsed into silence. Henry fidgeted. His eyes flickered over the water to the lush, green riverbanks and the distant sandy hills, pretending to look for crocodiles or whatever other fauna attracted the tourists. The movement allowed him to turn and take a glimpse at the other passengers, who had altogether too fine a view of his exposed back. He willed himself to continue the conversation.

"What are you writing in your journal?" he asked. "Are you watching and noting my habits to determine how best to avoid me in the future?"

"I haven't stared at you any more than you stare at me."

He couldn't deny that. "True. But I have reason. I'm your bodyguard. I must know what you are about at all times."

Truth, concealing his lie. He watched her because she intrigued him. Because he'd spent years watching people, and had no intention of altering his behavior.

She made a little noise of displeasure. "I can take care of myself."

"I never said otherwise."

One delicate brow arched. "As for the journal, it is full of my observations, so that I can remember this journey and give a report to my aunt of all the interesting things I have seen."

"Ah. You won't have mentioned me, then."

Elle flipped the journal to a new page and scribbled across the top, large enough that he couldn't miss it, *Henry Ainsworth is speaking to me at last. I don't know what he means by it.*

She snapped the book closed.

"I think I will return to my room for a rest. You'll see me all the way to the bed, I imagine?"

Heat rose in his cheeks. "I won't follow you into your room. It would be most inappropriate."

"And we wouldn't want that, now, would we?" Her voice had the merest hint of an edge, but he couldn't determine whether it was sarcasm or irritation.

He could have answered her with a simple lie, but he turned away instead and left her to depart in silence. A week into their journey and already he was fed up with Henry the servant, so proper and obedient. Damned if he didn't want to hang society's rules and barge right through her door as the equally fictitious Captain Ainsworth, sophisticated libertine.

VI

Inquiries and Accidents

$\mathcal{E}$LLE LEANED OVER THE RAIL, letting the breeze tug the pins from her hair while the sights and scents of the Nile flooded her senses.

"Don't fall overboard. I'm not in the mood for a swim this morning."

She glanced back at Henry, who had taken up his habitual seat, away from the edge, with his back to the wall. He rarely joined her for more than a few minutes at a time. She beckoned to him.

"I can see another crocodile. I love the way they lie there as if dead or asleep, waiting for unsuspecting prey to come along."

"Indeed. Quiet, unassuming. You might never even notice him lurking. But he is lightning quick and lethal."

"Are we talking about the crocodile, or you?"

"I don't bite."

Pity. She fancied a nibble. She held her tongue, keeping any saucy retorts bottled up. She couldn't do anything that might distract from their work or endanger the tentative camaraderie she and Henry had cultivated over the past few days. It frustrated her to have met a man she liked and not be able to flirt with him. She had done her best to cut back on the staring.

When he did catch her at it, she had no explanations. What could she say? "I think you are mysterious and fascinating, and

I want to discover more about you?" Or worse, "I was admiring the muscles of your arms and the breadth of your shoulders and hoping someone would come along with a task that required you to take your shirt off."

Most of the girls at the bar would have told her to jump him, Elle thought with a smile. But this was a mission, not a pleasure cruise. And she couldn't ignore Marie's all-too-accurate warnings about liaisons with aristocrats. *Never dally with a gentleman.* She'd seen girls get hurt. She'd witnessed the struggles of single mothers.

So no fantasizing. She would focus on her work. Earn her pay.

Henry closed his sketchbook and tucked it under his arm before joining her. He had either finished or abandoned his Arabic textbook, and now spent most of his time with a pencil in hand. Elle was dying to know if he had any talent.

He stopped beside her, planting his hip against the rail, his feet apart, as if bracing himself. A crocodile was an apt comparison. Suspiciously calm. Motionless, but primed for action. His eyes darted back and forth, searching, always moving.

"Are you afraid you might fall over the side?" she asked.

"No."

"You don't like it here by the railing."

He turned in a circle, making a pretense of examining the deck. "It's as good a place as any."

"Not as good as your favorite chair."

His eyes narrowed slightly, scrutinizing her yet again. "True enough. Where is your crocodile? Perhaps I'll sketch it."

"Just there." She pointed. "Though I'm certain you knew that. Will you share your finished drawing? I would love to see something of your handiwork."

A smile broke through his passive facade. "I've been waiting to see when your curiosity would get the better of you." He opened the book to a half-finished landscape. "This is my current project. I have completed a few others as well."

Her fingers brushed the page. Even incomplete, his work was remarkable. His eye for detail and the precision of the penciled lines lent a photographic quality to the art. He flipped to the next drawing.

"Incredible. You don't miss a thing."

His cheeks colored. She wasn't the only one uncomfortable with receiving praise.

"Thank you. I don't share them often. My family tired of looking years ago."

"I think they are lovely. You have much talent, monsieur."

Her gaze lingered on a drawing of the pyramids, thinking about their brief stop. She wanted to burn the memory into her mind forever. They were beautiful, yet eerie. To create such a structure for the glory of a single man... it struck her as the sort of madness that had led people like the French and the Americans to throw off the monarchy in favor of a more egalitarian system.

She reached to turn the page, thinking to see some of his older works, but he abruptly closed the book and tucked it away. What was he hiding?

"Shall we have a conversation," he asked, "or have you had enough of me for the day?"

"Walk about the deck with me," she requested. "I should like to hear your opinion of the pyramids. Do you think them mad?"

He considered her question for a time. "I think it not at all unusual to build a great temple to a god. If the pyramids are mad, then so are the great cathedrals of Europe."

"That is an excellent point, though one that smacks of blasphemy."

Henry shrugged. "I suffer from heretical tendencies. I can count on one hand the number of times I've set foot in a church in the past dozen years."

"May I ask why?"

"The sermons irk me. I don't like being told what to do."

"Yet you served in the army."

A wry smile touched his lips. "I also don't like doing what is expected of me. But enough about me. We are approaching Luxor and will have work to do shortly."

Elle leaned over the rail once again for a good look. Henry didn't stop her, but his hand settled on the railing scant inches away.

Luxor was a marvel of Egyptian civilization. The present-day city and the ancient one were mingled and inseparable, the pillars of ancient temples and monolithic statues jutting out between modern buildings.

"I had no idea the ruins here would be so close. I expected them to be off in the desert again, but they are right under our very noses!"

"I love the sight of that temple rising between the masts of the modern sailing ships," Henry added, opening his sketchbook to a blank page.

"It's beautiful. I look forward to seeing it up close. When we make land, however, I would like to visit the docks and warehouses along the river to see if we can find the place where Nenet's family picks up her ingredients. How do we question the merchants and warehouse owners while maintaining our cover?"

"I can handle that. As your servant, I won't look strange speaking with these people. By accompanying me, you will appear to be very controlling, but that's not too unusual for wealthy ladies."

Elle pursed her lips. "You will have to do as I say."

He just grinned.

The afternoon became a back-and-forth dance of business and pleasure. Elle and Henry stopped by shops, warehouses, and cargo ships, beginning every interview in the same manner.

"This fine lady who employs me is in search of additional quantities of a high-quality potion she purchased last week in

Alexandria. The seller tells us the shipments come from upriver and we thought to seek some out; but she has been unable to locate anything in the markets. Would you happen to have anything like this for sale, or know of someone who might?"

Most inquiries ended quickly, as few of the merchants dealt in potions. What potions they did find were the same cheap tourist variety as in Alexandria. Every few failures they would pause and take time to walk among the ruins. The sightseeing relaxed her, but the growing friendship with Henry was the true force keeping Elle's frustration in check. While he remained something of an enigma, she felt at ease with him and they worked well together. She headed for their ship with a smile on her face.

"Every tradesman in town knows there is a choosy young woman looking for good potions," Henry informed Westfield as they met him at the docks. They joined the line of passengers awaiting their turn to board the ship. "If there was anything here to find, we would have discovered it."

"My discussion with the owners produced similar results," he sighed.

"We'll try again at the next port," Elle said.

A large man in an ill-fitting uniform waved her toward a second gangplank. She changed course and gave him a nod of thanks, appreciating the efficiency. Henry and Westfield followed along.

"The day wasn't a complete loss," Henry argued. "I made a number of drawings of the hieroglyphs. I intend to learn to read them."

Elle smiled up at him. "Have you given any thought to the study of antiquities? I'm certain these excavators and Egyptologists would love to have someone of your talents to catalog their works."

He chuckled. "It's an interesting notion, but I find my current employment affords me plenty of opportunity for both travel and art."

The phrase "current employment" gave her pause. She had never considered whether he would be paid for his part in this venture. Logic said he would be, but she'd never imagined him as someone who needed to earn a living. Perhaps as the youngest son he didn't expect to inherit much. Though it had looked as if the Ainsworths had enough money for a dozen sons.

Henry motioned for her to go first up the gangplank. "After you, my lady."

She shifted her voluminous skirts and stepped onto the ramp. It creaked beneath her feet, swaying with the movement of the steamer. Henry followed a step behind. Did Mr. I-hate-standing-by-the-rail also dislike boarding? As she turned to ask him, a loud crack split the air. An instant later, the plank gave way beneath her. With a shriek, she plummeted into the waters of the river below.

Elle kicked for the surface, but the many layers of her fancy clothes weighed her down and impeded her movements. She clawed her way upward, straining to pull her head above water. She broke the surface gasping for breath, fighting the weight of the heavy garments. Henry popped out of the water nearby, looking as stunned as she was. He swam toward her, reaching for her hand, but her fingers slipped past his as she sank once more.

In desperation, Elle snatched at the hooks and buttons of her skirts, trying to wriggle free. Her eyes failed her in the murky water. Her lungs burned from lack of air. She had a mad thought that if she drowned at least it wouldn't hurt when the crocodiles came for her.

Something tugged at her clothing. Her head swiveled. Henry was underwater beside her, his hands clenched on her skirts. He yanked again, and layers of petticoats tore loose, giving her enough freedom to propel herself above water for a breath. A cork flotation ring bobbed nearby, and she grabbed hold and pulled it to her chest. She sagged atop it, coughing, her breathing labored. Exhausted from fighting her garments, she could do no more.

Crew members towed her to shore, where a flurry of onlookers rushed to her side, offering assistance. She waved them away. Dry clothes and a rest would restore her. If she felt poorly, she could drink the weak health potion she had bought in Alexandria. It wasn't as potent as the one Nenet had made, but it would be sufficient for her needs.

"Elle, are you quite all right?" Henry dropped to his knees at her side, dripping wet and disheveled. He looked wild and enticing, with his skin flushed and his shirt plastered to his skin. She hugged him.

"Thank you," she murmured, her lips only a breath away from his cheek. "Thank you ever so much."

His assistance merited more than a quick embrace, but with so many eyes on her, she let her arms slide away from him. His cheeks, previously pink, were bright red. He ran a hand through his wet hair.

"I, uh… I'm sorry for tearing your clothing."

"Don't be. I hate the petticoats," she whispered. "It saved me. That's all that matters. I'm much more sorry about your sketchbook."

"What?"

He looked about for a moment, spied the book floating not far from the pier, and went to fish it out. A moment later, he shuffled back to her, flipping through the soggy pages.

"It's pencil, so the drawings haven't washed away," he said, his glum expression giving lie to the optimistic words. "I don't know how well the paper will dry, however."

Elle patted his arm in sympathy. "I think I can do something about that."

VII

Stirred, Not Shaken

ELLE'S ACCIDENTAL SWIM IN THE NILE made her something of a celebrity. For the next half hour, ladies and gentlemen bustled about her, offering clothing, medicines, help from their servants, and anything else they could think of. Elle declined everything, thanking her fellow travelers for their concern, but her words did little to stop the hovering.

"What do you mean you haven't a lady's maid to fetch?"

She winced. Not that question again. She steeled herself with a deep breath.

"As a modern and independent woman, I have no need of such assistance."

"Yes, but, dear, this is precisely the sort of situation where one cannot do without," the woman persisted. "Perhaps my maid might be of use to you?"

Elle adopted her best working smile. This woman—a proper English lady with an elegant pale yellow dress and a wide-brimmed floral hat—had sent for a warm blanket and didn't deserve rudeness; but all Elle wanted was to return to her stateroom and dry off. Alone. She stood tall and did her best to appear composed despite her sopping condition.

"Henry provides quite enough help for both my uncle and myself."

"He does seem quite devoted," the woman replied, a trace

of suspicion in her tone. She studied her perfectly manicured nails, which peeped from the ends of her half-finger gloves. "If somewhat overfamiliar."

Elle bit back a curse. She shouldn't have hugged him. She'd broken character and committed an impropriety, drawing attention and risking exposure. Still, she wouldn't take it back, given the choice. Henry had saved her life and deserved her thanks.

An idea sprang into her head for how to placate this woman and help herself at the same time. "You know, I believe after such an ordeal I could use something to eat and some herbs to make tea. You were so gracious to offer the assistance of your maid. If I gave her a list to take to the kitchen, could she bring those things to my room? I would greatly appreciate it."

"Aila!" the woman snapped. "Can you do as this lady requires?"

A young woman rushed over, dropping an awkward curtsy. "Aye, my lady."

The teenager's simple dress hung loosely over her skinny frame, and several strands of hair had escaped her twisted braid. She looked up at Elle with an eager smile, eyes bright despite the dark circles beneath. She curtsied again, this time to Elle.

"I'm at your service, miss."

"Thank you. Let me make you a list of what I need. I won't keep you from your other duties too long."

A short time later, Elle found herself alone in her room at last. Divesting herself of the wet clothes seemed the easiest of tasks after her struggle to remove the heavy garments while underwater. She would never again complain about doing up the awkward buttons.

She dried herself and slipped into a new dress, leaving off most of the underthings, including her wet corset.

A knock sounded as she sat brushing the snarls from her towel-dried hair. She set the brush down and rose to unlock the door. Aila stood just outside, holding a tray with all the ingredients Elle had requested.

"Thank you so much, Aila," Elle said. "You've been most helpful."

"My pleasure, miss, though I must say the kitchen did think it an odd sort of lunch."

Elle laughed. "The bread and butter and cheese I will eat. The remaining ingredients I plan to mix up into an herbal tisane. It's something I learned from my grandmother."

"Ah. To ward off a chill?"

Elle answered only with a smile. She thanked the girl again, then took the tray into her room and set it on her table. She plaited her hair into a neat braid, nibbled on some of the bread and cheese, and got to work.

From her trunk, she removed her own personal potions kit, one she had carried for many years. It contained the tools of her trade and one half-empty vial of precious serum.

Using a fine-bladed scalpel and her set of pharmacy spoons, she measured exact amounts of each ingredient into a glass, smelling and tasting as needed. The recipe she had memorized wouldn't give her what she needed, but a few adjustments would do the trick. She poured one dram of scotch whisky and two of water over the dry ingredients and stirred the concoction several times.

The mixture steeped as she finished her meal. The bread and cheese wasn't quite enough to fill her, and she thought she might have to request something else. Never in her life had she been able to simply take as much food as she wanted. Someone—Westfield, probably—was paying for it, but in this she wouldn't deny herself. There would be no going hungry unless necessary.

When the mixture had rested, she strained out any remaining bits of herbs and spices and stirred in two drops of the reddish liquid serum. The serum was the consistency of molasses and took some time to dissolve fully, but Elle knew better than to hurry. Agitating the potion too much resulted in a lower quality product, and she had learned to have patience in her craft.

Satisfied with the final result, she rose from her seat and took the potion next door. Westfield answered her knock and ushered her in, inquiring after her health.

"I'm perfectly well, now that I have dried off and taken lunch. I was wondering if you might tell me where I could find Henry?"

"I believe he went to his room to change, as you have done."

"And where would that be? The smaller rooms are toward the interior of the boat, I imagine?"

Westfield's brow furrowed. "You can't mean to go to his room."

"Why not? Because he is supposedly a servant?"

"Because he is a man. And you are an unmarried young lady without a chaperone."

Elle's jaw tightened. What was wrong with these upper class people that they thought women so helpless? She had gotten along perfectly fine on her own for many years. She walked the streets of Paris alone and earned her own keep. She didn't need a maid to help her dress, and she certainly didn't need a chaperone to visit a friend.

"I don't need to go inside," she lied. "I have a potion to give to him."

"Of course. To ward off a chill?"

Only her barmaid's training kept her from rolling her eyes. As if anyone could take a chill in this warm climate.

"I can take it to him," Westfield offered.

Elle shook her head. "I have very specific instructions. I should like to do it myself."

"I believe his is the third door on the right, in the interior hall, one floor down. Let me check the number, and I will..."

She dashed off as soon as he turned his back.

VIII

Between the Pages

"*E*LLE!" HENRY GAPED AT HER. "Er, pardon, Miss Deschamps. I'm pleased to see you looking so well, after our misadventure this afternoon."

She looked better than "well," in fact. She hadn't puffed up her skirt with layers of underthings, and her green dress was simpler than her previous ensemble, with a low, square-cut neckline. He didn't even think she was wearing a corset. Her breasts seemed... bouncy.

God.

He forced himself to look away, his cheeks burning, trying not to think about how it had felt with her arms around him, the tickle of her warm breath on his skin. She brushed past him into the room, and even that slight touch made him shiver.

"I've mixed up a potion for you." She held up a glass of what looked like whisky.

Henry blinked at her, words escaping him, scandalized at the impropriety of her presence in his bedchamber. He was a bloody prude. This would not do. A sophisticated libertine would welcome the intrusion.

He collected himself and shut the door, triggering the familiar thrill of willful disobedience. No one had seen her. Etiquette be damned.

"A potion? I didn't suffer in any lasting way from our

plunge into the river, so I don't believe it necessary, though I thank you for your concern."

"It's not that sort of a potion," she replied. "It's to help with your book. Have you any sort of painter's brush among your things?"

"I'm afraid not. I have a hair brush, and a brush in my shaving kit..."

"That one will do. Could you fetch it, and your sketchbook as well?"

"Of course." He hurried to bring her both, eager to see what she would do with them.

Elle seated herself at the tiny desk and opened his damp book. Dipping the shaving brush into the potion, she used long, even strokes to apply the mixture to the first page. She brushed both sides of the page, fanned it a few times with her hand and then continued to the next.

"This potion is one my grandmother taught me long ago," she told him. "The chemists wanted younger girls at their shops, so after a certain age she turned to other work. She did the washing for wealthy families, and used this potion on their laundry—and ours. She would sprinkle it onto the wet clothes, shake them out a bit, and then hang them to dry. They would dry more quickly than those of our neighbors, especially in damp weather, and the fabric would dry unwrinkled. She had a flatiron, but she never used it, and the clothes were always crisp and without creases."

"So, by applying your potion to my book, the pages will dry neatly? That is marvelous!"

"Don't give me too much praise, just yet. I had to tweak the recipe for paper rather than cloth. It's thinner, and must be applied more evenly. We will see the results soon enough. It should be some improvement, but the book will likely not ever be as good as new."

"The first page looks better already. I refuse to be anything other than amazed by your skill."

Elle gave him an awkward smile. Compliments flustered her. Perhaps if he gave her enough she would grow more accustomed to them.

He watched her continue on to the second page and the third, her fingers swift and dexterous. Her hands lacked the unmarked perfection of a true lady, but they moved with an elegant certainty that had him enthralled. Too late he realized that she had gone further into the book than he intended. He reached to pick it up, but she had already flipped to the next page.

Her hand stilled. *"Mon Dieu."*

Henry's gaze fell to the hand-penciled map of Alexandria that spanned two side-by-side pages. As always, the map bore no labels, only symbols such as stars and crosses to mark locations of import. He never added words or a key to any map until he turned it in. Better to leave it difficult to decipher for anyone who might stumble across it.

"This is Alexandria," Elle gasped, her superior mind deciphering the image with ease. "These are the places where I made purchases. Lord, it's laid out so neatly a stranger could use it to find a particular stall in the marketplace. When did you draw this?"

"That same day. In the evening, after you told Westfield about the potions." No sense in lying about that.

"You did it all from memory?"

He nodded. "I've been drawing maps my entire life. Treasure maps as a child, and maps like this during my time with the army. It wasn't something I could often do on the move, so I became accustomed to committing the streets to memory and drawing them out later."

His hands itched to snatch the book away, but he stuffed them in his pockets. She'd caught him out sooner than expected and now he owed her a confession.

Elle stared at him, then back at the book, flipping more pages. Cairo. Luxor. This very ship, with her room marked only by a dot that could easily be mistaken for a smudge. He watched her face, seeing in her expression the pieces falling into place, solving the puzzle that was Henry Ainsworth.

Her lips pinched together. Her brow furrowed. When she looked up again, her brown eyes flashed in anger. "Languages, maps, your never-ending surveillance—I am beginning to understand the nature of your military service, Captain Ainsworth."

The scorn in her voice stung, but he had received similar wounds too many times to let it show. "I have done certain work as an intelligence agent," he replied diplomatically.

She pushed the chair back and stood up to glower down at him. "No. Not 'have done.' You *do*. You are a spy."

"Yes." It would be ridiculous to deny it.

"A spy for whom? What do you want from me?"

"I want to help you discover serum sources, as we have been doing. Nothing more."

A knock on the door provided him temporary relief from the harshness of her gaze. He opened it only a few inches, to conceal her presence. The new visitor didn't surprise him. Westfield's brow was creased with worry.

"Please tell me Miss Deschamps is not in there."

Well, that made the lie simple. "She is not."

"She was looking for you. She had some sort of potion."

"Yes, she delivered it."

"But she is no longer here? Do you know where she has gone?"

"Back to her room, I would imagine. She had quite the ordeal this afternoon, and I expect she will want time alone."

"Yes, yes. I hope you are right. I worry for her, though. She is so independent-minded."

"An admirable quality."

Westfield rubbed his temple. "Perhaps. I fear it will make it difficult for you to protect her."

"I look forward to the challenge."

Westfield looked pained. "Young people these days. I will leave you be, Henry. I must track down my wayward niece. Let us meet again tomorrow after breakfast."

"Until then."

He closed the door and turned back to Elle. She regarded him in silence, her posture stiff, her lips still turned downward.

"You lie very smoothly, monsieur."

The formal address was like salt to his raw wound. He was no longer Henry to her.

"Most of that was the truth."

"Which makes the lies all the more convincing. You are well practiced."

"Yes." Perhaps honesty would help smooth this over.

"What other lies have you told, I wonder. Are you who you claim to be? Are you even English? Your accent is odd."

"What? How?"

He didn't even think of himself as having an accent. It was his native tongue. He spoke how he had always spoken. What was odd about it?

"I should have known," she continued, not bothering to answer. "There is no other reason for you to befriend me. I apologize if I haven't proved enough of a challenge."

"I haven't lied to you. I swear it."

You're lying to her now, you ass.

Probably true. Certain things he lied about by habit, and chances were good he had mentioned one or another of those. But he had never intended to deceive her, only to keep his work private.

"You make it very difficult to believe you." She started for the door.

Without thinking, he grabbed her arm to stop her. "Elle, please."

She shoved him aside. "Leave me be. I have no time for your games."

She stalked off, closing the door behind her. He wished

she had slammed it. Her cold, rational anger cut more deeply than a passionate outburst would have. He sank down on the bed and put his head in his hands.

It was no less than he deserved for not being frank with her from the start. He had seen immediately how intelligent she was, and he'd known she would uncover his secrets. But he'd liked keeping her guessing. He'd liked the way she watched him and scrutinized him, trying to unravel the mystery. He'd toyed with her, and paid the price.

Pushing the melancholy thoughts aside, he rose to follow her to her room. Nothing she could do or say would keep him from protecting her. She was crucial to this mission, and he would see to it that she came through unscathed. He didn't intend to let her out of his sight unless she was safely behind lock and key. Not when someone knew what they were about and was determined to put a stop to it.

During the ridiculous fuss over Elle's lack of a maid, he'd snuck a peek at the broken gangplank. The boards had split too neatly, as if they'd been chopped or sawn. Their swim in the Nile was anything but accidental.

IX

A Woman's Work is Never Done

*A*SWAN, THEIR NEXT PORT-OF-CALL, was known for its quarries. The Egyptologist aboard ship gave a detailed lecture on theories about how the ancients had cut and moved the massive stones for their great monuments. It was fascinating. Truly. Yet Elle couldn't enjoy it, nor shake her somber mood. Not while trapped aboard the tiny steamer with Henry Ainsworth her constant shadow.

Her anger had faded to a simmering resentment. It was her own fault, after all, for letting his awkward charm and shapely body sway her. She knew full well that gentlemen didn't strike up real friendships with penniless barmaids. Still, her lack of judgement didn't excuse the lying scoundrel of a bodyguard.

Henry wasn't an enemy, of that she was certain. His father was Westfield's closest friend, and she believed Henry's affection for his family genuine. He was also far from stupid. If he had meant to keep her in the dark, he would have concealed the existence of the notebook entirely. He'd been making sport of her, seeing what she would discover and when. It felt an insult, though in moments of weakness she wondered if it were, perhaps, a compliment.

For his part, Henry followed her about in taciturn misery.

When he did speak, his sentences were short, his words clipped. Elle avoided his wide, sad eyes and told herself he'd gotten what he deserved.

"Are you well this morning, Niece?"

Elle swallowed her irritation. Since the accident, Westfield had been a fretting, hovering mess.

"Yes, Uncle, I'm quite well, thank you."

"You need not fear for your safety today. Henry and I will be by your side at all times."

She had to glance away to hide her grimace. Henry noticed, naturally, and a hint of a smile flashed across his features. It was the first smile she'd seen from him in days.

"I'm not concerned," Elle said. She didn't fear the sort of coward who would sabotage a gangplank to rattle her. Their investigation had hardly begun. She would press on until she located Nenet's serum source.

"Perhaps not," Westfield said, "but we are walking into dangers unknown, and you need not put on a brave face for my sake."

Elle gritted her teeth. Westfield was the one afraid. She hadn't needed the help of a man since she was a little girl and her Papa was still alive. And yet, here she was, stuck with two men following her about as if she were helpless.

She endured their presence throughout the morning, hanging on Westfield's arm because he talked less the nearer she was. Henry followed behind except where he was needed to open doors or carry packages. His sullen demeanor had given way to predatory energy and watchful eyes—not that anyone noticed outside herself. It was remarkable, really, the way people overlooked him. Perhaps the role of servant was convenient for a spy.

After several hours exploring the city and declining offers of cheap European potions and scented oils, they paused to rest and fill their bellies.

"After lunch I would like to walk back to the docks," she

suggested. "We have been told more than once that the smaller boat owners bring goods from beyond the first cataract."

"Briefly, perhaps," Westfield replied. "I fear we have been taken on a wild goose chase. The ship returns north tomorrow, fortunately. Come, my dear, there is a restaurant at the hotel where we can dine."

Elle wasn't so quick to declare defeat. The moment Henry was shunted off to see to his own lunch, she excused herself to go wash up. Then she slipped out the front door and headed out on her own. Her stomach growled for lack of food, and Westfield was certain to panic when she didn't return, but she wouldn't be deterred.

Investigation proved difficult. Most of the boat owners either didn't wish to do business with a strange foreign woman or didn't speak a word of English or French. She wandered from boat to boat, doing all she could to make herself understood.

She was near to declaring her quest a failure, when a voice said, in accented English, "I can help you, my lady."

Elle whirled toward the speaker. He was a tall man, with skin so dark as to be near black, close-shaven hair, and large, intent eyes.

"My name is Durere. I am at your service."

Elle nodded in greeting. "Hello. You know something of potions in this region?"

"Yes. I have carried them, and I know villages up the river where they are made. Good potions, not like the ones those other men will offer you. Let me show you."

A shiver of excitement raced down her spine.

Durere withdrew a small vial from his pocket and presented it to her. "I carry this. I haven't needed it yet, but it will cure me of bad food, snake bite, small injury."

Elle uncorked the bottle and took a sniff. The same unusual tang she had discovered in Nenet's potions filled her nostrils. Her heart thudded in her chest. She had found her path to the serum. At last!

She passed the vial back to him, her hands trembling with anticipation. "Would you be willing to take passengers to some of these villages?"

"Yes, my lady, if you wish to hire my boat, but it is not large and comfortable like your British steamship."

She waved a hand. "That doesn't matter. We need only the clothes on our backs and enough food to last the journey. There are but three of us: myself and two men. How many could your boat carry?"

"All, if you truly bring no more than you have said."

"Excellent! I will speak with my uncle, and he will make arrangements to pay you your fee. We can find you here at the dock later today? Perhaps in an hour?"

"Yes, but I cannot wait all day. If you will not return to hire my boat, I will take on other work."

"I will return. You have my word."

He smiled at her. "Thank you, my lady. I am happy to assist you."

"Thank *you*, Durere. You have been most helpful." She gave him a gracious bow and hurried off to find the others.

A short way down the street, Henry stepped out from the shadows of a building, startling her.

"Have you been following me this whole time?"

Ridiculous question. Of course he had. There was no sense being angry about it. It was his profession. She would never best him at it, and she couldn't fault him for making a living.

"I'm a spy, mademoiselle. You told me so yourself." He both looked and sounded cheerier than he had anytime since their fight. "I wasn't close enough to hear your conversation with the Nubian gentleman. I assume you have arranged passage on his boat?"

"Gentleman?" she echoed, shocked by his use of the term for a lower class, native man. Too many of Henry's class would allow none but a landed man such a moniker.

"Is he a scoundrel, then? I hadn't thought you would consort with such."

"The only scoundrel around here is you, monsieur." Her retort fell flat. Taunting a man was far less effective after he had shown himself complimentary of someone most members of his station would disregard.

"My mistake. You do consort with the likes of me, though perhaps against your better judgement."

"Henry Ainsworth, you are the most singular man I have ever met."

He cocked an eyebrow. "Am I?"

"Absolutely. And you are correct. I have hired the boat. We will collect my uncle and be off."

"Very well."

Silence fell between them as they made their way back to the steamship. Henry bounced and fidgeted, full of nervous energy. Halfway to their destination he spun to face her and stopped.

"Are we speaking to one another again?"

"I don't think so. I've been waiting for an apology."

"An apology for what? For upsetting you? For that I'm very sorry. For following you? Drawing maps? Keeping my work private? I cannot apologize for those things. Those are the habits and necessities of my profession."

"What about the lying?"

"I told you, I haven't lied to you."

Elle didn't know if she could believe him, but she was surprised to find she wanted to. She considered him for a moment. His face was calm now, unreadable.

"I will give the matter some thought."

His cheeks dimpled. "Good enough."

X

Beyond the First Cataract

"Greetings, my lady," the boatman welcomed Elle. "My boat is prepared for you. Are these the gentlemen who will be coming along with you?"

Henry stopped a few feet behind her, carrying the cumbersome pair of boxes with several days' rations inside. A bag with necessities and extra clothing dangled from his elbow. Elle glanced over her shoulder at him. He'd seen that look on her face before. She hated it when he carted all their things about. He knew part of it was her desire for self-sufficiency. He hadn't yet decided how much of the rest was guilt for making him do all the work, and how much was worry he wouldn't be up to the task. She had no cause to fret on either account. He liked having physical work to keep his body strong, and he'd had far worse jobs than baggage handling.

Elle had her personal satchel, and a blanket draped over one arm. Westfield hovered over her, his arms laden with several more blankets, a frown of anxiety on his face.

"They are indeed, Monsieur Durere. This is my uncle, Lord Westfield, and Lord Henry Ainsworth. And I'm terribly sorry, but I neglected to introduce myself when I was here earlier. I am Elle Deschamps."

"I am happy to see you again, Lady Elle. Please, follow me and we will load you and your things onto the boat."

The boat was small, at most fifteen feet long. Half-full with boxes, it had but a single bench for passengers to sit upon. It was simple in design, with no cargo hold in which to shelter, and no awning or other covering to protect from the elements. Their host had laid a cloth across the bench to provide some amount of comfort.

Despite its austerity, the vessel was tidy, carefully maintained, and possessed of both a fine sail and a small steam engine attached to a paddle wheel which could be raised and lowered as needed. Henry admired the serviceable little boat and the pride its owner clearly took in its upkeep.

"A beautiful craft, sir," he said. "And the engine and paddle you have added to her are quite marvelous. You must put a great deal of work into her care."

"I try to do right for her. She carries me swiftly, she has no leaks, and she rides smoothly on the river."

"A testament to your seafaring, I'm sure."

"The gentleman is most kind. Please, let me load your things for you, and you may take your seats."

Henry handed over their luggage and turned to help Elle into the boat. She hesitated, then accepted his hand. The warmth of her skin flowed all the way to his chest.

"This is madness," Westfield hissed. "Miss Deschamps, you can't truly intend to undertake this voyage. Why, there is hardly room to sit. Where will we eat? Where will we sleep?"

"I assume we will sleep on the ground, Uncle. That is why I brought a blanket."

Westfield groaned. "Henry, do help me talk some sense into her."

"Where is your spirit of adventure, sir? I, personally, am looking forward to seeing where Miss Deschamps will take us next."

Truth be told, he was thrilled at the direction their journey had taken. Tailing Elle through Aswan had provided more fun than he'd had in months. Camping out in the wilds of Africa promised to be even better. He had a sharp knife, fire starting tools, and plenty of tea. What else did a man need?

"A fine thing to say for a lad like you, accustomed to soldiering. I haven't slept on the ground in twenty-five years!"

"I have blankets for sleeping," Durere assured him as he rigged the sail. "I have taken passengers before, do not worry."

"I'm not worried. I am… hesitant," Westfield replied. "I don't think this is a proper conveyance for the young lady."

"The lady is an explorer. I have carried many explorers. She will have no trouble. Are you comfortable? We will be off soon."

Durere untied the boat, pushed it away from the dock, and took his place at the helm. The water levels were falling at this time of year, and were too low to allow large boats such as the steamer past the cataracts. Durere's small craft had no difficulty. When the wind died down, or the rush of the water grew too fast, he lowered the paddlewheel and the little steam engine carried them until the sailing became smooth again.

Elle asked his permission to examine the potion he used to run the engine, and he cheerily agreed. Henry watched her poke about in the back of the boat, smiling as she worked.

"It is good?" Durere asked. "I buy it from an honest man. The other sellers, their potions are weak."

"It's very good," she replied. "I think you have found an excellent supplier."

"It is worth the price I pay. This engine takes me upriver very fast and when others sometimes cannot sail at all. I earn many more commissions that way, and it has made me popular with explorers such as you."

"I'm not an explorer, monsieur."

"Ah. You may not call yourself one, my lady, but you are in your heart."

Elle blushed. She looked lovely this afternoon, with her pink cheeks and bright eyes. A cute and practical bonnet shaded her face just enough to add an aura of mystery. Henry turned away before his thoughts could venture into inappropriate territory. Damn. Sitting close to her for hours would be an exercise in forbearance. Hell, this was the adventure of a lifetime. He couldn't comprehend how Westfield could dislike it so.

Long before Durere moored the boat for the evening, the frustration of inaction began to rankle. Henry resorted to playing mental games, the sort he used to keep himself awake and focused during surveillance missions. Tomorrow he would ask their linguistically-skilled guide to teach him Arabic and Nubian.

The moment the boat hit the shore, Henry hopped over the side and busied himself unloading their things. He allowed himself a few minutes to walk up and down the river bank to stretch his legs and familiarize himself with the area, then he set about starting a fire.

Durere cast two fishing rods into the river and sat on the bank watching them and sharpening his knife. He was an excellent guide—quiet, efficient, and knowledgeable. This flat, open area would be good for sleeping, and let them see any danger long before it reached them.

Elle walked about with Westfield, speaking in quiet tones. Henry couldn't hear what they were saying, but Elle was using her false smile, so he guessed she was again enduring questions about her well-being. After a time, her smile turned genuine, and she patted Westfield on the shoulder. Henry chuckled. She had turned the tables and was offering him help.

Westfield looked baffled and exhausted. The poor man was not fit to be a field operative. His skill was in diplomacy: resolving conflict and making connections. He lived to reconcile enemies and make new friends.

Henry could count his own friends on one hand. His bungling of the situation with Elle was testament to his lack of skill in that regard. He wasn't social by nature, and espionage was an anti-social profession. Their small group might be better off splitting up if future outings such as this were necessary. Or at least they'd be better off leaving Westfield behind.

Elle and Westfield started back toward the fire. Henry rose to greet them and tossed a few more sticks into the flames.

"The fire looks marvelous, Henry," Westfield complimented him. "Thank you."

"I'll fetch some vegetables from our stores for dinner," Elle suggested. "They will taste excellent roasted."

"She's quite the girl," Westfield said softly, watching her walk to the boat.

"Indeed. She is the most remarkable woman I have ever met. And, as you know, my family is full of women of courage and spirit."

"I greatly admire her sharp mind, her kind heart, and her determination to do good. I only wish she would take more care to respect social proprieties and stay clear of potentially dangerous situations."

Henry grinned. "I wouldn't change her for the world."

Westfield gave him a sharp look. "Take care, lad. It wouldn't do to go falling in love with her."

Henry schooled his features into an expression of neutrality. No, it wouldn't do at all. He was well on his way there, though, and he likened it to riding a bicycle down a steep hill—the heady rush of excitement and the uncertainty of what lay at the end. He had a chance to walk away unscathed, but the odds favored a crash. In this scenario, he wasn't a skilled cyclist.

Elle started back to the fire, her arms full of turnips and carrots. One of the turnips slipped from her grasp and rolled across the ground. She sighed and bent to retrieve it.

"Stop!"

Elle froze at the boatman's shout. Henry dropped to a knee, hiking up the left leg of his trousers to draw his knife. He cursed his decision not to wear the breeches and tall boots that gave him better access to the weapon. He followed Durere's gaze, looking for the danger.

Durere had risen from his place near his fishing poles, and he stood in a slight crouch, his own knife ready to strike. A snake lay coiled in the rocks near the fallen turnip, little more than two feet from Elle's outstretched hand. It lifted its head, hissing its displeasure.

Elle sucked in a horrified gasp, jerked her hand away, and took a stumbling step backward, losing a carrot in the process. She quickly regained her composure and inched away, careful not to startle the creature. Durere sprang into action. He came at the snake from behind, slicing its head off with one smooth stroke of his knife. He picked up the turnip and the carrot she had dropped and handed them to her with a slight bow.

"I'm sorry to startle you, my lady. I should have warned you to look for the snakes. They like to hide among the rocks." He bent and picked up the headless reptile. "We will have an excellent dinner. I have a fish also."

Henry felt a rush of relief, followed by a pang of guilt. Some bodyguard he was. He replaced the knife and turned back to the fire. Elle lowered herself to the ground beside him, depositing her load of food between them.

"Are you quite all right, Niece?" Westfield fretted. "What a frightful thing to be lurking so near to us."

"Yes, I'm fine," she answered. "Only surprised. I'm not accustomed to the sorts of creatures that live here."

"We'd best stay by the fire," Henry suggested. "Animals shy away from it." If he couldn't protect her, he could at least offer good advice and cook dinner. He reached for the food she had brought. "Thank you for getting these. I'll make us something to eat."

Durere brought both the snake and the fish over to the fire and began preparing them for cooking. Westfield watched him, frowning.

"Is that snake not poisonous? How can it be safe to eat?"

"The only danger is in the head. The body is good for eating. You should eat some. It will fill your belly better than those vegetables."

Henry had eaten unusual foods before, but never a snake. "I'll try it," he said. "How about you, Miss Deschamps?"

"Yes, I will try it," Elle answered without hesitation. "We may as well make good use of the poor creature." Her mouth twisted into a little half-frown, as it so often did when she was thinking. "The venom is still in its head, I imagine? Is there a way to extract it?"

"Yes, my lady, if you are careful."

She hopped up from her seat and scampered over to the boat, watching where she stepped. She returned carrying her bag and drew out an empty vial.

"Can you help me fill this with the snake venom?" she asked Durere.

"Yes, I can."

"Excellent! Thank you."

"What on earth do you want a bottle of poison for?" Westfield asked in astonishment.

"Snake venom can be used in many potions. Small amounts can be wonderful for medicines when mixed properly. It's hard to procure back home. I can't pass up a chance to collect it fresh from the source."

Henry tried his best not to burn the vegetables while he watched her. She knelt beside the severed snake head and listened as Durere pointed out the glands where the snake stored the venom. Her patient and steady hands wielded the scalpel with precision, swiftly dissecting the head. She filled the bottle as full as possible and then held it up, examining it in the firelight. The delight on her face was infectious. Henry grinned, even as he rolled a blackened carrot from the fire. He'd eat that one. He didn't care.

"This is excellent," Elle enthused. "Well worth the fright."

Henry couldn't suppress a laugh. "I love your attitude, Miss Deschamps. You like to find the good in things." Durere had the right of it. She was an explorer at heart. She possessed all the qualities of a first-rate adventurer: intelligence, tenacity, curiosity, self-reliance, courage, and a solid work ethic. Henry wished he could take her on all of his missions.

Bloody hell. He was further gone than he'd realized. He was going to crash, and his heart might never recover. He ate in silence, watching her, wondering what he might do to get her speaking to him again. He thought he might agree to just about anything.

When they spread their blankets out around the fire, he put his fully opposite hers. Westfield gave him a nod of approval, but in truth Henry didn't care a whit whether their sleeping arrangements were improper. It was a matter of practicality. If he lay down beside her, he would be up all night with a raging cockstand. He didn't expect to sleep well as it was.

"I'll take first watch," he told the others.

Elle nodded. "Wake me in a few hours. I will take second watch."

"Thank you. I'll do that," he replied, before Westfield could jump in to exclaim that it wasn't appropriate to make a woman take a shift on watch. She had volunteered. Henry wasn't going to be the one to tell her no.

XI

All Dried Up

$\mathcal{D}$URERE MOORED THE BOAT at a small dock on the western bank of the river and escorted his passengers into the village. Brightly painted mud-brick buildings lined the dirt road, the smell of spicy foodstuffs wafting from their open doors. Elle breathed deeply, hoping she would have the opportunity for a taste of the local cuisine.

According to Durere's information, a potion maker lived here, distributing her wares to people up and down the river between the first and second cataracts. Elle walked with a spring in her step. Soon she would have another genuine Nile valley potion in her hands. If it matched Nenet's, this first leg of her mission would be a true success.

She jumped when a nearby door slammed. A boy cried out in a language Elle didn't understand and scampered off into the fields. Several other villagers ducked inside their houses, leaving the visitors alone but for a single, disinterested goat.

"They are skittish," Henry observed. "I wonder why."

"Shy of strangers, perhaps?" Westfield mused. "We are unarmed and there are but few of us. I cannot imagine we appear threatening."

"Explorers have passed this way before," Durere said, his typically cheerful face pulled into a tight frown. "It should not be so unusual."

He led them to a small house at the end of a long row of similar buildings and knocked on the door. A woman answered promptly. She was tall, with ebony skin, penetrating, dark eyes, and a few wisps of gray in her tightly-braided hair. She held herself with the confident posture of a woman who knew what she was about. She started upon seeing the strangers, but allowed Durere to engage her in a serious and lengthy conversation.

"The Lady Tabiry is the potions woman I told you of," he said sometime later. "She will speak with you, but only to Lady Elle. The gentlemen must wait with the boat."

Westfield's brows rose in alarm. "I don't think it appropriate to leave the young lady alone in a strange place."

Henry took Westfield's arm and steered him away. "Don't fret, sir. Miss Deschamps is quite a capable woman, and she has our excellent guide to translate for her. We had best be out of their way."

His words were calm, but his expression tight. Elle felt a flutter in her belly. He didn't like this any better than Westfield did. He was fighting his own instincts to let her work unobstructed, giving her a chance to learn something. That alone was reason enough to renew their friendship.

Elle quashed the upwelling of happiness. This was business. Nothing more. It was easier, safer to remain silent and distant.

Inside the house, Elle introduced herself through Durere's translation, and explained why she had come. "The serum used to make this potion comes from a source unknown to us." She showed Nenet's potion to Tabiry, who uncorked and sniffed it. "We are interested in determining the location of that source for our research. We aren't here to steal, only to learn."

"You won't find the source," Tabiry told her. "It is dried up or cut off. We don't know for certain."

Elle's heart sank. "We have the same problem with our sources. That's what prompted our expedition—to see who else uses serum and where they find it."

"Our supply has been dry this past month," Tabiry explained. "Since the first of your kind came through here."

"My kind? What do you mean?"

"Europeans. Potion-seekers. The first were few and seemed pleasant. They were followed by others who were not. They came with guns, and made demands. They stole food and took shelter in our houses without permission. They poked through my belongings and destroyed much of my work. We suffered no more than that in this village, but we have heard of other places where they killed the men who stood up to them and... *used*... the women."

Elle suspected Durere had softened that last sentence for her ears. Fury flared inside her. Her fingers curled into fists. She couldn't speak for several moments, and when she did, her words came out in French. She stopped and began again in English.

"I'm shocked and angered to hear this. My heart hurts for your people. Please, if you have a chance, tell your village and tell the others that my friends and I oppose these men, and we will do everything we can to see that they are stopped before they do further harm."

"It may be too late for that. Search out other potions makers in other lands. Warn them of these evils so they will be prepared."

Elle bowed to Tabiry. "Thank you, Lady Tabiry. You have been kinder than we deserve. I will ask for help to be sent. If at all possible, we will hunt down the wrongdoers."

"Thank you, also, Lady Elle. I wish you and your companions safe travels."

Heart heavy, Elle returned to shore, where she found Henry pacing about in an agitated fashion. Westfield stood stiffly by the boat, looking at his pocket watch. They both turned when they heard her footsteps. She rushed to them and gave them the unhappy news.

"Mother of God," Westfield swore. "They must think us monsters."

"Is there something we can do?" Elle inquired. "Can you send word back home? Ask for soldiers to search out these men?"

"I'd like to take down the bastards myself," Henry growled. His face was pale, his jaw clenched.

She gave him a grim smile. "That would be ill-advised, monsieur."

He blinked at her, as if just realizing she had heard him.

"I apologize for my coarse language, Miss Deschamps. I was overwrought. You are right, of course. One man against a group of unknown size would be like to suicide. Were I alone, I would go further for reconnaissance, but that is outside the scope of this mission. I will telegraph back home and ask that they send someone else."

"I, too, will do all I can," Westfield assured her. "We must return to Cairo at once. I can telegraph from there to Ainsworth in Rome and to others in London. Mr. Durere, I will pay you a handsome bonus if you can get us to Aswan quickly."

"We will be going with the river now, Lord Westfield. We can sail very quickly, indeed."

"Thank you. Your help is much appreciated."

Durere gave a nod. "I, too, will be fighting these criminals. I will spread the word to my people and along my route."

Henry gave the boatman an assessing look. "Something tells me you and I could flush out these brigands on our own, given the right tools and information."

A true smile touched Durere's lips. "I will learn all I can. If you come back this way, Lord Henry, we will test that idea."

Westfield frowned at Henry and shook his head before turning to Durere. "I wish you luck, my good man. We will ask any men that come this way to use a code so you may know they are friendly. If they declare themselves 'a friend of the miller,' you will know they are allies. If they do not know that code, do not trust them."

Durere nodded. "I will remember. Now we must be off."

Henry handed Elle up into the boat. The fierceness in his eyes had given way to sadness.

"I'm so sorry you had to hear of these terrible things, Miss Deschamps."

Elle's mouth pinched tight. Had he not minutes ago acted as though he believed her an equal? And now he thought her unable to withstand bad news? He wouldn't have said such a thing to a man. "I grew up poor in Paris, monsieur. This isn't my first encounter with rape and murder."

His expression grew pained. "And for that I'm also very sorry. No woman, no matter who she is or where she lives, should have to fear such things."

There was a slight hitch in his voice. He was more sensitive to the matter than she was, she realized. His concern was perhaps not so illiberal as she had thought.

"No," she agreed. "Nor any man. But such is the world we live in."

His eyes hardened. "Then we will have to change it, won't we?"

XII

Traveling Companions

*T*HE DAYS DRAGGED ON. Traveling downriver shortened the journey considerably, but with no progress possible until they reached Alexandria, Henry passed the time in a state of restless ennui.

Elle no longer avoided him, meaning following her had become more chore than challenge. And while they were again on speaking terms, conversation between them hadn't regained its prior ease. They watched one another in silence, Henry wondering all the while what she might be thinking.

He had never met anyone with a mind like hers. Even during restful moments she never stopped taking everything in, processing it and storing it away until the time came when she could put it to good use. She was like his pocket watch: quiet on the outside, but humming with internal energy. He wondered if her dreams were as full of life as her waking self. She had certainly looked peaceful enough when he'd watched her sleeping by their campfire, the glow of the coals casting a soft light on her delicate features.

Dammit, Ainsworth.

The moment they hopped off the train in Alexandria, Henry excused himself to send telegrams. A few moments alone would do him some good.

His messages were so numerous and lengthy as to cost him

all his pocket change, but the trouble in Egypt merited the expense. His employers would send additional funds.

Finished with his own work, Henry made his way to the hotel, armed with a list of possible serum sources and the timetables of the ships in port.

Elle answered his knock promptly and waved him inside her room. The violation of her personal space caused a thrill of anticipation and a surge of guilt he attempted to quash. If she could enter his room, why shouldn't he enter hers?

He scanned the entire chamber out of habit, his eyes coming to rest on her trunk. It stood open, offering an indecent display of feminine undergarments. A mental list formed automatically. Half-a-dozen pairs of silk stockings: two each, blue, green, and white. Matching ribbon garters. Six pairs linen drawers, frilly and white. Silky purple corset with pink laces and trim.

Heat rose in his cheeks. What the hell was he doing? And damn, what would she look like in that glorious corset? He'd seen bawdy stage shows where the women wore scantier things, but his body hadn't reacted half as much as it did to the image in his head.

"Henry?"

He turned to face her, trying to pull himself into some semblance of control. Naturally, she had chosen the worst possible moment to resume the intimate address.

"Would you prefer we take our conversation elsewhere? I know you were raised to be a proper gentleman, and I wouldn't wish you to be uncomfortable."

The embarrassment smarted. Thank God he wasn't a boy anymore. Schoolboy Henry would have run and hidden and never spoken to her ever again. Adult Henry would persevere, even if it meant exposing himself to her ridicule.

"No, thank you. My career necessitates occasional situations or behaviors that many would consider improper.

It's only sensible that I practice such things whenever the opportunity arises."

Good Lord, did that sound indecent. Running away and hiding seemed better every second.

"Very well," she replied. "Please, have a seat."

Her skirts brushed against his thigh when he took a place beside her. He shoved his chair tightly against the table to conceal his reaction to her touch, scolding himself for letting her distract him from work. He handed her the papers and gave her a moment to look them over.

"My recommendation is to sail for America," he said. "There are numerous locations worth investigating, and the States are far enough away that perhaps they haven't yet fallen prey to the bastards who are destroying supplies. Pardon my language, Miss Deschamps."

As usual, she appeared unfazed. "I agree with both your word choice and your assessment of our options."

She consulted the list of upcoming departures, wearing her thinking frown, then tapped the paper with a single finger. "If we sail on this ship, it will carry us straight through the Mediterranean to Lisbon. Passage across the ocean should be easy to come by there."

"Good thinking. We will have our pick of ships in Lisbon. Most will be bound for New York, I imagine, but we should have other options. Charleston, in the Carolinas, has a large port."

"And is among the top sites on the list. It would be excellent if we could find a ship directly there. Good." She smiled up at him. "When Uncle Edwin returns we will tell him the plan so he can purchase our fare."

Henry chuckled.

Elle's smile vanished. "What's so funny?"

"You didn't even consider asking for his opinion on the plan."

"It's a good plan. He would be foolish to disagree with it.

Even if he did, there are three of us, and two of the three have already approved it. He would be out-voted."

"Very democratic."

"Yes, I suppose it is."

"I approve."

Elle pursed her lips, and Henry could tell she was pondering the meaning behind his words.

"Thank you," she said a moment later. "Though I don't require your approval, it's not unwelcome."

Her words were a perfect Elle response. Polite, yet firm, she asserted her independence while showing she still valued his opinion. He opened his mouth to tease her about it, but snapped it shut at the last instant. There was no sense risking the delicate balance of their reemerging friendship.

Their reentry into polite society was another important consideration. Henry didn't look forward to reprising his role as her servant. What did interest him, however, was her transition from explorer to fine lady. She had proven she could take charge when she was working. How much of that would carry over? All, he hoped. The world could stand to learn a thing or two from her.

· · · 👤 · · ·

Elle gawked at the ocean liner waiting at the dock in Lisbon. She would have thought the many grand sights she had seen thus far would have made what was really no more than a big boat less imposing, but no. The ship was as long as the Great Pyramid was high, with four towering sailing masts and a massive central smokestack. Giddiness spread through her body. The long transatlantic journey would allow her days of exploration, and the size of the ship would give her plenty of places to curl up on her own with a book.

Westfield took her arm, steering her about as if she were helpless. The more time she spent as a lady, the more it seemed that no amount of money was worth the trouble. She would rather be poor and independent.

"Miss Deschamps! Hello!"

Elle froze at the sound of the voice. Turning, she spied the over-attentive woman from her Nile dunking, dressed once more in a pastel gown and an enormous hat. Her maid, Aila, trailed behind. The woman hurried to Elle's side and kissed the air beside her cheek, as if they were great friends.

"How are you, dear? I trust you had time to recover from that terrible accident?"

Elle adopted her working smile. "I'm quite well, Lady... Pardon, I don't believe I ever learned your name?"

"Charlotte de Winter."

"A pleasure, Lady de Winter."

"The pleasure is mine, I assure you. I'm so thrilled to see we are once again traveling the same route. You and I are kindred spirits, I can tell. I have only just left my cousins who must return to England. They were loathe to leave me, naturally, but I have told them that, in these modern times, it is not unseemly for a widow of means to travel solo."

"Quite right, Lady de Winter," Westfield agreed. "You seem a most capable woman."

Elle's smile tightened. Apparently not all women needed protection in his mind. Only the young, unmarried ones. Pity she hadn't thought to invent a dead husband.

"You are too kind, sir," Lady de Winter cooed. "I've been dying to travel to America. It will be such fun to see what the colonies have gotten up to."

"I suspect you'll find them to have achieved a tolerably united state," Henry quipped.

Lady de Winter scowled at him. "Haven't you anything to do?"

"No, ma'am. Not at present."

She made a tutting noise and turned back to Elle. "This is a most fortuitous meeting, though."

No. It's really not.

"We are the answer to one another's problem."

"I don't have…" Elle began, but Lady de Winter talked right over her.

"I will be able to wire my cousins to reassure them I am not alone, and I can provide you a much-needed female companion. I know how difficult it must be for you, with only your uncle and an insolent manservant for company."

Westfield beamed. "That is so kind of you, Lady de Winter. It's most gratifying to know my niece will not get lonely on the voyage."

Elle bit back a nasty retort. The last thing she needed was to make a scene. Remaining unobtrusive was important to their investigations and she was trapped. For now.

As they boarded and made their way to her cabin, her eyes roved the decks, analyzing her surroundings. There were, indeed, many good places to curl up with a book. She would have to find the least obvious.

XIII

Therefore I'll Hide Me

$\mathcal{H}$ENRY SAT ON THE UPPER DECK of the ocean liner, enjoying the fine weather, and sketching a map of the ship in his journal. Every time he opened it, he thought of Elle and how remarkable her potion was. Nearly as remarkable as the lady herself. He resisted a preposterous urge to mark her stateroom with a tiny heart. God, but he was a fool.

"Ah, Henry, there you are!"

Henry closed the book and rose to greet Westfield.

"And how are you this afternoon, sir? Have you need of me?"

"I do, indeed, Henry. Have you seen my niece anywhere?"

The question surprised him. Henry had spoken hardly a word to Elle since they'd planned this route in Alexandria. He'd taken his meals in the third class dining room, and kept his own company. It was difficult to spend time with her when he was all but banned from the first class areas. He watched her as much as he could—chiefly when she was here on the deck—but even then they couldn't converse without looking improper. His frustration with Henry the servant grew by the hour.

"I have not. I thought you wanted us to remain apart to maintain the servant-employer distinction." He hoped his words didn't sound too bitter. Their ruse had seemed a good idea when the expedition began.

"Yes, that is correct. It's helping, I believe, but I'm concerned that acting the part of a wealthy lady has been a strain on her nerves."

"I hate to disagree, sir, but I don't think her nerves strain so easily. She may be unhappy with the role, but she is quite capable of playing it. If she seems stressed, then there must be some larger cause."

"There may be, but I cannot even speak to her present mood. I can't find her anywhere. She did not come to the dining room for luncheon, she isn't in her room, and she is nowhere I have looked."

Henry frowned. Because of the attack in Egypt, they had arranged certain precautions for the journey. With Henry limited in his ability to follow her, Westfield had counselled Elle to remain with himself or Lady de Winter as much as possible, and to keep to public spaces or her room when alone. She had promised to carry defensive potions, and to let the others know at once if she noticed anything suspicious.

That she had deviated from the plan didn't surprise Henry greatly, but her absence did concern him.

"When was the last time you saw her?"

"She was at breakfast this morning. She did not say a great deal, but she has been rather silent of late."

"I wonder if she has hatched some sort of plan."

"I cannot imagine what that would be. We can't make any progress on our work while we are at sea."

"True. But she may have plans of her own."

"For what purpose? I cannot think her devious."

"Not devious plans, sir. Personal. Perhaps she is off writing a letter, or reading a book. Maybe she wanted to go exploring on her own."

Elle valued her private time. She would need it all the more if something was bothering her.

"Would you be so good as to search the ship for her? I am

becoming worried for her safety. You know the second and third class areas and can look there."

"Hmm…" Henry considered the matter for a moment. "I doubt she would go anywhere in the lower class areas. She would be too conspicuous in her fine clothes, and she doesn't know the layout of those decks. She would stick to the first class and common areas. If she wishes to be alone, she will have found herself a nice little hiding place. I would guess she has had a place in mind since the day we boarded."

"You are thinking like a spy, my boy. Do you really believe she planned this disappearance in advance?"

"I do. She likes to be prepared. I wouldn't be surprised if she spent most of our first day here walking about this vessel thinking up hiding places, escape routes, and the like. I know I did. I admit I have been trained to assess every location and situation, and it is second nature to me now. Part of the reason I was chosen for this career was that I already had a tendency to view things in such a manner. Miss Deschamps shares that tendency. She has the makings of a brilliant spy. She wants only for training."

"I'm not wholly certain I approve of your career, Henry. I certainly don't wish you to lure my niece into such things."

Henry sighed. "I'm not luring her into anything. I'm merely making an observation. You wish me to find her? Very well, I shall do so."

"Thank you. Please let me know her whereabouts as soon as you know them."

"If she desires time alone, I don't think it polite to reveal her hiding spot. I will report back to you, but I make no promises."

Westfield shook his head. "I remember your father saying years ago that he didn't know how you could manage a military career, because you habitually question authority. I'm wondering the same thing now."

"I believe Father thought me quite daft, at the time.

There are many reasons my superiors herded me into an unconventional role, and I imagine that is one of them."

"Well, it seems to have been a success."

"Indeed. I enjoyed the challenge of my military service, and it continues to be of use in our current work. Now, if you will excuse me, I will see what I can learn of our missing partner."

. . . &. . .

The tarpaulin covering the lifeboat shifted, startling Elle so badly that her pencil slipped and poked clear through the page.

"Ah, there you are!"

"Henry! Mon Dieu! You gave me a fright."

He climbed into the boat, tugged the canvas back into place, and slipped down between the benches to sit beside her. The tight quarters put them nearly shoulder-to-shoulder.

"Apologies, Miss Deschamps. Westfield was concerned by your disappearance and asked me to locate you."

She nodded. That wasn't unexpected. Henry was too good at these games, however, and he'd found her much too quickly. She'd hoped to get more than one day's use from this location.

"Well, it's better, I suppose, than having been found by one of the crew and thought a stowaway."

"Your name is on the passenger manifest, Miss Deschamps. You needn't worry on that account. More likely, you would be assumed to be awaiting a lover for a secret tryst."

"Ridiculous. This is hardly a romantic venue."

Henry lounged against the curved hull, folding his arms behind his head. "It seems comfortable enough to me, but then, I've been sleeping in third class. Any place that doesn't reek of human sweat and other unmentionable things would be more comfortable."

"That is uncharitable. Those passengers have likely paid every cent they have to move to a new country."

"True, but their poverty ought not prevent them from

bathing. You have never spent time among a large group of single men, mademoiselle. They often take a lax attitude toward personal hygiene. I had rather sleep near the families and the women, but that, of course, would be most inappropriate."

As was everything, it seemed. Elle would have been happy to never hear the word "inappropriate" again in her life.

"You ought to share Uncle Edwin's quarters. There are two beds in the room, and it doesn't lack for space."

"And then people would suspect me of being more than a servant."

"Don't they suspect you already by the way you talk?"

"I can talk in all sorts o' ways, if need be, miss. Now, if you'd be excusing me, I'll be gettin' on back t' yer uncle and tellin' him yer well."

Elle closed her journal and reached for the book and the lantern she had brought. "I suppose I shall have to find a new hiding place. I will try to think up a better one so I can have a bit more time before you come poking about again."

Henry frowned at her. "I had no intentions of revealing your hiding place, Miss Deschamps, and I'm happy to leave you to have time alone. I sought you out only to reassure Westfield and myself of your well-being. Rest assured you will be left in peace."

He pulled back the tarpaulin and poked his head out to check the surrounding area. He then swung one leg over the side of the craft and began to climb out.

"Henry?"

"Yes?"

"I…" She paused, a bit embarrassed to ask him for anything. "I have had nothing to eat since breakfast, and it's near to tea time. I wondered if you might…"

"Of course, my dear lady! I wouldn't dream of leaving you to go hungry. I will return shortly."

Mere minutes later, he surprised her with a tray containing a steaming teapot, a pair of matching cups, scones and jam, two varieties of sandwiches, and even some cold meats and deviled eggs.

"Good heavens!"

"What have I done wrong this time?"

"Nothing. I was expecting perhaps some bread and cheese, but you have brought me a tea fine enough for your queen. How did you come by this?"

"Simple. I went to the kitchen and informed them that Lord Westfield and his niece would be taking tea in private today and could I get a tray made up for them? The results are as you see them."

"I was right. You are a spy *and* a liar," she teased.

"One begets the other, I dare say. I haven't had a decent cup of tea in days, and I'm not above telling falsehoods in order to procure one."

She laughed as he poured out two cups of tea from the first pot. He left hers black, as she liked it. To his own, he added a precise amount of milk, stirring it until the two were only just blended. Then he took a sip and leaned back against the side of the lifeboat, giving a small sigh of pleasure.

"Ah. That's so much better. Someone should campaign for better provisions for the lower class passengers. You wouldn't believe the swill they tried to pass off as a Darjeeling."

Elle liked seeing him this way, relaxed and spouting witticisms. She had missed his company. Here in secret, there was no playacting, no social divide. They could be themselves and be friends. A warning sounded in the back of her mind, but she shoved it away. This was her time to relax.

She smiled and sipped at her own tea, enjoying the warmth and the brisk flavor. She wondered if Henry had chosen it and steeped it himself.

"You ought to learn potions."

"I haven't the talent for it, as I believe I have mentioned before."

"So you say, but you are mistaken. You possess the necessary skill set for potions work. You select and prepare your tea with great care, and you can taste or smell subtle differences not only between varieties, but in the quality. You have a good memory and a steady hand. You are not likely to ever be a master, but you could be proficient enough. You only lack training."

Henry selected a scone and smothered it with jam. "I said much the same thing to Westfield about your talent for espionage. Perhaps we ought to swap knowledge."

Elle's hand froze with a sandwich halfway to her mouth. "You would teach me to be a spy?"

"Certainly, if you would like to learn. And if you are willing to teach me in return, I would love to learn something of potions. I promise to try my best, though I offer no guarantees of success."

"Ha! If I teach you, you will have success. Don't doubt it."

"It's difficult to doubt anything that you say, Miss Deschamps. You fairly exude certainty."

"Good. That will serve well when you teach me to lie."

His grin was broad, his dimples deep. "Perhaps your first lesson ought to be when to keep impertinent comments to yourself."

"I possess that skill already," she retorted. "I wonder, though, if you do."

Henry looked away from her and finished his tea in silence. Elle felt the tremor rattle their fragile relationship. She wouldn't let it break again so easily. She'd only meant to tease, not to scold.

"I think we ought to skip that lesson. I find your impertinence much more agreeable than your silence." She picked up the teapot. "Another cup?"

"Please."

She poured for them both and tried one of the eggs. "This is by far the most pleasant meal I have had since we boarded this ship. We ought to do it again."

His smile returned. "I would not be adverse to such a plan." He pointed at the remaining scone. "Did you want to eat that?"

She shook her head. He snatched it up and scraped every last drop from the jam jar. He almost had more jam than scone.

"Teatime again, tomorrow, then?" he asked. "Or some other meal? Perhaps every meal. I wouldn't say no to that."

Elle laughed. "I will have to think on it. I can't leave poor Uncle Edwin alone too much. He will suffer an apoplexy. I think we strained his nerves near to breaking with that trip up the Nile. He will be horrified if he learns what we are about."

Henry's eyes sparkled. "Then we had best not tell him."

XIV

Into That Good Night

$\mathcal{A}$S IT HAPPENED, ELLE DIDN'T SEE HENRY at all the next
day, but their clandestine tea had left her in such a good mood
that even Charlotte de Winter's repeated badgering couldn't
dampen her spirits. Elle explained her disappearance as
seasickness, and rambled on about what she was reading, to
make a day spent abed sound plausible. Lady de Winter didn't
believe the tale, but Elle stuck with her story, and by dinner the
questioning stopped. She went to bed plotting to find Henry
and arrange tea the next day.

She awoke some time after midnight to a tapping at her
door. Blinking away sleep, she rose from her bed, turned up
the lantern, and cracked the door. Henry awaited her in the
darkened corridor, dressed all in black. She surveyed him in
the dim light. A simple, fitted shirt. Snug breeches tucked into
knee-high boots. He even wore a black cap to hide his blond
hair. He put a finger to his lips and passed her a bundle of cloth.

"Put this on and meet me at the end of the hall."

Elle closed the door and unrolled the bundle. It proved to be
a black dress, along with a scarf to cover her hair. She donned the
outfit quickly, forgoing the usual layers of undergarments. The
dress was plain and comfortable, lightweight and easy to move
about in—vastly better than the fancy outfits she'd been wearing
of late. She tied up the scarf and slipped out into the hall.

Henry stood deep in shadow, and it took Elle a moment to spy him. He motioned for her to follow, and they moved silently past the first class cabins until they reached a common sitting area. The room looked empty, but Henry steered her over to the darkest corner regardless. Putting his back to the wall, he motioned for her to do the same.

"Welcome to your first night of training," he whispered. "We won't be using any lights. Give your eyes a few minutes to adjust."

"I do wish you had warned me we would be sneaking about tonight. I would have gone early to bed."

"In this profession we don't always get a warning. We must be prepared for anything at any time."

"I see."

"We are in a good position to observe the room here. When it is dark and you wish to move about unobserved, stay in the darkest shadows you can find. Walls are your friend. The way we are standing here, no one can come at us from behind. We can take stock of the whole room without having to move or turn around."

"What if we were to be attacked?" Elle wondered. "Couldn't an enemy trap us against the wall?"

"It's a possibility. We will discuss defensive moves another day. This location is for observation and stealth, not fighting. If you are attacked, flee. Moving laterally along the wall can defend your back, if needed. Always head toward an exit. This segues nicely into my next lesson. Where are the exits in this room, Miss Deschamps?"

"Where we came in, and there, off to our left," she replied quickly.

"What about the opposite wall?"

Her brow furrowed in puzzlement. "The portholes? You can't be serious."

"They are a way out of the room. I wouldn't fit through one, perhaps, but you certainly could. It's far from ideal, but in an emergency it would suffice."

"I would fall into the ocean."

"I doubt that. You climbed to the upper deck where the lifeboats are stored and into the boat in a dress much more cumbersome than the one you currently wear. You are perfectly capable of escaping through a window. If it concerns you, we can arrange to practice it at another time."

Practice climbing through portholes? The idea was preposterous, yet so intriguing that she almost laughed. She thought to reply, but the sound of a footfall kept her quiet. Henry grasped her about the waist and pulled her deeper into the corner, pinning himself between her body and the wall.

Elle's eyes had adjusted well, and she was certain the two of them would be visible to anyone, despite the shadows. Would they be thought spies? Thieves? Lovers? She could hardly breathe, whether from the anticipation of being caught or the shock of their sudden embrace.

Her admiration of his physique hadn't prepared her for the feeling of his solid body pressed against the length of her. Henry was a wall of muscle, taut with barely-restrained energy. No wonder he didn't struggle with their baggage. If he took it in mind to restrain her, she would be powerless.

The way he held her now, though—his arm cradling her, but not squeezing, his hand resting lightly on her hip—she could slip free at any time. He protected, but made no attempt to control. She doubted he could have dreamed up a stranger way to win her trust.

A man hurried through the room, not even glancing in their direction. Elle remained frozen in place, not daring to move until Henry nudged her. The tickle of his breath on her ear caused her to shiver.

"We'd best be moving on now."

Elle let him lead the way, keeping close enough to brush against him. Henry didn't seem shy of her touch in these circumstances, and she took full advantage of it. She wasn't afraid to admit she enjoyed touching him. With the excitement of their clandestine outing pumping through her veins, even the slightest contact sent chills across her skin.

"I can't believe we weren't spotted," she whispered.

"We were well-concealed, despite how it may have felt. The people we might encounter tonight aren't out looking for us. They won't be poking their noses into corners to see if anyone is hiding. They have their own concerns, and that is to our advantage."

"Romantic liaisons, do you think?"

"Almost certainly. There could be a bit of thievery, also, if anyone were to be foolish enough to leave his door unlocked. This company has a good reputation, which usually means the crew isn't above searching all of third class for missing belongings. A wealthy thief would fare better."

"Why would a wealthy man be a thief?"

"Why not?"

They had come to a portion of the ship Elle had never seen before. The halls were narrower here, and the ceilings lower.

"Where are we? I don't recognize this area."

"Heading toward the working areas of the ship. Have you been paying attention? Do you think you could find your way back?"

"Um…" She thought back to when they had left the sitting room. They had continued down the hall, gone down a set of stairs, and then turned… right?

"I think I could get back, but I'm not completely certain."

"You need to be completely certain. You were lost in your thoughts. You have a very analytical mind, and that is a wonderful thing, but when you are working in the field, you must put that tendency to rest. You want to gather as much information as possible. Later, when you are in a safe, private location, you can sit and think and sort through all you have collected."

"I'm not certain I can remember so much at one time."

"It takes practice. I will share some tips with you in another lesson, and we can do some memory work. Tonight, I want you to concentrate on observation and knowing your surroundings. Exits, entrances, hiding places, obstacles, weapons. Don't forget to look up and down."

She nodded. This was how he could draw those maps so well. He memorized every place he went in exacting detail.

"May I ask, do we have a destination in mind?"

"The kitchens. They ought to have plenty of supplies we can use when you teach your portion of the training."

"Supplies?" Elle stopped in the middle of the hall. "You mean to steal ingredients?"

"I don't think they will miss anything."

His casual attitude stunned her. Her possessions were few and much prized. To her mind, theft was a serious crime. Clearly, he didn't see it in the same light.

"You make me question your moral judgment, monsieur!" She glanced down at her clothing. "How did you come by this dress?"

"Do lower your voice, mademoiselle, if you don't wish to be discovered here."

"Answer the question," she snapped.

"I purchased it, if you must know, from a young woman of about your size. I paid her quite a handsome sum, too. She seemed rather happy with the transaction."

Elle pondered that for a moment. She had seen how smoothly he could lie. Would he lie now, just to soothe her? Did it even matter? She hesitated too long before replying. Even in the dim light she could read the expression of pain in his features.

"Ah, Miss Deschamps, you have brought us to the most difficult lesson in all of espionage, and one I still struggle with myself. When your work is by nature one of secrets and deception, no one ever trusts you. I think perhaps we should call it a night. Why don't you lead the way? I will let you know if you take a wrong turn."

Elle traced their path back to her cabin, acutely aware of the space now between them. She couldn't reconcile his lying, thieving habits with the artless good-humor he displayed at unguarded moments. He seemed equal parts knight and knave. Her gut told her she could trust him with her life, but his career of choice and its attendant moral ambiguity gave her pause.

"Not a single mistake," he commended her when they arrived at her door. "You have a natural talent, Miss Deschamps." His praise was polite, but cool.

Her chest tightened. She hadn't meant to hurt him. The truth and an explanation had been all she desired. Her shock had made her words harsh and she couldn't take them back.

"I won't keep you from your rest any longer. Have a good night. You may keep the dress. I have no need of it."

He bowed to her and started off down the hall. Elle jogged after him. She couldn't leave it like this.

"Henry!"

He looked back. "Yes?"

"I'm sorry."

He gave her a nod.

Before he could turn away, she grabbed hold of his shirt and kissed him.

His body went rigid, his lips parting in a gasp of surprise. She slid her tongue into the gap, and he groaned and pulled her to him, crushing her uncorseted bosom against his chest. He kissed like the spy he was, delving, searching, leaving nothing unexplored. And lord, was he ever a thief. He stole her very breath away, crept inside her to crack open and expose her deepest passions.

She broke the kiss with reluctance, trembling, her chest heaving, even hungrier than when she had begun. Her fingers were clenched in the fabric of his shirt. In the darkened hall it was difficult to decipher his expression, but she could hear his ragged breathing and feel his pounding heart.

"Elle." Her name was a hoarse whisper. "Bloody hell."

He slid from her grasp and staggered backward, raking a hand through his hair. "*D-dormez bien*, mademoiselle," he stammered. An instant later, he had disappeared into the shadows.

XV

Tabula Rasa

*E*LLE STIFLED ANOTHER YAWN. Breakfast seemed inter-
minable. She had begun to think she should have feigned
a headache when Westfield had knocked on the door that
morning. She certainly had one now.

"You seem tired this morning, Elle, dear," Charlotte de
Winter observed. Her lips curled in just a hint of a smirk.

"A bit," Elle replied. "I didn't sleep well. Strange dreams."

"Ah. I'm sorry to hear that."

She didn't sound in the least sorry, and she clearly didn't
believe the lie, either. Elle didn't want to deal with her superior
attitude today. The moment the meal was ended, she would
escape to the deck and read in the morning sun. The fresh air
and breeze would help keep her awake, and perhaps she could
be dull enough to bore Charlotte into finding other amusement.

Her plan was delayed when a crewman stopped by their
table as they were finishing up.

"Miss Elle Deschamps?" he inquired.

Elle blinked, startled. "Oh! Yes, I am she."

"A letter for you, miss." He bowed and handed her a small,
folded slip of paper.

"Thank you."

She looked down at the paper. It bore only her name, in a
neat, even script.

"A letter!" Charlotte exclaimed. "How exciting. Whoever could it be from?"

"I can't imagine."

Her surprise made the lie sound credible. She recognized Henry's writing from his sketchbook. She had no idea why he'd written to her, and why he'd chosen to deliver the message in such a public fashion.

"Curious," Westfield observed. If he recognized the handwriting, he didn't comment on it.

"Well, you must open it," Charlotte urged. "You cannot leave us in suspense all day."

Elle unfolded the note with care, angling the paper so no one else at the table would be able to observe the contents without behaving rudely. Even Lady de Winter wouldn't be so obvious in her snooping.

To her complete shock, her caution proved unnecessary. The inside of the letter was completely blank. She turned it over in her hands, but could find no writing or mark save her name.

"It... it doesn't say anything at all," she told the others, flattening it on the table for them to see.

"Well!" Charlotte exclaimed. "How mysterious! This is quite a fascinating addition to our morning, don't you think, Lord Westfield?"

His face creased in a deep frown. "It seems to me highly inappropriate, to be sending a young lady cryptic, unsigned messages. It could easily be taken as a threat of sorts."

"I don't think so, Uncle. A joke perhaps, but not a threat. Anyone who knows me knows I'm not so easily frightened." She refolded the letter and pocketed it. "I will pay it no mind."

She rose from her seat. Westfield and Lady de Winter did likewise.

"Charlotte," Elle said pleasantly, "I was thinking just now that I would like to have some fresh air. Would you like to join me up top? I plan to take a book and sit out for a time."

"Thank you, but no. I have some letter writing of my own

to do. Mine, I assure you, will contain actual words, and I intend to sign them."

"That would be best. I don't think blank letters a very effective form of communication."

"I will see you for luncheon?"

"Of course." Elle smiled, nodded to the other woman, and then took her leave.

Westfield followed her. "May I see that note?"

"It was addressed to me, monsieur. I would prefer to keep it private."

"Was that Henry's writing? What is the boy about?"

"I didn't recognize the writing. You must be mistaken. I'm certain it's no more than a joke or a mistake. If you would excuse me, I will see you again at noon."

Elle walked up to the deck, looked about to make sure neither Westfield nor Lady de Winter could see her, then took another staircase back down into the first class section. She stopped briefly at her room to grab her potions kit before retracing last night's path into the heart of the ship. When she reached the place where she and Henry had turned back, she continued on. She had to try several different corridors before finding the correct passage, but eventually she located the kitchen.

A woman in an apron and flour-covered hands spoke to her.

"May I help you, miss?"

"Yes, if you please. I'm looking for some herbs and oils that I might use."

"Oh, you are the lady who makes potions! I ought to have known. Come with me, dear." She ushered Elle into the kitchen. "That man of yours was down here before breakfast—a sweet boy, he was—and I gave him a few things, but he said you might have more specific needs. Now, here are our spices and herbs, powders are off to the right, and I will fetch you the oils as well. You just gather up what you need."

Elle studied the shelves of ingredients before her. The well-stocked kitchen had nearly everything she wanted.

"How much is the fee for the ingredients?"

"Oh, goodness, there is no fee, child. You take what you like. Some folks eat more in one sitting than you could possibly use up for your potions. You'll just be getting your fair share."

"Thank you. You are most kind. Do you keep any spirits here? Cognac? Gin?"

"I can fetch you both, my dear. How much?"

"A few ounces of each is plenty, thank you."

Elle opened her bag and refilled many of her ingredients. She also filled several empty bags with additional substances. She had emptied and cleaned all the potions bottles she bought in Egypt, save Nenet's special one, and used those bottles now to hold the oils and alcohol. She had everything she would need for her current project.

"One last question before I go. Have you any saltpetre?"

"Of course, my lady. Let me show you."

Elle collected a small amount and closed up her bag. She thanked the woman again, and walked back to her room with a spring in her step. Her excursion had turned out better than she had anticipated.

Alone in her cabin, with the door locked, she measured out tiny amounts of several ingredients into a small dish. She added a single drop of serum and a few drops of the gin, and stirred until she had a thin paste. She drew the note out of her pocket and spread it on the table. Using a brush intended for cosmetics, she coated the paper with an even layer of the potion.

It took only a few seconds for the words to become fully visible. The note was short and to the point.

Meet me for tea.

The same location.

H.

Henry held the lit cigar to the handkerchief until it burned a hole all the way through.

Willful destruction of property.

He didn't know whose property it was. He'd found it abandoned on the ground, and it bore no monogram, embroidery, or other distinguishing marks. Did it count as stolen property, regardless? The cigar was stolen. He'd taken it from Westfield, the first night aboard, when he'd been learning the ship, and needed a door to practice on to assess the quality of the locks.

Unlawful entry.

It seemed pointless to break into a room and not steal anything. He'd enjoyed it at the time, and he was enjoying the benefits now. He ought to feel guilty for it, he suspected, but his only real concern was that Elle might think ill of him.

He had no idea what to expect from her. She'd been furious with him for his casual thievery, and then, out of nowhere, she'd kissed him like no one had ever kissed him. She'd left him reeling, and he wasn't certain he'd recovered.

A noise nearby snapped him back to attention. His hand went for his knife. The tarpaulin shifted. Elle. At last. He leaned back and took another draw on the cigar.

Use of tobacco products in the presence of a lady.

Elle wrinkled her nose and fanned away the smoke.

"Lord, Henry, that's vile."

He ground out the cigar against the bottom of the lifeboat and pushed the tarpaulin further open to give her more fresh air. The sunlight and blue skies he had hidden from were welcome now that she was here.

"My apologies. I had begun to think you wouldn't come and needed something to pass the time."

"Ugh. Where did you get that thing?"

"Westfield gave it to me."

Telling untruths.

She nodded, not even questioning the statement. He wasn't certain if that was good or bad.

"I wish he wouldn't. I hate them."

"I will keep that in mind in the future. Tea?"

"Yes, please."

He poured a cup for her and one for himself.

"I apologize for my tardiness. It's such a beautiful day that the deck is teeming with people. I had to make two circuits of the entire area before I could sneak up here. And prior to that, there was Lady de Winter."

"Ah, yes. Your new friend."

"She is in no way a friend. She is nosy and insufferable in her superiority. I think perhaps she has latched on to me because she suspects I am not who I claim to be and is eager to expose me. She may have the birthright and outward appearance of a lady, but her true manners show her to be nothing of the sort."

Henry nodded. "We have but two more days before we arrive in Charleston. I trust you can outlast her, and I will continue to teach you something of spying, if you desire, to help you sneak away from her more easily."

"I would appreciate that. She has been tailing me since lunch, and I had to feign needing use of the washroom to be rid of her. I was almost ready to consider climbing out a porthole."

A smile played across Henry's lips. She was enough at ease to make jokes, and didn't seem upset with him, despite the cigar. A bit of tension left his body.

Elle selected a sandwich from the tea tray. She looked over the collection of herbs and other potion ingredients arranged beside the food.

"I see you intend this to be a working meal. I have my potions kit if we need it, but these are good basic ingredients for a first lesson."

"And I assure you, I have come by them honestly, so you don't need to worry on that account."

"Henry, I'm sorry. I didn't mean—"

He held up a hand to stop her. "Your apology is unnecessary, mademoiselle. I fully intended to steal these items last night, and I never even gave it a second thought until you objected. In my six years of spying I have done much worse than pinch a few herbs. You are fully within your rights to call me both a liar and thief."

"You are too hard on yourself."

He waved one hand. "It's of little import. Let's get on with this potions business. I'm interested to find out what, if anything, I can do."

They spent the next hour going over the steps for some simple potions. Henry had always been a disciplined student. For the potions work, his attention to detail served him well, as did his patience. He never spilled or mismeasured, and he crushed herbs and stirred mixtures precisely as directed. The work didn't feel natural, but he persevered, mopping the sweat from his brow with the burnt handkerchief. They mixed up several different concoctions together, leaving out only the serum that would make them potent.

"I think that's good for today," Elle said. "You are an exceptional student. Others have greater natural talent, but your hard work makes up the difference. You will be quite competent when we are done."

Her praise more than compensated for the difficulty of the work. He wanted to go another hour, just to earn a second compliment.

"Thank you, Miss Deschamps. I'm certain I owe it all to your quality teaching."

"Tomorrow we will add the serum and make a full potion." She took his letter out of her pocket and waved it. "You find your magic ink useful, I imagine?"

He nodded. "I have but a small amount, and I take great care with it."

Elle smiled. "That is what we will make tomorrow, then,

along with the antidote for reading it. They are best made together, as the one comes from the other. This morning I made such a small batch of antidote to read your letter that I didn't make any ink with it, as I should have done."

"Same time and same place?" Henry inquired.

She nodded. "Oui."

"Excellent. I look forward to the lesson."

"So do I," she replied. She started to rise, but stopped halfway, frowned, and sat. "I think I should like to remain here somewhat longer and enjoy the sunshine. Will you sit with me awhile?"

"As long as you wish." He thought he might lie on a bed of nails if she asked it of him. He was a bloody fool.

"Good."

She slid over until she was snugged up against him, shoulder-to-shoulder, hip-to-hip. He caught a whiff of her subtle perfume. Her proximity made his head spin.

"Why do you want to be here with me? I'm an admitted criminal, and I feel no remorse."

"You feel remorse for upsetting me."

"True. But not for the crime."

"I pondered that throughout the night. I think..." She paused for a moment. His eyes fell to her mouth. The turn of her lip when she was lost in thought made him ache for another taste. "It seems to me you have very little care for things. But you have a great deal of care for people. You have a kind heart."

She placed a hand on his chest. His pulse quickened. He dared to put an arm around her, and she laid her head on his shoulder. The urge to haul her into his lap and kiss her senseless was near irresistible.

Her nose wrinkled again. "You smell of smoke."

"My apologies. Do I need to change clothes?"

"It isn't worth the trouble. It simply means I won't kiss you today."

God, those lips of hers. Plump, teasing, delectable. The searing heat in her cognac-colored eyes lanced through him.

"I'll change," he blurted. "Wash. Whatever you'd like."

She grabbed his shirt sleeve to hold him down. "Tomorrow, Henry. For now, sit with me. I have a book of Shakespeare's plays we can read."

"I will die of anticipation before tomorrow."

"You can read the part of Hamlet. I understand he likes to wear black and is overly dramatic."

Her teasing mouth curved in a beautiful smile. He drew her close, feeling the curves of her body, inhaling the scent of her. He closed his eyes and let her melodious voice wash over him. Today, he would feast on her with his other senses. Tomorrow there would be no cigars.

XVI

A Suspicious Mind

CHARLOTTE DE WINTER CAUGHT ELLE crossing the deck, altogether too close to her hiding place for her liking. Elle brandished her book like a weapon.

"Please excuse me, Lady de Winter. I've done with my reading and am off to change for dinner."

"A word, before you go." She grasped Elle's arm and guided her toward the nearest staircase. Elle twisted to try to get away, but Charlotte's hold was strong enough that she couldn't break it with so slight a movement.

"Do you think to prevent me running away with such a grip?"

Charlotte gave her a simpering smile. "It seems wise, seeing as you have done quite often of late."

Elle was sorely tempted to stomp on her foot. She was fed up with this nonsense, and intended to give Lady de Winter a piece of her mind. All she needed was a location private enough not to cause a scene. She jerked her arm free and glared at the other woman.

"Perhaps if you wish me to accompany you, you might make a polite request and show a sincere desire for my company rather than manhandle me."

"What good would a request of any kind do?" Charlotte laughed. "You would invent some excuse and then disappear in a most unladylike fashion."

"I will not have this discussion here on the deck, madame. If you wish to have it out with me, I'm willing, but I have no desire to ruin everyone else's evening."

"You have something to hide, then?" Charlotte taunted.

Elle's eyes narrowed. She folded her arms across her chest—an unladylike stance, but she wasn't in the mood to be a lady just now.

"I have nothing to hide," Elle replied, her voice firm and cold. "You would like a public row? The crowd here has abated, I'm afraid. Let's to the lounge, so as many people as possible may witness whatever slanders you wish to heap on me."

She stomped down the stairs at so great a pace that Lady de Winter had to lift her skirts and scurry to catch up. When they reached the main lounge area, Charlotte gestured to an unoccupied sofa by the wall. It was a relatively private area for the space, an indication that she didn't intend to make a scene after all.

"Let's sit, Elle, dear," Lady de Winter said with a falsely conciliatory air. "I don't know what has gotten you so overwrought, but I only wished to talk."

"Ah, yes, make me the guilty party."

"Oh, I'm certain you are guilty of something. The question is: What?"

She sat and arranged her skirts around herself. Elle plopped down beside her, forgoing any attempt at elegance. Her mind was occupied, scanning the room, making note of all the exits. It seemed a sensible time to put the spying lesson to good use.

"I haven't seen anything lately of your servant, Harry, or whatever his name was," Charlotte remarked.

Realizing where the conversation was headed, Elle adopted a similarly casual tone. "Henry," she corrected. "He's traveling down in third class. The service here is so good we hardly have need of him."

"Is that so? Why, then, is he sending you mysterious notes?"

"What makes you think he sent that paper? It was unsigned. It could have been from anyone."

"I'm not stupid, Miss Deschamps. Disappearing for hours at a time, appearing unusually tired at breakfast... it is quite obvious you have been sneaking off to your lover."

"I have not."

"You have another explanation for your behavior, then? I would certainly like to hear it!"

"I have taken tea in private, read books, and mixed some potions, which I believe you know is a hobby of mine. I am entirely within my rights to take time for myself, and I daresay I wouldn't have such need of it were you not so insufferable a nuisance!"

"How dare you?" Charlotte spluttered. "I will be reporting this to your uncle."

"Go right ahead. He won't believe you."

"Oh, I think he will. The evidence is clear, my dear. He chose to indulge you with your 'modern' notions, and what happens? A young woman is taken advantage of by some scoundrel."

"Henry Ainsworth is a gentleman," Elle snapped, her voice now loud enough to turn heads. "He wouldn't dream of taking advantage of any woman, and he certainly has done nothing of the sort to me." She rose from her seat. "You may believe what you like, but I won't listen to your slanders. Do not seek me out at dinner or at any other time for the duration of this voyage. I have nothing more to say to you."

She stalked from the room, wondering if Charlotte would make good on her threat to tell Westfield. If that happened, Elle knew she would have to tell him the truth about her recent activities. She doubted he would like that any better than the lies.

XVII

Pale and Deadly Looks

*H*ENRY SCANNED THE TWO PIECES of paper, just to make certain he hadn't missed anything. The one sheet was a copy of the passenger list for this ship, the other, a list from the boat that had taken them up the Nile. He'd gone through every name and noted anyone who appeared on both.

His own name was there, of course, along with Westfield and Elle. Charlotte de Winter and her maid appeared, and four men: two in first class, and two in second. The only other names that matched were extremely common names, such as Smith, and those he couldn't be certain were true duplicates. He refolded the papers and stowed them in a pocket.

He'd located the four men over the past few days and had made brief observations. The men in second class looked to be the servants of those in first, and the two first-class parties didn't appear to know one another. They were ordinary, unremarkable men and behaved exactly as expected. He wasn't ready to completely eliminate them as suspects in his and Elle's unwelcome swim, but none had caught his particular attention. He would have to move on to investigating some of the Smiths on the list, and there was always the possibility the perpetrator had used a false name, making anyone on board a suspect. He kept a constant watch for familiar faces, but with more than a thousand passengers on the ship, he'd had little success.

As he took his breakfast, he scanned the men in the crowd, watching for any behavior that might seem unusual. Lady de Winter's maid, Aila, came scampering up to him the moment he rose to leave the table.

"Hello, Mr. Henry," she said in a cheery voice. "I'm sorry I couldn't join you for breakfast."

He wasn't sorry in the least. The girl had been flirting with him for the past two days, and couldn't seem to get it through her head that he wasn't interested. He wondered if he found her as frustrating as Elle found her employer.

"I had to take a breakfast tray to my mistress today," Aila continued.

Henry arched an eyebrow. "She isn't dining with Miss Deschamps this morning?"

"Oh, no, sir. She tells me that Miss Deschamps was terribly rude to her last night."

Henry couldn't hide a grin. "Was she? Good for her." She had either gotten the knack of being a lady or was rebelling against it. The former would be more practical, but he found himself hoping it was the latter.

Aila looked confused. "I beg your pardon? Good for which lady, now?"

"Never mind, Aila. Thank you for the information. Good day to you." He gave the girl a nod and headed off to get some work done.

The better part of his day was spent trailing people named Smith and getting nothing out of it. By mid afternoon he changed tactics and outfits, donning his best attire and making his way into the first class area. He would seek out Elle early and enlist her help, or at least distract himself with a conversation. Then he was bloody well going to kiss her.

He went directly to the library, and was happy to see he had guessed correctly. Elle stood perusing books on the shelf while she chatted with Westfield, who sat upon a nearby sofa, holding a newspaper that must have been a good two weeks old. Henry picked a book off a shelf at random, using it to shield his face, and slipped into an easy chair within hearing distance. His back was turned to them, which afforded him a good view of most of the room as he listened in on their conversation.

"Do you have a volume such as this, Uncle?" Elle inquired.

"What's that?"

"Shakespeare's sonnets. The book you gave to me has only plays."

"Ah, yes. I have a similar book at home, but not with me. I also have a larger collection that includes all the plays, and not just the selected ones you have in your possession."

"Will you lend them to me when we return home? I have enjoyed everything I have read so far. I believe they are my second favorite British thing, after tea time. I must say, however, that I found your popular lovers Romeo and Juliet rather disappointing. They could have gone away together and lived happily had they been more intelligent."

Westfield chuckled. "You do not find dying for love to be romantic, my dear?"

"Not when it can be easily avoided by some common sense."

Henry bit his lip to contain his laughter. He loved her opinionated assertions.

"Regardless, I would like to read more," she continued. "I haven't yet read a single one of the history plays."

Henry would have to remedy that. The histories were his favorites, in no small part because seven of them were about the King Henrys. He had become enamored of the stories as a boy, and his father had teasingly called him Henry IV, since he was fourth of the five children.

"I think I'll borrow this for the afternoon," Elle decided. "The poems are short, so I can return the book whenever I need to and not have to worry that I haven't finished a story."

"Will you be taking tea in the dining room this afternoon?" There was a note of hopefulness in Westfield's voice.

"No, thank you, Uncle," she replied. "I've found my private time very therapeutic. I've been able to take some time to practice my potions, as well."

She wore her work bag slung across her body today. It was far more utilitarian than an ordinary lady's purse, but Henry thought it suited her. It wasn't unheard of for an upper class woman to dabble in potions, and therefore not likely to attract negative attention.

"Very well," Westfield sighed. "I can understand…"

Henry stopped listening to the conversation, because a man across the room had caught his eye. He had seen the stranger's face before, but in another context. He looked down at his book, read a few sentences, and turned a page. Keeping his head down, he glanced up, wishing he had spectacles to hide his eyes.

The man was tall and powerfully built, though not so much that he stood out based on his looks alone. He wore a proper gentleman's suit, but the fit was poor, and he didn't stand with his hands in his pockets or leaning on a cane, the way men so often did when at leisure. His posture was stiff, wary. He was part of a group of passengers, but not engaged in their conversation. His eyes were fixed on some point behind Henry's chair. There was nothing in that area except Elle, Westfield, and the bookshelves.

"I think I'm ready to head up top for a time," Elle said. "I'll see you again at dinner, for certain, and perhaps sooner."

The suspicious man withdrew a small flask from his coat and took a swig. He then turned to his companions and spoke for the first time since Henry had spotted him. The move put the man in a position to watch the exit. It also gave Henry a better chance to assess him, unobserved.

The man's head turned to follow Elle's progress across the room, confirming Henry's suspicions. A fiery anger raged through him, settling in seconds into a simmering hatred. He had no doubt this hired thug was connected to the "incident" in Luxor.

The man excused himself shortly after Elle left the room. Henry dropped his book on the chair and followed. She would be safe in public, but she'd just announced her intent to have private time, and she was headed for the lifeboat, not the locked door of her cabin.

"Henry!" Westfield called out, catching him halfway across the room. "What are you up to, lad? I thought you were keeping your own company of late?"

"Excuse me, sir, I have pressing business," Henry replied, not interrupting his stride.

Westfield took hold of his arm and pulled him to a stop.

"One moment, if you please. I'd like an explanation of what you mean by sending my niece strange blank messages. Have you been meeting her in secret? I'd like to believe I can trust you…"

Henry broke free from the older man's grip.

"I'm sorry, sir, I must go. I will explain later."

He rushed out of the room, leaving Westfield calling after him, and looked down the hall in both directions. Neither Elle nor her pursuer was in sight.

"Damn and blast."

He ran for the nearest staircase and took the steps two at a time up to the deck. He couldn't see Elle anywhere, but it didn't take long to find the man following her. His swaggering gait made him easily identifiable, and most passengers had begun to retreat from quickly darkening skies. Henry zigzagged around empty chairs as he raced across the deck. The man had already reached the far side of the ship and would soon disappear around a corner. If Elle were on her way to the lifeboat, which Henry was certain she was, she would be out-of-sight of anyone else, and in danger.

He reached the rail just in time to see Elle pause at her favored climbing spot, waiting for the man to pass by. Her pursuer reached into his jacket and withdrew a thin wire, stretched out between two wooden handles.

Elle gasped, her hand going to her throat. Henry's heart pounded in his chest. The distance between them was agonizingly far.

"You, there!" he shouted.

The man turned to look at him, deemed him unimportant, and continued after Elle. She ran.

Henry knelt to draw his knife, cursing the long trousers that slowed his progress. He would wear his breeches and boots from now on, and to hell with fashion.

The thug raced after her, gaining easily with his long stride. Elle pulled something from her bag and dashed it on the ground. A cloud of smoke billowed up from the shattered bottle, but the assassin plowed through it without pause. Henry held his breath, closed his eyes, and followed.

He emerged on the other side coughing, his eyes stinging and watering. Elle strained to climb up to one of the lifeboats, while the thug grabbed at her skirts. Henry ran at him, slashing the knife across the back of the man's leg.

The wound should have crippled him with pain, but he seemed hardly to notice. Henry grabbed hold of the man's jacket and hauled him down, stabbing this time, going for the belly.

The man seized the blade with his bare hand and tossed it away, growling not in pain, but in fury. His pupils were big, his eyes crazed. He was mad, or drugged. He seized Henry's lapels and flung him almost as easily as he had the knife.

Henry tucked, protecting his head as he crashed against the hard, oak planks. Elle shouted his name. She raced across the upper deck, the assassin chasing her from below, preventing her from jumping down. He reached the next climbing point well before she did. She spun around, but he was already halfway up.

Henry scrambled to his feet, wincing in pain. There was

no time to go for the knife, and he wasn't even certain it would be of any use. He needed a crippling blow to stop the madman.

He had wandered this deck dozens of times and knew every potential weapon in the area. The rigging for the tallest mast ran above his head. Racks of belaying pins lined the rail, and no more than half of the foot-long wooden rods had been used to secure the ropes. Henry whirled around, snatching the nearest unused pin.

Elle took the only route left to her, and jumped from the upper deck, landing in a heap of tangled skirts. By the time she struggled to her feet, the thug had landed beside her. Henry caught her eye, but she didn't cry out for help, or even let her eyes linger on him, too savvy to alert her attacker. She stumbled backwards, eyes wide with fear, whimpering helplessly—uncharacteristic behavior, but convincing enough to fool her attacker. The man laughed in triumph and grabbed at her. She dropped to the ground and when he bent over her, she kicked at his arms and legs, not to hurt him, but to keep him busy, stalling for time.

God, was she brilliant!

Henry flew down the deck. The thug stomped on Elle's skirts to hold her still, but Henry was on him before he could get a hand on her. He brought his improvised weapon crashing down on the man's head. The shattering skull made a sickening crack, and the man crumpled to the floor.

Elle skittered backward and scrambled to her feet. She ran toward him.

"Henry, are you all right?"

He stumbled away from her outstretched arms, his heart pounding, lungs burning. His eyes still stung from the smoke, and his left ankle throbbed from his crash. His mind whirled as it tried to process everything. There was still work to be done.

He scanned the area in all directions, but could see no witnesses. Drops of rain splattered the deck and lightning flashed in the distance. Anyone with sense would be indoors.

He threw the belaying pin overboard and checked his hands and clothes for blood. His jacket was a loss. Splattered with gore and too badly torn to repair, it followed the belaying pin into the ocean. The rest of his clothing had a few spots, but nothing highly visible. He could clean it himself and leave no one the wiser. He retrieved his knife, used a handkerchief to wipe it clean, then threw the handkerchief overboard as well. He replaced the knife and set about examining the area for other evidence that might need disposal.

Unfortunately, he couldn't dump the body. Doing so would leave him noticeably bloody, and he didn't have tools or time to clean the blood and brains spattered on the deck. The best option was to leave the area as soon as possible. There would be no way to trace the deed to him. The entire thing had been remarkably simple and efficient.

He staggered, suddenly lightheaded.

Elle took hold of his arm.

"Henry, are you all right?" she repeated. "Are you hurt? That was a nasty spill you took."

He pulled away, but she didn't release him. What was wrong with her? Why wasn't she upset? She'd been attacked. There was a bloody mess on the deck that had once been a man.

Oh, God, oh, God.

"It seems you can add murder to my list of sins, mademoiselle." His voice sounded flat, distant, as if it were coming from someone else entirely.

Oh, God, what have I done?

Her grip tightened. "No," she vowed.

Henry swayed on his feet. He was a scout and a thief, not an assassin. Usually spared from direct combat, he'd killed no more than half a dozen men over the entire span of his military career. Each time it had made him queasy, and never had it been in such a brutal, personal manner. His ears rang with the snapping of bone. He could still feel the skull caving in. His stomach heaved. He retched and nearly had to dive for the side of the ship.

"You must excuse me," he choked. "I... I..."

He fled, unsure if he would ever feel worthy to speak with her again.

XVIII

Lessons Learned

*E*LLE DARTED INTO HER ROOM and locked the door. She slumped against the wall, shaking, her heart still hammering. She had seen no one, yet her skin crawled and her mind painted images of people coming after her, demanding answers for the body on the deck.

She took a few deep breaths to calm herself. Worry for Henry consumed her. His face had been void of all color, and he hadn't sounded at all like his usual self. If anyone questioned him in his current state, he would confess to the deed, and then he would be hanged.

She trembled. She couldn't even bear the thought of him being locked away in prison. Killing the villain out to murder her was deserving of a reward, not a punishment. She doubted others would believe that, however, and worse, she wasn't certain Henry would believe it, either.

Something had to be done.

Elle shed her cumbersome dress and corset and slipped into the simple black gown she had worn during her spying lesson. She yanked the pins out of her hair and plaited it into a single braid down her back. She slipped a perfume bottle of peppery liquid into one small pocket. The pepper potion wasn't as easy to use as the smoke potion, but it would have much the same effect if she sprayed it in someone's face.

Assuming said *someone* wasn't altered by a berserker potion.

A shiver ran down her spine. When the assassin had grabbed the knife bare-handed and then thrown Henry like a doll, Elle had never been more terrified in her entire life. She prayed she would never encounter anything like it ever again.

In the middle of the day, sneaking would be next to impossible, so Elle planned for deception instead of stealth. She gathered up the books she had been reading, piled them into an untidy little stack, and took off toward the library. Halfway there, she paused to ask a passing gentleman for directions, over-emphasizing her French accent. He waved her down the proper hall, but didn't so much as look her in the eye. It was treatment she was accustomed to from her work as a barmaid. She was a working girl. Unremarkable.

Emboldened by the success, she dumped the books on a table and headed down to the lower decks.

After a bit of wandering and backtracking, she found the general layout of the second and third class sections mirrored the familiar halls of first class. She could only hope Henry had chosen to keep to his bed and hadn't hidden himself somewhere as she had done.

Watching the other passengers, it became quickly apparent that the third class women's quarters were along the port side, and the men's off to starboard. She took a right turn and soon found the first of the bunk rooms. She poked her head inside, hoping it would be Henry's room. As he had warned her, it didn't seem the cleanest of places. One man lay snoring in his bunk. Two others were playing at cards. She saw no sign of Henry, so she moved on to the next room.

She was reaching to open the door, when she realized one of the card players had followed her.

"Looking for someone?" he sneered.

"Yes, I am," she answered, keeping a level tone, but slipping her hand into her pocket to find the perfume bottle.

The man put one arm out on either side of her, trapping her between himself and the door.

"I think you ought to look for me instead. How 'bout it?"

"No, thank you."

Elle pushed the door open, thankful it swung inwards, and ducked away from the man. He followed her and grabbed hold of her arm.

"Now, missy, don't be coy," he scolded. "I'm sure I can pay you better than the other fellow."

His rough hands pulled her against his body. She could smell his foul breath and his unwashed clothes.

"Unhand me at once!"

Elle lifted the perfume bottle and sprayed it in the man's face. As he howled and clawed at his eyes, she thrust her knee up into his groin. He collapsed to the floor, moaning in pain.

Across the room, Henry sat up so abruptly he came near to smashing his head on the bunk above.

"Elle!" he cried, leaping from his bed. He rushed to her side. "Bloody hell! What are you doing here?"

"I came to see that you were all right."

"That *I* was all right?"

"Oui, monsieur." She looked up at him. His face was still pale and his eyes were red-rimmed. "I was very worried. You look distressed. Have you been crying?"

"For God's sake, Elle!" He took her arm and pulled her into the hall. "Whatever possessed you to come here?"

"Release me, if you please. I don't wish to be dragged about."

He let go at once.

"My apologies."

"Thank you."

She smoothed her skirt and pocketed the perfume bottle, then started back toward the dining room, Henry close at her elbow.

"I told you already why I came," she told him. "I was concerned about you. You seemed terribly distraught when you left me."

"I'm fine, mademoiselle," he replied stiffly, regaining some manner of composure.

"You are not fine, Henry. You are sad in your heart and your nerves are overwrought. I can tell because you have been calling me by my Christian name and cursing more than usual."

"My nerves would be perfectly well were you not sneaking about putting yourself in danger. These are the men's quarters! Not only is it inappropriate for you to be here, but there are men about, such as that lout you just dispatched, who are not only willing, but eager to assume the worst!"

"I'm not afraid of them. My perfume bottle remains nearly full."

Henry threw up his hands. "You aren't afraid of anything! A man has tried to kill you, and instead of seeking shelter or staying close to friends you choose to run about on your own?"

"Perhaps we should find someplace quiet to talk, before you make a scene."

"I'm not making a scene," he snapped.

Elle didn't bother to argue the point with him. "The dining room is just ahead. Let's have a cup of tea and something to eat. We are late, but I believe they are still serving."

"The tea here isn't worth having."

"Then let's go up to my cabin. I will run to the kitchen and fetch us something."

"You will do nothing of the sort!"

She put her hands on her hips. "Do not think to order me about, Henry Ainsworth. You have no say over what I choose to do."

"I'm trying to protect you," he protested.

"And I'm doing the same for you. Please, don't remain down here alone thinking dark thoughts. I cannot bear it."

"Very well," he sighed. "I will come along, provided we go together to the kitchen."

She nodded. "A fair compromise."

By the time they reached Elle's room with the tea things, a hubbub had arisen among the first class passengers. People rushed about, whispering and avoiding the gaze of others.

"They have found the body," Henry whispered. "There will be an inquest."

He sounded resigned, and Elle didn't like it. She linked her arm with his.

"If anyone asks, we are lovers, and you have been with me in my room all afternoon."

Henry nearly upset the tea tray.

"Miss Deschamps, you cannot mean that!"

Elle unlocked her door and all but pushed him inside. She closed and locked the door and spoke to him in low, but earnest tones.

"I do mean that. I won't see you hanged."

"Damn it all, Elle, I can't do that to you!"

"You prefer the noose?"

"To destroying your life? Absolutely."

She rolled her eyes to the ceiling. "You don't think me capable of making a life for myself after a scandal? I believed you thought better of me."

"But everyone would shun you! They would be like to throw you out on the streets without a second thought!"

"Out on the streets where I come from?" She laughed mirthlessly. "No one there will care what a few rich people think of me. I never desired to be part of high society. What would I lose? Only the chance to lie my way to a wealthy husband, and I assure you, I have no interest in marrying such a man."

"No, I don't suppose you do," Henry sighed. He sank into a chair. "You win, Miss Deschamps. We will do it your way. But only—*only*—if it will prevent an execution."

He looked pale and dispirited again. Elle poured him a cup of tea with milk.

"Drink your tea before it goes cold. And have something to eat. It will make you feel better."

"Better is a relative term, mademoiselle. I could scarcely feel worse."

"You may feel worse later on, I fear."

He frowned at her. "Why is that?"

"We are going to have to explain all this to Westfield."

XIX

All My Sins Remembered

"*Y*OU HAVE BEEN DOING ALL THIS BEHIND MY BACK?*"

The look of disappointment on Westfield's face reminded Henry altogether too much of his father. He was the disobedient child, receiving a scolding.

"Yes, sir," he replied. "I didn't think it fair to Miss Deschamps to reveal her whereabouts, considering how you were encouraging the relationship with Lady de Winter that she wished to escape."

"That was an error on my part," Westfield acknowledged. "I was so hopeful that some female companionship would do her good, and I regret I misjudged Lady de Winter's character. But sneaking out at night? Spy lessons? Henry, what were you thinking?"

"I told you, sir, she has a natural talent for the business. She was interested in learning from my experience."

Elle nodded. "I have already seen the benefits of the training."

"You shouldn't need the training! Henry, you weren't hired to teach her, you were hired to protect her!"

Elle's eyes narrowed.

"Sir, Miss Deschamps will be far better protected if I teach her something of the spy business. You've seen firsthand her tendency to take initiative and do things on her own. I can't be with her every moment of every day."

"Out of the question! It's inappropriate and dangerous."

"Dangerous?" Elle echoed. The edge in her voice hinted at the anger bubbling underneath. Henry would have been terrified, had it been directed at him. "Learning to recognize and avoid enemies is *more* dangerous than remaining ignorant?"

"Sneaking about is dangerous. Henry possesses all that knowledge. I see no reason to burden you with it."

Fury flashed in her eyes. "I think what you are trying to say is that, as a woman, I am a weak and fragile thing, and I must be coddled and watched over by men, because I cannot possibly do anything worthwhile all on my own."

"Only a damned fool would believe such a load of horse shit," Henry declared.

Westfield gaped at him. "Captain Ainsworth, such language is not fit for a gentlewoman's ears, or a gentleman's tongue!"

"Oh, for God's sake, she's not going to break if she hears a bad word." He was done apologizing. She'd made it clear his colorful language didn't bother her, and he wasn't sorry for it, in any event.

The affectionate smile she bestowed on him melted his heart. He turned back to Westfield.

"Sir, the lessons have helped, and will help her protect herself in the future. Nothing you can say will convince me to give them up. We would prefer your support, but we *will* continue. Had Elle had a bit more training, she likely wouldn't have needed me…"

He let his words trail off. His eyes locked with Elle's, and she nodded.

"Excuse me, sir, there is more I must tell you." He took a deep breath. "As you know, I have been examining the passenger lists and searching for any signs the person or persons responsible for the accident at Luxor had followed us. I believe the man found dead this evening is such a person."

Westfield looked from Henry to Elle and then back. "Why do you say that?"

"He followed Miss Deschamps out of the library this afternoon when she left to prepare for our potions lesson. I was there myself, if you will recall, and he seemed more interested in her than he ought. I followed him to see what his intentions were."

"And that convinced you he was a villain?" Westfield asked. "Did you see how he died?" His displeasure had given way to worry. "I heard he was garroted. Did he fall prey to another criminal? I cannot rest easily knowing there are such men aboard this vessel."

"He was not garroted, sir. He had a garrote in his possession, and he followed Miss Deschamps with intent to strangle her."

Westfield gasped. "No."

"It's true, Uncle," Elle replied. "He was a villain of the worst kind. I will be always in debt to Henry for his timely action. His attention and training stopped the man before he could do me any harm."

"You stopped him... how?" Westfield asked, understanding dawning in his eyes.

Henry stared past him at the wall, trying to gather himself. He didn't want to speak of it. His stomach churned at the memory of the carnage on the deck and the sickening feeling of death that still roiled inside of him.

"Henry, how did the man die?"

"I hit him over the head with a belaying pin." The words spilled out, uncontrolled. "He was deranged, drugged. I cut him with my knife, and it did nothing. Only a killing blow could stop him. I did the only thing I could. I may be bound for hell because of it, but I would do it again in an instant."

"Good heavens." Westfield put his face in his hands.

"I couldn't have done it alone," Henry continued. "If Elle hadn't run, hadn't fought, my help would have come too late. She defended herself, and it made all the difference. You can't stop me from teaching her more. The slightest bit of knowledge could mean the difference between life and death, for any of us."

"Dear God in heaven," Westfield moaned. "Henry. Elle. I am so very sorry. If I had known I would be putting you in such danger, I would never… I ought not to have undertaken this journey. Forgive me. If you wish to return home…"

"Certainly not!" Elle exclaimed. "If anything, this has furthered my resolve to continue with our mission. These people, whoever they may be, must be discovered and stopped before they can do more harm. If chasing serum will lure them out, then that is what we must do."

"I agree with Miss Deschamps," Henry added. "If we quit now, then they win. If we continue on, we have a chance to discover them and thwart their plans. Return home yourself, if you so desire, but I intend to continue on."

"As do I," Elle vowed.

Westfield gazed at them for a long moment. "Henry, please continue with the lessons," he said at last. "Teach my niece all you can of how to protect herself."

"I will, sir. To the very best of my ability."

Westfield nodded. "I will do what I can to see that neither of you encounters such dangers again. May God help us all."

Henry walked Elle to her room next door. He wouldn't say it, for risk of insulting her, but he wanted to be certain she was locked safely inside for the night.

She gestured for him to follow her, but he shook his head.

"Thank you, Miss Deschamps, but I should return to my own quarters."

She seized his hand. Her fingers were warm and soft. "Henry, please, stay here, or with my uncle, if you must. I don't want you all alone down there."

He gave her a smile. "You needn't worry for me. I'm well enough, thanks to you. Your courage, determination, and insistence on seeing to my well-being…"

He placed his free hand over his heart. He couldn't find the words. Whatever he had felt for her before was a mere shadow of the emotion that now ravaged him. He was losing the war with love, and surrender was tempting.

"You have my eternal gratitude," he finished.

"And you have mine. You have saved my life twice now."

He shook his head. "I meant what I said. I couldn't have done it had you not fought for yourself."

"We are a good team. We ought to stick together." She gave him a pointed look.

He sighed. "You can't watch over me every minute of every day, just as I can't do the same for you. But I will promise to take utmost care, if you will promise me the same?"

She nodded and released his hand.

"Good night, Miss Deschamps. I hope you are able to sleep better than I expect to."

He bowed to her and turned away.

"Henry, wait!"

"Yes?"

"I had promised to kiss you again today."

She threw her arms around his neck. The room spun as her lips covered his. Longing coursed through his veins. The softness of her lips and the sweetness of her mouth consumed him. Her body was all perfect, womanly curves beneath his hands. So soft, so feminine, around her core of iron. He couldn't think, couldn't breathe. He was lost in the taste of her.

The sounds of someone approaching echoed in the back of his mind. He jumped, his body tensing. Elle drew back, her eyes blazing with a smoldering desire that matched the fire inside him. A middle-aged woman walked past, on the way to her cabin, giving a shake of her head and a knowing half-smile. Henry was too overwhelmed to feel embarrassed.

Elle backed into her room, still holding his gaze. "Would you like to come in?"

Yes.

"I don't think that's a good idea."

She nodded. "Another time. Good night, Henry."

"It is now."

A smile lit her face. "Now you can think happy thoughts when you go to sleep."

He waited until she had closed and locked the door before departing. He could, indeed, think happier thoughts, but he wasn't going to sleep a wink.

XX

As Men Drink Potions

ELLE GLARED AT THE ENORMOUS BRICK EDIFICE that loomed over her, watching the painted columns of the front portico shift from one color to another to match whomever stood nearest the entrance. The three-story house with its large windows and long balconies could have been grand, perhaps even beautiful. Instead, the facade had been painted over with this garish, wasteful...

"That may be the stupidest use of potions I have ever seen in my life," she muttered, unable to hold back her irritation. "And I worked at a bar, where customers get drunk and request appallingly stupid things."

"Now, now, my dear," Westfield said. "You must remember potions here are all about fashion, and Mr. Randolph's parties are the height of fashion. This will be a fine opportunity for us to observe something of that culture."

Elle cringed. She hadn't meant for him to hear. She gave him her working smile. "How fortunate we could procure an invitation."

"Diplomacy, young lady, not fortune. You don't think I spent so much of our voyage at cards simply for the pleasure of losing money, did you? Befriending the right people gets us the information we need without sleeping outdoors and eating snakes."

"I hope you are correct, Uncle."

The paint faded to match the creamy yellow of her gown as she ascended the stairs. The color of the fabric gave her a sallow complexion and the frilly bodice pinched. She didn't want to suffer this awful dress and ridiculous party for nothing.

They were ushered into the atrium by a servant dressed in a suit almost as fine as the ones Westfield wore for everyday wear. He checked their invitations, and took Westfield's hat and coat. Elle tied her Egyptian scarf about her waist rather than surrender it. It had too much purple in it to look correct with the dress, but it was all she had of her own style, and she wouldn't let it out of her possession.

"Potions for you, sir, and miss," the butler offered, beckoning to a dark-skinned, gray-haired woman with a tray of small cups. "Lavender cups are for the ladies, green for the gentlemen. You may proceed through the doors at your leisure."

He bowed and turned to carry their outerwear to the cloakroom.

Elle eyed the cups of potion. They were both a thin amber liquid, the ladies' a bit lighter in color than the men's.

"*Pardon, madame,*" she said to the woman with the tray. "May I smell the potions before I take one?"

The woman quirked an eyebrow. "Yes, miss, if it pleases you."

"Thank you."

Elle picked up a lavender cup, noting the mirror of Venus symbol etched into the tinted glass. The female marker had crept into potions work recently from the world of biology. The green cups were marked with its male counterpart, the spear and shield of Mars. She swirled the liquid and took a brief sniff. She thought for a moment, sniffed once more, and then set the cup back down. She repeated the process with a green cup.

"You would do better to take a lavender cup, Uncle. It will suit you well. I prefer the green, myself, so I will swap with you."

"What is it?" Westfield asked, sounding a bit suspicious.

"A stamina potion," Elle replied. "Mild and long-lasting. Intended to ward off drowsiness during the long evening. You may as well drink it. It will do you no harm."

"Why the different colors for men and women?"

"The woman's brew is less potent. That isn't unusual, since potions are often weakened or strengthened based on body size. What the makers don't seem to realize, however, is that women's bodies process this particular mixture more efficiently than men's. Even the stronger potion would be less effective for a woman than a man. The weaker one is next to useless. Its effect will wear off within an hour."

The woman with the tray smiled. "The lady knows her potions."

"Thank you. You know potions yourself? Did you have any hand in these?"

Her smile vanished. "Oh, no, miss. Mr. Blake won't hire any black help. Only white folks work on his potions."

Elle scowled. "And just who is this narrow-minded Mr. Blake?"

"Ellison Blake, miss. King of the potions. Anything you drink tonight, that'll be his doing."

"Hmm," Elle mused. "Thank you for the information. You've been most helpful."

She picked up one of each potion, nodded to the woman, and walked with Westfield through the double doors that led to the party. She took a tiny sip from the green potion to confirm her conclusions. Pleased with the findings, she finished her cup and handed the lavender one to Westfield, who drank his own in similar fashion.

"Ah," he commented. "I can taste something of it now. It's been too long since I tried making these things myself to remember the details, but there is a familiarity to this particular brew. And something of a spicy aftertaste."

"That is the serum. Like Nenet's potion in Egypt, it has

a flavor of its own. It is subtle, but different. Your list is two-for-two thus far."

"We have been lucky. You are the one who deserves the praise, my dear. I am amazed at how much you have discovered in just these few minutes. Let's see what else we can learn."

He took both the cups and deposited them on an empty tray. Offering Elle his arm, he led her through the house, nodding and smiling at the other guests.

"Ah, Westfield, my good fellow!" exclaimed a tall American in a smartly tailored white suit. Elle recognized him from their voyage, but they hadn't been formally introduced. "Welcome to my humble home. I was ever so pleased to hear you were able to attend our little soiree."

"We are happy to be here. May I introduce my niece, Miss Elle Deschamps? Elle, our host, Mr. Hunter Randolph."

Randolph bent low over her hand. "Miss Deschamps, it is my pleasure." He pronounced her name Day-Shahmp, elongating each syllable in his slow drawl.

"I'm pleased to meet you, also, monsieur."

"Thank you, thank you. Allow me to show you-all the house and introduce you to some of the other guests."

Elle breezed through introductions using her best upper-class manners, but the other guests were forgotten the moment she left them. Her senses were occupied by her surroundings, marking exits and watching for unusual behavior. She was determined to prevent anything like the incident on the ship.

"You will be well on your own?" Westfield inquired. "Several of us gentlemen have an appointment for a game of billiards."

"Of course. There looks to be plenty to keep me occupied." She leaned in close and whispered, "Take care with any potions you drink. Some of them can put you in an altered state of mind."

"Thank you, my dear. Enjoy your evening. You know where to find me."

Elle took her leave of the gentlemen and headed for the ballroom, pondering how she might mingle effectively with the guests without revealing her lack of knowledge. She didn't know whist or other popular card games, she had never so much as pressed a key on the pianoforte, and her dancing skills were limited to a simple waltz. Her masquerade as a fine lady was in jeopardy.

"Potion, miss?" asked a servant carrying a tray of drinks. "I have one here to improve your balance as you dance, or one to increase your allure, not that you are in need of such."

Elle examined the tray. She could guess several of the potions by looks alone. She had made some of them so many times when working at the Folies that she thought she might be able to make them in her sleep. She picked up one potion that puzzled her, sniffed it briefly, and then set the glass back on the tray. The scent turned her stomach.

"That one is for boosting the spirits, miss," the servant told her. "If you are feeling bored or melancholy, it comes highly recommended."

Elle thought it was likely to cause impaired reasoning and possible hallucinations, but she thanked the servant and gave him a pinched smile.

"I think I will pass on a drink for now," she said. "There is much of the party still to come, so I may seek you out later."

He nodded to her. "Ask any one of us," he told her. "All of the servers carry a variety of potions, and we can always go fetch you something special if you don't see what you are looking for. Mr. Randolph brings in many potions for his parties, so we ought to have anything you require."

She thanked him once more and he left to offer his tray to another young woman nearby.

Elle made a circle of the room, trying to maintain a casual and inconspicuous air. The buzz of voices mingled with the lively tune of a country dance. Smiles and laughter abounded, and drinks flowed freely. Even several of the dancers held glasses. At every chance, Elle picked up discarded glasses for examination. Some had held champagne or other spirits, but most smelled of potions. The crowd was energetic, carefree, and thirsty for questionable beverages.

Satisfied that she had made a thorough investigation of the ballroom, she ducked out onto the balcony for a breath of fresh air. She could avoid the dancing here, and take a moment to consider her worrisome findings. Even out here, there was a servant with potions, hanging back in a shadowy corner, waiting for any requests.

Elle wandered to the rail and looked over the gardens, letting her eyes adjust to the darkness.

"Would you care for a potion, miss?"

Elle turned to refuse and froze with her mouth agape when she noticed a freckled face and a pair of twinkling blue eyes. Henry wore spectacles and a false moustache, but the same black clothes he had worn for their spy lessons.

"What are you doing here?" she hissed, glancing over her shoulder to see if anyone was in earshot.

"Serving potions, miss," he replied. His American accent was flawless.

Elle's pulse raced. These secret meetings were altogether too intoxicating. They dared her to push beyond the boundaries of friendship, tempted her with sensual thoughts of romance. She could scarcely believe she'd been foolish enough to invite him into her room on the ship. Here on dry land she had regained her senses. He was a spy, an Englishman, a gentleman. Born to wealth and title. Not for her.

She took a deliberate step back. She would never regret kissing him, but it had to end there.

"I had to climb to the balcony," Henry added in a lower voice. "All the doors and windows are shut tight, and it would take enough time to pick the locks that I'd risk being seen. The kitchen area is highly guarded, both inside and out. Mr. Randolph takes his security very seriously, especially where the potions are concerned. If he is to be fully protected, however, he might want to consider removing the trellis."

Elle leaned over the rail and examined the vine-covered trellis that stood nearly as high as the balcony itself. Any child could have climbed up.

She checked again for any eavesdroppers. "I don't think Westfield understands the nature of this party," she said. "I have found potions for increasing sexual appetite and stamina, potions to alter one's state of mind, and stimulants of dangerous potency. The guests grab them and drink them with little care for what they are imbibing."

"Such parties are not uncommon among certain circles in London, as well. Some wilder than others."

"Have you ever been to one?"

"No. I avoid things that might impair my judgment. I suggest this potion for you, miss," he said louder, lifting a glass from the tray.

Elle accepted the drink as another guest joined them. Henry's potion was only water with a bit of mint. She downed the glass, happy to have something safe to slake her thirst.

"Very refreshing." She set the empty glass upside-down on the tray and pretended to look at something in the other direction. When the other guest departed, she turned back.

"Did you make these yourself?" She picked up another glass, the largest on the tray, and sniffed at it. "How?"

"This party is full of extra hired staff, not all of them competent. I snagged a tray from an inebriated fellow near the refilling station and emptied a pitcher of water into the cups. Then I sprinkled in whatever I could find at the refreshment table and a few pinches of your ingredients."

"My ingredients."

"I stole them from your potions bag and stuffed them in my pockets. You don't have even a small purse tonight, and I thought you might need something."

"I'm not certain whether to scold you or thank you."

His eyebrows twitched. "You're welcome."

Elle took a drink and pulled a face. "Henry, this one is vile. Does it have pepper and… hibiscus?"

His eyes glinted mischievously. "I thought they ought not all taste good. Some potions have horrid ingredients."

She tossed the contents of the glass off the balcony. "Hand me another good one. I'm thirsty and I don't trust the refreshments here tonight."

He passed her a different cup, and she drank it down.

"Thank you. You should go now. I haven't spied any dangers that would require your expertise, and I have a favor to ask of you."

"Of course."

"Ask around among the servants about a Mr. Ellison Blake, known as the 'potions king' in these parts. Find out all you can. The black servants may be particularly helpful, as he apparently has no love for their people."

"I imagine he's bitter his side lost the war and he had to give up his slaves."

Elle shuddered. "Ugh. What a thing, to think you can own a person."

"Not something a modern and independent woman would approve of, clearly."

"Not something any decent person ought to approve of," she retorted.

He set down the tray and gave her a sweeping bow. "You are correct, as usual." He swung a leg over the rail. "I will find out what I can of this Mr. Blake. We can share our findings in the morning."

"Very good," she whispered. "Oh, and Henry, the spectacles are nice, but the moustache is ridiculous."

"Does it look false?"

"Oh, no. Just silly."

"It's the very height of fashion," he argued.

"It's horrid."

"I suppose I will give up any notion of growing a real one, then. Good night to you, Miss Deschamps."

She watched him disappear over the edge, then scooped up another one of his concoctions and carried it into the ballroom. It may not have had a drop of magic in it, but it was better for her spirits than anything she would find in the house.

XXI

What Vile King is This

"Good evening, once again, my good sir," Henry greeted the stable master. The man had been friendly earlier in the evening. With luck, he would have some information on Elle's Potions King.

He glanced up from his work. "What brings you back here, boy? Still looking for a way inside?"

"The household does seem quite determined to keep people out, as you said."

The man nodded. "I did warn you. What do you want in for, anyway? Looking to meet a girl?"

That was, in fact, exactly what he had done, though not in the way the man meant. The idea of meeting Elle for that other sort of purpose made his cheeks burn.

"Aha! I have the right of it. I can see that blush on your face."

"It's difficult to hide such things with my pale skin," he admitted. "I also freckle terribly in the sun. Very unbecoming. The ladies don't like it."

"Perhaps your lady inside won't mind so."

"I'm not certain. She seldom remarks on appearances. I doubt she has considered mine much at all." Except that he'd decided he ought not grow a moustache.

"If I may offer you some advice, young sir?"

130

"Certainly."

"If your young lady cannot overlook your spotted complexion, you find yourself a different gal. No sense wasting your love on one who doesn't love you back."

"Thank you, sir. I will keep that in mind. Now, may I ask a favor of you?"

The man frowned. "You may ask, but I won't say for sure I can do it."

"I seek only a bit of information. Let me begin this properly." He held out a hand to the man. "My name is Henry Ainsworth. And you are?"

"Caleb."

The two men shook hands.

"It's a pleasure to meet you, Caleb. There is no more to your name than that?"

"Not that I use. If you need more than that, you can call me Caleb Freeman."

"Very good. Now, the young lady inside whom we have been discussing is concerned about the prevalence and casual use of potions at parties such as this. I am investigating the matter on her behalf. Should I be concerned about the nature of the potions? Is she in danger?"

"Folks who go to these parties know what they are getting into. They are there for their own pleasure, not to do harm to others. That said, there are times when they act a bit... unusual. Certainly there are goings on that would shock a young lady of virtue."

"The lady is difficult to shock, and she knows her potions too well to drink something that might harm her. I'm more concerned about the behavior of other people at the party."

"I don't think anyone will harm her. No such thing has yet happened at Mr. Randolph's place."

"Glad to hear it. I'm also somewhat concerned about possible criminal activity in the area. It looks to me that Mr.

Randolph has placed a heavy guard at the kitchen entrance. Is he worried about theft?"

"He is a cautious man," Caleb replied.

"I see. I do understand if you feel a certain loyalty to your employer, so if I ask anything untoward, do not feel obligated to answer. Does Mr. Randolph pay well?"

"He pays me. It keeps a roof over my head."

Henry nodded. But the pay wasn't enough that Caleb would lie to protect the man.

"I understand that Mr. Randolph gets his potions supply from a Mr. Ellison Blake?"

Caleb frowned. "The guards at the kitchen are employees of Mr. Blake. He sends them along with big shipments to all his best customers."

"And Randolph is a good customer?"

Caleb nodded. "His parties are famous for their potions."

"What of the other good customers? Are there many of them?"

"Most rich folks buy from him," Caleb explained, "but few throw parties such as this one. Mr. Randolph has had folks come from as far as New York just to attend."

"Interesting. And what can you tell me about Mr. Blake himself? Where does he procure the potions?"

"He makes them," Caleb explained. "Has a whole team of folks who mix them up. White folks only. Won't let a black man near the factory, not since the war. Doesn't want to have to pay us, you see. Never mind that we were the ones mixing the potions in the first place and we still know better than his people how to do it."

"Were you a potion mixer once?" Henry asked, surprised.

"No, I've always worked with horses, but I know folks who were. Mae, in the house, she was a great mixer once. Blake wouldn't pay her a cent, but Mr. Randolph gives her a living wage. She doesn't mix potions anymore, but she's got a roof over her head, just like me."

Henry nodded. "A few more questions, if you don't mind."

Caleb chuckled. "You just keep right on asking, boy. I've got nobody else to talk to but these horses, and while I like 'em better than a lot of folks, it's not the same as chatting with a person."

"Thank you. I appreciate your time and your knowledge. Since you know something of the potion making business—or at least what it was before your civil war—could you tell me what you know about the source of the serum? Does Mr. Blake import it from somewhere?"

"No, sir. He collects it himself. Used to be slaves did the picking, but these days it's the poor white folks. And he doesn't pay 'em much or treat 'em well, as I hear it."

"He sounds a rather unpleasant sort of person."

Caleb laughed so hard he almost doubled over. "Son, you are the most well-mannered man I ever did meet. 'Rather unpleasant.' Lord Almighty. Ellison Blake is the meanest son-of-a-bitch in the whole of Charleston, and everyone knows it. But he controls the potions, and the potions control the wealthy folks. The rest of us are just trying to get by."

"I would dearly love to break his stranglehold on your city," Henry mused. His mind began to turn over ideas for what it would take to overthrow a potions king. He had to work to bring himself back to reality. "Is the source of serum local? You mentioned picking. Does it come from a plant?"

"Comes from the ground. The plants suck it up and folks pick 'em and draw it out from the roots and stems."

"Could you show me where to find some of these plants?"

"The Well, as they call it, is out in the islands, oh, maybe twelve miles or so from here."

"Only twelve miles?" Henry felt a rush of excitement. "We can cover that in under an hour by steam car."

"Woah, woah. Hold on there, young sir. Mr. Blake owns that land, and he doesn't take kindly to strangers poking their noses in his business. Besides, that's only half the journey.

Once you get to the right island—and mind you, they all look the same to outsiders—you have to take a boat down to the point nearest the Well, and then you have to walk a mile inland to find it."

"That will be no trouble. I can handle a rowboat or canoe, and a mile walk is nothing. Besides, I will have a guide to give directions and warn of any dangers."

"Oh, you will, will you? Where you gonna find this guide of yours? And where you gonna get a steam carriage from?"

"The carriage won't be difficult. I will simply borrow one." *Or steal one, if necessary.*

"As for the guide, I was hoping you would be so good as to lead us. You will be well-paid for your work, of course."

"Sneaking onto Mr. Blake's land? I don't suspect you can pay me or anybody else enough for that sort of caper."

"I'm prepared to pay two hundred dollars for your trouble."

Caleb stared at him for a moment, then let out a low whistle. "Two hundred dollars? Who are you, boy, that you are able to play free with such a sum?"

"It's not my money," Henry confessed. "Expenses are covered by my employer, but I am authorized to make decisions of this sort."

"Employer. Hmm. Thought you were asking questions to help out your young lady. Tell the truth now. You work for a competitor, is that it?"

"No. We aren't interested in selling potions, only in learning where the serum comes from and who controls it. This is a research mission, not a business one."

Best not to explain that his employer was, in fact, Her Majesty Queen Victoria. He'd rather the Americans took him to be an industrial spy than a political one.

Henry withdrew a handful of coins and handed them over. "Payment for your information, even if you decline my offer."

Caleb pocketed the money, looking thoughtful. "So, for two hundred dollars, you want me to show you and this employer of yours the way to the Well, just so you can take a look?"

"You will be taking myself and the young woman," Henry corrected. "She is a potions master, and I need her expertise in this matter."

"And this is the young lady who is in Mr. Randolph's house right now? The one who made you blush so?"

"The very same," Henry admitted. "Don't worry about her ability to make the journey. I assure you, she is extremely capable."

Caleb chuckled. "You have yourself a deal, boy." He patted the horse he was brushing. "With two hundred dollars, I can move to Kentucky with General Sherman here, and set myself up as a breeder."

Henry coughed to cover a snort. "You named your horse General Sherman?"

"Well, he used to be General Lee, so I changed the name when I bought him. Got him cheap when he injured a leg and they wanted to put him down. He doesn't run anymore, but his blood is pure as a king and he's a randy devil. He'll do me proud. I think I'll ask Miss Mae to come with us."

Henry caught a hint of a shine in Caleb's cheeks. "Aha! You, sir, may hide it better than I, but you blush over the ladies, too."

Caleb grinned. "Course I do, boy. Did you think you were the only one who's climbed that trellis to meet a girl?"

Henry's laugh echoed off the stable walls. "Caleb, it has been a pleasure speaking with you. I will meet you here tomorrow night. Half-past midnight."

The older man nodded. "Tomorrow, then. Now, go back in that house and tell your lady."

XXII

Crime and Drama

$\mathcal{E}$LLE TUCKED HER SHIRT into the trousers and examined herself in the mirror. Thank goodness the outfit was intended for stealth and not deception. She was clearly a woman. Very clearly. In fact, the trousers fit so snugly that her hips and bottom were on full display.

As indecent as an acrobat at the Folies, she thought with a rebellious smile. Not a lady tonight. She opened her door and beckoned for Henry to join her.

"How do I look?"

He stared at her for a long moment, his gaze lingering on her curves. "Er… uh… quite, uh, quite like yourself, in fact."

"Not like a boy, I think."

"I should say not. You look very, er, feminine, despite the trousers."

She was oddly charmed by his blushing and stammering. He had a bizarre sort of innocence that both amused and intrigued her.

This is a job, she scolded herself. *Keep your mind on what matters.*

Ten thousand francs. Care for her aunt. Not a fling with a British spy doomed to end in disappointment.

Never mind that he had given her the best kisses of her life. The moment this mission ended, he would be hustled off to the next dangerous assignment. Or perhaps to a London ballroom, to waltz with *real* aristocratic ladies. Meanwhile, she would be back in Paris hoping for a job that was one step up from barmaid.

Suddenly it seemed ludicrous that they had ever interacted.

"Do I need a lantern?" she asked.

He shook his head. "We will use only moonlight. Artificial light brings too great a risk for discovery."

"That is sensible," she agreed. "I do have my pocket torch, should we have need of it."

"Your what?"

She took the small device out of her bag to show him. Cobbled together from old lantern pieces, the five-inch metal cylinder didn't look like much, but the light shining from its glass tip was focused, and strong enough to illuminate anything it might point at.

"I call it '*une torche de poche.*'"

He took it from her and looked it over. "You made this?" He waved it around, watching the light bounce off the walls. "It's brilliant!"

She shrugged. "It's only a lantern, with a mirror to focus the beam. It requires an unusually concentrated potion because of its small size, but really it's no more innovative than a foot lamp at the theater."

"On the contrary. You ought to apply for a patent and start selling these. You could make a fortune."

She shook her head. "I haven't the time or the spare parts to make more."

"Buy parts with your earnings from this venture." He paused. "They had better be paying you well for this."

She smiled. "Yes, they are. It's something to consider for the future, I suppose." He handed back the torch, and she stashed it in her bag. "Is it time for us to depart?"

Henry checked his watch. "Indeed. It's quarter past midnight. We oughtn't delay any longer, as this is likely to take three or more hours. The carriage is out back, and we will pick up Caleb on the way."

Elle slung her potions bag across her body. "Let's be off, then, before we wake Uncle Edwin. You know he won't approve of this scheme. He wouldn't even approve of my outfit."

"I approve of your outfit." His voice was husky, and desire sparked in his eyes. Elle looked away, making a pretense of checking her bag.

The carriage house behind the hotel contained a number of steam carriages. She didn't ask how Henry had procured a key. He pointed to a particular vehicle, and they pushed it out into the street, then paused to check the potion level.

"Do you think this is enough to take us twelve miles out and then back again?" Henry asked.

"If it's a quality potion, yes."

She dipped a finger into the liquid and rubbed it between her fingertips.

"A bit oily, but it should do."

"Excellent. Let's be off, then."

He opened the door for her and helped her in before walking around to the driver's side. Sneaking out in the dead of night, yet always the gentleman.

"To whom does this car belong, if I may ask?" she queried, when they were some way down the road.

"An associate of Mr. Randolph," he answered. "One of the men Westfield befriended at the party last night."

"Borrowed, then? Not stolen?"

"Borrowed under false pretenses," he admitted. "I told him I would be driving Westfield around the countryside this afternoon, but as you know, I did no such thing. It's due to be returned tomorrow."

"Good. I find I'm far more concerned with the thought of someone looking for it than with how you procured it. And I'm not at all bothered with the notion of trespassing on Mr. Blake's property and stealing his serum. This spy business changes one's perspective, does it not?"

Something of Henry's former melancholia appeared in his expression.

"I'm terribly sorry for dragging you into this mess, Miss Deschamps. You are a woman of great moral character, and I have never intended to change that."

"I'm not afraid for my morals, Henry. What I mean is that I have begun to understand the way you look at things. Previously, I would never have considered stealing serum. But whatever crimes we may commit tonight, they are next to nothing when compared to the crime of letting men such as Ellison Blake and the murderers in Egypt use potions to gain power over the rest of us."

His frown faded. "Well reasoned, as always, mademoiselle."

They met Caleb down the street from Randolph's home, and he hopped into the carriage and gave Henry directions out-of-town. He introduced himself to Elle, who shook his hand and thanked him for his assistance.

"I understand you are a potions master, miss," he said.

"Yes. I've been mixing them since I was a girl. I'm excited to see the source of the serum tonight. I have never had an opportunity to visit such a place before. This 'Well' is the only source in the area?"

"As far as I know, miss. It's been owned by the Blakes my entire life, and always fiercely guarded. It's the basis for all the potions in the Charleston area, and nowhere else. Ellison Blake won't let a drop of it out of his control."

"Does he have men who patrol the area?"

Caleb nodded. "Yes, miss. We can avoid them if we take care. I've never heard tell of any attempt at thievery, so they aren't likely to be expecting us."

"The man seems to have his own personal army," Henry pointed out. "It's no wonder no one dares to cross him."

"If he owns all the serum-producing land, legally there is little to be done to stop him," Elle mused.

"I could think of no way to stop him at all, short of murder," Henry agreed, "and even such a drastic measure would likely be for naught. He must have heirs, and someone would take up his role were he to die."

"Then the best thing we can do is what we are doing," Elle decided. "We must find additional sources of serum and make it as accessible as possible. Tonight, we will learn what a source looks like."

As they neared their destination, Caleb directed them to a wooded area where they could conceal the carriage. The sky was only partly clear, and the moon ducked in and out of the clouds as they made their way to the water's edge. Several rowboats were tied up along the bank, some in better repair than others.

"Who owns these?" Henry asked.

"Part of Mr. Blake's estate," Caleb explained. "We've been on his land for the last half-mile or so. These are the boats his people use for moving around the islands. He has them scattered all over."

"And other people don't take them?"

"Oh, people do. Heard of a fellow who claimed one for himself and only put it back on Blake land once a month when they took inventory. Could be a tall tale, could be true. Blake's stingy with potions, but careless with his possessions. Prides himself on being able to buy anything he wants."

"Well, then." Henry walked back and forth past the boats. "I suggest we take the nicest one."

"Or perhaps the fastest one?" Elle suggested.

"I believe the two are one and the same, miss," Caleb said. He paused beside a small, trim rowboat.

She nodded. "I'm no expert, but it looks serviceable."

Caleb climbed aboard and offered her a hand into the boat. Henry stepped in after her.

"I'm happy to row," Henry offered.

"No, no," Caleb waved him off. "You already drove that

carriage, and I grew up in these parts. I can row quicker and quieter than those slippery water snakes. Excitable young thing like you will splash so much you'll wake half the county. You sit with the young lady."

Henry shrugged. "I will defer to your expertise."

Caleb untied the boat and pushed them out into the narrow channel that wound around the island. For the next quarter hour, they glided silently through the water, lit only where slivers of moonlight fell between the trees. Elle shivered, unnerved by the eerie quiet of the unfamiliar landscape. Only the croak of frogs and the buzz of insects disturbed the still night air.

By the time Caleb pulled the boat up on shore, she was beginning to have doubts about the mission. Had her time sneaking about on the ocean liner prepared her enough for such a venture? If she were caught now, she wouldn't simply cause a scandal. She could be arrested and jailed. She jumped when Henry touched her arm.

"Everything all right?" he whispered, leaning close to her ear to keep his voice as low as possible.

"I worry about the guards. They may be armed and are certainly unfriendly."

"If we do this correctly, they will never see us."

She nodded. She wouldn't let her fears keep her from her work. She swung her potions bag around to her back, tightening the strap so it wouldn't bounce. She was grateful for the trousers that let her walk unencumbered through the underbrush.

Caleb gave the directions, but Henry led the way, his steps completely silent. Elle felt clumsy by comparison. Twigs snapped beneath her feet and leaves rustled as she brushed against them. His every movement was smooth and effortless. This was his career, she reminded herself, just as potions were hers. She concentrated on watching him and learning from his expertise, and found it calmed her nerves. With her mind occupied, she had less time to dwell on her worries.

The trees began to thin out, and Henry stopped abruptly, holding up a hand to signal the others to do the same. He ushered them into the shadows beneath a massive tree dripping with gray moss. Indicating to Caleb that he ought to wait, Henry took up the bucket and spade their guide had insisted on carrying. He turned to Elle.

"Are you ready?" he mouthed to her.

She answered with a single nod and ducked down beside him in the brush. Henry touched her arm to make sure he had her attention, and pointed off to the left. It took Elle a moment to see what he did. A trio of guards, sitting on a fallen log, with playing cards in their hands.

Henry crawled toward them. Elle swallowed hard and followed. Every second seemed an eternity. She inched closer, her eyes darting back and forth between the guards and the ground, searching for anything that might tell her where to find the serum.

A curse broke the silence. Elle froze.

"Dammit, Toms, you're cheatin' again!" the voice continued.

"I ain't! Swear to almighty God."

Henry nudged her, and her limbs began to function again. Best to do this now while the guards were preoccupied with their gambling.

"You're a cheatin', lyin' son-of-a-bitch!"

"I tell you, I ain't!"

"Shut up, both of you," the third guard snarled. "You want Blake to find out we're not patrolling?"

"Who the hell's gonna hear us out here?"

Elle stifled a laugh. Who, indeed.

She crawled on, determined to take advantage of their carelessness. A rock dug painfully into her leg, and she twisted to move away from it. As she turned her body, she saw it: a place where the plants changed suddenly. She clapped a hand over her mouth to stifle her gasp of awe and grabbed Henry's shirt to stop him. When he turned toward her, she pointed and scrambled closer, her heart hammering with excitement.

Up close, the difference was clear. Two plants of the same variety, one with stems and leaves that shimmered in the darkness like a potion-enhanced pigment. It stretched out in a neat arc in front of them, a patch of otherwise unremarkable brush, glittering in the soft moonlight. She scanned further, finding the plain, wooden stakes that marked the boundary of the Well.

Henry passed her the spade, and she accepted it with trembling hands. Her whole body was afire with excitement. They had found it! She lifted a handful of dirt to her nose. The spicy scent of serum mingled with the wet, earthy odor of the dirt. She held it out to Henry, who sniffed and nodded to show he could tell the difference.

Elle dug up several plants and enough dirt to fill the pail, keeping an ear out for the guards. They had fallen silent again, with only the occasional grunt to mark the progress of their game. She was reaching to hand Henry the spade when one of them sprang from his seat without warning.

"I fuckin' quit!" He spun around and stomped straight toward Elle.

Her heart skipped a beat. The spade slipped from her fingers, the soft thud echoing in her ears. Her eyes darted to Henry. The blade of his knife gleamed in the moonlight.

One knife against three men who surely had guns? Elle's body remained frozen, yet her mind raced. What potions were within easy reach? Could she incapacitate even this one man, let alone all three before they could harm her?

The crunch of trampled foliage continued toward her. She squirmed her hand into her potions bag, feeling for a defensive potion.

"Don't be an ass," called one of the other guards.

Elle's fingers found her spray bottle. She flinched when Henry's arm brushed hers. He had risen slightly onto his hands and knees, prepared to spring into action. She held her breath. A boot crushed a plant inches in front of her face.

"How 'bout dice?"

The boot swiveled. "Dice?"

The decorative pattern of the spray bottle dug into Elle's palm. Sweat trickled down the back of her neck. The guard took two steps away from her.

"Dice might be all right."

Another step. Another. She began to breathe again. Henry tugged on her shirt, and they began to back away, watching the guard's back as he reluctantly tromped back to his friends. The moment he sat down Elle and Henry turned and scrambled back to where Caleb waited.

Without a word, the trio slipped among the trees.

The walk to the water and the boat ride back to the carriage were both carried out in silence. By the time they reached the steam car, the fear had subsided, leaving only the elation of their success. Words and exclamations burbled inside her, but Elle kept her mouth closed until the car was several miles down the road to the hotel.

"I wouldn't want to suggest we do such things every night," she said at last, "but I must say that was one of the most exciting experiences of my life. When I realized we had truly found it… I cannot describe the feeling. It was amazing."

Henry gave her a grin, then turned his eyes back to the dirt path that led to the city. "Now you know why I like it."

Even such a quick flash of dimples caused a flutter in her belly. She pulled her pocket torch from her bag and occupied herself studying the serum-filled plants. In the light, the shimmer faded to a shiny, reddish tint. The exact color of the serum she had used so often.

Her studies kept her so preoccupied that they arrived back in town in no time at all. Henry stopped near Mr. Randolph's house, where Caleb's lady-friend Mae hurried up to greet him, leading a donkey laden with saddlebags and a stallion that walked with a slight hitch, but nonetheless held his proud head high.

Caleb shook Henry's hand and accepted a stack of banknotes. "This is more than two hundred dollars, son."

"Is it? I'm terrible with figures. Consider it an investment in your business."

Caleb shook his head, but chuckled softly. He made his adieu to Elle, and then he and Mae started off into the night.

Elle and Henry arrived at the hotel a short time later. She yawned as they made their way through the silent building to their suite. She checked the time. Nearly four in the morning.

They left their muddy boots by the door, and Elle took the bucket to her room. Henry waved to her to say goodnight, but she beckoned him over. He hesitated a moment, then followed her into her room.

"I wanted to ask," she began once the door had closed, "is spying always so riveting?"

"It can be. Tonight the danger heightened your senses, and then the success made it seem thrilling. Much of the time, however, it's terribly boring. Quite a lot of waiting and watching. During waking hours, it's just like what we've been doing: playing a role and learning the area and the people. So, no, it's not all crime and drama."

Elle yawned again. "Excuse me. I'm not accustomed to staying up so late."

"We ought to be getting to bed," he agreed, "or we shall get no sleep at all."

Despite his words, he made no move to leave. His blue-eyed gaze seared her. Her hand twitched, itching to wipe away the smear of dirt across his cheek.

Don't kiss him. Don't kiss him.

He reached out and tucked a loose strand of hair behind her ear. A tingle ran the length of her body and she stepped closer.

"Henry," she breathed.

"Elle, darling."

His fingers caressed her hair. His other hand slipped around her waist. She placed a hand flat on his chest, feeling the warmth of his skin through the thin fabric of his shirt.

Push him away. Go to bed.

She kissed him.

His response was immediate, and passionate. Their mouths crushed together. He ran his tongue across her lips, coaxing them apart. Elle drew him in, matching his efforts, driving their kiss deeper, wilder. Her fingers tightened on his shirt and she hauled him against her. Every nerve in her body thrummed with a mad, sensuous heat. The slow caress of his fingers on the back of her neck made each sensitive hair stand on end. She teased him with her tongue, begging for more, drowning in the hot taste of him.

His hand lifted to cover her breast. Without a corset, only the soft fabric of her shirt separated his flesh from hers. She arched her back, pressing herself further into the heat of his eager grasp. When his thumb flicked across her nipple, she let out an audible gasp of pleasure.

Henry jerked and stumbled back, his chest heaving, cheeks flushed with desire.

"God, Elle, I…" He took another step away from her.

"Thrilling," she breathed.

"I'm sorry. I shouldn't have done that."

She shouldn't have done it, either, but she could feel no guilt over it, standing here savoring the heat of him, desire raging through her like an inferno. Maybe just this once. It couldn't hurt that much, could it? To have him this one time?

"Why not?" She took a step toward him, challenging, and ran a finger down the length of his torso. "Because you are a proper gentleman?"

His hand went back to her breast, stroking, teasing. His lips raked over her jaw, her cheeks, her neck. "Apparently not," he mumbled.

Elle tugged his shirt open, splaying her hands across his warm skin, relishing the strength of his muscled torso. Desire pooled between her legs, and she reached for the fastenings of his trousers.

Just this once.

Henry wrenched himself away, chest heaving. "I think... I think we should stop now." He groped for the doorknob, fire still burning in his eyes. "Sleep well, Miss Deschamps. I will see you in the morning when we are both less... overstimulated." He darted out the door.

Elle sank onto her bed, rocking back on her hands, her skin hot from his touch, her heart hammering out a rapid beat. Definitely a gentleman, and not only in name. A rake would be in bed with her now. Her eyes slid closed and she exhaled slowly, her sigh half disappointment and half reluctant acceptance. She had taken leave of her senses, and they were slow to return. *This can't go on. We are not a suitable match.*

The upper classes didn't dally with barmaids unless there was an exchange of coinage. It was a casual, businesslike transaction. There was nothing casual about what had happened tonight. It was raw and primal, and she had no control over it.

She sprawled on the sheets, arms and legs spread wide, hoping to cool her overheated body. Her restless mind churned on, and only with the first stirrings of dawn did she fall into an uneasy sleep.

XXIII

Enemies in Our Midst

*T*HE SOUND OF A DOOR OPENING jolted Henry from a deep slumber. He shot up, hand going to his knife. Only Westfield. He relaxed and slumped back down.

"Good heavens, lad, whatever are you thinking, sleeping on the sofa half-undressed at this hour? Miss Deschamps could walk out at any moment. Do you want her to find you in such a state?"

Yes.

Last night's kiss was burned into his memory. Her tousled hair. The boy's clothes hugging her curves. The sweet, wet heat of her mouth. Her body molded to his, soft and luscious beneath his hands.

God, yes.

"No, I suppose not." He glanced at the clock on the mantelpiece. Half past nine. Damn. "I apologize. I'm rather tired this morning."

"And you looked flushed. Are you ill?" Westfield spied the muddy boots by the door and put a hand to his temple. "Oh, for pity's sake. You two have been sneaking about again, haven't you? What are you up to this time?"

Elle's door opened, and she stepped out, wrapped in a dressing gown. Her gaze fell on Henry, raking over his bare chest before lifting to meet his eyes. She gave him an appreciative smirk. He snatched up his shirt to cover himself.

"We found the source of the serum, Uncle. It isn't suitable for our purposes, but we know how to recognize such things now, and I have collected plant and soil samples for testing. It was a very successful investigation."

"And why did this investigation need to occur in the middle of the night? No, don't tell me. I don't want to know. Get dressed, both of you, we have things to do today."

Elle ducked back into her room, and Henry made himself presentable while Westfield chided him in low tones about the impropriety of taking innocent young ladies on late-night adventures. Henry didn't catch much of the lecture.

"Today we can make real progress in a proper, diplomatic way," Westfield informed Elle when they sat down for breakfast. He avoided Henry's gaze. The "servant" was to be left behind again, it seemed.

"I have arranged, through my friendship with Randolph, for us to join a small group on a tour of Ellison Blake's potions factory. We may even meet the man himself."

"I don't want to meet him," Elle said firmly.

"Nor do I," Henry agreed.

"You won't be going, Captain Ainsworth. I don't want you following us and sneaking about, either. Stay here and make preparations for the next leg of our journey. Miss Deschamps and I will let you know any information we discover."

"I doubt there is much to learn that we don't already know," Elle argued. "The source of the serum was the important thing, and we know that."

"We shall see," Westfield replied. His voice and expression were still colored by his displeasure with their behavior. He wasn't going to back down.

Neither was Elle. Her eyes were hard, her jaw rigid. Henry caught her eye and gave a slight shake of his head. She frowned at him, but didn't argue further.

When she excused herself to begin her study of the serum-laden plants, Henry followed her into her room, ignoring respectability and Westfield's harsh stare.

"You should go on the tour," he whispered. "It will give us a better picture of the industry here."

"I know. It's a sensible plan. But I despise it. I don't want to meet that man."

"I told you spying wasn't always enjoyable."

She appraised him in silence for a moment, then handed him an empty jar. "Hold this while I slice this plant open."

They passed the remainder of the morning extracting the serum from a single plant. Elle worked methodically, making incisions of different sizes in various locations, evaluating each one and taking careful notes. Over and over she pried stems open, observed the innards, and squeezed liquid out, until she had collected half a teaspoon of thick, reddish-brown serum. The dissected plant littered the table, looking green and ordinary.

"It isn't much, but we should get a better result from the next plant, now that I have the process down. Next time I will try to see if I can make the incisions small enough to allow the plant to heal and continue to grow. I want to see if it will replenish its serum from the soil."

"I'm looking forward to the experiment," Henry replied. "I've enjoyed watching you work."

"Thank you." She grinned at him for a moment, but her happiness quickly faded. "I must clean up now or my uncle and I will be late for our appointment."

"Of course. I will await your report."

She gave him a knowing smile.

The moment they departed, Henry swapped his spy clothes for his nicest shirt and trousers. He rummaged through Westfield's trunk for a jacket that almost fit, along with a hat, tie, and handkerchief. The man had good taste—quality items, but not flashy. It felt good to step outside as a gentleman again. He wondered if Elle would like seeing him like this, or if she preferred him in servant's garb. She certainly had no love for the idle rich.

As he descended the hotel steps, he heard a feminine voice call his name. Aila, Lady de Winter's maid, rushed up to him.

"Henry! My, you sure do look fine today. Like a proper gentleman, I think." She giggled.

"I wouldn't wish to be thought improper," he quipped.

She giggled again, and stepped uncomfortably close. "Lady de Winter said you've been looking for me."

Henry frowned. "I'm afraid she was mistaken. You must excuse me. I have business to attend to."

"I don't understand," Aila puzzled. "She sounded very certain. She told me you've been asking after me for some time." Her eyes darted about. "Is it because we are in public? Should we go somewhere private?"

"No, I don't think that would be wise."

Aila's face fell. "Is your business so pressing? Shall we meet after? Or would you like me to accompany you?"

Henry mulled over the situation. The girl sounded sincere. What the devil had Lady de Winter told her? And why? The woman's contentious relationship with Elle made him wary. He wouldn't stand for anyone troubling her.

"You know, Aila, I think perhaps I have changed my mind," he told her. "I think we ought to go somewhere we can talk privately. Would you care for a walk in the park?"

She blinked up at him. "Oh! Yes, please. That sounds nice."

"Follow me. It's not far."

She floated along happily behind him for the few blocks it took to reach the park. Henry chose a side path, and they followed it some way in silence. He spoke again only when he was confident they were alone.

"Now, Aila, if you don't mind, could you tell me again what your employer has said about me?"

"Oh, she told me you had approached her more than once to ask after me."

"Could she have been mistaken? Could it have been another man seeking you?

"I don't think so. She seemed sure of herself, and she is not often wrong. She is a woman of great intellect."

"Yes. I believe that."

So the woman had been making up lies designed to increase Aila's interest in him. He could think of no reason to do so other than to drive a wedge between himself and Elle. He didn't think Lady de Winter above such vindictiveness, but she was savvy enough to recognize that Elle wasn't so naive.

"What of today?" he wondered. "What made you look for me outside the hotel?"

"She told me you wished to meet me, and she suggested I wait outside. She said you would appear after the lady and the gentleman had gone out."

Dread washed over him.

"And where is she this afternoon?" He was certain he knew the answer, but held out some faint hope that Aila would tell him otherwise.

"Oh, she is taking a tour of the potions factory."

Henry spun on his heel and started back in the opposite direction.

"Bloody hell! She has contrived to keep me away, and I have fallen for the scheme like a rank amateur."

"Henry?" Aila jogged after him. "I don't understand. What is happening?"

"Your mistress is up to mischief, young lady. I don't know for certain what her purpose is, but if she is deliberately separating myself from Miss Deschamps, I cannot believe it anything good. I suggest you return to the hotel and remain there. I also strongly suggest you make no further attempt to contact myself, Miss Deschamps, or Lord Westfield in the future."

"But…"

"Go home, Aila," he ordered. "Go back to England, if you can. This is no sort of place for an innocent girl."

He broke into a run, leaving the bewildered youngster gaping at his flapping coattails.

XXIV

Unto the Breach

ELLE TRIED TO EXAMINE the factory the way she thought Henry might. It was an unadorned brick edifice with small, high windows, reminiscent of a fortress. It occupied a corner lot, with a warehouse entrance that opened onto the main street. Workers carried crates in and out under the watchful eye of several security guards. The steam car turned down the side street to drop off Elle and Westfield at the visitor entrance. Like the commercial door, this one was guarded, but only by a servant dressed in blue and gold livery.

She composed herself and settled into her work mode. Only years of practice kept her from cursing aloud when she discovered Charlotte de Winter was one of the other tour guests.

"Elle, darling, how delightful to see you!" Lady de Winter's saccharine smile made Elle want to retch. Or slap her. "Have you been enjoying your stay here? This is such a delightful town. Everyone is so friendly, and they have potions for just about everything! That must interest you, I'm sure."

Elle met her gaze coolly. "My stay here has been interesting, yes."

"I see you did not bring your man Henry with you today. That is good. We can't be getting too familiar with the help, now can we? Imagine if they started getting ideas beyond their station?" She laughed. "How absurd. They don't belong in *our*

153

world, do they, Miss Deschamps?"

The Nile snake Elle had dissected contained less venom than Charlotte de Winter's smile. Lady de Winter knew. Somehow she knew Elle to be a fraud and wished to rattle her, if not expose her entirely.

"I try to adhere to the modern notion of ladies and gentlemen, where they are defined not by birth but by actions."

Charlotte studied her nails. "How very peculiar and French of you."

"Oui, madame." Elle smiled and turned to one of the other ladies in the party. Lady de Winter would get no greater reaction from her. This barmaid was well-trained in the art of holding her tongue.

The tour stopped first in Blake's warehouse. Crates lined the walls on all sides. Workers, dressed in the same colors as their tour guide, bustled about, loading and unloading the crates and shuttling things in and out of the room.

"This is where everything begins and ends," the guide told them. "Here, on the right, are all of the raw ingredients that go into the manufacture of our potions. The area directly behind me contains the dry ingredients, all carefully labeled and arranged for easy access. We pride ourselves on using only the finest quality goods, whether they come from right next door, or all the way from China. For some items, freshness is a concern, and those ingredients are brought in daily. Many of them are grown right here in Charleston, on Mr. Blake's own lands."

Elle couldn't have cared less where Blake got his ingredients, but she nodded, as she saw many of the other tourists doing. Her attention was focused on the workers. Their uniforms were clean, but of poor quality. They spoke very little, and never looked at the tour group. They didn't look angry or unhappy, but resigned. It was an attitude familiar to her. They were getting by. Their work didn't bring them pleasure, but it kept them alive.

"On the opposite side of this storage bay are the outgoing potions," the guide continued. "Some potions store well, and are kept in the labeled containers until a client makes a purchase. Others are made on-demand and shipped out as soon as they are finished. Now, if you will follow me, I will show you where the heart of the operation takes place."

Westfield stepped close to Elle as they left the room.

"I am impressed already by the scale of this place," he told her. "It is very different from the European model. What do you think of it thus far?"

"I have only begun to form my opinion. Ask me again when we have seen more."

He nodded and took her arm as they continued on.

Inside the central factory room, more people, men and women both, were hard at work. All throughout the space, they stood at tables, mixing potions in a mechanized fashion. Blake's man began to discuss the process, but Elle heard little of what he said.

She watched a nearby woman at work. Her table held a tray laden with ingredients, a large mixing bowl, a wooden spoon, a funnel, and at least a dozen potion jars. She dumped the ingredients into the bowl in a haphazard fashion, stirred for a time, and then poured the mixture into the potion bottles. Elle hadn't seen any serum go into the mixture.

She turned to look at a man at a different table. He was in the process of squeezing liquid from a cheesecloth into jars. When he had gotten as much out as he could manage, he dropped the cloth into a bucket at his feet, and repeated the process with a second cloth, steeping in a bowl nearby. The two mixtures didn't quite match in color. Elle could find no indication the steeping had been timed in any fashion. The man finished filling his array of jars with the liquid in the bowl, and then began to wrap up some new ingredients for steeping. As with the woman, she saw no sign of serum use.

All throughout the room, she found more of the same. The potions were made in large batches by jaded workers, without much care for precision. Quantity was favored over quality.

After their walk through the mixing room, the tour guide led them into a smaller room at the back of the building. Two men and one woman stood at a round table. They had droppers, stir sticks, and a single bottle of serum between them. A guard watched them from the far corner. These workers looked weary and dispirited. They dripped serum into potions by the trayful, stirred and capped them, and placed the trays on racks along the walls.

"This is the key to the whole process," the guide intoned. "Here is where the magic happens. When the potions leave this room they are ready for shipment and use."

Several people *oohed*.

"Do you not find it marvelous?" one over-enthusiastic man asked Elle. "To see it up close! Such tiny drops transform simple tisanes into the remarkable potions we use. Have you sampled many of the potions here? I have found them wonderful. So invigorating!"

Elle nodded, hoping he didn't mean invigorating in the way she thought he might.

They were ushered back out of the room to the front hall where they had first gathered. A servant offered them a tray of potions, which Elle declined.

"Not thirsty, Miss Deschamps?" Lady de Winter taunted. "Do you not appreciate all the work that has gone into making these lovely concoctions?"

"Everyone here seemed to be working hard, and I admire that," Elle answered. "I simply prefer to take my potions in moderate doses. I will pass on the offer now, so that I have greater opportunity to imbibe this evening."

"Ah, I understand." Charlotte stepped closer. "You do not lie well, Miss Deschamps," she whispered. "I can see through all your oh-so-polite responses."

Elle stepped away from her, hoping she could draw Westfield out of his conversation so they might depart as quickly as possible.

Before she could say anything, the doors opened, and a

towering man entered, flanked by two servants in the same livery as their tour guide. The man had a neatly-trimmed silver beard and was dressed to the nines, his cufflinks and watch fob glittering with gold and diamonds. Elle needed no introduction to know she was looking at Ellison Blake.

The tour guide bowed to Mr. Blake and announced him to the crowd.

"I do like to meet the folks who come to visit," Blake drawled. "I'm always looking to add new customers to our business. I know you are all great fans, and we would be most grateful to you for any purchases you make."

Elle kept her smile pasted on her face. He didn't look grateful, not with his puffed up chest and smug smile. Blake was possibly even more false and condescending than Charlotte de Winter.

"We are the ones who are grateful to you," Charlotte simpered, making her own claim to the title of most insincere. "Being allowed a glimpse at your operation is a rare opportunity, and your generosity will not soon be forgotten. The sample potions you offered were so energizing, though there were some who did not partake."

She cast a frown in Elle's direction, and Elle broke her facade long enough to return the expression.

"You are too kind, Lady…?"

"De Winter. Charlotte de Winter." She offered her hand and Blake shook it.

"A pleasure, Madam. If the rest of you would be so good as to also tell me your names and where you are from?"

Elle would sooner have punched the man than shaken his hand, but she was forced to maintain decorum or risk drawing unneeded attention to herself.

Westfield took care of the introduction for her, and she was happy to play the bashful girl while he carried the conversation.

"I wonder, Mr. Blake, if this factory is representative of the American potions industry as a whole?"

"I can't rightly say," Blake replied. "I serve only the populace of Charleston and its environs. Other areas, they do things for themselves, and they may do it differently. Having said that, I can tell you we make the most potions and the finest potions in all the States. People travel from all over to sample our wares, as you can see by those assembled here."

Heads nodded all around.

"While I dearly love to have you-all visiting our fair city, it seems a shame that other places lack what we here take for granted. My goal, therefore, is to spread my business model to other cities and to create a thriving potions culture across America. My business associates and I have been working diligently to that end, and we hope to open our first remote factory in New York by fall."

"I wish you much luck, sir," Charlotte replied. "Perhaps someday you could bring your business across the ocean."

The idea made Elle shudder. Was this Lady de Winter's true goal? Spreading this horrid business across the globe? Did she know of more than Elle's deception? Did she know of her mission?

Elle touched Westfield's arm to get his attention. She wouldn't stay here a moment longer.

"We should be off now, Uncle."

"Elle, one moment," he began, but she was outside before he could finish the thought. She tore into the street, colliding with a gentleman running in the opposite direction.

"Oh!" She staggered backwards, collecting herself to apologize, and looked up into a pair of startlingly blue eyes. "Henry?"

"Elle! Thank God."

"What's wrong?"

"Everything. Where's Westfield?"

"Just behind me," she answered, glancing back over her shoulder.

Westfield emerged from the building, looking rather put out.

"Elle, whatever are you about—" He lurched to a stop. "Henry? What on earth are you doing here? I told you—"

"Urgent business, sir," Henry interrupted, taking hold of Westfield's arm and drawing him away from the building. "We need to leave town immediately."

"What? Why?" Westfield spluttered.

"I will explain in private. We must go."

Westfield continued to frown in displeasure, but he accepted Henry at his word and agreed to walk back to the hotel rather than waiting to hail a cab.

"Elle, I must ask, what possessed you to leave so abruptly?" Westfield asked. "I had hopes of chatting longer with Mr. Blake and arranging a visit to the source of the serum."

"It would be pointless, Uncle. Henry and I have already been there."

"I wish the two of you would let me show you there is a safe and lawful way to handle these things."

"I must beg to differ in this instance, sir," Henry said. "Ellison Blake is the sort of man who is accustomed to getting his own way. When his way includes keeping the serum to himself, no amount of pleasantries will get you where you want to go."

Westfield could only shake his head. "It cannot hurt to try. Now, I expect you to have a good reason for dragging us off in this manner. And for borrowing my things. I do wish you would learn to ask permission. Were you this much trouble for your parents?"

"Much more, I'm sure."

Elle laughed, and Henry gave her his dimpled smile.

"How did you find the factory, Miss Deschamps?"

"Horrid. The workers were bored and mixed potions that were mediocre at best, without adding the serum. That ingredient was added by just a few people, and I didn't like the way they looked at all. I don't believe they do the job by choice. They are harried and kept under guard. The only reason for them to be there is fear of what might happen to themselves or their families were they to try to leave.

"I was also displeased with the variety of potions. I didn't see a single medicinal potion, and few useful ones. Some of the ingredients make me suspect certain potions are deliberately addictive."

"Brilliant business model," Henry said. "Evil, but brilliant."

"Indeed."

Henry led the way to the hotel at a blistering pace, but Elle wasn't bothered by the rush. She was eager to put distance between herself and Blake's factory. She would be all too happy never to see the place again.

A wild fantasy flitted through her mind of watching it burn to the ground. Last night she'd had her first experience as a thief. Perhaps she could add arsonist to her resume. All it would take would be one good explosive potion, and she still had the saltpetre she'd acquired on the ocean liner.

Her lips pinched into a frown. Blake might be the sort to have people working 'round the clock. She couldn't put innocents at risk.

"Are you plotting, Miss Deschamps?" Henry asked her. "You have a secretive sort of look on your face."

"You are altogether too observant, monsieur."

"Of course. I'm—"

"A spy. I know."

He smiled. It was becoming their own private joke.

She decided to be completely honest and see what he thought of it. "I can't burn the factory down because of the people inside," she whispered.

Henry looked thoughtful. "Pity. I should like to try arson."

The moment they were inside the suite, Westfield folded his arms across his chest and demanded to know Henry's urgent news.

"Charlotte de Winter is an enemy," he replied. "I'm certain she is responsible for the attacks on Miss Deschamps. Look what she has been doing—tracking Elle's whereabouts, trying to learn her habits, testing her. Could she be scared off? Could she be distracted? The answer was no, so she sent an assassin."

"I knew it!" Elle blurted. "I knew her presence at the tour today was suspicious. She was trying to expose me. Why didn't I see it before? She goes everywhere I do. She is nosy as anything. And she would have the means to supply a thug with a berserker potion. It is difficult to make and requires expensive ingredients."

She'd been blinded by Charlotte's upper-class snootiness. She'd let herself believe that someone who never needed to lift a finger to get what she wanted couldn't be bothered to think, either.

Henry nodded. "She is hiring people to do her dirty work. We escaped the attack on the ship, so now she will try something new. She will sic Ellison Blake on us."

Westfield's brow crinkled. "Why would a well-bred lady do such things? This seems rather speculative."

"It's not," Henry asserted. "It's obvious." He began to pace. "Glaringly, disgustingly obvious. I should have seen it earlier, but I'm a damned fool! And, so, sir, are you."

Westfield gasped at the curse and the insult. He tried to express his displeasure, but Henry was in a rant and wouldn't be stopped.

"We're all fools, the whole bloody lot of us! And do you know why? Because from birth we've been reared to think of women as the 'weaker sex,' to see them as somehow lesser than us. Why? Because they are smaller and bear children? Goddamned idiotic!"

A grin spread across Elle's face. The words could just as easily have come from her own mouth.

Henry prowled about the room, hands waving as he shouted, betraying his Italian upbringing. "I've spent years learning to uncover secrets and identify enemies, and I couldn't see one in front of my face! Do you know what they taught me about women? Do you? What they pounded into my brain so damn hard I haven't yet bedded a woman at twenty-seven-bloody-years-old?"

Ah. So he *was* innocent. That certainly explained his tendency to stammer and run from her embrace.

He had paused for an answer, but Westfield was too stunned to say anything. Elle smiled expectantly, silently encouraging Henry to continue. His hair was mussed, his cheeks scarlet, the passion inside him on full display. She could watch him like this all day. Or all night. His virginity was a tricky, yet not insurmountable, obstacle.

Or perhaps yet another reason she needed to stop fantasizing about him.

"Well, I'll tell you," he thundered. "They told me the cheap whores will sell your secrets for money, and the fancy ones will knife you while you're fucking! As if the only useful thing women have is their stupid bodies!"

He stopped in his tracks and turned to look at Elle.

"No offense, Miss Deschamps. I find neither your body nor anything else about you stupid."

She replied with a nod and a broad smile.

"We've made asses of ourselves," Henry continued, resuming his pacing. "Utter, unmitigated asses. Christ Almighty, we've wasted the talents of half the population! This isn't right. It's not bloody right, and I won't stand for it any longer! No one had better treat my daughters like that, and you can be damned sure I'm going to teach my sons some common bloody sense! Now if you'll excuse me, I need some fucking fresh air." He stormed out of the room and slammed the door. Elle stared after him, wondering how long he needed to calm down before she could follow. He deserved some vigorous kisses.

"Miss Deschamps, I am so sorry..." Westfield began.

Her eyes remained locked on the door. "I love that man."

Westfield gaped at her. "I beg your pardon?"

Her words sank in. Her heart jolted.

Merde.

She loved him. A dangerous, possibly disastrous truth, but a truth nonetheless. One she couldn't spare time to dwell on just now.

"I wouldn't expect you to understand. Don't fret over it. It's clear Henry is correct about Lady de Winter. You, yourself, witnessed her interest in Ellison Blake and his business. Let's see to our departure. I will need one hour to extract the serum from the remaining plants and bag up small soil samples. If you could go arrange for our transportation, I will ask Henry to pack up our baggage as soon as he returns."

"But you… That is…" Westfield stammered.

"Please, Uncle?

"Yes, yes, you are right. I had rather leave now and be safe than stay and find out too late these people do mean us harm."

Elle ushered him out the door and turned to her work.

XXV

The Journey North

BY SUPPERTIME ELLE FOUND herself comfortably settled on an overnight train in a well-appointed dining car, filling her belly with a hearty first-class meal. Across the table, Henry lounged against the plush upholstery, sipping on his third cup of tea. He was silent now, having finished his latest burst of chatter about the tea and jam tartlets.

Elle said little, equally content with quiet Henry and over-enthusiastic Henry. It was a pleasure to spend time with him in public with no disguise or false persona. While the train lacked the excitement of their secret lifeboat tête-à-têtes, the warm glow of the lamplight gave her a chance to admire all his freckles and the brilliancy of his blue eyes.

She had come to a decision this afternoon. She would seize what she could, wring every bit of pleasure possible from what could only be an acquaintance of limited duration. Better that than nothing.

"You have been staring at me for a full five minutes, mademoiselle," Henry teased. "I must conclude that either you are madly in love with me, or you are plotting my demise."

Elle smiled at him over the top of her teacup. "Both."

His brows raised at her bold statement, and then his mouth curved into a smile. "Sounds like a tragedy in the making."

She set down her cup and leaned across the table. "Perhaps

I only contemplate *la petite mort*."

He choked on his tea. The fit of coughing lasted several seconds, and left him with a pink complexion that she didn't think entirely due to bashfulness.

"Lord, Elle, you will be my undoing!"

"I hope so." At the very least, she intended to relieve him of his unwanted innocence. "In truth, I have been thinking you look more yourself than I have seen in some time."

His expression relaxed. "A good dinner and hot tea will do wonders."

"And a seat in the corner where you never need look over your shoulder?"

His cheeks dimpled. "*Naturalmente, signorina.*"

"Has it come as a relief, to cease playing servant?"

Henry now leaned forward as well, and spoke in low tones. "The work is welcome. I like to keep busy, and I don't mind carrying the baggage because it gives me some exercise."

"Yes, to keep all your lovely muscles strong."

For once, he didn't blush. "I do it to stay healthy and agile, not to attract the ladies. But, yes, I'm tired of the role. It irks me to be unable to speak to any man as an equal. How did you stand it all those years serving customers, knowing you were a good sight better than those looking down on you?"

"I disciplined myself not to let it show. It was necessary to put food on the table. And no one knows my work smile isn't genuine."

"What?" he exclaimed. "That ridiculous false thing you use? It doesn't look at all like your true smiles. You hold it very rigidly—there is no life in it, no sparkle in your eye. Your lips don't curve as widely, or appear as plump. That smile doesn't make me want to kiss you."

He sat back abruptly. He'd spoken loud enough for nearby passengers to hear, and across the aisle, Westfield frowned. His dining companion—an American widow who was traveling north to visit her grown son and his family—whispered to him, and he chuckled and relaxed. He seemed quite taken with her, and Elle thought it might do him good to have some companionship.

"Perhaps we should speak in your native tongue," Henry suggested, switching to French. "Then we can have some measure of privacy."

"*Absolument*," Elle replied, though they both knew full well Westfield lived in France and was fluent. "It's best if you don't subject the other passengers to your jests."

He put a hand to his heart in mock pain. "You wound me, mademoiselle."

"Then I will make it up to you by telling you that your French is beyond compare. You sound like a native."

"It's a gift. And an obsession. I began studying languages even before I could read, and my father indulged my passion with excellent tutors. I was fluent in half-a-dozen tongues by age ten."

"It's no wonder they made a spy out of you."

"I was born to it, I'm afraid. Let me tell you the story of what I did when I was a boy. I was nine, I believe, and my elder brother was studying in London. We went as a family to spend the summer at a country house in Kent, so he didn't have to travel far to see us. I spent a great deal of time playing with the local children in the nearby village. For whatever reason, I decided it would be more fun if I pretended not to be British at all."

Elle laughed. "Did you claim an Italian heritage to match your place of birth?"

He shook his head. "While that does seem a logical choice for my charade, I had spent my entire life hearing people tell me I didn't look at all Italian."

"It's true. You are much too fair of coloring."

"There are, in fact, plenty of blond Italians, but no matter. I told my playmates in the village, through gestures and few words, that I was Swedish. I didn't speak a word of the language, but I used alternating sentences of Latin, French, and Italian, and a ridiculous made-up accent I believed sounded northern. It was a month before my parents discovered what I was up to and made me apologize. None of the boys cared, but one girl I played with often was devastated. She had been convinced I could teach her to be a Viking. I think I cried for an hour when she told me she didn't wish to see me anymore."

"I can well imagine your poor broken heart. I'm certain that was a far greater punishment than what anyone could have devised."

"Indeed. It didn't stop me from lying, as well you know, but it did make me far more careful to whom I lied."

She smiled at him. "Your story is sweet and funny and has a moral as well. It's a tale you can tell your grandchildren someday."

"I hope so. What of you, mademoiselle? Have you any entertaining exploits from your childhood?"

"I don't have much to tell. I had rather listen to your stories."

"That was my best one, I'm afraid."

"Then tell me something else about yourself. Is there anything at which you don't excel?"

"I'm hopeless at mathematics. Anything beyond basic arithmetic and my head begins to hurt."

"I can't believe that. Your maps are drawn with mathematical precision. You must have some innate understanding of geometry and trigonometry."

"Perhaps, but I have yet to find anyone who can explain it in a way I can understand."

She shook her head. "You have been looking in the wrong places, obviously. I will teach you."

"And how did you come by your knowledge of such subjects? That's not at all what I would expect a poor girl in Paris to learn. I knew you had childhood tales of your own to tell!"

"You win, monsieur. You are correct that it wasn't from

any formal schooling. My family values knowledge, due to our history of potions work. Books are especially prized, as my mother and grandmother believed it was important to read and write to record our recipes and experiments. I learned to read as a very young girl. My uncle, who had no wife or children, took a job at a book bindery. When misprinted or damaged books were to be disposed of, he would salvage them and bring them to me. The bindery sold books to university students, so I learned mathematics, medicine, biology, philosophy, and history. I have almost two dozen books at home, and I have read them all many times. Some of my books are even in English, so I would read them and then practice speaking to international customers—first my mother's and later my own. I did lack for literature and novels, however, which I believe is why I have enjoyed Lord Westfield's books so."

Henry grinned at her. "You are a remarkable woman, my dear," he said, slipping back into English at last.

She glanced away, even now unable to accustom herself to such praises.

"You are kind to say so."

"I'm not kind at all. It's just the bloody truth," he exclaimed. "And for whatever reason, I cannot seem to prevent myself from swearing in your presence."

She reached out to cover his hand with her own. "It is who you are, Henry. Your natural exuberance is at war with your fine manners, and I find it charming." She leaned close and whispered again. "If you were to stop, it would be a fucking shame."

Shock flashed across his face, giving way to a stare so impassioned that Elle sucked in a sharp breath. He flipped his hand over and his fingers raked her palm, sending sparks of arousal along her skin. "My undoing, indeed." His eyes flicked to Westfield, and he sat back, withdrawing his hand. "More tea?"

"No, thank you. I find it's rather warm in here."

Henry poured for himself, his eyes never leaving her. "Very."

Their train car had been prepared for the night during dinner, with the seats folded into beds and the upper bunks pulled down from above. Clean sheets and pillows adorned each bed. After the rickety third-class dormitory on the ship and the lumpy couch in the hotel room, it looked like heaven to Henry. He caught a tantalizing glimpse of Elle's stockings as she clambered into an upper bunk in a delightfully unladylike fashion. Suppressing a groan of desire, he climbed into the next bunk over, laying the wrong way in order to face her. Close enough to whisper, if desired. Close enough to touch her.

"Wouldn't this lower bunk suit you better, Niece?" Westfield asked, a note of pleading in his voice.

"Oh, no. I like being up here. And with these fluffy pillows, it's like sleeping on a cloud."

"If you insist," he sighed. "I trust you had a pleasant dinner?"

"It was lovely, thank you. How was yours? You looked to be enjoying your conversation with Mrs. Fulton."

"Yes, it was enjoyable." He glanced about to see if anyone could overhear him, lowered his voice, and spoke in French. "Although, I introduced the two of you as my niece and nephew, and after observing your dinner conversation, she is now convinced you are a recently married couple. I had hoped to pass you off as brother and sister, but I suppose this will have to do."

"Brother and sister with different accents?" Elle argued. "Peculiar."

"And I'm not such a good playactor as to be up to *that* task," Henry added.

"However we proceed," Westfield continued, "I think having the two of you—and on occasion, myself—conversing in French is a fine idea. It will be easier to keep things confidential if we use a language that few people here speak."

"I think you missed the perfect stratagem, Uncle," Elle said. "You should have told everyone that Henry was a good-for-nothing wastrel from Rome who had convinced me to run away with him, and you had only now caught up to us. You would be free to chastise us in English, I could weep in French, and Henry could swear in Italian while gesticulating wildly. No one would understand a word we were saying, and it would be better entertainment than most stage shows. We could throw bits of real conversation into the mix, with none the wiser."

Westfield's mouth pulled into a tight line. "Amusing as the suggestion is, I would prefer we not actively draw attention to ourselves. Besides, despite his growing up there, Henry does not look at all Italian."

Henry looked at Elle. "As I said, my whole life. Next someone will comment on my freckles, and then I will be told to watch my tongue and not blurt out the first thing that pops into my head. Welcome to the entirety of my childhood."

Elle's laughter rang through the car. "I like your freckles."

Westfield rubbed his temple. "Heaven help me," he muttered. "I am going to bed. Good night, both of you."

"Sleep well, Uncle."

"Do you need me to escort you to the ladies' washroom before you turn in?"

"No, thank you. I know my way if I have need of anything, and it seems absurd to even contemplate changing clothing in so cramped a setting. I will read awhile and then sleep as I am."

She pulled her torch and a book from her bag and drew the curtain around her bunk.

Henry closed his own curtain and propped himself up on his elbows. From this position the modesty panel between their two beds did not entirely conceal her from view. The cheaper upper bunks didn't provide the same privacy as the lower berths, and Elle had pulled aside the pillows that ought to have covered the gap. She looked up, caught his eye, and smiled. After a few minutes, she tossed her reading aside and sat up.

"This isn't the best outfit for lounging," she muttered, tugging at the buttons of her bodice.

Henry's eyes went wide. She discarded the garment, and he shifted for a better look. She glanced at him, just for an instant, before her dexterous fingers unknotted her corset strings and tugged them loose.

Fucking hell. She was undressing in front of him. Was she *trying* to seduce him?

She tugged on the corset until her breasts looked in serious danger of springing free, then flopped on her belly.

"Much better."

His mouth had gone dry. He couldn't tear his eyes away. Elle didn't look at him again, but the corner of her mouth quirked upward in a satisfied smirk. She returned to her reading, angling her torch to illuminate her entire bunk.

Her chest rose and fell with every breath. Henry could see the dusky circles of her areolas peeking over the edge of her untied corset. She kicked up her legs, and her skirts fell away, exposing her clear up to her knees. He imagined running his hands over every part of her, remembering the taste of her mouth and the way her breasts fit *just so* in his palms. The moniker of sophisticated libertine remained beyond his reach, but he was making progress. He sat motionless, watching her in rapt adoration until she turned out the light.

Several hours later, he woke with a start. An eerie silence had fallen over the train car. They were no longer moving. He sat up and peeked out of the curtain, but could see nothing out of the ordinary in the compartment. He reached between the bunks and gave Elle a gentle shake.

"Henry?" She yawned. "What has happened? Are we stopped?"

"It seems so." He pushed the curtain open and slipped soundlessly to the floor.

Elle's bed creaked as she sat up. "I thought there were no stops until morning."

"There shouldn't be. Something is amiss. I will investigate."

A pair of stocking-clad legs poked from beneath the curtain and she slithered from her bunk, her upper half still covered only by her loosened corset. "I will join you."

"I think you had better stay here. It could be dangerous."

"You think there may be danger, yet you would leave me here, unprotected?"

Henry rolled his eyes. "You are too clever by half, you know."

She grinned and presented her back to him. The corset laces dangled down across her rump. "Tie me up."

He made a hash of it, but she was gracious enough not to complain. He donned his suit coat, she grabbed her bag, and they set off, Elle buttoning up her bodice as they slipped out the door. Behind them, Westfield and the other passengers slept on.

Henry ducked under the chains and jumped to the ground beside the train. Elle landed next to him before he could even offer her a hand.

He made a quick survey of the area. A strip of weeds and grasses ran alongside the tracks, melting into the woods several yards further on. No buildings, farms, or other signs of civilization were in sight.

"What do you think has caused our unexpected delay?" Elle asked.

"I haven't a clue. I hope it is no more than an animal or a fallen tree on the tracks, but given our previous experiences during this expedition, I'm suspicious."

"Perhaps we are waiting for another train to pass by on a shared portion of track? That happens, doesn't it? If the train starts to move again while we are here on the ground..." Her voice trailed off.

"Miss Deschamps, you are plenty agile for such an occurrence. We will simply hop back aboard."

He motioned for her to follow, and started toward the front of the train, keeping in its shadow to avoid being spotted in the moonlight. He didn't need to ask her to stay close or to keep silent. These shared nighttime excursions were becoming a habit.

Ordinary men take their girls to the theater.

He scolded himself for thinking of her as his girl. She was far too independent to let any man make that sort of decision for her. If she chose to attach herself to anyone, it would be because he wasn't just out-of-the-ordinary, but extraordinary. He would never qualify.

Tonight's mystery prevented him from brooding too long. As they neared the front of the train, his eye caught a bit of movement, and he paused. Behind him, he heard Elle gasp.

"*Gendarmes,*" she whispered.

He nodded. He could see two men patrolling, perhaps twenty yards beyond the engine. They moved in and out of sight, making their rounds. He turned around and nudged Elle toward their own car.

"They must have set up a roadblock," he murmured. "Someone has betrayed us to the authorities."

He wasn't surprised. Their trespass wouldn't have gone undetected, and Ellison Blake certainly had law enforcement officials in his pocket. What scared him was that someone had identified and caught them up already.

"Lady de Winter colluded with Blake," Elle guessed.

"Undoubtedly." He didn't know who Charlotte de Winter was or what motivated her, but he was determined to find out as soon as possible. "We will wake Westfield and make a run for it. Take only what you can carry."

"You don't think we can talk our way out of trouble?"

"I don't trust anyone will let us talk. I doubt they will shoot us on sight, but I don't expect to be treated pleasantly. They will expect to catch us sleeping. We can put some distance between us before they discover we are gone."

They hurried toward the back of the train, but the sound of a door sliding open stopped them in their tracks. They flattened themselves against the side of the train as several armed men passed between the cars.

"We're too late. We shall have to go as we are. On my word, we run for the woods. As quickly and quietly as possible."

"What of Westfield?"

"We can't help him if we are arrested, too." He watched the sky, waiting for the brief burst of darkness as the moon ducked behind a cloud. "Run. Now."

She clutched his hand and they raced into the woods, sprinting until Henry was confident they were out of range of the police rifles. He slowed his pace by half. Elle was breathing hard, but she didn't falter or lag behind. Her palm was sweaty against his. He didn't dare let go.

They had gone nearly a mile, by his best estimation, when they heard the train rumble past. Henry staggered to a stop, leaning against a tree for support. His legs felt like jelly. They had been too inactive of late, and he wasn't as fit as he ought to be. He sank to the ground and lay on his back, staring up through the trees and trying to catch his breath. Elle collapsed next to him, her skirts tumbled about, her chest heaving. Good Lord, he had made her run a mile in a corset. He was a right bastard.

"We shall have to continue on," he said as soon as he was able to speak normally.

"Oui. Do you think they are searching for us?"

"I don't know." He sat up, feeling an urge to start moving again. "How are you?"

"Tired, but not unwell. You?"

"I'm fine. We should depart whenever you are able."

He took his time rising, and gave her a hand up. He could see, even in the moonlight, how her cheeks were flushed from the exertion, and her brow damp with sweat.

"Do you need to rest longer?" He knew she would never

ask for more time of her own volition. She was among the hardest workers he knew.

"Only if you do."

He shook his head. "We should go as far as we are able tonight. The further from here we are, the harder it will be for them to find us."

"Where do you plan to go?"

"We will head north, following the train tracks. I have money, our train tickets, and our passports in my jacket. If we can get to a station, we should be able to arrange to board another train."

"And Westfield?"

"He has done nothing illegal—it wasn't he who stole those plants, after all—and he has many diplomatic connections. I think he will have little trouble freeing himself. We will make inquiries as soon as possible."

She nodded. "Let's be off, then. We have rested long enough."

They started off through the forest. After a few moments, Elle tugged on his sleeve.

"How do we know we are following the tracks when we can't see them?"

"We can hear the trains go by, as we did before. I may like to put a bit more distance between us and the tracks tomorrow, but we shall see. Regardless, we will take a northward path." He pointed up at the sky. "That is the North Star, Miss Deschamps. As long as we can see it, navigation will be easy."

"And what of the clouds?"

"They are spotty. We can wait for them to pass over if we must."

A distant flash of lightning lit the horizon for a split second. Henry cursed under his breath and picked up the pace.

XXVI

Chills and Heat

*E*LLE TRUDGED ON, mile after mile, eyes on the approaching storm. A chill had stolen into the night air, and the wind whipped at her skirts and tugged tendrils of hair from her chignon. Clouds covered most of the sky, allowing only an occasional sliver of moonlight to break through. A fat droplet splashed on her arm.

"It's raining."

Henry shrugged out of his coat and draped it over her shoulders. "The storm is nearly upon us. We should find shelter."

The coat was heavy on one side, and Elle put her hand in the pocket to see why. Her fingertips found the cold metal of a pistol. She let out a yelp and jerked her hand away. The urge to throw the jacket to the ground and run from it nearly overwhelmed her. She stumbled to a halt.

"What's wrong?" Henry asked.

"I... I cannot carry this gun. Please. It terrifies me."

He pulled the pistol from the pocket and tucked it into the back of his trousers. "I'm terribly sorry. I didn't realize."

Elle took a steadying breath, the fear easing as the shock wore off. He was a spy. He'd served in the army. Of course he carried a gun. The thought of him using it turned her stomach.

"You couldn't have known," she said. "It's a very old fear. A phobia."

He nodded. "I understand. And I'm certain you have good reason for it. I can't say the same for myself. I'm deathly afraid of sharks. Beyond terrified. I won't swim in the ocean."

"I've never seen a shark."

"Neither have I. But there you have it. I don't even like boats."

"You made it across the Atlantic with no trouble."

"If we had used the lifeboats for their intended purpose, I assure you, I would have embarrassed myself. More than usual, that is."

She laughed, grateful for his empathy and humor.

"It was very trusting of you to allow me to carry your gun at all." She patted his coat pockets. "You gave me all of our money and documents and our only weapon. What was to prevent my running off, or even shooting you, and taking it all for myself?"

"Your common sense?"

"There is that, I suppose."

"I believe you also possess a certain amount of affection for me. I hope it's enough that you wouldn't harm me."

She reached for his hand, threading her fingers through his. "I will never hurt you, Henry."

"The gun isn't our only weapon, in any event."

"Oh. Your knife?"

"I carry it at all times." He held his free hand out to gauge the rain. "We ought to stop and build a shelter. The rain is coming harder now, and we will be soaked if we wait too long. Grab whatever large logs and sticks you can find."

They worked quickly, gathering broken branches and piling them into a tent-like formation against a downed tree. Henry directed the operation with calm efficiency, giving instructions as he hauled the largest of the limbs. Elle gathered smaller sticks and leaves to plug up the holes in his framework. The rain grew heavy even beneath the trees, and thunder rumbled in the distance. They ducked inside the shelter, closing the entrance with a few leafy branches.

Inside there was only enough room for them to sit side-by-side, their backs against the fallen tree. The shelter was dry and kept the wind out, but Elle shivered nonetheless. Henry put an arm around her, and she leaned into his warmth.

"I'm sorry for dragging you into this mess," he said.

"Dragging me? I insisted on participating, if you recall."

"I should have refused."

"It's true your effort was rather half-hearted. I believe you secretly wanted me to join you."

"You seem determined to uncover all my secrets, mademoiselle. Yes, there was some part of me—a large part, rather—that wanted you to come with me. But I never wanted this. To make you run all that way, and then walk many miles more, all in the dark, wearing such inappropriate clothing. And now, huddling in a dank little hovel of sticks to wait out a horrendous thunderstorm. I can only imagine what you must think of me."

"I think even more highly of you than I did before. I'm impressed with your navigational skills and your knowledge of how to get by in the woods. This shelter may be small, but it was quick to build and seems effective."

"You are the most resilient woman I have ever met. We have no idea where we are, we have no food, and there may be armed men hunting us down. How does that not bother you?"

"It bothers me quite a bit, to be truthful. I'm scared, Henry. I'm scared we are lost. I'm scared enemies may be after us. I'm scared to be out here in the woods, so different from any place I have ever lived. But I would be far more scared were I not with you. Things that may sound unbearable aren't as bad when you don't have to face them alone."

"You are far kinder than I deserve," he insisted. "You may not wish to blame me for our predicament, but..."

"Oh, Henry, do shut up." She kissed him before he could say another word.

His arm tightened around her. His tongue delved into

her mouth. Elle slid her hands over the silken fabric of his waistcoat. She was done with waiting. Done with flirting. She would sate this unrelenting desire inside of her, and the consequences be damned.

"Elle," he sighed against her lips.

Her fingers, cold and stiff from the rain, fumbled with the waistcoat buttons. "Your sneaking clothes are more practical."

He hoisted her up onto his lap, crushing and tangling her skirts. "So are yours."

His hand came up to cup her cheek. He trailed his fingers along her jaw, then down her neck to her shoulder, taking advantage of her square-cut neckline. His touch was the lightest graze against her skin, a tingling tease full of promise. A quiver filled her belly and raced down to settle between her legs.

She left his waistcoat hanging open, and tugged at the shirt buttons, squirming her hand inside when they were but half undone. He sucked in a breath at her cold touch, but kissed her with an even greater vigor.

Her fingers tangled in the fine hairs splayed across his chest. She sucked on his bottom lip while her hand explored the contours of his muscles, loving the softness of his skin over his wiry core.

"Elle. God." His voice was thick with desire. She could feel his arousal, long and hard against her bottom.

Henry slid his hand into her dress, his fingertips skimming across the swells of her breasts. His every touch was like fire in her veins. Her nipples strained against the fabric of her chemise.

"Touch me," she groaned.

His hand burrowed beneath her corset, taking advantage of his poor lacing skills. She grabbed for his other hand, pushing it up beneath her skirts.

"More."

She squirmed atop him, grinding herself against his

erection. He moaned as if in agony, then drew back, gasping her name again.

He lifted her off of him. "I—I can't. We mustn't."

"Henry..."

"I'm so sorry." He dove for the shelter entrance, leaving her holding empty air.

Cool air blew through the opening, but did little to relieve the heat that suffused her. Even now the intensity of her body's response to him was staggering. He was right, of course. They shouldn't. But her mind was made up. She *would* have him.

She leaned toward the shelter entrance, seeking his shadowy form in the darkness. Cold droplets splattered her face and arms. She shivered, the loss of his warmth coming in a sudden, unwelcome rush. His stifled groan cut through the steady patter of rain. What she wouldn't give to be able to see him taking himself in hand, strands of wet, blond hair plastered to his face while rivulets of water streamed over his bared skin.

Someday, perhaps.

Elle sat back with a sigh. A short time later, Henry ducked back inside the shelter, only moderately wet.

"I'm so sorry," he babbled. "I got carried away. I should never have..."

She placed a finger to his lips to silence him.

"Don't apologize. I began it and fully encouraged it."

"Your senses were heightened from the danger. I know better. I ought to have stopped it immediately."

"You regret kissing me, then?" she challenged.

"No."

"I thought not. You are worried about being immoral, and you are making excuses."

"It's not an excuse. It's true that danger can over-stimulate the nerves, and..."

She poked a finger at his chest, finding his shirt still open. "The only thing stimulating my nerves is you, Captain Lord

Henry Ainsworth. You and your lean, hard body, and your cute freckles, and your never-quiet mind, and your too-quick mouth. You make me yearn for you, and I'm not ashamed of it."

"I... But..." He gave up and fell silent.

"We will sleep now," she commanded. "Our adventures grow more exciting every night. We will need our rest." She dragged a lingering kiss across his mouth, laid her head on his shoulder, and closed her eyes. *"Bonne nuit, mon chéri."*

"Gute Nacht, meine Liebe."

She didn't know a word of German, but he lifted her into his lap and cradled her against his chest, and that needed no translation.

XXVII

A Discovery

ELLE SHIVERED AGAINST HENRY'S CHEST. He kissed her brow and tugged his coat tighter around her shoulders. The damp cloth provided little relief from the chill.

"Good morning." He knocked away a portion of the shelter, exposing them to the warmth of the morning sun. "We should walk, if you are able. It's too wet to light a fire, so we must rely on exercise to shake off this cold."

"If you give me a moment, I can help. I know a recipe for a warming potion, and a basic stamina potion will ward off fatigue and hunger."

"Excellent! Have I mentioned I want to take you on all my missions? You are a splendid traveling companion. You mix up your potions, while I scatter these logs. We cannot erase all evidence of our stay, but there's no sense making it obvious."

Four potions left her original jar of serum all but empty. She had toyed with the idea of using some of the newly extracted serum, but with her own well-being and Henry's at stake, she preferred her own trusted supply. She held the bottle up to the light, watching the amber droplets ooze along the bottom. She blinked away a tear.

"Elle? Is something wrong?"

"No. It's only that I have had this jar of serum for near to five years, and it feels somewhat as if I am losing my protection."

"You have your harvest from the plants, I thought?"

"Yes, but…" She bit her lip. Talking about herself didn't come easily. She didn't want his pity. "My family had very little money," she explained. "When I was young, a terrible fever came through the city. We had no medicines to combat it, or serum to make our own. The illness took my father, my brother, and the baby in my mother's womb. My memory of the time is dim, but the pain of losing my family was deep, and I feel the pangs even now.

"I learned potions as I grew older. My grandmother taught me without serum, but I was at times allowed to make real potions when helping my mother at the chemist's where she was a shop girl. Her employer, Monsieur Martin, was very fond of her. They may have been lovers, but I'm not certain. She didn't talk much about her paramours. I think she compared them all to my father and found them lacking. When she died—also of an illness—Monsieur Martin gave me a sum of money in her memory. I used it to buy this bottle of serum."

"To defend what little family you had left," Henry murmured. "Christ, Elle, I'm so sorry." His stricken expression brought new tears to her eyes. Her pain was his pain.

He reached for her, but she busied herself with the potions to avoid his embrace. She would not cry on his shoulder.

"It has been many years. I have adjusted. But I feel it more than usual just now. Here, drink your potions. I have spirits as well. Would you like a swallow of cognac to fortify you?"

"Thank you, no. I drink liquor only on occasion, and never on an empty stomach. It addles the brain, and I cannot often afford such a risk."

"That makes a great deal of sense given your profession."

"The potions are quite sufficient. I feel better already."

"Good. I hope it lasts until we can get some real food."

He took hold of her hand. "We will manage. As you said last night, we are not facing this alone."

Under the clear skies, the air warmed quickly, and the trees soon gave way to farmland. They skirted the farms, keeping a good distance from any houses and barns. From afar their dirty, rumpled clothing would be hidden, and they could pass as a couple out for a walk.

It was mid-afternoon when they reached a town with a train station. Amidst the commotion of a train arrival, they slipped into the washrooms to clean up. Elle brushed the dirt from her skirts, washed her hands and face, and repinned her hair. She emerged feeling refreshed and comfortable.

Henry, too, looked tidy and proper, with the lone caveat that he hadn't been able to shave. The shadow of stubble along his jaw was oddly appealing, and she almost dared to kiss him in public. Instead, she hooked her arm through his, and they joined the crowd, just one couple among many.

"When we arrived, I noticed a lovely grove of trees west of town," Henry said. "I think it would be a fine place for a picnic. Shall we take a look?"

She nodded, watching the other people walking to and fro. No one paid them any special attention.

"I don't want to spend too much time together in town," he added when they were far enough away not to be overheard. "If anyone is searching for us they will be looking for a man and woman together. If you wait at our picnic spot, I'll go back to town and buy us something to eat and some supplies. I need to send a few telegrams as well."

"To whom do you send all these telegrams? Westfield's people?"

"My own people. I honestly don't know how much the two overlap. Also to my father, who will wish to know that I am neither dead nor in prison."

"I had rather go into town than wait for you. We don't have to walk about together. I could purchase the food while you run other errands, perhaps?"

"I understand your need to feel useful, Miss Deschamps, but I can fake an American accent, and you cannot. No one will remember me. They will remember the pretty French woman."

"Blast," she muttered. "You're right. I hadn't considered that." She sighed. "Very well. I'll wait here for you. Don't take too long."

"I won't be but a moment. I want to get this mission back on track as much as you do. I'm certain Westfield will blame me for all the trouble. It's a good thing dueling has been outlawed, or he would call me out for dishonoring you."

"Oh, Henry, don't be so melodramatic. You Englishmen worry about the silliest things. Go run your errands. I will be fine here until..."

She gasped and he froze.

"What's the matter?"

"Look!"

She raced toward a haggard old tree several yards beyond. It had lost many branches over the years and its bark was peeling. Up close, she could confirm what she thought she had seen. Where the bark had fallen away, thin veins of shiny red ran up the trunk.

"Serum! Henry, it's just like the source in Charleston!"

She bent down and dug up a small sample of dirt. She sniffed it, then searched through her potions bag for the dirt samples she had collected. She took a whiff of one, then held out both to Henry.

"Do these smell the same to you?"

He smelled both the old dirt and the new, and nodded. "Yes, but your nose is better than mine."

"They smell the same to me, too," she replied. "It's just good to get a second opinion on the matter." She grinned at him. "It appears I have found something to do after all. I will investigate the area while you fetch us something to eat."

"Splendid! I'll try not to take too long."

She waved him off. "Don't rush yourself. I will be fine here for some time."

She sat down beside the tree to get a look at the grass as Henry scurried off. By the time he returned, she had done a thorough investigation, and had two full pages of notes in her journal. She looked up when she heard his footsteps, to find him with an armful of packages, including a ceramic water jug and a powder-blue hat box. He also wore a brand-new bowler hat.

"You paid a visit to the milliner, monsieur?"

"I felt silly as the only bare-headed person in the entire town. I bought something for you, as well. It will help us blend in better. We can use the box to carry what food we don't eat."

He set down the hat box and his other packages and took a seat beside her. Elle opened the box to find a stylish velvet bonnet the exact green shade as her dress. She lifted it out carefully and tried it on.

"I wasn't certain what you might like, but this one matched."

"It's lovely, thank you." She tied up the strings, her delight at the gift warring with her discomfort that he would buy her something so fine on a whim.

"You look fetching in it." He glanced away and changed the subject. "Tell me what you have learned while we have lunch."

"Lunch?" she laughed. "It's nearly teatime."

"I can't stand the thought of calling it tea when I can't even have a cup of the stuff."

He unwrapped several packages and spread out the food. The scent of fresh bread made Elle's empty stomach grumble. There was jam to spread on it, two types of cheese, and an assortment of fruits. Simple fare, but it looked a veritable feast to her. The last package held two tin cups so they wouldn't have to drink directly out of the water jug. Elle found it hilarious and delightful that Henry troubled himself over such trivialities.

She beamed at him. "I think I can solve your problem." She flipped open her potions bag and poked through it for ingredients.

Henry frowned at her. "I'm sorry?"

"The tea." She passed him a small tin. "We will have to

put the leaves directly into the cups, and you'll have to drink it black, but it's better than nothing."

It took no more than a minute to mix up a warming potion identical to the one they had drunk that morning, but completely undiluted. She dripped the base of the potion into a small metal capsule and added the last drops of her serum. It was a good way to finish it, bringing joy to someone dear to her. She snapped the capsule closed, shook it for a few seconds, and passed it to Henry.

"Drop this into the water jug, but take care. It gets hot very quickly."

He squinted at the capsule, turning it over a few times.

"What in blazes is it supposed to... Ow!"

He dropped it into the jug and shook his burned hand.

"Blast it all, that hurt. That damned thing is dangerous!" He shook his head. "I suppose you did warn me."

"The water will boil eventually. It may take some time, but we will have tea."

His smile was all the thanks she needed. "You are brilliant. Bread?"

"Yes, please."

"Jam?"

She shook her head. "Only cheese at the moment."

He handed her a thick slice of each, then slathered jam onto his own bread.

"And now will you tell me about your discovery, or do you wish to keep it all to yourself?"

"There's not much to tell, I'm afraid. The source is only about as big as the spot we sit now, and is not dense." She ran her fingers through the grass. "If you look here, you can see streaks of red in the blades of grass, but if you look off to your left, you won't find anything."

Henry checked the grass to each side of him.

"You're right. And the red is very faint. I wouldn't notice it if I weren't looking for it."

"I think the source must be directly under the tree, somewhat to this side of it. I checked the other side of the tree, and the red streaks are difficult to see. This, here, is the only spot where it's strong." She put her hand to the tree.

"Were you able to extract any serum?"

She shook her head. "I don't have a spile, like one might use for collecting sap, and when I tried scraping the wood with my knife I got nothing."

His mouth twisted. "So it's useless, then?"

"I don't think so. I compared several samples of soil from around the base of the tree and from the affected grassy area. At first I thought only the dirt along this side of the tree compared to what we collected in Charleston. But when I took a deeper sample from underneath the grass, it, too, had that same feel and scent. There is serum here, but it's underground, and not much is getting up into the plants."

"Interesting. It seems we need some way to extract it directly from the ground."

"Yes, and I intend to spend some time playing with the soil samples I have collected to see what can be done with them. If we can find a way to extract serum from the ground, it could be the answer we are looking for."

"One thing is certain. Sources are not so difficult to find as we have been led to believe."

"No, they're not. I won't be surprised if we find another on the next leg of our journey."

He only nodded, his mouth full of bread. There was a smear of jam on his upper lip, and her gaze lingered on it. She wanted to lick it off, but she settled for watching him lick it away himself. Now wasn't the time.

"I believe the water is ready. I will make us some tea."

"No bloody milk," Henry grumbled, when the brew had steeped. "Damned uncivilized. But an excellent blend. I promise to restock your supply as soon as I'm able."

Revived by the tea and with their bellies full, they stashed the uneaten food in the hat box. Plenty remained for both dinner and breakfast, and they had used only a third of their water.

"The railroad split a few miles south of here," Henry briefed her. "This station is the first on this branch of the track. It veers off to the west. We need to make our way to the other track, which continues on to the north. We can pass through town and then continue north-east until we find that track and follow it to the next town. I'm not certain we can make it there by nightfall, so we may need to spend another night out-of-doors. If that happens, I will try to find us a better shelter."

"I thought the one last night was quite adequate, given the circumstances."

"It was horrid. It was so cramped you had to sleep sitting in my lap the entire night."

Elle gave him her best seductive smile. "That was the best part. Particularly when you warmed me with your exhilarating kisses."

A touch of pink tinted his fair cheeks. "When I kiss you next, it will be somewhere more appropriate. I can't think of a less romantic location than a dank pile of sticks."

"Then you don't have a very good imagination, mon chéri."

He made a noise that was part grunt, part laugh. "Thank you. Now my mind is conjuring up some truly hideous settings, and I'm certain I would kiss you and worse in any of them. I'm rather a cad, as it turns out."

"No. A rogue, perhaps, but always a gentleman."

He bowed and helped her to her feet. "Please tell my father. He will want to know I absorbed some small part of his instructions. Come. If we walk quickly, perhaps we can sleep indoors after all." He picked up their provisions and led the way.

"Let me know if your arms grow tired," Elle said, knowing he would refuse her offer. "I'm happy to take a turn carrying something."

"That won't be necessary, thank you."

"I'm perfectly capable, you know."

"I'm well aware of that."

"I have heard your bold statements on the equality of the sexes, monsieur. I'm certain you realize, therefore, that despite our smaller stature, we females are plenty strong enough to, say, carry a hatbox full of food. After all, we carry children in our bellies for some months, and when they are born we continue to carry them, strapped onto our backs or in our arms, for any number of years."

He grinned at her, showing even white teeth, his eyebrows arching. The smile of a rogue. "All the more reason for you not to have to carry anything just now. It's the least I can do."

"I suppose I should be grateful you don't insist upon carrying my potions bag."

"Don't tempt me."

She took hold of his arm and leaned in close enough for him to feel her breath. "That will come when we are in private."

XXVIII

Of Marriage and Money

GOD, WAS SHE GORGEOUS. Henry snuggled up to Elle's warm body, twisting a lock of hair around his finger. She had again removed her bodice and loosened her corset, and he'd stripped down to his shirtsleeves, but nothing had come of it. They'd reached the hotel well after midnight and tumbled into bed, exhausted.

Now with the sun slanting through the curtains he had a glorious view of her bare arms and generous bosom. Hair tumbled about and clothing askew, she looked disheveled and utterly delicious. He wanted to ravish her.

All he needed was to wake her and ask, he was certain. God knew why, but she was enamored of him. Her eager, confident sexuality suggested she was no virgin, which didn't surprise him. As a barmaid, she would have had no image to protect, and the French took a more liberal approach to such matters. The word *affaire* was theirs, after all.

Westfield—who treated her like some fragile icon of chastity—would be aghast at the very suggestion. Henry dismissed it as irrelevant. There was nothing lewd or immoral about her. If she thought such things immoral, she would never have done them.

What would he want with Westfield's sort of girl, anyway? Icons of chastity didn't sneak out at night with a man of questionable integrity. They didn't plead for his caresses, or writhe unabashedly against him. The interlude in the woods played repeatedly in Henry's mind. The torturous pleasure of her rear stroking his cock had nearly sent him over the edge.

He shoved himself from the bed. He couldn't be there when she woke.

A few splashes of cold water from the wash basin calmed him enough to function, and he took a seat at the desk and busied himself with work. The combination of mental and physical effort required provided a brief respite, and he didn't look up until the bed creaked. "Good morning," he greeted her. He glanced at her and then refocused on his task.

"Good morning to you. What time is it?"

He consulted his watch. "Quarter to ten."

"Goodness! I hadn't thought to sleep so long. Why didn't you wake me?"

"We all need our rest, mademoiselle. I have only been up this half-hour myself."

"I will wash up and then we must eat breakfast and prepare to leave."

"No need to rush. The train we want doesn't get in until half-past noon. There's no reason we shouldn't spend a lazy morning in bed." His damnable cheeks flushed. In bed. Together. In a state of wanton dishabille. "My apologies. I didn't intend for that to sound so suggestive."

Elle shook her head. "I don't know why you insist on apologizing to me, when you are the one distressed about such things. I assure you, I wasn't in the least offended." She started for the door. "Excuse me while I go down to the washroom. I won't be long."

"You must find me completely ridiculous," he muttered.

How could he be anything but a disappointment to her? He'd already confessed to his absurdly virginal condition. Too proper to touch an innocent, too chivalrous to pay for a woman like a commodity, too naive to find anyone else.

His pen marked smooth strokes across the paper. This, at least, he was good at.

Elle returned momentarily, clean and properly attired. From the corner of his eye, he could see her inching toward him, craning her neck for a look at his papers. She hovered, her skirts rustling as she shifted, curious but unwilling to interrupt.

"You needn't stand there all day, chérie. I can tell you are dying to know what I'm about."

"I don't wish to be a bother."

"Not possible. Come take a look. I don't mind."

Elle stepped up beside him. He waved his free hand over the array of passports, his pen still drawing careful marks on the last, incomplete document.

"New travel papers."

"You have turned forger, now?"

"Not now, no. I've faked documents in the past. I must have failed to mention it was on my list of ignoble accomplishments."

"It does seem obvious, given your good hand at drawing. How did you get the seal and the stamp so perfect?"

He chuckled. "I didn't. I started with a blank, pre-signed passport. I have only to add your information. My profession provides certain advantages."

"This is yours?" she asked, leaning in. "Henry C. MacAlaster. It sounds Scottish."

"Aye, lassie, that 'tis. And many a cousin ha' I still in tha' part o' the world."

"*Quoi?*" She squinted at him. "Oh! That explains your accent."

"My accent?"

"Oui. You have a funny lilt on certain words. You are part Scottish."

"Aye. Fully half, in fact. My mother's family has an estate near Edinburgh." He held out a hand to her, as if introducing himself for the first time. "Henry Charles MacAlaster Ainsworth, at your service, mademoiselle."

"Elle Deschamps," she replied, taking a firm grasp of his hand. "No middle names, no great family history. Just some girl."

He lifted her hand to his lips and kissed it. "You are anything but just a girl." He turned back to the work before he could lose focus, finishing her name with a few strokes of the pen. When the ink had dried he handed her the paper. "Here you are, Mrs. MacAlaster."

"And just like that, we are married."

Henry's gut clenched. He ought to have asked her beforehand. "I hope that doesn't bother you."

She waved a hand at him. "I was prepared to pose as your unwed lover, if you recall. I don't see how this would be worse."

"That was only in an extreme emergency, and never proved necessary. It's too late to prevent this new fiction, however. I registered us at the hotel last night as a Mr. and Mrs. MacAlaster."

"As you should have. Traveling alone together and sharing a hotel room is unremarkable for a husband and wife. If we presented ourselves as an unmarried pair flouting social customs, we would draw unnecessary attention. The choice is obvious. We will continue with the tale at least until we are reunited with Westfield."

"Still, you have my apologies for imposing on you."

"You *have* been somewhat of an inattentive husband thus far." She fluttered her lashes at him. "You haven't even kissed me."

"I was thinking of our public image," he pressed on, trying to ignore the curve of her mouth. "My own situation is affected very little, but you will be expected to defer to me and abide by my decisions, and I don't think you will like that. We have grown accustomed to speaking frankly with one another."

She pursed her lips. "I do defer to you on many matters. You possess knowledge I don't. But you're right to think it will look unusual when you ask me for *my* expertise. Perhaps men would make fewer mistakes if they were more willing to openly consult with their wives."

"And educate our women properly. I'm proud to say my own alma mater has recently begun to award degrees to female students, but their numbers are still few."

"Be careful, Henry. You may be accused of being a feminist."

"I may well be," he replied. "I shouldn't want my own daughters to grow up needing to bind themselves to some man in order to secure a comfortable future. I had much rather they be able to provide for themselves."

"Which we do, in the working class," Elle replied. "But, then, most of us don't have a choice in the matter. It is work or let your family starve."

"No wonder men and women alike scheme to marry someone of wealth to escape such circumstances."

"Many scheme, but few of my class ever move up to yours."

"My father clawed his way to the top. Not that his Italian title means much in England, but it was enough that when he wandered up into the Highlands and fell madly in love with a proper Lady, her family allowed them to marry. Little did she know his title came with no money and his villa was a wreck. Mother claims she refused to speak to him for an entire week and nearly returned to Scotland. In the end, they dumped her entire fortune into restoring the villa and starting a winery. To this day they sell overpriced wine to clueless foreigners, but I'm not sure what they intend to do with their wagon loads of money."

"Make sure all you children have no financial worries, I'd imagine."

"True. Though there are other ways of dealing with that. My father is a master of the marriage market. Both my older brothers wed extraordinarily wealthy ladies, and my sister's husband owns the British half of the Ainsworth wine cabal."

"And what of you? Does he throw heiresses into your path?"

"He keeps a list of suitable wives. I burned the last copy he gave me. I'd rather earn my own keep than marry for so mercenary a reason."

Elle put on her thoughtful frown. "Do spies make good money? My own pay for this particular journey feels outlandish. I can only imagine what they would give to an agent of the crown."

"Five thousand pounds sterling, assuming the venture is considered successful. My travel expenses are paid as well."

Her jaw dropped. "Five thousand," she echoed. "Mon Dieu. I wouldn't expect any government to part with so much."

"I agree, it's outrageous. But this mission is vital. Without potions the empire will grind to a halt—no lights, no factories, no transportation. The economy will collapse. And not just in Britain. All Europe is in danger. The whole world, perhaps, given what we saw in Egypt. In any case, I don't get paid unless we succeed."

"How did you come by this job?"

"Luck. My father and Westfield had been talking to their friends all over Europe about the troubles. They were determined to enlist the aid of a potions expert. I was in a position to take advantage of all the work they had done. Westfield was given the money to hire you, provided I came along, supposedly as your protector."

"So you pose as a bodyguard and steal their secrets." She sounded neither surprised nor upset. Apparently she had accepted the fact that he was a scoundrel. "Does Westfield know?"

"That I have my own agenda? Certainly. More than that, I doubt. What of you? What is your objective?" He grinned at her. "Clearly not listening to Westfield."

"I will do what I was hired to do. Find serum. I will fix the problem, because someone must. I will earn my pay."

"I don't doubt it. Might I inquire what your pay is?

"Of course. Ten thousand francs in total, a portion of

which has already been paid in order to cover the costs of the care of my aunt while I am away. I dream of using the rest to open my own potions shop, but I'm not certain it will be enough."

"Ten thousand francs? What would that be in pounds?" His brow furrowed as he did the arithmetic in his head. A pound was close enough to twenty-five francs for an estimate, and twenty-five into ten-thousand... Ugh. Twenty-five into one hundred...

"That can't be right," he grumbled. He worked the figures again, muttering and counting on his fingers. "It's only about four hundred pounds! It's a pittance! You are far more vital to this operation than I am. How can they pay you so little?"

Elle ticked off the reasons. "I'm poor, I'm not British, and I'm a woman. I'm surprised they are willing to pay me at all."

"It's disgraceful. I ought to give you half of whatever I earn."

"I couldn't accept that."

"Why not? I don't need it. I already have twelve hundred pounds in savings in my own name. Even if I gave you half my pay, I would..." He paused a moment. "Triple my net worth. Now, I don't expect future jobs to pay as well as this one, but it has been hinted that even less critical work will earn me upwards of five hundred pounds per annum. As you can see, I won't be starving any time soon."

"Does your father know that?"

"Of course. He would still prefer I give it up and become an idle gentleman, but I don't fancy being bored out of my mind."

"I wonder that he didn't protest when you set off on this quest."

"Oh, he complained plenty in private. I'm certain he told Westfield to see that I didn't get into any trouble."

"And here you are, having broken several laws, run from the authorities, lost touch with Westfield, and concocted a false marriage to a former barmaid. I don't imagine your father would in any way approve of our current charade."

"Certainly not. But that hardly matters, as I don't ever intend to tell him of it."

"Wise." She looked down at the false passports. "You know, I believe I envy this Elle MacAlaster and her husband. Their life seems less complicated than that of Elle Deschamps and Henry Ainsworth."

"No doubt. Perhaps the MacAlasters could run away together. I hear America is a good place to make one's fortune."

She laughed, as he had intended. If only he'd been joking.

XXIX

Reunited

𝒯HE TRAIN RIDE TO NEW YORK proved uneventful. Henry slept fitfully, and when he awoke feeling groggy and cranky he told himself it was due to the rocking of the train and the proximity of so many strangers, and not at all related to the fact that he wasn't snuggled up next to Elle.

Upon arrival, they made inquiries and left messages for Westfield, then spent a few hours walking about town, in their guise as the MacAlasters. They stopped into several apothecary shops to evaluate the potions, but it still felt like a day of leisure. They wandered like tourists and had a nice lunch at a little cafe. Henry bought Elle a pretty little tortoise-shell box to hold potion ingredients. She accepted it with a smile and only minimal scolding that he oughtn't buy her gifts.

In mid afternoon they returned to the train station to check for replies to their messages. Instead of a note, they found Westfield himself awaiting them. He was seated on a bench, reading the newspaper, and when he caught sight of them he jumped up so fast the pages scattered.

"Good afternoon, sir," Henry greeted him, bending to pick up the papers. "It's good to see you again."

He rose and handed the disorderly newspaper back to Westfield, who snatched it from him in an irritable fashion.

"Good afternoon? Is that all you have to say? I've been

sick with worry over the two of you. What on earth were you thinking?" He shook his head. "No. This is not the place. Let's return to the house where we can discuss matters in private."

"And have a cup of tea, perhaps?"

Henry had had one weak cup with dinner on the train the night before, but nothing more since Elle had used her warming potion. He was certain a cup or two would help ease his general crankiness and the nagging headache he had suffered all day.

"I am certain Herbert has something of the sort. I can tell you firsthand he has excellent coffee to offer."

Henry pulled a face. "No, thank you. I don't understand how anyone can drink such a repulsive beverage."

"Henry, you are a terrible snob," Elle teased.

"It's hardly my fault so many people suffer from a lack of good taste."

"I happen to be very fond of coffee."

"Then I'm terribly sorry, my dear, that you should find yourself a member of such a sad group."

"Enough, I beg you," Westfield groaned. "We are only a few of many house guests this week, and if you insist on flirting so vigorously, everyone will assume you are romantically involved."

"That would be unfortunate, indeed," Elle replied. Westfield completely missed her sarcasm.

"Pretend we are married, as you did before," Henry suggested. "Then you needn't fret about it."

"Impossible. Herbert has met your father, and I have already mentioned you both by your real names."

"How, then, did you explain that we have been off alone together?"

"I haven't attempted to do so. I only mentioned that you were each coming, and not that you would arrive together." He sighed. "I should have thought to employ a chaperone for Miss Deschamps. That would have prevented this sort of thing."

"I'm a grown woman and perfectly capable of taking care of myself and making my own decisions," Elle snapped. "I have no need for a chaperone, and I certainly wouldn't wake such a person to ask her to accompany me when I go sneaking out at night."

"It would take one hell of a chaperone to prevent Elle from doing what she's set her mind to," Henry chuckled.

"Thank you, Henry. You are very kind to say so."

"You must use the proper forms of address, dear, now that we are all of the same social sphere," Westfield pleaded. "You may address him as either Captain Ainsworth or Lord Henry, but nothing more familiar. Perhaps we should review?"

He yammered on while they rode to their destination, Elle nodding and smiling. Her eyes surveyed the streets, focused on the things that mattered.

Their current conveyance was a steam carriage that had been hastily modified to allow a horse to pull it. Not a single steam car passed by during their ride, a shocking statistic for a well-to-do neighborhood in a large city.

Their host, one Admiral Herbert Johnson, was a cheery and talkative man some half-dozen years older than Westfield. He greeted them with enthusiasm, assuring them they had rooms prepared and staff at their service for anything they might need.

"I must apologize, Captain Ainsworth, that your trunk has not yet arrived. It was misdirected, it seems. Please, if there is anything we can do in the interim to provide for you, do not hesitate to seek out any of the household."

Henry played along with the baffling apology, nodding graciously. "You are most kind, Admiral. Like yourself, I am a military man and know something of making do, but could I possibly trouble you for a cup of tea?"

Shortly thereafter, he had a steaming pot all to himself and a comfortable seat in a charming little parlor. Elle sat beside him, sipping a cup of coffee and nibbling on a biscuit, the picture of elegance. No one would guess this wasn't her natural habitat. Until she opened her mouth to express some scandalous opinion, Henry thought with a grin.

"The admiral believes Elle to be your niece in truth?" he asked.

"Of course," Westfield replied. "Everyone here believes it. I've been telling the same story from the very beginning. It feels quite real, these days."

"No one suspects we aren't what we claim, then?"

"As far as I am aware, no, which is why I would like the both of you to behave in as proper and inconspicuous manner as possible. No more sneaking about."

"It's difficult to conduct an investigation without any sneaking. People tend to be unhappy when you pry into their business right in front of them."

"That is quite enough flippancy, young man. I'm still owed an explanation as to why you two disappeared from the train the other night."

"We woke when the train stopped and went to see what the trouble was," Elle explained. "By the time we saw the police boarding the train it was too late to do anything but set off on our own. I'm sorry there wasn't time to wake you. It does seem to have worked out for the best, however. We wouldn't have been released so easily as you were, I don't think. I hope they didn't trouble you too much?"

"It was no great burden. They allowed me to send telegrams and treated me respectfully. The worst was my worry for you, which did not diminish when I was released."

"We are quite well, as you can see. Now, let us tell you what we have learned during the last few days." She gave him a brief summary of her discovery. "While we are here, I would like to take a few days to travel about the countryside and see how many more small sources I can find. We can go by train, since there don't seem to be many steam carriages in use here."

"I was wondering about that myself," Henry said. "Have

the combustible potions become too expensive, or are they simply unavailable?"

"I don't know," Westfield replied. "I've seen a few other converted carriages, like the one we rode in today. Herbert mentioned a friend who has converted his carriage to burn ordinary combustibles, such as wood and coal. He complained it creates clouds of smoke and bad smells."

"If so many people have converted their carriages already, the potions must have run out some time ago."

"The potions I saw in the stores here used serum imported from overseas," Elle added. "They were just like those in France, though weak and overpriced. At such a distance, the shortage has hit them harder than it has hit us."

"Now that I think on it," Westfield mused, "there were few lights last night. It didn't seem so odd, as there were no after-dinner activities, and the household turned in relatively early. This evening, however, there will be a house party, as a number of other guests are due to arrive this afternoon. If the lights are still used minimally, we will know those potions, also, are hard to come by."

"I assume I'm invited to the party and won't need to climb any trellises to gain entry?" Henry asked.

"I'm going to pretend I don't know what you are talking about."

"What am I expected to wear? This suit is both filthy and inappropriate for evening dress. Everything else I have would be worse."

"I ordered a new dress for Miss Deschamps, since I had her measurements. You may borrow something of mine."

"Sir, you are a full three inches taller than I. I don't think that will suffice. This was the smallest of your coats, and it is still somewhat large."

"Well, we shall have to make do until the trunk with your things arrives. Herbert believes it was misdirected, but in reality your father only sent it along two days ago. It will be some days yet before it arrives. I believe he is including your dress uniform, which would be most appropriate for this sort of thing."

"He must know how much I despise wearing it. I'd rather wear my working clothes and have people stare at me."

"I'm fond of the all-black outfit you wear for sneaking," Elle said. The twitch of her brows made him shift uncomfortably in his seat.

"Let's move on," Westfield urged. "Miss Deschamps, I received a very lengthy and interesting telegram from my physician, regarding your aunt." He pulled a paper from his pocket and offered it to her. "Here it is, for your reading pleasure."

Elle took the telegram, looking at it with a puzzled frown. Henry watched her eyes grow wide as she read. Finally, she laughed.

"Well!" she exclaimed. "I suppose I don't need to worry she is suffering without me."

"Oh?" Henry inquired.

"Doctor Lambert has been attending my aunt in my absence. It seems Aunt Madeleine has become a great friend of his father. He walks her to the market every day, and now the good doctor writes to tell us they are plotting to move in together and he hopes we don't mind, as he doesn't think he is able to prevent it."

Henry burst out laughing. "Elle, the women of your family are a delight. I regret I never had the opportunity to meet more of them."

"I hope to have daughters of my own someday," she replied. "God willing, there will be more of us for you to meet."

God willing, I will be their father.

Henry stared down into his cup of tea, reprimanding himself for even considering such a thing. He had to force himself to look back up at her.

"I look forward to meeting the next generation of Deschamps girls," he said at last.

"What, not 'Ainsworth girls'?" Westfield muttered into his teacup.

Henry's good mood abruptly turned sour. He wouldn't stand for having his most private thoughts aired and mocked. He slammed his cup down on the table, rattling the saucer. "Excuse me." He bowed to Elle and bolted for the door.

"Henry, where are you going?" she called.

He didn't look back. "To buy a suit. I imagine my father will want me stalking heiresses all evening."

XXX

But Not Remember'd

ELLE'S NOSE WRINKLED at the scent of oil and candles permeating the house. Their flickering lent an antiquated feel to the residence, and the decorations had been played up accordingly. Gauzy fabrics dripped from the walls and flower petals lay strewn across the floor. Wrought iron candelabras tucked into corners cast pools of light and shadow. Elle heard more than one person declare how romantic everything was. Personally, she found it annoying.

The poor lighting reminded her too much of her apartment, where even oil and candles were dear. She had spent many an evening sitting by the window in the fading sunlight, trying to read as much as possible before darkness fell. The more removed from that life she became, the more determined she grew never to go back. Her ten thousand francs could pay the rent on a nicer apartment, and with a reference from Westfield perhaps she could find an assistant chemist position. It would remain sadly far from her dream, but a good sight better than the bar.

Elle squared her shoulders and did her best to ignore the lighting. She wasn't enamored of parties, but Westfield had promised champagne and fancy desserts, and she loved her new clothing.

The ball gown was a pale blue silk ensemble, with a low, square neck and tiny sleeves that sat just off her shoulders.

Lightweight and airy, it was the exact opposite of the cumbersome, conservative outfits that made up most of her wardrobe. It had a matching pair of shoes and a pretty, jewelled purse, into which she slipped her defensive potions.

She had spent the better part of the afternoon bathing and washing her hair. Every inch of her felt clean and smooth. She could still smell the soap under the touch of perfume she had dabbed on.

Admiral Johnson had sent one of the housemaids to help her prepare for the evening, but she only had the girl help with buttoning her dress, declining the offer to have her hair done. Instead, she braided it herself, twisted it and pinned it atop her head, and added a single flower for decoration. For jewelry, she chose only a pair of silver earrings. It was simple compared to what she expected from the other ladies, but she liked it, and she wanted to feel herself, even in the finery.

The ballroom was abuzz. She made a slow circuit of the crowded room, squinting in the poor lighting, searching for Henry, or even Westfield.

"*Voulez-vous danser*, mademoiselle?" a husky voice murmured from behind her.

Henry caught her hand and bowed over it as she turned. The soft leather of his gloves against her bare skin made her realize she'd forgotten an essential part of her costume. She shunned gloves because she needed her fingers free for potions work, but to be bare-armed at such a party was a terrible faux-pas. She risked exposure as an imposter. Dancing would only draw more attention.

"I'm afraid I don't know how to dance."

"Nonsense." He led her toward the center of the room. "You can't possibly be worse than I am."

"Henry…"

The orchestra struck up a waltz, and he swept her into his arms.

"I won't be dissuaded. You are the most radiant woman in

the room, and I must seize my chance before you are inundated with admirers."

"You exaggerate."

"Not at all."

They spun across the room, Elle trying her best to mimic the other dancers and remember the basic one-two-three pattern.

"One dance only." His eyes drifted away from her. "I won't monopolize your time this evening. I have done so too much of late."

"Is this about my uncle's comments this afternoon? It was a joke, Henry. No one expects you would make such an ill-advised match."

His jaw tightened. "So it would seem."

"I hope you don't think I meant to... I'm not a fortune hunter. I would never use a friend so meanly."

His blue eyes blazed with anger. "While my 'fortune' may seem vast to you, Miss Deschamps, I assure you I don't spend my days fretting that women are plotting to ensnare me. I don't envision matrimony in my future."

He jerked her into a spin and nearly trod on her dress, stomping around the dance floor as if he meant to put a foot straight through the parquet. She had never seen him so furious. Was it Westfield's thoughtless insinuations or something she had said?

"I'm sorry if I have upset you."

"You haven't," he growled.

They finished the dance in awkward silence, while she racked her brain for a way to soothe him.

When they made their final bow, she said, "I have neglected to mention how fine you look this evening. Your suit becomes you very well, though it is a bit... prim." She ruffled his hair and tugged on his cravat until the knot looked negligent. "There. Now you look a proper rogue, and ladies will fling themselves at you."

His smile was tight-lipped. "I appreciate your efforts, but I'm certain you are the only one who will note them. I will take my leave of you. We have work to do, and I can make my observations best alone. No one sees an ordinary man in a crowd."

"Henry, you are anything but ordinary."

"But I am. I'm not tall, I'm not handsome, my voice is neither loud nor compelling, and there is nothing noteworthy about my looks or my clothing."

"I disagree. You are quite handsome, and your voice is lovely, regardless of what language you are speaking."

The pinched smile didn't twitch. "Our friendship clouds your reasoning. Please excuse me, I must... Well, I'll be damned."

"What's the matter?" She followed his gaze across the room, but saw nothing remarkable.

"I've spied a way to prove my point. Come, let me introduce you to an old friend of mine. I'm quite certain she won't remember me at all."

"She can't be much of a friend if she doesn't remember you."

"An acquaintance, then, though that doesn't convey the reality of the situation, either." He took Elle's arm and steered her through the crowd. "She is the daughter of Colonel Wilton-Bowles, who first recommended me as an intelligence agent. I have dined with her dozens of times, and danced with her even more than that. I believe I followed her about for a full three months."

Elle set her jaw. "She must have been quite something to inspire such devotion."

Henry shrugged. "She was pretty. I was a boy."

"I see."

"I was far from alone in my admiration, of course. I learned some years later she had married an American, leaving half a regiment's worth of broken hearts."

Elle spotted a lady near the beverage table who had to be the woman in question. Pretty was an understatement. She was flawlessly beautiful. Her skin was alabaster, with pink cheeks that needed no rouge. Her long, glossy hair had been curled and pinned atop her head in an elaborate arrangement, with beads and flowers woven throughout. She wore a resplendent dress of rose red, and though the neckline was no lower than Elle's, her ample bosom made it look much more so. She was as tall as Henry, and carried herself with an air of supreme confidence. Elle disliked her immediately, and felt guilty about it. She resolved to withhold her judgment until they had spoken.

Henry paused at the edge of the circle of admirers and waited for a lull in the conversation. "Rachael!" he exclaimed, as if only just noticing her. "How good to see you!" His brows twitched at her revealing ensemble, but he was polite enough not to stare.

Rachael frowned at him. "I'm sorry, do I know you?"

"Henry Ainsworth," he introduced himself. "Lord Henry, in fact. My father is a marquess, you know. But, of course, you would know me by my military rank. I served under your father a number of years ago. We were quite good friends until my duties parted us."

"Ah."

That single syllable was full with condescension, and Elle concluded that her first impression had been correct.

"I'm terribly sorry, er, Lieutenant…?"

"Captain."

"Captain Ainsworth, but I'm afraid I don't recall our acquaintance."

"Oh, that's a shame." His frown lasted only a fraction of a second, before morphing into an over-enthused smile. "Well! It's wonderful, then, that we have this opportunity to renew it!"

He took hold of her hand, which she had offered only perfunctorily, and pumped it with vigor.

"It's such a pleasure to see you again," he gushed. "I heard you were lately married and moved to America?"

Rachael yanked her hand away from his grip. "These five years," she replied primly.

"Ah. Of course. Splendid, splendid. Please, allow me to introduce my great friend, Miss Elle Deschamps. I'm certain you will get along excellently. Elle, this is Rachael... er, formerly Wilton-Bowles, and now?"

"Rachael Fasching."

"I'm pleased to meet you, Mrs. Fasching," Elle greeted her. "It's always interesting to get a new glimpse into Henry's past."

Rachael's manicured eyebrows twitched at Elle's casual use of Henry's first name. "Do the two of you have an understanding?" she asked.

Elle laughed off the rude question. "Oh, no. We simply spend a great deal of time together. My uncle and Henry's father are the greatest of friends, you see."

"A pity. You two seem..." She looked them both up and down as she sought out the right word. "Suitable for one another."

They were equally plain and unsophisticated, was what Elle suspected she meant. Rachael's eyes darted around, looking for an escape from their conversation. Henry's exuberance had chased off most of the crowd.

"Allow me to introduce you to my husband," she offered, breezing past the drinks to the far end of the table.

Much to Elle's surprise, the table held an array of common potions ingredients, with spoons, stir sticks, and small glasses stacked neatly to one side. A woman stood in front of the table, muddling ingredients together in a haphazard fashion. She handed her mixture across the table to a man, who carefully dripped some serum into it, then handed it back. The woman stirred her potion, thanked the man and wandered off, sipping at her poor-quality concoction.

Rachael gave the man a wide smile. If she was Aphrodite, he was Adonis. Every bit as beautiful as she, he was tall and broad-shouldered, with a strong jaw, pouty lips, and gleaming hazel eyes. His dark, wavy hair was worn on the long side, and he had carefully trimmed sideburns and a neat moustache. His well-tailored suit had been accessorized with a silk tie and handkerchief in the exact red as his wife's dress.

"Henry, dearest," she cooed, "I have some new friends for you to meet. This is Miss, uh..."

"Elle Deschamps," Elle introduced herself, holding out a hand to Henry Fasching.

"A pleasure, Miss Deschamps."

He kissed her hand rather than shaking it, and his eyes lingered on her chest for an unseemly long time. She didn't see why he bothered when he had his large-breasted wife to ogle.

"And I'm Henry Ainsworth," Henry interrupted. "I served under Colonel Wilton-Bowles and I know your wife from her unmarried days."

Fasching inclined his head in the slightest of nods. "Ainsworth," he acknowledged. "Your parents named you well."

"The name suits me. I see you know something of potions?"

"Mr. Fasching is a potions master," Rachael declared proudly. "He oversees all potions imports here in New York, which is terribly demanding and important work, but as you can see, he is gracious enough to share his skills with friends at parties. Have fun." She waved a hand at his set-up and scampered away.

"This is my favorite of the games," Fasching explained. "I offer advice and handle the serum, and the guests are free to mix themselves a potion. People love to feel they have worked a bit of magic."

"It seems dangerous," Elle argued. "It wouldn't be difficult for an ignorant person to harm themselves with an inferior potion."

"Not to worry, Miss Deschamps. I'm here to supervise the entire process."

"Of course. Perhaps I shall try my hand at it."

"Please, do."

She scanned the ingredients and began to mix without another word. The potion was one she had made hundreds of times, and it took her mere seconds to get everything blended in perfect proportion. Instead of handing the glass to him to add serum, she held out her own hand for the bottle.

"May I?"

Fasching handed her the serum, watching her hands now, rather than her décolletage. She dripped the serum in, swirled the glass, let it rest for a moment, then swirled it once more. She passed the serum bottle back to Fasching, and handed her potion to Henry. He tossed it back in a single gulp, then set the empty cup on the table beside several similar ones.

"Very refreshing. What was it?"

Fasching chuckled. "A stamina potion. First class. You won't grow tired this evening."

There was something of a leer in his voice. Henry's eyes narrowed.

Fasching turned back to Elle, who held his gaze, challenging him to make the next move in this strange chess match.

"That was most excellently done, Miss Deschamps. You are quite skillful."

"Thank you. I like to try my hand at potions work now and again."

"I can tell."

They could both read the lies in the words. He knew she was a professional.

"Allow me to make something for you," Fasching offered. "I always enjoy sharing knowledge with potions proficients."

Internally, she bristled that he hadn't called her a master. Outwardly she smiled at him.

"What did you have in mind?"

"One of my specialties. It will relax you and bring a glow to your cheeks."

"Sounds like whisky," Henry quipped.

"Ah, but you see, Mr. Ainsworth, my potion will cause no tipsiness. It calms and brings a feeling of happiness and warmth without any ill effects."

"Very interesting," Elle said.

"Thank you, Miss Deschamps." Fasching gave her a wide smile. "Inventing new recipes is another hobby of mine."

He began to select ingredients, one at a time, holding each one up and talking about it as he added it to the mixing bowl. He held her gaze as he worked, rarely casting even a glance down at the table. His voice carried well and drew the attention of others in the area. This was a performance, though he spoke as if to her alone. Elle smiled and looked where he wanted her to look, but kept her attention on the table and the bowl that she could see at the edge of her vision. Each ingredient went into the bowl as he mentioned it, but as he showed her the final ingredient, praising its quality and odor, she caught a glimpse of an unnamed substance that trickled from his other hand.

It happened so quickly she couldn't guess at what he had added, or how much. From the first, she had disliked the idea of drinking one of his potions. His attempt to deceive her had just assured she would never take so much as a sip.

Fasching muddled the herbs, stirred serum into the mixture, and strained it into a glass of water. He passed it to Elle, who swirled it slowly and sniffed.

"Very fragrant."

The potion wasn't familiar, and she couldn't discern from the scent alone what he had snuck into it. The odor caused a sense of unease, validating her decision not to drink it. She turned to Henry, as if to show off the potion, and deliberately bumped into him. She staggered and sloshed the potion across the table.

Fasching's handsome features twisted into a scowl.

"Are you quite all right, Miss Deschamps?"

"Heavens! I have ruined your hard work. You have my

sincerest apologies, Mr. Fasching. This crowd has left me overheated and a touch faint. I think it best if I stepped out for a bit of fresh air. Henry, would you be so good as to escort me out?"

Fasching was momentarily confused. "I beg your pardon?"

"*My* Henry." Elle took a firm hold of his arm. "Goodnight, Mr. Fasching."

She steered Henry through the crowd with her usual brisk pace. It belied her claim to lightheadedness, but she didn't care. She wanted to get away from Fasching and his insidious potions as quickly as possible. Henry came along without complaint, and said nothing about the matter until they reached a secluded corner.

"So, I'm your Henry, am I?" A hint of wistfulness colored his voice.

"Apologies for sounding possessive. I wanted to set you apart from that *fils de pute*!"

"What did he put in that potion?"

"I don't know. The recipe he showed made sense for what he claimed it would do. It used aspects of familiar potions. But I couldn't see what he snuck into it. He is much practiced at sleight-of-hand, it seems."

Henry's hands clenched into fists. "He meant you harm, then."

She gave a single nod. "I believe he saw me as both a rival and a potential conquest. There is more than one sort of potion that can be used to make a woman compliant, and anyone of his skill could manufacture them."

Henry called Fasching a name so vile that even Elle, accustomed to his outbursts of profanity, gasped and blushed. He blushed as well, when he realized he had shocked her.

"My sincere apologies, Miss Deschamps. That was not at all fit for a lady's ears."

She waved her hand in a nonchalant fashion. "It wasn't without cause. There is a great likelihood the man is a rapist."

Henry shuddered. "What sort of madness drives a man to such things? Surely his wealth and fine looks would win him many willing women. And why look elsewhere when he has a lovely wife?"

"Yes, she is quite beautiful," Elle muttered.

"You're jealous!" he laughed.

"Certainly not."

"You are. You're jealous because I admired her all those years ago, when I didn't know any better."

"Admire her all you want. It's not my place to say whom you should and shouldn't love."

Henry slipped both his arms about her waist.

"Darling, you could give me forty Rachaels, and they would still not be so fine as the one of you."

"What would you do with forty women, anyhow? You would have neither time enough to spend with them, nor money enough to feed and house them. You could open a factory, I suppose."

He laughed again. "The thought of any number of Rachaels working in a factory is ludicrous. I knew years ago she was spoilt, and it appears she has only become more so. I do feel for her, though, if her husband is as odious as you suspect. I will begin investigations into his business first thing in the morning."

"Leave that task to my uncle. You and I should concentrate on the more important task of searching out new potion sources."

"You have concocted some plan, I take it?" He led her toward the dance floor. "Come, tell me while we dance. I promise to be a better partner this time around."

"I intend to prove small sources, such as the one we found along the railroad, are abundant. We can start tomorrow morning visiting city parks, and then expand the search to other areas."

"This search involves overnight travel?"

"You have the MacAlaster passports, yes? I have a perfect story."

"Westfield will disapprove," he opined.

"That may be, but I'm not seeking his permission. I'm the expert, here."

"You are, indeed." His eyes sparkled mischievously. "I will, of course, defer to your judgment in this matter."

She returned his flirtatious smile. "Just as I thought. I'm glad to see I haven't chosen the wrong Henry."

"Not to worry. I am irrevocably your Henry."

She leaned in closer and kissed him.

XXXI

Above the Bounds of Reason

$\mathcal{T}$HE SECOND HAIRPIN jutted from the keyhole in Henry's door. Elle slipped a third one into the lock and wriggled it about. She had it nearly in position when the door swung open and she tumbled into the room, swallowing a yelp. Henry stood over her, studying her with a curious frown.

"Do you think to rouse the entire household with that racket?"

She struggled to her feet, huffing in indignation. She would have had the door open if he'd given her only a bit more time.

Henry dangled his lockpicks in front of her. "Perhaps the proper tools? I would have left them with you had I known you intended to practice this evening."

Elle pulled her pins from the lock and closed the door behind her. An oil lamp on the bedside table illuminated a chamber identical to her own save for color scheme. Henry, attired only in a pair of old trousers, surveyed her in the flickering light, arms crossed over his bare chest.

"I hoped to sneak in without waking you," she admitted. "I'm sorry to have disturbed your sleep."

He chuckled. "You didn't disturb me, mademoiselle. I've been wide awake all evening."

She gasped. "The stamina potion! Oh, Henry, I'm terribly sorry. If you engage in some sort of vigorous activity, your body will use it up and you will be able to sleep."

"Vigorous activity?" His voice had darkened, and he shifted nervously.

A quiver started in her belly.

No. Stop. You aren't here to seduce him.

"You could go for a run or do calisthenics. It isn't the sort of stamina potion intended for bedsport. I wouldn't have done that to you."

A grin tugged at the corner of his mouth. "I would never assume you had. Naturally, you have snuck into my bedchamber in the middle of the night for entirely virtuous and sensible reasons."

There was nothing virtuous about it, standing in his room in her nightgown, staring at him in his current state of undress. She enjoyed the view here in private, where he made no attempt to cover himself. He had a fine body. Marie would have called him too small, but Elle thought him much superior to her friend's bulky dock workers. He was strong and compact, and she yearned to touch him again.

A long, white scar ran diagonally across the inside of his left forearm. She wanted to run her fingers along it while he told her the circumstances behind it. He'd been a spy for many years. It was probable he had other scars she could search for.

Fine. I'm here partly to seduce him.

"Neither virtuous nor sensible. Silly, in fact. I felt nervous and unsettled tonight. I couldn't sleep, so I thought to pay you a visit. I'm certain it's only the novelty of being alone in a strange room after so many nights spent in your close company."

"Fasching has frightened you," Henry guessed. "Is his room in your wing?"

"It is," Elle confessed. "He and his wife have side-by-side rooms across the hall from my door."

"Separate rooms? With such a crowd of visitors? Why can't they share?"

"Because he wants the freedom to slip out unnoticed and commit heinous acts?" She let out a small sigh. "You see, these thoughts are what have me wandering the halls in the dead of night. More likely they have a marriage of convenience and little interest in one another. We have already established Fasching doesn't seem satisfied with the marriage bed."

"In that case they oughtn't be married at all."

A smile rose to her lips. "Henry, you don't make a very good aristocrat. Valuing domestic felicity over money and hard work over idleness? It's shocking. Perhaps you read too many sentimental novels."

He bristled at her jest.

"Or perhaps I have spent enough time among people of all sorts to know there is at least as much misery among the elite as there is among the middle classes. The poor, I'm afraid, have additional hardships, as well you know, but even they can find pleasure in simple things. It's not sentimentalism. It's common bloody sense."

"I can see you aren't in a particularly jovial mood tonight. I'll leave you to your own devices. Good night, Henry."

She turned toward the door, but he caught her arm.

"Elle. Please, don't leave on my account. If you leave, let it be for yourself alone."

She looked back at him. His blue eyes were wide, his face creased with concern.

"You are at least as scared as I!" she marvelled.

"Yes, I am. I learned long ago to have a healthy respect for fear. It has kept me safe many a time. Truly, tonight I have been apprehensive since we parted."

"Why didn't you come to see me, then?"

"I trust you to be capable of defending yourself, and I didn't wish to insult you by doing anything that might suggest otherwise."

"Oh, Henry. You are so sweet, and so silly." She slipped her arms around him, her hands gliding over his back, only the thin cotton of her nightdress between their two bodies.

"How am I silly?" he protested. "It bothered you in the past when I implied you needed my help. Do you wish me to seek you out if I'm worried, or not?"

"Neither. I wish us to stay together so there is no need to seek me out. That's why I came here."

He planted a kiss in her hair. "If only we could."

"And why can't we?"

"You've already taken a risk coming here. If we continue sneaking about, night after night, it's only a matter of time before we are caught."

"I find I don't much care whether we are caught."

Seduction was a certainty now. She nudged him toward the bed, nuzzling his neck. He shivered and sighed her name, his hands moving over her, warm through the fabric. She looked up to see his face flushed with desire, the reflection of the oil lamp glinting in his vivid blue eyes. He caught her mouth in a savage kiss, greedy hands grasping at her curves, taking everything she would give him. Elle stroked his chest, flicking at his small, flat nipples until they stiffened beneath her fingers.

They backed into the bed and stumbled, breaking apart. Henry took a halting step away from her, gasping, flushed clear down to his chest, moisture glistening on his lips. Ravishing. Lust coursed through her like a drug.

"I, uh…" He ran a hand through his hair. "I think I had better go for a run. The stamina potion…"

"For heaven's sake, Henry, it's sex, not differential calculus. What are you so afraid of?"

He cringed and turned away. "You cannot want me for a lover, mademoiselle. I know nothing of the business save for the lurid tales of soldiers and a book of erotic drawings I stole from my brother when I was fifteen."

She started. "You have a book of erotic drawings?" She grasped his arm to turn him around. "Really? Is it interesting? May I see it?"

"I no longer have it. My father burned it when he found it. Then he dragged me to the nearest church and demanded

I confess. I refused, naturally, and have avoided churches ever since. God, I was so angry. I must have hidden in my room for days. Father never did find the photographs, though. They have no instructions and aren't as explicit as the book—simply actresses posing in various states of undress—but I rather like them. I'm sorry. I'm babbling."

"I like your babbling."

He turned pink once more, eyes now brimming with adoration. The path to seduction unfurled in front of her, and she seized his hand between both of hers.

"I like your blushes and your freckles. I like your easy humor and your quiet seriousness. I like your determination to improve the world, and your kleptomaniacal tendencies. I like the passionate fire inside you that flames up with the slightest provocation. I like every single thing about you, Henry Ainsworth, and I'm going out of my mind waiting for you."

"Elle." He kissed her again, his lips a soft breeze against hers. "Elle, *mon amour.*"

"Come to bed." She pulled him after her, and they tumbled together onto the sheets. Her hands resumed their explorations of his lean, muscled body. "Touch me the way you have before," she urged. "Touch me the way I touch you."

He kissed her neck and slid a hand over her belly to cup her breast. "We ought to lock the door," he murmured.

The tickle of his tongue against her earlobe sent a shiver down to the tips of her fingers.

"Later."

"I will forget."

"Hah! You... ooh."

When his thumb stroked her nipple, she forgot what she had meant to say. His second hand lifted to her other breast, teasing her with gentle strokes and squeezes. She sighed with pleasure.

"Lord. You cannot be entirely innocent."

"Mostly."

"Fondled a few barmaids, have you?"

"None that can compare to you." He paused in his caresses long enough to unbutton her nightgown and bare her chest to his gaze and his hands. "Ah, *ma chérie*," he breathed, "*tu es la plus belle femme que j'ai jamais vue.*"

He trailed kisses down her neck and across her breasts, murmuring additional endearments in a combination of English, French, and Italian.

Little gasps of appreciation sprang unbidden from her lips while his hands and mouth roved across her skin. His tongue flicked over her nipple, and she shuddered. He repeated the motion, slow and deliberate, gauging her reaction. Lord. He was using his spy training on her. He caught every noise she made, every twitch of her body.

She moaned his name, fumbling with the buttons on his trousers. A hoarse groan rose from deep in his throat when her fingers curled around his rigid shaft.

"Elle. Oh, God, Elle." His fingers crushed the thin fabric of her nightgown, pushing it up past her waist. He ran his hands over her naked thighs. "God, do I need you."

Elle quickened her strokes, and he squirmed away from her.

"Wait."

A pang of disappointment constricted her chest. Didn't he realize what he was doing to her? She was so hungry for him. So hot and wet and ready.

"Henry..."

She had no more than spoken his name when his trousers hit the floor. She feasted on the sight of him fully nude in the lamplight. Her legs parted for him, beckoning him to come to her and satisfy her aching desire. His gaze raked across her, his smoldering eyes the sizzling blue of a candle flame's innermost core.

He wore a knife strapped to the inside of his left calf, and he didn't remove it before clambering back atop her. He hadn't been lying when he'd said he was always armed. Dangerous man. But not to her. Never to her.

She embraced him and pulled him down on top of her, kissing him hard, thrusting her tongue between his lips. Her hands meandered across his backside to pull him closer.

His hand slipped between her legs. Another gasp of pleasure escaped her lips as his fingers explored her. She covered his hand with hers and guided it to her most sensitive spot, showing him what she liked. His thumb rubbed a slow circle against her clitoris and her desire flared into an all-consuming need.

"Don't stop," she moaned. "Mon Dieu, Henry, don't ever stop."

The tension swelled within her, as he continued to stroke. He slipped a finger inside of her, and she lifted her hips to press against his hand. All of him. She needed all of him—on her and around her and deep within her.

Just when she thought she could stand the urgency no longer, her passion peaked, and she cascaded over the edge. A delicious shudder trembled through her. She cried out and arched her back as the tension poured out of her in a torrent of exquisite release.

Henry shifted to align their hips and slammed into her, his initial gasp of wonder quickly giving way to a moan of ecstasy.

"Christ, Elle. Fuck."

More curses spewed from his mouth as he began to move inside her. Still reeling from her orgasm, Elle rocked against him as he thrust, prolonging her own gratification, yearning to give him the satisfaction he'd so long denied himself.

"Yes," she sighed, pulling him to her, her nails digging into his back. "Yes, Henry, you feel so good."

"You," he groaned. His fingers clenched in the sheets as he drove harder, faster. "You feel good." His eyes slid closed in an expression of exquisite bliss. "Fuck, Elle, you are everything."

He stiffened as his own climax ripped through him, clutching her, thrusting deep one final time. "Everything."

He collapsed atop her, and lay there for some seconds before forcing himself onto his back with what looked to take a superhuman effort.

"Bloody hell," he gasped.

Elle rolled onto her side and put her arm across his chest. All the muscles in her body had relaxed and a soothing sleepiness had begun to settle over her. Henry's arm encircled her, drawing her close, his fingers a light caress against her back.

"I hope that was satisfactory?"

"It was exquisite," she sighed. "Do you feel you burned off the stamina potion?"

"Good Lord, yes."

She giggled, but her laugh soon morphed into a yawn. Her eyes closed, and she snuggled up against his warm body. "Goodnight, my Henry."

He kissed her brow and pulled a blanket up over the both of them. "Goodnight, love."

XXXII

Arguments and Plans

DAMN, BUT I COULD GET USED TO THIS.

Waking beside his lover, gazing upon her, half-naked in her rumpled, unbuttoned nightgown, Henry felt something of the libertine he had aspired to become. Her presence in his bed mingled the rebellious thrill of rule-breaking with the tantalizing promise of renewed physical passion.

He trailed his fingers across her bare shoulder, his lips close behind, savoring the salty-sweet taste of her skin. No more avoidance or excuses. He would take care with her reputation, but he would deny her nothing, and he'd managed not to bungle things last night.

Unless she woke regretting the whole business.

He didn't think he'd performed especially well. The timing of it all baffled him. He'd started too late and finished too quickly. She had acted pleased enough, but he determined to do better. As if he needed a reason to repeat the exercise.

Elle stirred beside him. He watched her wake, her eyelids fluttering, her slim body twisting and stretching as she yawned.

"Good morning, Henry." She sat up and tossed back the sheets, giving herself a full view of his still-naked form and jutting erection. "You are looking well-rested."

"I am, though it's terribly warm in here. You must be sweltering in that nightgown."

It was, in fact, chilly without the bedding, but Elle lifted her arms, and Henry yanked the nightgown over her head and cast it aside. For a moment he basked in the radiance of her in all her naked glory. Then she drew him close for a kiss, and he settled between her legs, his hands and mouth eager to explore all the soft curves of her body.

He acquitted himself better this time, drawing her to a climax while buried deep inside her. The sensation of her tight, hot flesh quivering around him brought a shocking intensity to his own release. The pleasure of making love to her was so acute he worried he could never make her own enjoyment match his.

She graced him with a tender kiss and a sleepy-eyed, satisfied smile. He'd done something right. They dozed in one another's arms as the sun crept higher.

Henry woke feeling refreshed and hungry. He reached across Elle to retrieve his pocket watch from the night table, and flipped it open to check the time.

"Bloody hell!" He shook Elle awake. "Darling, you have to get up."

She blinked up at him. "Something is wrong?"

"It's nearly half-past nine. The household will be breakfasting. I don't know how you'll get back to your room undetected."

She shimmied from the bed and picked up her nightgown. "You're a worrier. I'll be fine."

He shook his head, watching her button the garment. The fabric was wrinkled, her hair in a tangle, and her cheeks still pink. The smile she bestowed on him carried an intimacy that hadn't existed the day before.

"Impossible. You look as though you've been ravished."

"Yes, and I enjoyed it very much. I look forward to the next time."

"Do be serious," he pleaded. "I don't want you subject to scorn or ridicule. Perhaps you can stay here until after breakfast and play that you were ill?"

"I'm much too hungry to skip breakfast. I will do my best not to be seen." She reached for the door handle. "You did lock the door. I knew you wouldn't forget."

"I couldn't sleep thinking someone could get in easily."

"Always the spy," she teased. "I will see you again shortly."

He could think of nothing to say to stop her, so he watched her go and prayed no one would trouble her.

He was down to breakfast first, and he suspected she would be some time yet in arriving. Her clothes were far more complicated than his, and she would also have to do up her hair, possibly apply cosmetics, and do anything else ladies deemed necessary to make themselves presentable in society. He could see why she preferred a less formal lifestyle.

The houseguests were taking a casual breakfast as they arose, so Henry gathered himself some food, requested a pot of tea, and sat down across from Westfield, who sat at a small table in the corner, sipping his coffee and reading a newspaper.

"Good morning, Henry. How are you today?"

Worried about Elle. "Well enough. Yourself?"

"Fine, fine. Have you seen my niece yet this morning?"

"I haven't. She may be sleeping late. Or perhaps she was up before us all and has already moved on."

"I have been here since eight. She has not been down."

"Ah."

"I have some business to discuss with the both of you. I've received several messages this morning, some of which are relevant to our work."

"Excellent. We have business to discuss, as well. Elle has come up with a plan for the next part of our operation. She told me of it last evening, and means to get started today."

Westfield's brow crinkled in a wary frown. "What does this plan entail?"

"I think it best if Elle explains it herself. It's her plan, after all, and she is the expert in these matters."

"More spying? It must be something I will dislike, if you won't tell me of it."

"It doesn't involve spying, nor anything dangerous. It's fine idea, and I think it unfair if we don't wait for Elle to arrive…"

"Would you kindly cease referring to my niece in such an intimate manner?"

Henry blinked. "Pardon?"

"You have thrice in a row used her given name. I do not recall giving you permission to do so."

Indignation burned through him. "I have *her* permission." He lowered his voice. "And since you are not truly any relation to her, I don't see how your opinion on the situation has any relevance whatsoever."

"It may interest you to know," Westfield countered, also keeping his voice down, "I have already spoken with my solicitors. I have no family, and she has very little. She is all I would wish for in a daughter or niece: intelligent, hardworking, and kind-hearted. I intend to make her my heir."

Henry was taken aback. He stared at Westfield a moment, then shook his head. "She doesn't want your money."

"It will be hers nonetheless. How does that affect your marriage prospects, Captain Ainsworth?"

His fingers clenched, Westfield's words rekindling yesterday's fury at the world and all its stupid divisions and rules.

"It changes them not at all." He would never marry. Elle had declared an alliance to be an impossibility, and he would marry none but her.

"I can't believe that. It's obvious you are in love with her. I don't blame you. I love her dearly, myself. I suspect if I were twenty years younger, we would be bitter rivals."

"You might be bitter," Henry scoffed, "but not I."

Not after last night. He had slept in her arms and taken pleasure in her embrace. She had given all of herself, taken all of him, and he had no doubt of her loyalty.

Westfield's eyes narrowed at him. "Pride goeth before a fall, Captain Ainsworth. You have my permission to court her. I expect you, however, to distance yourself from casual friendship and common flirtations and to conduct yourself instead as a man hoping to marry an heiress."

"Seduce her in some public fashion so she has no choice but to marry me?" His anger burned so hot that the rude reply brought a deep satisfaction. Marry an heiress? Bullshit.

It was damned bullshit, the whole lot of it. Money, titles, ranks—for what? So others could condescend to grace him with their approval? They could go to hell, for all he cared. Only Elle mattered.

"That is not funny," Westfield sputtered.

Henry leaned back in his chair and poured himself a cup of tea, a cold indifference supplanting his anger. "Ah, but it would be practical, were I so mercenary as you seem to think."

"I don't think you mercenary. I think you are interested in my niece, and I see no reason why you shouldn't be more interested when there is an inheritance due to her. You are the fourth child and the third son. Your father cannot have all that much to settle on you."

"Very well. I will play along. You have a large fortune, sir?"

"It is ample enough," Westfield replied. "Much of it has already been put aside in trusts to ensure the continuance of the work your father and I do, but there will be enough remaining to provide my niece with a comfortable home."

Henry suspected Westfield's definition of 'a comfortable home' was rather more elaborate than his own. He was less interested in the financial particulars, however, than in the aforementioned trusts.

"Trust funds to provide for your work? Have you established a registered company, then? Guardians of International Peace, Limited, or some such? I had thought of you more as a diplomat than a businessman."

Westfield frowned at him. "I do not run a business, lad, I

provide a service, fostering positive relations between people and nations."

"Still, it's clear you have an eye to turning that service into a self-sustaining operation. Either a company with private shareholders, or a club with members would be needed to pool resources and allow for controlled use of funds. My father loves finances and regulations and organizational matters. I assume he has helped with that side of things?"

"He is always willing to offer his expertise, of course. He is still disappointed you did not study business or law."

Henry stabbed at a piece of sausage with enough vehemence that the fork clinked on the plate.

"I'm well aware of my filial inadequacies, sir. But to continue our conversation, I must own I'm still puzzled by this club of yours. I don't believe I understand your goal. Improving relations between peoples? That's terribly vague."

"It seems clear enough to me."

"The international cooperation is clear. Father is in Italy, you live currently in France, there is Neufeld in Germany, several in England, of course... who else? Batista? Most likely. Also your physician, Dr. Lambert, I suspect. You mentioned multiple trusts, so I must assume the finances are similarly spread between countries?"

Westfield glared across the table. "I will not stand to be interrogated by you, Captain Ainsworth."

"I'm only curious."

"You are a damned spy!" His voice carried far enough that more than one other guest turned to look at them.

"We are on the same side," Henry replied calmly.

"I think not. What all have you done? Stolen information from your father? Read our private correspondence?"

"I have done neither of those things."

He had, in fact, done both of those things, and in such haphazard fashion his father would be sure to know. George Ainsworth had never spoken a word about it, which suggested he secretly liked having someone in the family privy to his affairs. Henry wasn't privy to the financial information, however. He suspected it was mixed in with the books for the wine business, which he avoided like the plague.

"How much have you told them about us?" Westfield demanded.

"*That* I'm not at liberty to say. However, you might consider when it was that Her Majesty's government at last began to take you and your friends seriously."

Westfield's eyes grew wide as he made the connection.

"You scoundrel! You sold us out to advance your own career."

"I did nothing of the sort. I was asked about my father and his friends as part of a routine check into my own loyalties, and I recommended you as honest men and excellent sources of information. As I stated, we are on the same side."

"No. You are loyal to your British Empire. I am loyal to the people of all the world."

"The two are not incompatible. We all wish to prevent war and improve trade and communications between nations. Why else are we here?"

"I couldn't say why you are here. I feel I hardly know you, Henry Ainsworth."

"You don't trust me, and yet you expect me to trust you and even to obey you? My father, as I'm sure you know, was a staunch supporter of Italian unification. He has some mad notion of a centralized government for all of Europe. I know it's only a fantasy, and he doesn't actually intend to attempt to achieve such a thing, but who is to say that others of you, with whom I am merely acquainted, have the same restraint? What if you set out to overthrow governments? What if you intended to achieve peace by bribing high ranking officials and murdering anyone you saw as a threat?

"I believe you to be a good man, but your friends I have met only in passing, if at all. Can't you see why I wish to understand your business and your intentions? We could be far more effective working together rather than in parallel."

"Excuses. You wish to report my personal business to your government."

"It's your government, too, and if there is anything untoward happening, it is my duty to report it!"

"Enough. This conversation is at an end. Stay out of my business and stay away from my niece. I rescind my permission for you to court her."

"I neither need nor want your permission. Elle doesn't belong to you or to anyone."

Elle entered the room as he was speaking. She wore a modest, high-necked dress, dark blue in color, with little adornment. Her hair was done up in a neat bun. She could easily have passed for a school teacher or governess. It was the exact sort of outfit Westfield wanted her to wear. Henry hated it. It was an affectation. A damned lie.

She met his gaze and gave him a radiant smile. Her brows quirked, adding a hint of mischief to her expression. There was the real Elle. Smart, strong, passionate. The sort of woman who would wear trousers for nighttime thievery, carry nasty spray potions to fend off enemies, and seduce a man who carried a knife to bed. His irritation faded, squelched by the thrill that he knew her as no one else did.

"Here she is, now. Perhaps you could ask for her opinion on the matter." He rose from his seat to greet her. "Bonjour, chérie. I hope you are well this morning?"

What he really wanted to know was whether anyone had caught her out, and he was pleased when she answered with another smile.

"I'm very well, thank you."

"Could I fetch you something to eat?"

"No, thank you. I prefer to select my own breakfast."

"Yes, I suspected as much. Will you permit me to accompany you? I should like more toast."

"Of course."

Westfield looked daggers at him. "Watch yourself, boy. I'm reporting your behavior to your father."

"I know you are. You have been his spy since we left Italy. I trust you are giving him a full account of my personal business?"

Henry walked with Elle to the buffet where the food had been laid out. The room had grown crowded. He and Elle weren't the only ones who had slept late.

"I don't know what that was about," Elle said, "but Uncle Edwin looks furious. What did you do?"

Henry took a piece of toast and slathered it with marmalade.

"I was asking questions about his friends and their finances and motivations for this odd diplomacy they do."

"Ah. You've been spying on him."

"No more than he's been spying on me. And you must admit that secretive groups of men are bound to arouse suspicion."

Elle finished gathering her food and turned toward the table.

"Well, for the sake of our mission, I suppose you will just have to apologize."

"Certainly not. I have done nothing wrong. He is being unreasonable. He insists I stay away from you."

"Sound advice. I have corrupted you quite enough already." She gave him that same mischievous smile.

Henry trailed after her, pulling out the chair for her to sit. "I must respectfully disagree. I believe you have a great deal more work to do in that regard."

"Perhaps." A hint of a blush crept over her cheeks, though she was nowhere near as red as he was.

Westfield cleared his throat. "Now that you are here, Niece, I will update you on the plans for the day." His voice still held an edge, and he looked only at Elle.

"I have a plan, too. Did Henry tell you of it?"

"He insisted on waiting for you."

"Thank you, Henry, that was kind of you."

He gave her a brief nod.

"Would you like to tell us your plan first, Uncle, or shall I explain mine?"

"Why don't you begin? I have a feeling it could lead to much discussion."

Elle glanced around the room to check that no one was eavesdropping. Their secluded table was sufficient for private conversation, provided they kept their voices low, but Henry kept an eye on the crowd, nonetheless. He had already drawn too much attention by arguing with Westfield.

Elle sliced her food into neat bites as she talked. "After all we have discovered so far, I believe it important to further investigate the possibility of small serum sources. The fact that Henry and I just happened to stumble upon one suggests they are not at all uncommon. I would like to explore the countryside for a time to see how many more I can find."

"That doesn't seem unreasonable," Westfield answered. "There must be more to it. Where is the part I will dislike?"

"Henry and I will go alone," Elle explained, her voice near to a whisper. "We won't tell anyone where we are going or when we will be back. I don't want anyone to follow us. I want time to explore and experiment free from outside interference."

Westfield folded his hands atop the table. "Well. There we have it. I don't like that at all."

"Nevertheless, I don't intend to change my mind."

"Might I suggest I accompany you instead?"

"I don't think you and I would do well posing as husband and wife."

Westfield opened his mouth to comment, but Elle continued on.

"I realize you speak out of concern for me. I would like to remind you that our goal is to help increase the supply of serum throughout the world, not to parade me through high society to win me a rich husband. I'm far more concerned someone might attack me physically than that someone might attack my reputation."

There was a long pause before Westfield answered. "That is a valid concern," he admitted. "Seeing it in that light, I can understand why you would want Henry as your escort. He is a far better bodyguard."

Henry's eyes locked with Elle's.

I will guard every last inch of your body, day and night.

Damn. He was blushing again. He made a pretense of stirring his tea.

"Is there a particular reason all three of us cannot undertake this venture together?" Westfield wondered.

"There are several. Firstly, it takes away the cover story of a young married couple. A husband and wife is much less memorable than three unrelated persons traveling together. Secondly, you would be here to keep an eye out for anyone who might be asking questions about our absence or other suspicious behavior. Finally, it leaves you free to pursue other angles of inquiry, such as looking into Fasching's import business and the severe shortage."

"It seems the two of you have thought of everything."

"Elle thought of everything," Henry said. "For once, you can't blame me for any of it."

Westfield frowned at him. "I will think on it. We can discuss it further after luncheon."

"I intend to begin immediately," Elle argued. "There are several large parks here in the city to explore today, and we will leave this evening or tomorrow morning, depending on train schedules."

"Impossible. We are already engaged for lunch. We will be meeting with a number of people who do business with potions here in the city. You met Mr. Fasching last night?"

Henry was sorry he didn't have more sausage to stab at. "Yes, unfortunately," he growled. "The man tried to poison Elle."

Westfield's coffee cup rattled. "What!"

"Drug me, I believe," Elle corrected. "I don't think he wants me dead."

"You must be mistaken."

"Possibly," Elle replied. "But in the world of potions I rarely am. I consider the man an enemy."

"He is the owner of New York Imports, the main supplier of potions to the entire region. I thought he might be able to confirm our suspicions about the shortage and tell us whether his serum comes from any sources other than ours." He rubbed his temple. "Now I am concerned about this meeting."

"Who else will be there?" Henry inquired.

"Our host is James Richards, Fasching's right-hand man. I believe other associates from the import business are joining us, and our old acquaintance Lady Charlotte de Winter. It seems she has followed us here."

"Has she?" Henry replied, his tone deadpan. "I'm shocked."

"I have had news of her, finally, that explains somewhat her involvement in this matter."

Henry cut in before Westfield could finish. "She is the largest shareholder of the Imperial Potions Company."

Westfield gaped at him. Henry pulled a paper out of his pocket and slid it across the table for the others to see.

"You aren't the only one to have received messages this morning, sir."

"I see. In any event, upon finding out she was in town and also planned to meet with Mr. Fasching, I decided to arrange for us all to come together in a social setting. I hope if we speak frankly to her, we might learn more of her own intentions. Perhaps we can come to an understanding."

Elle leaned over the table and said with quiet ferocity, "She had me dumped into the Nile, sent a murderer after me, and tried to have us arrested. There can be no understanding."

"I thought the presence of Fasching and the others would be a mitigating factor. With what you have told me, however, I'm not certain that will be the case."

"Call off the meeting," Elle ordered.

"Then we lose our chance to learn something."

"We have already learned something. Either Lady de Winter and Mr. Fasching are working together against us, or they soon will be, just as was the case with Ellison Blake. She is making deals with whatever powerful and unethical businessmen she can find."

"Maybe we can learn the names of others."

"It's not worth the risk. I'm not going. Nor am I staying here any longer. Henry and I will be leaving immediately."

"Miss Deschamps, please be reasonable."

She rose from her seat, forcing him to do the same.

"I'm being quite reasonable, thank you very much. I refuse to dine with a table full of enemies. We are leaving. Good day, Uncle."

"How will I find you? Where will you go?"

"I will decide when the time comes. No one else is to know. That is part of the plan. Excuse me. I must go pack my things."

She turned and marched from the room, her head held high.

"Damn, I love that woman."

Westfield rounded on him. "This rash independence is a direct result of your bad influence, I have no doubt."

Henry laughed so hard he choked. "I'm afraid you are mistaken, sir. She has simply grown comfortable enough to express her true self."

"You see to it she does not come to any harm," Westfield demanded. "Don't use this as an excuse to seduce her. You will treat her as an heiress, not a barmaid."

"I respect all women equally, sir, regardless of their status."

"I've seen the way you look at her. No seductions."

"And what shall I do if *she* seduces *me*?"

"Don't be ridiculous. Innocent young women don't go about seducing people. How would such a thing even be possible?"

Henry chuckled. "You don't understand our relationship at all, do you? Excuse me, I, too, must prepare for the journey."

"Behave yourself. I will already be writing a lengthy telegram to your father."

Henry inclined his head in farewell. "I look forward to reading it. Good day, sir."

XXXIII

In the Out-of-Doors

*E*LLE RAN HER HANDS THROUGH THE GRASS, trying to determine the boundary of the source. In the bright sunlight, she could see faint traces of red running up the blades. Out here, miles from the nearest town, she could take all the time she wanted to examine the plant life and do a thorough analysis.

Working conditions were perfect today, unlike the previous morning, when a foggy drizzle had made their search all but impossible. Even with the umbrella Henry had purchased, they had gotten soaked to the skin within an hour. After slogging for several miles through the mud, they'd given up and spent the day in their room with hot drinks and a crackling fire.

The memory brought a wistful smile to Elle's face. She had finally taught Henry how to make the disappearing ink, and she'd honed her lock-picking skills. They had shared good food and a warm bath. Lazy hours passed by, filled with nothing but reading, cuddling, and lovemaking. It had been the happiest day of her life.

Today reality weighed on her. Try as she might, she couldn't dredge up enthusiasm for cataloging yet another serum source.

Henry, too, looked to have little interest in work. He lay on his back, arms crossed behind his head, his eyes closed. His notebook lay face down atop his chest, and his pencil had rolled off into the grass. She wasn't even certain if he was awake.

"Henry, dearest, you are supposed to be my indulgent husband, not my indolent husband."

His eyes opened. "I don't think my behavior out-of-character. It's a fine day for enjoying the sunshine, and, regardless, I've grown weary of drawing plants. In fact, the very thought of drawing more plants makes me feel very ill indeed. The only remedy is to lie here and rest."

She rolled her eyes skyward. "It's not so bad as all that. You did a fine job blathering on about your drawings at the inn this morning. The other guests must have found you exceedingly dull."

"Thank you, my dear, for that tender sentiment. What man doesn't want to hear his wife term him 'exceedingly dull'?"

"Do not sass me, Henry Ainsworth."

"MacAlaster," he corrected.

"Henry MacAlaster wouldn't be so impudent."

"Nor would Elle MacAlaster."

"I'm tired of her, anyhow," Elle grumbled. "Tromping around studying nature as if she could be a female Charles Darwin? It's ridiculous."

Henry sat up, catching his notebook just before it tumbled into the grass.

"Elle, what's wrong?"

She threw up her hands. "I don't know." A wave of despair cascaded over her. "It has been near a week, and we have been able to work the entire time unmolested. We have found five sources in as many different locations, proving me correct, and making the journey a successful one. You have been my constant friend and companion, and you make love to me every night, and sometimes more. I ought to be happy, but I'm not at all."

Hot tears stung her eyes, and she wiped angrily at them. Henry crossed the space between them in a heartbeat and took her in his arms.

"Darling, don't fret. No one will think ill of you if you are unhappy, and you need only tell me, and I will do whatever I can to improve your mood."

She pushed him away.

"No, don't. Doubtless you will succeed, and that will only make it worse when I come to my senses."

He looked hurt. "I don't understand."

She put a hand to her temple and closed her eyes, fighting the flood of emotions that clouded rational thought.

"It's a beautiful day," she said. "Warm, sunny, a perfect day to spend out-of-doors. But when we stepped outside this morning, I was disappointed. I had no desire to go out searching. I felt none of my usual enthusiasm when we found this source."

"You have been unusually quiet today. I thought perhaps our work had become routine. Go out walking, find a source, catalog it, collect samples. There is nothing particularly exciting about today's find, though you always seemed to enjoy the process before."

"I did. I do. I would gladly spend months traveling the world, studying and recording sources. But I can't." Her frustration boiled over. "I hate Elle MacAlaster! I hate her with a terrible, burning, jealous passion. She is free to go wherever she likes, doing just as she likes, with no one to tell her no or to try to stop her. Her husband will follow her anywhere, because he is an artist, and all he wants is to be with her and draw things. No one ever mocks their dreams or questions them. They don't have to answer to anyone but themselves."

Henry took hold of her hand. "When this is over, you can take the money you have earned and buy your way to freedom. If you don't have enough, I will give you some. Not charity," he quickly added. "A loan. You can pay me back. With interest, if you like. If you want to travel around the world and record serum sources for the rest of your life, then so be it. I won't stand in your way, and if you want me to chase off any naysayers, I'll do that, too."

Elle brushed a tear from her cheek. "I don't wish to record

sources all my life. It would be mostly an excuse to see the world. And what would be the purpose if we don't discover a way to use these sources?"

"That's something else for you to do, then."

"It's the dirt that bothers me the most. I can tell there is serum in it, but even under a magnifying glass I can't see it. The plants suck it up somehow, but to have enough to collect when you slice them open requires a large source. All this grass is useless. There is serum in every blade, but it's so little we can't even extract it."

"You'll come up with something," he said with absolute confidence.

She shrugged. "I'll try. I think we're done for the day. The soil and plants here are no different than those at the previous source. I won't make you draw any more plants this afternoon."

He heaved a melodramatic sigh. "Thank God."

Laughing, she put her arm around his waist and laid her head on his shoulder. "And there you go, improving my mood without even trying." She kissed his cheek. "This has been the most pleasant week I can remember. The MacAlasters, with their fictional life, can do this forever. That's the thing I'm most jealous of. You and I must to return to the city where we must face reality. Where I will be told not to spend my nights with you. Where I won't be able to work at my own pace, studying what I think is important or interesting. Where other people will dictate what we do, to whom we talk, where we go, what we wear. There is nothing unusual about it, but after a week of independence, it feels like returning to prison."

His arms encircled her. "It won't be forever. One way or another, this job will come to an end and you can have your independence. I promise I'll give you that loan. You can be the world's foremost serum hunter. Or open that shop. Deschamps Potions, finest in the world. Rich Londoners will flock to your store. Anything that comes from Paris is fashionable."

"I will keep that in mind the next time a rat gets into my

apartment. It will make a fine pet for a lady like Charlotte de Winter."

She expected a chuckle, but instead he scowled. "We won't live anywhere infested with rats."

We.

Such a tiny word, to tear so big a hole in her heart. She wanted nothing in the world as much as Henry. She wanted to see his smile each morning, when she felt a mess but he thought her beautiful. She wanted to rush to tell him first when she had a new idea for a potion. She wanted to hear his voice and his laugh, to see the sparkle in his eyes and the dimples in his cheeks every day for the rest of her life.

It was time to face facts. She had ignored all good sense and involved herself with a titled gentleman, knowing there would be consequences. Knowing "we" wasn't possible.

Shop girl was little better than barmaid. His family and friends would do all they could to prevent him marrying so far beneath him. He had a job that took him around the world and was so dangerous that he went armed at all times. A job he loved. She wouldn't take it from him.

Class, title, money, nationality, on and on. Their affair would end, and all too soon.

"You're looking sad again." He pulled her into his lap. "I'll have to chase that frown away." One hand roved across her breasts, the other tugged at her skirts.

"Out here in the open?" she exclaimed. "Who are you, and what have you done with my Henry?"

"You've corrupted me. I'm now a sophisticated libertine."

"Ha!"

"We're in the middle of nowhere. No one will bother us."

She cast a wicked smile at him. "You have become quite insatiable, *mon coeur.*"

"Yes."

He leaned in for a kiss, parting his lips for her eager tongue. She plunged inside, drinking deeply, savoring the hot sweetness of him. His hands groped her beneath the layers of fabric, trying to find their way to the slit in her drawers.

"You have far too many undergarments," he complained between kisses.

Elle pushed him down onto his back, and brushed his hands away.

"A sophisticated libertine would know how to handle a woman's clothing," she teased, shaking her skirts into some semblance of order.

"I know how. It simply takes too long to undress you."

"No need." She straddled him, pinning his muscled thighs between her own. Grasping his hand, she guided it up beneath the layers of her clothing, to where they both wanted it. "Now was that so difficult?"

"Saucy wench."

"*Absolument!*" Her fingers worked the fastenings of his trousers. "It hasn't yet been a full week since we began. You will improve. In the meantime, I will undress you."

He sucked in a breath as she touched him. She stroked him with languid caresses, enjoying his arousal beneath her fingers, soft skin over a rock-hard core. This strong, powerful body was hers to explore. Hers to tease and pleasure. She could take all that she wanted and give to him in return.

Her fingers tightened and she increased the speed of her strokes, little by little. She loved the look of bliss on his face, loved that she was the cause of it. Sunlight slanted through the trees, illuminating the heightened color of his skin and his moist, pink lips, which parted on a throaty moan. Delicious. She bent to kiss him, swallowing his noises of pleasure.

The world might conspire to separate them, but here and now he was hers and hers alone. She would indulge every desire, give herself up to the craving that heated her skin and quickened her breath. She shifted her skirts aside, sliding over him until his thick erection strained against her wet core. She let out a sigh of her own as he sank into her.

"Henry."

"Elle," he gasped. "God."

She placed her hands flat on his chest, riding up and down, her need growing more urgent with each stroke. Beneath her skirts, Henry squeezed her buttocks with one hand, his other flicking teasingly across her clitoris. She ground her hips atop him, moving faster, pulling herself ever closer to the moment of release.

Henry trembled beneath her, groaning and clutching at her, thrusting upward to meet her movements. It sent her over the edge. Her fingers clenched in his shirt and she convulsed in ecstasy. She rocked hard against him, feeling him shudder as he spent himself deep inside her.

She collapsed atop him, breathing hard, the rapture ebbing away into relaxation. Slowly, she eased herself off of him and lay beside him in the grass, her hand resting lightly on his chest.

"Lord," Henry murmured. "That was extraordinary. Why didn't I do this years ago?"

It took a moment before he realized what he had said.

"Er, of course, I didn't know you," he sputtered, "and, er…"

Elle laughed. He was so charmingly honest with her.

"I didn't mean I would want anyone else," he continued lamely.

Elle laughed harder. She lay her head against his chest as her whole body shook. Tears of mirth ran down her cheeks.

"Oh, Henry," she gasped, "you are adorable." She kissed and squeezed him. "You know I don't care in the slightest what you've done before or with whom, as long as right now you love me and are with me."

"I love you madly, and I will stay with you for as long as you will have me."

She snuggled against him, her sour mood a thing of the past.

He yawned. "Don't let me nap too long. I'd like to be back in time for tea."

"Tea does sound nice," she murmured. "You never know with these Americans if they will be serving anything at that time, but we have bread from lunch and I can brew us up..." She gasped and sat up. "Tea! Of course! Why didn't I think of it before?"

"What?"

Henry levered himself up on one elbow as Elle began to yank fistfuls of grass from the ground.

"I can brew this! Like tea! To extract the serum!"

"You think that will work?"

"I think it has a very good chance, and if it does, I may even be able to do something similar with the dirt."

He grinned at her. "See? I knew you would solve the problem."

She returned the smile. "Thank you for being my inspiration."

"It was my pleasure."

There was not even a hint of a leer in his voice, but his eyes smoldered. She tackled him and kissed him until they were both breathless.

"Mine too." She climbed off of him and began to adjust her clothing. "I'm afraid we ought to get back to work. I would like to test this idea this afternoon."

He nodded, buttoned up his trousers, and collected his things. Elle stuffed several handfuls of grass into her overflowing potions bag.

"I have decided," she added, "that we shall take a leisurely trip back to the city. This adventure may be ending, but I intend to savor every last minute of it."

Every last, precious minute I have with you.

Henry showed his dimples and offered her his arm for the walk back to town. "Whatever you think best, my dear. After all, you are the expert."

XXXIV

Brotherly Love

It wasn't until Admiral Johnson's house came into sight that Henry became properly apprehensive about their return to society. He had to assume anyone remaining at the house would believe them to have eloped. Part of him wished they had done. It would certainly make explanations simpler.

"Do you have your story straight?"

Elle gave him a puzzled look. "Pardon? What story do you mean?"

"The story you are going to tell everyone to explain why you disappeared for a week."

"Oh. I hadn't planned to tell one."

"They will ask. Repeatedly, I'm sure."

She shrugged. "I will tell the truth. I will say I was working."

"The niece of a lord does not work."

"Well, this one does."

Henry sighed. Once again she refused to care how others would react to her unusual behavior. He wondered how much of it was willful rebellion against social norms and how much was an assumption that she would soon return to her old life and never see any of them again. He adored her independence and poise, but feared for her regardless. She didn't deserve the public shaming that felt perilously close.

"Why don't you tell them you were visiting a friend?"

"That doesn't sound very plausible. What friend would I have in this part of the world?"

"Westfield has friends here. Why not you?"

"I'd rather tell them I was working."

He slashed at a hedge with his umbrella to vent some of his frustration. Sadly, he did no harm to the overgrown monstrosity.

"Very well. You tell them what you want. I will spread the rumor that you are one of those Parisian feminists. I trust everyone will be suitably horrified."

She gave him an eye roll that said he was overreacting. "What is your story?"

"I am not at liberty to say."

"Whyever not?"

"That's my story. 'I am not at liberty to say.'"

"Convenient."

"Your uncle rather loudly declaimed that I was a 'damned spy' at breakfast the day we left, so rumors have been circulating since then, I imagine. I will take advantage of that by being silent and mysterious and implying I have been engaging in some sort of vital espionage."

"Which is exactly what you have been doing. You get to tell the truth and you want me to lie? How is that fair?"

"I'm not telling the truth. I'm telling nothing. I will leave it all up to the imagination."

"Why don't we ask Uncle Edwin to let it slip that I'm also a spy?"

Henry's eyes widened. "Good Lord. We may as well tell them you're an actress or a courtesan!"

"Or a barmaid?"

"Fine, fine, have it your way. But when I'm out at dawn fighting to defend your honor it will be your fault."

"Don't be so melodramatic. You know dueling is illegal."

"Which would stop me, why?"

Elle sighed in exasperation. "Fine. You know dueling is extraordinarily stupid."

"Which would stop me, why?"

She gave him a playful shove. "Impudent rogue."

He paused at the bottom of the steps. "Perhaps we should enter separately."

"That only makes it look as if we having something to hide."

She strode up the front stairway and rang the bell. A servant admitted them, but before they could even ask after Lord Westfield, a woman barged into the entrance hall. Blond-haired and blue eyed, with freckles dusting her nose and cheeks, she looked so like Henry that they could have been pressed from the same mold and merely stamped "male" and "female."

"Henry Charles Ainsworth, where on earth have you been?" she demanded.

"Hello, Emma."

She jerked her head towards the parlor and strode off, expecting them to follow.

"Your sister?" Elle asked.

"What gave it away? The freckles or the lack of tact?"

"The fiery emotions. Shall we see what she wants?"

Henry shrugged and offered his arm to escort her to the parlor. The moment the door closed behind them, Emma rounded on him, hands on her hips.

"Where have you been?" she repeated. "I've heard all sorts of terrible reports about you. Sneaking about, disappearing for days at a time, corrupting young women." She stomped toward him. "And you've been spending far too much time in the sun. Your freckles are horrid."

"I'm very fond of his freckles," Elle said.

"Is this the girl you corrupted? I was told you taught her spy things."

Henry refused to spar with her. "Emma, this is Lord

Westfield's niece, Miss Elle Deschamps. Miss Deschamps, this is my sister, Lady Emma Faraday." Addressing Elle so formally felt more of a lie than his usual falsehoods.

Elle held out a hand. "It's a pleasure to meet you, Lady Emma. Are you any relation to Michael Faraday the scientist?"

Emma blinked and frowned. "Who?"

"No? That's a shame. Mr. Faraday did a great deal of important work. His research in the field of electropotions was especially interesting to me. It led directly to the coatings we use to protect and strengthen our telegraph cables. It has increased the efficiency so much that speeds have been doubled and prices cut dramatically."

Emma seemed at a loss for words. "I see."

"I'm highly grateful for his contributions," Henry said. "I send many telegrams when I'm working."

A noise came from just outside the door. Henry walked silently across the room and yanked it open before the person on the other side had a chance to realize what was happening. He wasn't at all surprised when his nine-year-old nephew tumbled through the entryway. The boy sprang to his feet and flung himself into Henry's arms.

"Uncle Henry!"

Henry picked him up and swung him in a big circle, knowing Emma would disapprove of the roughhousing.

"Georgey, my lad, how are you?"

"I'm well, Uncle Henry. Were you away spying? Mother thinks you were doing something awful and wouldn't tell me about it. Was it terribly secret? Do you want to see how fast I can run now? I've been doing lots of training. Did you know I was listening outside? I was trying to be very quiet. I'm going to be a spy like you when I grow up."

"So you've told me."

Henry, accustomed to Georgey's babbling, was able to answer the boy with a straight face. Elle needed to cover her mouth to hide a giggle.

"Who's the lady?" the boy asked, pointing at Elle. "Is she a spy, too? Are you going to marry her, Uncle Henry? Grandfather says you ought to be married at your age. He wants you to come home and stop being a spy because he thinks it's dangerous. Mother doesn't want me to be a spy, either. She says it's a 'disgraceful profession,' but I think it's exciting!"

Henry glanced at his sister, suppressing the urge to laugh.

"Georgey!" Emma exclaimed. "You shouldn't say things like that."

"But that's what you said, Mother."

"Your uncle is an adult and is free to make his own life choices," Emma said primly.

Georgey frowned. "Then why do you scold him about it?"

"You know," Elle spoke up, before the conversation could grow even more awkward, "It's nearly time to eat, and I need to change out of these traveling clothes. I could use a smart young man, such as you, Mr. George Faraday, to be my escort through the house. Do you think you are up to the task?"

"Oh, yes! I know my way through the whole house," the boy declared.

"Excellent. Why don't we go and give your mother and your uncle some time to chat in private."

"You mean time to quarrel more?" Georgey asked. He offered Elle his arm in an attempt to play the gentleman. "Mother loves to quarrel with Uncle Henry. She says younger brothers cause lots of trouble. I have two younger sisters, but Mother and Father have been trying ever so much to make a new baby, so maybe it will be a boy."

Emma turned red as a beet. Henry feigned a cough to hide his laughter. He shut the door after Georgey and Elle, and didn't look back at his sister until he'd had a moment to compose himself.

"You might consider disciplining the child now and again."

Emma's cheeks were still pink. Henry was glad of the reminder that he wasn't the only family member to suffer from oft-flushed skin.

"Georgey is a good boy. It's only that he hasn't learned what things are best left unsaid."

"That would be his Ainsworth blood. I still have yet to master that particular skill, and I've noticed you have similar difficulty."

"I don't know what you are talking about."

"Why are you here, Emma?"

"I brought you your trunk. Father seemed to think you needed more clothes and things."

"You could have shipped it. Or he could have sent the one I left in Italy. I don't think my suits need an escort."

"It was a wonderful opportunity to expose the family to a new part of the world."

Henry rolled his eyes. "It was a chance for you to assert your superiority over me."

"That's not it at all. I only want to verify you are well and offer my advice. I want you to live up to your full potential, Henry."

"Your favorite pastime: telling me what to do."

"The girl, Henry," Emma switched topics abruptly. "Who is she?"

"I just introduced you. She is Westfield's niece."

"Oh, bah! No one believes that. Who is she, really? She sounded very scholarly, talking about science. I was told Westfield had some scheme to get you to marry an heiress. I also heard something about you with a barmaid. Which is she? Or is she someone else entirely? How many women are you involved with? It is most unseemly."

"She is both and neither."

"Don't be cryptic."

"Miss Deschamps is a potions expert. She has a very keen mind and has been the key to the success of this mission. I don't doubt she will go on to great things."

"What of the others?"

"There are no others. You don't need to believe every rumor you hear."

"They aren't rumors. Westfield sent several telegrams to Father."

"Who, suffering from the same Ainsworth curse as you and I, clearly doesn't know how to keep his damned mouth shut."

"Henry! Don't say such things about Father. And watch your language."

"As I said, a curse."

He saw the corner of her mouth twitch upwards at the pun, but she quickly suppressed it.

"Don't wander off topic. I want you to explain who this girl is. You've been dashing about all alone with her. You're going to have to marry her or there will be a scandal."

"Why should there be a scandal? We both spent the week working. It's what we were hired for. Feel free to ask Miss Deschamps yourself. She will tell you the same thing."

"Now you are being deliberately obtuse. I don't know why you are protesting, in any event. Westfield told Father you had fallen in love with her. She seems polite and well-bred enough. Is she from a good family? Is she actually an heiress?"

"She hasn't a penny to her name other than what she has been paid for this work, and her only family is an aged aunt, with whom she lives in a tiny, rat-infested apartment in a rather unsavory area of Paris."

Emma frowned at him. "You must be joking. She looked a perfect lady."

"She is a perfect lady. She just happens to be a lady by her actions, not by wealth or birth. You were asking about a barmaid. That is she. Her previous employment was mixing potions at a follies house. That's where Westfield found her."

"Henry, you can't be serious."

"I'm perfectly serious. Ask her yourself. She won't lie to you."

"You can't marry a barmaid! What would Father say?"

"In case it wasn't clear already, dear sister, I don't care what he would say, nor do I care what you say on the matter. Not a one of you gets to decide whom I will marry, or, indeed, if I will ever do so."

"There is going to be a scandal no matter what," she lamented. "Oh, Henry, why can't you be like our brothers? They are so normal."

"I don't fancy their lifestyle. I have told you many a time I will never marry an Italian heiress and join the family business of cheating tourists."

She looked insulted. "We don't cheat anyone."

"You sell them 'authentic Italian wine' that is so bad the locals refuse to drink it. You would be better off letting it all turn to vinegar."

Emma blinked. Then her eyes grew wide. "Henry, that's brilliant! Father has stores of bottles lying around that are much too old to drink. One of the children broke one when we visited at Christmas, and thinking upon it, it had quite a pleasant scent."

"Emma, it will taste vile!"

"Perhaps. I will notify Thomas and Robert and tell them to pull everything out and evaluate it. I think they could do better in the vinegar market than with wine. There is much less competition."

Henry could only stare at her and shake his head.

"We will start by selling whatever we have lying around. If that is successful, we can then look into refining the process and producing more of a variety." Her eyes were shining. "This is excellent. Father will probably give you a bonus in your next monthly share."

"I'm twenty-seven and gainfully employed. I don't understand why he insists on providing me an allowance."

"It isn't an allowance, Henry, it's your share of the business."

"I don't work in the business!"

"That's why your portion is small. But you are still part of the family. Now, you must excuse me. I want to go discuss this with Reggie."

"Reginald is here as well?"

"Well, of course he is here! You know we always travel as a family. He is upstairs minding Daisy. You don't think I would let a two-year-old run about the house on her own, do you?"

"Is Lily up there as well?" Henry inquired after his six-year-old niece.

"Actually… well, I may have told her she could dig in the garden for as long as she liked. I'll pay for repairs if she does any damage."

"This is why most people hire a governess."

"And let someone else dictate what my children do and do not do? No, thank you. I'm off now. We will talk more over lunch."

She swept from the room, leaving him staring after her, reminded once again that he was not the runaway favorite for the title of oddest member of the family.

XXXV

A Bad End

"*It's* a conspiracy," Elle muttered, tugging the gloves up her arms and flexing her fingers. "He arranges parties every day I arrive." The only good thing about the arrangement was the chance to dress again in her blue ball gown.

Henry kissed the back of her neck. "I'm not complaining. It afforded me the opportunity to lace you into that slinky purple corset. I look forward to removing it."

"Don't tell Westfield you are my substitute for a lady's maid. No, on second thought, do tell him. Perhaps then he will stop thinking of me as a helpless child. How do I look?"

"A picture of perfection. Wise as Athena and luscious as Aphrodite." He cracked the door and peeked out. "Empty hall. Shall we be off?"

She took his arm. "Let's."

A pleasant and productive afternoon had fortified her somewhat for the evening's activities. Her experiments with the serum-laden soil samples had gone well. She could now consistently extract serum, and had moved on to a series of efficiency tests. This afternoon's work had compared hot water versus cold, agitation levels, and even soaking the dirt in alcohol. An ongoing experiment had samples soaking overnight. Excellent progress.

"Ah, Niece, there you are." Westfield rushed to her side,

the tightness around his eyes fading when she allowed him to draw her away from Henry's side. "I've been worried. Rumors are floating all over about the two of you."

"I'm uninterested in rumors. Tell me about your meeting. Has anything happened since? Are Fasching and Lady de Winter colluding?"

"I..." His brows scrunched in confusion. "I don't know. The meeting was odd. I only remember discussing the weather, and perhaps the food? I'm sorry, it's all a bit hazy."

"Hazy?" Elle glanced at Henry, who met her frown with one of his own. Westfield's mind was sharp and his memory good.

"Yes. It's peculiar. I feel as if I ought to have learned something, but nothing happened at all that I recall. It seems we didn't even discuss business, though I cannot determine why."

He'd been drugged. With Fasching's talent for noxious potions and Westfield's trusting nature, it would have been all too easy to dose him into forgetfulness. Had they interrogated him as well? She would have to assume her enemies knew all about her and her purpose.

"But, perhaps it does not matter," Westfield continued. "Mr. Fasching's business is legitimate and has had no legal troubles."

Henry sniffed. "He must be paying the right politicians."

"Lady de Winter is simply touring and attending ladies' social events. Her maid rushed home to England—an ailing family member, I believe—and she is rather flustered by the loss. She is relaxing by visiting a friend in the country for a few days."

Elle's stomach clenched. In the country? It was too much of a coincidence. The MacAlasters had ended their journey just in time, it seemed.

Admiral Johnson led the group into dinner, escorting Elle to the place beside him, at the exact opposite corner of the table from Henry. Westfield's attempt to quash the rumors? She couldn't ask, because he, too, was at the far end of the table. Worse yet, Henry Fasching sat directly across from her, beside Emma Faraday.

Elle wasn't certain what to make of Henry's elder sister. The woman scolded him like a child, but somehow their morning conversation had ended amicably. He had been cheerful at lunch and all afternoon.

Elle removed her gloves and picked up the menu card beside her plate. It amused her to no end that the fashionable menu was in French. *Côte De Boeuf à l'Anglais*? She almost snickered. American beef, served English-style. Obviously much fancier with a French name.

Regardless of the names, the food sounded extraordinary. She had never tried oysters or *aspic de foie-gras*. She wasn't sure what sort of iced dessert *"glaces de fantaisies"* might be, but she wanted to taste them.

The plates she was meant to eat from were gilt-edged, the silver shined to a mirror finish, and the napkins embroidered. Everything about the dinner was lovely, in fact, with the exception of the company. Sitting at a table with strangers, she couldn't be herself. Sitting at a table with enemies, she couldn't relax. Unfortunately, she still had a role to play, and until she could make arrangements to leave New York she was stuck with it. At least Fasching's proximity meant she could keep an eye on him.

"I hope there's an alternative to oysters for the first course," Emma said, reviewing her own menu. "My brother is allergic to shellfish, and he will be terribly ill if he eats even a small amount. He really oughtn't even touch them."

Even from a distance, Elle could see Henry blush at his sister's lack of tact.

"You need not fret, Lady Emma," the admiral assured her. "The gentlemen have already discussed the matter, and our chef has arranged a lovely tray of stuffed olives for anyone who wishes to pass on the oysters, or, indeed, for anyone at all."

Elle plucked an olive from the tray as it passed by her. The cheese-filled bite popped in her mouth, flooding her tastebuds with its salty tang.

"Can't get enough of these," said the man sitting across from Henry, a Mr. Parker from New Jersey. "I think I could eat olives all day, and these Greek ones are particularly delicious."

"Those are Italian," Emma sighed. "He has the types reversed. Poor Henry is going to have to spend half of dinner explaining about olives."

Elle chuckled and sampled an oyster. Perhaps dinner would be bearable, if the remaining dishes were as fine as this first course.

The time passed faster than she expected. None of the men had anything to say, so Emma Faraday carried the conversation for the entire end of the table. She peppered Elle with questions, though none that gave away her humble origins. They talked about the food in France versus that in England and Italy, how she enjoyed traveling, and what she liked to read. The interrogation allowed her to ignore Fasching completely. Whenever she ran out of things to say, she remarked on a new dish or savored another bite of dinner. It wasn't as enjoyable as it could have been, but she was neither bored nor irritable.

She swallowed the remaining few sips of her champagne, the only alcohol she had taken during the meal. Many of the guests downed a different drink with each course, but she wouldn't risk overindulging with enemies so near. Henry, true to his word, had only a single glass of sherry.

When the dinner was finished, Mrs. Johnson rose from her seat and invited the ladies to join her in the drawing room for coffee and tea. Her husband led the men to the library for the same refreshments, adding the offer of some fine cigars. Elle cast Henry a stern look, and he grinned and winked. If he indulged in one of those foul things, he wasn't getting kissed tonight.

Rachael Fasching looked down her nose at Elle as they passed one another on the way into the drawing room.

"I see you are wearing the same dress you wore to the ball last week."

Elle put on her best rude-customer-smile. "Yes. I'm quite fond of it."

"You may wish to pay more attention to your wardrobe, unless you want the rest of the world to think Captain Ainsworth is so short on funds he cannot afford to keep his mistress properly attired."

She said this last loud enough to be heard by all the ladies. Elle steeled herself for an argument, but Emma Faraday beat her to it.

"How dare you slander Miss Deschamps and my brother in such a manner? Apologize at once!"

"Slander?" Rachael laughed. "Lady Emma, you have been here but two nights, so perhaps you are not entirely aware, but the two of them ran off together fully a week ago, and have only just returned. What do you think they've been doing that whole time?"

"Working," Emma snapped. "They are both highly dedicated to potions research, and have been busy for months now, under the guidance of Elle's uncle. I assure you, if Lord Westfield had been at all concerned anything untoward might happen, he would have accompanied them himself or sent a chaperone for Miss Deschamps. He is a very conscientious man."

"A ridiculous story. If you are clever enough to invent such a tale, you are clever enough to realize no one will believe it. Myself especially, since I caught Miss Deschamps outside her room in her nightgown the very day she disappeared."

"Mrs. Fasching," Emma said, her tone scolding and motherly, "as you well know, this old house doesn't provide private water closets in all rooms. I'm certain even you need to dash to the necessary in your nightclothes every now and then."

"With wild hair and tangled clothes, looking freshly tumbled from a lover's bed?" Rachael sneered.

"Not all of us are so fortunate as to have been gifted with such a flawless appearance as you no doubt exhibit first thing in the morning," Emma retorted.

"Yes, I notice you have to use powder to hide your spotted complexion."

"Apologize," Emma demanded.

"I will not. The girl is a common harlot, and you know it."

"If that is your answer, I must beg your pardon, but I will never speak to you again. Elle, dear, would you like to join me for some coffee? Perhaps we can find some company with a higher degree of civility."

"That would be most pleasant, thank you," Elle answered.

Emma took her arm, and they walked together to the table to pour their drinks, then sat side-by-side on a sofa while Rachael glared at them and the other ladies whispered.

"Thank you for that," Elle said softly. "You were far more effective sparring with her than I believe I would have been."

"Think nothing of it. No one speaks ill of my family in my presence and gets away with it."

Elle smiled. "You Ainsworths are very passionate."

Emma sipped her coffee in a calm, ladylike fashion. "Do you think so? I think I'm perfectly even-tempered at almost all times. The necessity of defending you and Henry roused my anger, but that is a rare case."

"Perhaps."

Emma was deluding herself. Between this incident and her shouting match with Henry earlier, she had shown herself to be a woman of strong opinion who wasn't at all hesitant to assert herself. She could present a cool facade, but her emotions ran deep. She was much like her brother in that regard.

"I do expect to be given a proper explanation of your recent activities before long," Emma remarked. "You and I can have a discussion later, woman-to-woman. Henry was entirely unforthcoming this morning. He can be so trying. Just because he is a spy doesn't mean he needs to keep secrets from his family."

Elle struggled not to laugh. She was certain that if anyone in the family knew any secrets at all, they would end up shared around the dinner table, until eventually Georgey or one of the other children would reveal them all to a complete stranger.

"Henry doesn't want to involve you in his work, I'm sure. There is always the potential for danger, and if you know anything, it might put you in harm's way. He would never do that to any of you."

"I hadn't thought of it that way. You make an excellent point, Miss Deschamps. He needn't be so secretive about his personal life, however."

Elle did laugh now. "He wants it to be *his* personal life, not some idyllic fiction you all have imagined for him."

"Hmm. I can see why he likes you. I hope father won't disapprove too much, because you are certainly not on his list."

"Choosing a wife from a list makes it about as romantic as purchasing a pair of shoes. Your father has no hope of getting Henry to comply with such a scheme."

"I don't think you understand how excellent father's lists are. I chose Reggie from his list and we don't lack at all for romance. I'm certain Henry could find someone well-suited to him."

"It will never happen," Elle vowed.

"We shall see, shan't we?"

Their private conversation ended, as one of the other women at last dared to approach them, and once again Elle found herself forced to endure chit-chat about dinner, the weather, and the latest fashion trends.

A door slammed, interrupting their discussion about the oddities of dress of the horseback-riding women in the American west, and the shouts of male voices echoed through the hall. Emma and Elle exchanged an alarmed look and dashed from the drawing room.

Henry and Fasching were at the center of the mayhem, surrounded by other gentlemen, all of whom were talking at once.

Fasching held a lit cigar, brandishing it as if it were a weapon. Henry, his pale cheeks red and his eyes flashing with fury, had to be physically restrained by Emma's husband Reginald. Reggie, a tall, slender man in his mid-forties, looked fit for his age, but struggled to hold back his stronger brother-in-law.

"Do you speak in earnest, Ainsworth?" Fasching asked.

"I do. I will give you one more chance to apologize." His words were slurred, as if he'd been drinking.

Fasching let out a condescending laugh. "I have nothing to apologize for."

"Then I will see you at dawn," Henry spat.

Emma gasped.

"So be it," Fasching declared. "You have a pistol?"

Henry nodded.

"Pistols at dawn, then." Fasching took a long puff on his cigar. "Unless you change your mind once you sober up," he scoffed.

Elle shoved two men aside to clear her way to the center of the circle. "What have you done to him?"

"I've done nothing, girlie. The man can't hold his liquor."

"Elle, what are you doing here?" Henry asked. "You should be with the ladies." He didn't seem to realize all the ladies had joined the crowd.

"Interfering bitch can't help but rush to defend you. Should we place bets on whether she'll come along tomorrow morning? I've never heard of a duel where a man brought his whore as his second."

Henry had gotten one arm free from Reggie's grasp, and it was all he needed. His fist connected with Fasching's pretty face, sending him crashing to the ground. Rachael Fasching screamed.

"I'll see you in hell, you bastard!" Henry shouted. He looked back at Elle. "Elle, you shouldn't be here."

Parker, the olive lover, cheered the fisticuffs. "Bravo!" he slurred, weaving drunkenly.

Henry tried to free himself from Reggie's grip, lost his balance, and knocked them both to the ground. Emma pushed her way to her husband's side. Westfield was right behind her.

"Get them away from each other," he urged.

Henry staggered to his feet, took one step toward Elle, and nearly fell again. She grabbed hold of his arm and he sagged against her. She detected no alcohol on his breath.

"What have you been drinking?"

"Tea," he replied, sounding confused. "I always have tea."

Westfield had placed himself between Henry and Fasching, who sat on the floor, his hand clamped over his left eye.

"Get him out of here. I will try to calm everyone down."

Elle dragged Henry toward the library. He couldn't walk in a straight line, and crashed into her repeatedly. She slammed the door closed behind them and headed straight for the table where the tea service had been set. Henry stumbled when she let go of him, grabbing the back of a chair to remain upright.

Elle yanked the lid off the teapot. It was empty. She sniffed at the wet leaves, but found only the familiar scent of freshly brewed tea. Tossing her gloves aside, she ran her finger along the bottom of the pot and touched a tiny droplet to her tongue. She spat immediately, as the bitter taste assaulted her senses. A whirl of dizziness swept over her, along with an urge to drink more.

"That monster!" she screamed, spinning back toward the door, ready to kill Fasching with her bare hands. "Where's a knife? I'll gut the bastard myself!"

Henry grabbed her. "Elle, no."

"Release me!"

"No, stay away from him. I'll kill him for you, I promise."

That wasn't at all a suitable alternative. "Let. Me. Go," she commanded, still shaking with rage. Henry's arms fell away from her. "Thank you."

"Elle, please..."

He stumbled after her as she started for the door, and

instinctively she turned to catch him. As soon as he was in her arms, she came to her senses. The blinding anger faded. Fasching could wait. Taking care of Henry was the first priority. She wrapped her arms about his waist. His head fell on her shoulder, affording him a good look down her dress.

"You have the most lovely breasts, mademoiselle," he slurred. "I should very much like to touch them."

He groped her, and she brushed his hand away. "Not now, Henry."

"Later?" His lips grazed her neck and she felt a rush of arousal. "No, now. Now is better."

She heard the creak of the door opening behind her and held him at arm's length. "Henry, you're drunk."

"Nonsense."

"You are, and it's disgraceful," Emma reprimanded him.

Elle turned, relief flooding her senses. "Lady Emma, you are exactly the person I need." She pulled Henry over to his sister and handed him off to her. "Take him up to my room. I'm in the east wing, second door on the right." She pulled the key from its concealed spot in her boot. "I will join you shortly. I need to gather a few things."

"Are you mad? You can't take him to your bedchamber."

"I must. I have need of my potions supplies. Take him upstairs, and whatever you do, don't let him lie down. He must not fall asleep."

"What?"

"Do it, Emma, if you value his life."

She flinched. "What's going on?"

"I will explain when I can. For now, please help him. And don't berate him too much, as this isn't his fault."

She sighed and nodded. "The things I do for my family."

"Don't be so sour, Emma," Henry scolded.

"Don't be such a brat," she shot back.

Elle fled the room. "Fight all you want, just keep him awake," she shouted over her shoulder.

XXXVI

Up All Night

"Can't I please lie down? I'm feeling very unwell." Henry slumped back in his chair.

Elle glanced at him and shook her head. The intoxication was wearing off, but his eyes had begun to glaze over and he was paler than she had ever seen. She poured a full ounce of stamina potion into a cup and topped it off from the steaming pot of tea. She slid it across the table to him and turned her attention to the second, much more complicated potion. Her mind felt muddled, and she wasn't certain how much was from the tiny taste of poison, and how much from stress. It didn't help that the nausea had set in so quickly.

"Is there no milk?" Henry queried.

"Just drink it," his sister insisted.

"Uncivilized." He took a sip regardless.

"I don't understand any of this," Reginald Faraday confessed. He ran a hand through his tousled, brown hair in an unconscious nervous gesture. "Henry drank very little liquor and didn't partake of anything unusual. Miss Deschamps, you must enlighten me."

"It was the tea," she explained. "It was poisoned."

Reggie lifted a single eyebrow. "I had tea after dinner as well, and I was unaffected. It wasn't very good tea, I must say. I ought to have had the coffee."

"You didn't eat any olives," Elle stated. "Otherwise you would be in the same situation."

"Er, no, I didn't have olives."

"You are fortunate. You won't be ill like the rest of us."

"How many foodstuffs do you think were poisoned?" Emma cried. "What sort of household is this?"

"The olives were tainted with a simple poison called salinide," Elle explained. "It's based on salt and easily disguised as such. It could have been sprinkled on or added to the brine. We will all feel poorly tonight and likely much of tomorrow."

"Emma, you had olives, didn't you?" Reggie fretted.

"I had a few," she answered. "I do feel a bit queasy, but I thought…" She looked at her husband. "I had hoped it meant I was in a family way." She sighed. "I would like one more child, but I'm getting old."

"You are thirty-three. That is hardly old," Henry scoffed. "Mother was older than that when Lucy was born."

"She was a happy surprise. We have fertility troubles in the family when we age. It took mother and father five years to conceive you, and neither Thomas nor Robert has had any children since turning thirty. You had better marry soon, Henry, or you might never have any family at all."

He snorted. "Elle is a potions master. She will no doubt feed me some concoction if I don't give her as many daughters as she would like."

Elle winced. He was still drunk enough to be inappropriate.

"The poison?" Reggie prompted.

Elle gave him a smile of thanks. "You needn't worry about the salinide. It's not lethal. The sickness will be uncomfortable, but won't do permanent harm. The tea was dosed with something much worse. I have never encountered it before, and knew it only based on my readings. No odor, bitter taste. Alone it is harmless. Taken with the salinide, it causes immediate intoxication and a desire to drink more. It can be survived in small doses, but because victims keep drinking it, it is nearly always fatal."

Henry's teacup clattered in its saucer. "So I'm to die, then?"

"Not if I have anything to say about it. Keep drinking the tea I give you and don't lie down. If you go to sleep before the poison is out of your system you will never wake up."

Emma grasped her brother's hand. "How do we get the poison out?"

Elle looked at Henry as she answered. "I'm going to try a new potion, taking aspects from one that promotes appetite and from a general poison antidote. I hope it will help your body process everything faster. Also, I will give you regular doses of stamina potions to keep up your strength. I will adjust the potency as necessary. Other than that, all we can do is wait."

"What of the rest of the household?" Reggie asked. "Others may have had both the olives and the tea. I should go warn them."

Emma rushed to her husband's side. "Reggie, one of them is a murderer. You can't go off alone!"

"It's Fasching," Henry said. "Avoid him and you will be fine."

"Are you certain?" Emma asked. "I know he ate olives because he was seated next to me."

"I'm certain. Why wouldn't he make himself sick to keep suspicion off him? In fact, if anyone in this household dies, there will be so many others ill that it will be assumed to be spoiled food, not poison. It's too bad I will likely die before our dawn appointment. I should like to have shot the bastard."

"You won't die," Elle insisted. "And there will be no dueling. He would cheat and kill you."

"I suppose, then, if you save me, I shall have to beg off and be branded a coward?"

"Or perhaps just a drunkard and a hothead." She shrugged. "I've been branded a whore. You would be in good company."

"We are, all of us, leaving this horrid place as soon as possible," Emma declared. "Reggie, as soon as you have alerted the household, go back to our rooms and see to the children. Pack up all our things, if you are able. I will stay here to chaperone Miss Deschamps and my brother."

He nodded and kissed her, then bowed politely to Elle before leaving. She turned her attention back to her potion.

"A chaperone," Henry chuckled. "How absurd. You're much too late, dearest sister. The bewitching Miss Deschamps has thoroughly compromised me."

"That's not funny," Emma chastened.

"It is to me, though I didn't expect you to find it so. You wanted the truth. There you have it. I'm the worst sort of reprobate and I have ruined the reputation of the finest of women with my moral deficiency and unslakable lust. Condemn me all you want, but I will never regret it."

His words could have been a jest, but a tear shone in his eye, and Elle realized just how afraid he was. She rose from her seat and walked around the table to embrace him.

"Neither will I," she vowed, kissing his brow.

He made no attempt to stand, but he wrapped his arms around her and held her tight. "I'm sorry. I shouldn't have said all of that. I'm rather intoxicated, I'm afraid."

"It will wear off eventually. Drink your tea and pick a fight with your sister. That will give me time to make the potion you need."

"We have nothing to fight about," Emma said firmly.

There were no other chairs, so she dragged the trunk that held the bedclothes across the room to sit beside her brother. She grasped his free hand between both of hers.

"Don't fret. Your sweetheart is a potions master. She will take excellent care of you. You have chosen far better for yourself than any of us might have done."

Elle spent the next half-hour preparing her experimental remedy, pausing only to give Henry a second dose of the stamina potion. He looked ready to nod off at any moment, but Emma kept him talking, even threatening to slap him if she thought he was falling asleep.

Elle squirted four precise drops of snake venom into a teaspoon of brandy, followed by an equal number of drops of laudanum, before adding the entire combination to the health potion base. A little chill ran up her neck as she stirred the dangerous, potent mixture. She'd never made anything so powerful, and the slightest error could take the potion from cure to poison. She checked the color and consistency, sniffed it, and took an experimental sip. An immediate sense of relief coursed through her. She had done it. She prayed it would be enough.

She passed the rest of the potion to Henry and instructed him to drink the whole thing. Within minutes, he perked up considerably. He still looked pale as death, but he was alert and no longer drunk. If she could keep up his strength long enough for her potion to neutralize Fasching's poison, he might pull through. She wouldn't leave his side, even for an instant.

Elle picked up the large book she had brought from the library and settled herself on the bed. She patted the place beside her. "Come, sit with me."

He stood and walked to her, no longer staggering. The movement seemed to exhaust him, however, and he dropped onto the bed with a weary sigh.

"Aren't you afraid I will fall asleep in bed?"

She shook her head. "I have a plan to keep you occupied." She deposited the tome of Shakespeare's works in his lap, then laced her fingers through his, stilling his trembling hand. "Read me your stories, King Henry."

"So shaken as we are, so wan with care," he recited, not even opening the book, "Find we a time for frighted peace to pant, and breathe short-winded accents of new broils to be commenced in strands afar remote."

"Do you have the whole play memorized?" she marvelled.

"No. Only some of the soliloquies."

"Good. Then we shall have the rest of the night to correct that deficiency."

He smiled, and it brought a bit of color back to his cheeks at last. "Challenge accepted."

XXXVII

A Sad Discovery

"*H*ENRY!"

His eyelids flew open at her panicked cry. "I'm awake," he mumbled, though he was certain he hadn't been only a moment ago.

Elle wrapped her arms around him. "I'm so sorry. I didn't mean to fall asleep. I had the most terrible nightmare."

She lay her head on his shoulder. Her warm breath tickled his neck, and he felt his body stir in response. The flip-flopping of his stomach warned him not to get too excited. She held him for a long moment before sitting up and looking him over carefully.

"You have a bit of color back. How do you feel?"

"Ill. But not dizzy or drunk. Queasy and very tired. That's all."

"Could you walk about a bit?"

"Certainly."

He eased himself out of bed and walked a lap around the room. He was bone tired, that was certain. He'd drunk enough stamina potions to rouse a dead horse, but he still felt he could sleep for a week. He was no longer unsteady, however, and he didn't experience any sense of weakness in his muscles. He sat on the edge of the bed.

"Was that sufficient?"

Elle nodded. "I think the worst is over. It should be safe to sleep now."

"I was asleep a moment ago and I had no trouble waking," he assured her.

Emma, who was curled at the foot of the bed, lifted her head. "Do you need me any longer?"

Elle shook her head. "No. Thank you ever so much. You have been a great help, and I have kept you too long from your family."

Emma sat up and smoothed out her dress. "You *are* family. The children can cope without me for a night, and Reggie is very good with them. He isn't the sort of father who begets offspring and then ignores them until they are of age." She slid off the bed, paused beside Henry and gave him a kiss on the cheek. "You are looking much better. I will see you at breakfast, or perhaps lunch, as it is dawn already, and you need much more sleep."

"Thank you, Emma. For everything. I do love you, you know."

She grinned. "Of course you do. I love you, too, baby brother." She nodded to them both and departed.

Henry lay back down on the bed and pulled Elle against him. "I have missed my appointment with Fasching," he observed.

"He won't have gone. He ate the olives to make himself ill, and he no doubt thinks you dead."

"True." He yawned. "I have an earnest request of you, once I have fully recovered."

She propped herself up on one elbow and frowned down at him. "Oh?"

"Teach me to recognize poisons. I have been schooled in ways to avoid them, but clearly a clever adversary can find ways to administer them, and I cannot forgo food and drink entirely."

"I will tell you all I know," she promised, "but in return I would like you to teach me to throw a punch. You were falling-down drunk, yet you still hit Fasching hard enough to leave him stunned. I should like to be able to do that."

"Of course. I know other moves, too. We will work on hand-to-hand fighting, in case you find yourself without potions."

"Thank you. It is a rare man who wouldn't balk at teaching a woman something so unfeminine."

"I would have done, once. As a gentleman, I was taught always to protect and provide for women. I needed you to show me that we can do better by encouraging our women to protect and provide for themselves. Which doesn't mean I will defend you any less fervently, but I do love that you can get by without me." He yawned again. "You must excuse me, but I can hardly keep my eyes open."

She kissed him gently. "Sleep well, darling."

He awoke several hours later, still feeling nauseous and in need of more sleep, but not so tired he could ignore the commotion in the hall. He pushed himself up out of bed and headed for the door, Elle right on his heels. He found he didn't give a damn if anyone spied him coming from her room. He was beyond caring what any of these people thought of him. As for Elle, she had won over Emma despite his misbehavior and last night's drunken confessions. Anyone who mattered would love her without reservation.

As it was, everyone was so occupied with the goings-on at the far end of the hall that no one even noticed them until they were at the scene. A housemaid, who couldn't have been more than thirteen or fourteen, wept hysterically against Westfield's chest as he tried to comfort her. He was still in his nightclothes, with his hair unkempt and bags under his eyes. His door, two down from Elle's room, was ajar. Two other couples stood nearby, all four of them talking at once. One of the women dabbed at her eyes with a handkerchief.

The door directly across from Westfield's stood open wide,

and Henry squeezed past the distraught men and women for a look. He beckoned for Elle to follow him inside.

"You can't take a woman in there!" one of the men exclaimed.

Henry ignored the remark, and even stepped aside to allow Elle to enter first. In the middle of the room, a man lay face down on the floor, still in his dinner clothes.

"Dead for a ducat," Henry muttered, his brain still rattling with the words of the Bard.

He bent beside the body and rolled the man onto his back. Parker, the olive lover. The body was stiff, his skin cold, and his lips blue. Henry glanced up at Elle.

"What do you think?"

"He's been dead for some time. My guess is he passed out shortly after arriving here and died some time in the middle of the night. It fits with what I know of the poison."

Henry rose, feeling a shudder run through his body. "Thank you for keeping me from such a fate."

"How could I have done otherwise? I would have saved this man as well, had I known."

Henry put an arm around her. "We did what we could. Reggie went out to alert the other guests, but finding everyone and getting them all to listen is a daunting task. Poor Mr. Parker may already have been unconscious by then. I know I was ready to nod off as soon as I reached your room."

Elle nodded, and they stepped back out into the hall. "The Faschings didn't come out to witness this sad scene. Let us pay them a visit, shall we?"

"Henry," Westfield spoke as they passed him, "I'd like you to contact the authorities."

"Hang the authorities!" one of the other men blurted. "Call a doctor! My poor wife has been ailing since last night, and I won't have her end up like that man!"

His wife, the woman with the handkerchief, wept harder.

"Don't fret, sir," Elle told him. "She will make a full

recovery. Madame, I can make you a potion to ease your symptoms, if you desire."

"Like hell you will!" her husband blurted. "Do you think I'd let some foreign tart serve unknown remedies to my wife? You probably tainted the food in the first place."

Elle spoke only to the woman. "I'm sorry to see your husband is so upset. My offer stands. You know where to find me."

"Don't listen to her, Beth. She's in bed with that spy. Those damned greedy Brits still can't stand the fact they don't rule us anymore."

"Now see here," Henry began, jumping to defend Elle, himself, and his country.

Elle took hold of his arm. "Save it for Fasching," she whispered.

"You, sir, need to watch your language in front of the ladies," he finished, as primly as his sister might have done. It was an absurdly hypocritical thing to say, but it left the man looking bewildered and prevented any further shouting.

Elle led Henry to Fasching's door at the end of the hall. Henry flattened himself against the wall and gave her a nod. She rapped on the door.

When no one answered, she tried again, pounding with her whole fist. She looked wild. Her dress and hair were tangled, she had dark circles underneath her eyes from the lack of sleep, and her skin was flushed red with righteous anger. Goddamn, he loved her.

The door opened at last. Elle took a deliberate step forward to prevent Fasching from slamming it in her face.

"Murderer," she hissed.

"Go away, girl," he sneered.

Elle didn't twitch. "You killed him. You will pay for what you've done."

He laughed. "I've done nothing. If your lover has gotten himself killed, it's his own fault."

Henry stepped into Fasching's line of sight. "What makes you think she's talking about me?"

Fasching was so startled he stumbled backwards. He looked unwell this morning. His skin had a sallow cast from eating the olives, and his left eye was swollen nearly shut.

"You ought to put something on that eye," Henry suggested. "You're skilled with potions. Why not make yourself a healing salve? Or do you only make poisons and tranquilizers?"

"Go to hell, Ainsworth."

Henry gave him a polite nod. "I'll see you there, no doubt."

"You may want to change out of your nightclothes," Elle advised. "I'm sure the police will want to have a word with you."

"You have nothing to tell them but your own nonsensical conjectures," Fasching snarled. "They are more likely to arrest the both of you. There are plenty of witnesses to your low morals."

"Don't be stupid, Fasching," Henry replied. "If I were planning to kill anyone, it would be you, and I would make certain to do the thing right."

Fasching did slam the door, then, and Elle danced backward to avoid being hit.

"Did you want to contact the police?" she asked. "We don't have to."

"I will contact them, and give a statement if they want it, but I don't expect it to have much effect. No doubt this will be considered an accidental poisoning from bad food. Too many of us are ill to prove otherwise."

"And the tainted tea is gone. Even if we had the leaves, the poison would have lost its potency by now."

Henry took her hand to lead her back to her room. "You should change out of that dress and pack your things. I would like to leave here as soon as we can."

"In a moment. I haven't spoken to Mrs. Fasching yet."

"What could you possibly have to say to her?" Henry wondered, but Elle stepped to the next door over and knocked.

Rachael answered her door promptly. She was dressed for the day and her hair was styled. Unlike the majority of the houseguests, she looked in perfect health. She gazed at them in suspicion, startled, but not shocked.

"Can I help you?"

"No," Elle replied, "but perhaps I can help you. I think you should know an innocent man has died and your husband is responsible."

Rachael's eyes narrowed. "Don't speak such lies!" Her voice was strong, but lacked conviction.

"I'm very sorry," Elle answered. Henry was impressed by the sincerity of her words to a woman who had been nothing but unpleasant to her. "I know it's painful, but you deserve to know the truth. He attempted to kill Henry, and in doing so has harmed another. He shows no remorse. If you don't believe me, ask him about the olives, and why he instructed you not to eat them."

Rachael blinked in confusion. "How do you know that?"

"I know potions. He has poisoned the household. I wish it were not so. I realize there is no love lost between us, but even so, I wouldn't have you at the mercy of such a monster. Return to your family, Mrs. Fasching."

"You're lying," Rachael insisted. It was almost a plea, and her fear showed in her eyes.

"I have taken enough of your time," Elle said. "I wish you all the best."

She started toward her room. Rachael's door closed with a soft click and the lock turned.

"That was very kind," Henry said.

"It doesn't appear she was complicit in this murder. She needed to hear the truth. He doesn't yet know she knows. It may be the only chance she has to be free of him. I will pray for her safety."

"I don't deserve you."

"Nonsense."

"I would never even have thought to approach her."

"You are still hurt because you loved her and she was cruel to you."

He shook his head. "I'm long over that. I don't care a whit for her. But she has sought to injure you, and that I'm not so forgiving of."

"You are overprotective of me. It's a flaw, true, but a charming one." She opened her door and gestured for him to enter. "Come, help me dress and pack my things. I would prefer not to be parted from you until we are away from this house."

"I can't disagree with that."

"Also, you are looking very ill, and I think you could use another dose of stamina potion."

Her bluntness made him smile. "Spoken like an Ainsworth."

"Indeed. You are a terrible influence."

He grimaced because he thought she might be right.

XXXVIII

Family Planning

$\mathcal{E}$LLE PERCHED ON THE EDGE OF THE SOFA in the hotel suite, opposite Emma and Reggie. After enduring police questioning about the dead man and a hectic exit from the Johnson household, the group had finally settled itself with a calm dinner and a bedtime send-off for the children that involved a made-up story about Henry narrowly escaping a tiger in India.

At least, Elle assumed it was made-up. Or grossly exaggerated. Certainly he didn't have "a scar from the beast's razor-sharp fangs in a place too private to share." She would know.

With the children tucked into bed at last, the adults had gathered in the sitting room to sip tea and finalize plans for their departure.

The Faradays sat close together, the intimacy between them clear, though they weren't touching. They shared private smiles and long looks, and Elle felt a twinge of envy. Westfield occupied the other half of her sofa, forcing her and Henry to sit apart. The attempt to thwart their affair infuriated her. When Henry lowered himself into an easy chair, she found herself tempted to sit upon his lap. She would have done, if not for her work.

"I booked our passage to England, as you requested," Reggie said to Westfield. "All our names are registered as passengers. We have one large room for my family and the two first class cabins you requested."

Westfield nodded. "Excellent. Henry, you will share my cabin this time. There is no need for you to suffer down in third class again."

Henry glowered, not liking the meddling any better than she did. "I can pay for a room of my own, if finances are an issue."

"I think not. There has been altogether too much sneaking about during this campaign. I would like the both of you where I can keep an eye on you."

Enough. Elle sprang from her seat, startling Westfield, who rose as well. Reggie began to stand, but Emma gripped his arm to keep him still. Henry leaned back in his chair and folded his arms across his chest.

"This ought to be entertaining."

"You don't need to get up, Uncle," Elle said, her casual tone a thin coating for the resentment bubbling underneath. "I thought, since you seated yourself before the ladies, we weren't standing on propriety this evening."

"I'm sorry, my dear. I wasn't thinking."

"You were thinking, just not about things that matter. I'm sick of this game. I'm a grown woman and I will do as I damn well please."

Westfield gasped at her cursing, but she pressed on.

"Henry will share my stateroom onboard the ship. He is my bodyguard, and he will see me safely all the way to London. What we do or do not do during that time is of no concern to anyone but ourselves. I will not be questioned, lectured, or ordered about.

"Do you know when our work was the most effective? When we were left alone. If you expect me to have a presentation of our findings prepared for your generals and courtiers and parliamentarians, then you had best do exactly that. I don't respond well to harassment."

"I have no intent to harass you, Miss Deschamps." The formality of his voice and address pained her. "I intend only to protect you from those who would do. I do not wish a repeat of what happened here in New York."

"I appreciate the concern, but I'm not a child who needs minding. I'm not even your niece in reality. In little more than a week, my employment will be at an end, and I will no longer need to pretend to your social class. I will be no more than Elle at the bar, and I will never see any of you again." Her voice caught, and she fought to control it. "The least you could do is give me a little bit of peace before that happens."

"Elle…"

Henry leapt from his seat and reached for her, but she brushed past him and slipped into the bedroom where the children were sleeping. Tears stung her eyes, and she wiped them angrily with the back of her hand, frustrated with her own show of weakness. She leaned back against the door to prevent anyone from following her. The doorknob rattled, and the door shifted. She banged it closed with her hip.

"Ow! Dammit, Elle!"

She didn't budge.

"Darling, please talk to me," Henry begged.

"I can't," she replied, still fighting the tears. She couldn't bring herself to look at him. She could hardly stand the sound of his voice. Every word was a stabbing reminder of what could not be. She slid down the door until she was seated on the floor.

A bed creaked, and George Faraday climbed out.

"Aunt Elle? Is something wrong? Are you and Uncle Henry quarreling?"

She shook her head. "Go back to bed, Georgey. I'm sorry to disturb you."

He stared at her in the dim light, stubbornly ignoring her instructions.

"You need a handkerchief!" He dashed across the room, dug through his possessions, and rushed back to her, thrusting the white square of silk into her hands. "A gentleman should always be prepared to offer a lady a handkerchief if she has need of one," he declared.

Elle dabbed at her eyes. "Thank you, Georgey. You're sweet."

The boy sat down beside her. "Why are you sad?" When she didn't respond, he added, "Did Uncle Henry make you sad?"

"No. It wasn't his fault." She was certain Henry remained by the door, listening to her every word.

"Then why don't you want to talk to him?"

"I don't want to talk to anyone."

Georgey frowned at her. "You're talking to me."

She couldn't help but smile. "That's true. I guess you're special." She patted her eyes once again, and then handed him the handkerchief. "Thank you, young man, for your kindness and good manners. You will make a fine gentleman one day. To do that, however, you need to mind your mother, so you must return to bed now."

He nodded vigorously. "I will. I hope you feel better soon. Good night, Aunt Elle."

He hugged her, and she gave him a squeeze and kissed his cheek. "Good night, dear."

He scurried off to bed, and she climbed to her feet, wondering how he had bolstered her spirits with just that bit of boyish charm. What was it about the Ainsworth blood that made the males of the family so endearing to her?

She opened the door. As she expected, Henry stood waiting for her.

"We have business to discuss," she said before he could open his mouth. She strode to the sofa, and sat with as dignified an air as she could manage. "I apologize for the outburst. The stress of these last few days has taken its toll. I think it best we drop the subject of our ocean voyage and concentrate on what work remains to be done."

The ensuing discussion was sober and focused. Elle gave a brief outline of everything she had learned, including the locations of the major serum sources, the discovery of the tiny sources, and her efforts at extracting serum directly from the dirt.

"We learned a lot during the last round of experiments. The warm water was more effective than cold, and the optimal steeping time seemed to be about an hour. Anything longer than that had no added benefit. The agitation test was somewhat inconclusive, so I wish to run that again. I will then combine all the best results into a single procedure and see how well it extracts the serum. We've made a great deal of progress, and I'm confident we will have good findings to report, even if some tweaking remains."

"Don't forget about distilling," Henry added.

"Yes. Once we are in London, do you think we could get access to a distillery?" she asked Westfield. "I should like to run the serum-laced water through a still and see how pure we can make it. I have so far boiled the water, as you might do making syrup. It works, but distillation may be better."

Westfield nodded. "We will see what we can do. I think once you present this information everyone will be eager to help you complete the research."

"Everyone who doesn't hold shares in the Imperial Potions Company, at least," Henry corrected.

Reggie looked concerned. "I hold shares in the Imperial Potions Company. Should I sell them?"

"Yes, immediately. The men and women who control the company are wound up so tightly in this mess that you risk an enormous loss. The whole business could well go under. There's a chance, of course, that I'm giving you terrible advice and the shares will increase in value, but since that won't happen unless we are all killed before we have the chance to denounce them, I don't think you would enjoy the profits."

"I should think not."

"I've requested a list of the largest shareholders, but I haven't yet received one. I know Charlotte de Winter tops the list, but I hope to learn the names of the others as well. There might be some among the crowd Elle will be addressing, and that could pose a danger."

Emma put a hand to her head. "How do you live like this, Henry? I swear, I would go mad if I were constantly worrying and calculating and avoiding deadly enemies."

"This is unusual," he replied. "Most of my missions involve sneaking into places I'm not supposed to be and making notes and maps to give everyone else some idea of the area. That and integrating myself into some particular group or culture, learning about it, and reporting on it."

"Trespassing and eavesdropping," Emma sighed. "It's a terribly unsavory profession, Henry."

He shrugged. "It suits me. Take that as you will."

The conversation dwindled, and they poured more tea and chatted about happier subjects. Emma kept the others talking. She offered to show Elle some of the sights in London, reported to Henry on how the rest of the family fared, and when all else failed, turned to the topic of books, which gave the opinionated group plenty to discuss until the hour grew late enough to retire.

With only two rooms in the suite, one had been designated for the women and children, and the other for the men. Henry lingered in the sitting room, and Elle approached him to have a word in private before turning in.

"I won't leave you," he vowed. "You will never be just 'Elle at the bar' to me. I swear it."

"I'm trying to be realistic, Henry. I don't belong in your world, and you don't belong in mine."

"I don't give a damn. I would follow you to the ends of the earth."

He reached for her, and she stepped into the embrace, laying her head against his shoulder as his arms tightened around her. It was a tantalizing dream, to believe they could be together. If Emma accepted her, wasn't there a chance others could as well?

But Emma had only ever seen her as a lady and had no idea of Elle's longing for her own potion business or her need for independence. The only way to keep both her dream and Henry would be to drag him down with her, and she couldn't do that to him. She wouldn't.

Henry stroked her hair. "We will manage," he whispered.

"Please, don't say such things. I don't want to see your heart broken."

"I'm a spy, love. Risk comes with the job. I will take my chances."

She looked up into his eyes and he kissed her. For that moment, she allowed herself to forget everything but the taste of him and the feel of his hard body crushed against her own. But there was no place here for them to be alone, and all too soon they slid apart.

"Pleasant dreams, chérie," he murmured.

She smiled at him and touched the tip of his nose with her finger. "Hopefully, I will dream of you."

Emma waited for her in the bedroom. "Things are well between you and Henry?" she asked, keeping her voice soft so as not to wake the children.

Elle nodded and began to undress. Emma stepped closer to help her with the buttons. It was a sisterly gesture, and Elle felt another tug on her heartstrings. How she longed to be a part of this family.

"He will never give it up, you know," she said.

"I beg your pardon?"

"The spying. I know you all disapprove, but Henry won't give it up, whatever you might say. He loves it. You haven't seen the way his eyes light up when he has made a discovery. You haven't heard the thrill in his voice when something is exciting or dangerous. You don't know the satisfaction he gets from the mental challenge of noticing and remembering so many minute details."

Emma pursed her lips in thought. "You mustn't tell him this," she said at last, "because I have been sworn to secrecy, but Father did similar work when he was younger. It's how he earned his title. He decided it was dangerous and gave it up to start a family."

Elle nodded. The family dynamic was clearer now. "He wants Henry to do the same thing."

"Yes. But Henry has too much of Mother's Scottish independence. He won't listen to us."

"You exhibit a certain amount of that independence yourself, Emma. And I see it in your children, as well."

"I know. It both pleases me and scares me. I hope you don't have too much difficulty in raising your own children, seeing how they will inherit it from both sides."

Elle lay a hand over her belly. She couldn't remember a time when she hadn't dreamed of children and a family of her own. And Henry would be such a wonderful father. Her eyes misted over. Another impossible hope. Another regret.

"If I am blessed with a child I will take her however she comes. Or he, if it is a son. Don't assume, though, that it's likely to happen."

"I think it very likely. You need only to ask him, and Henry will do anything you request. I'm certain of it. Ask him to give up spying and settle down with you. You will be well off. The family business is thriving."

"No."

Emma blinked in confusion. "No?"

"I would never ask that of him. I couldn't possibly condemn him to a life of boredom to satisfy my own selfish desires. And what would I do as the wife of a wealthy businessman? Attend fancy parties? Spend his money on fripperies? It has been enough of a trial to pose as upper class for as long as I have done. It's impossible. We would each end up resenting the other and our life would be a misery."

Elle unfastened the last hook of her corset and slipped it off, then pulled her nightgown on over her chemise and drawers. She preferred to wear the gown alone, but modesty won out when sharing a room. Emma's nightgown had a low neckline and was nearly thin enough to see through. Intended to entice her husband, perhaps? In spite of their conservative public appearance, they were a deeply passionate couple.

"I will think of something," Emma decided. "I'm determined to make you my sister-in-law."

"I wish you luck," Elle replied. She slipped into bed and let her silent tears dampen the pillow, wishing she knew how to end things easily, how to quash that futile spark of hope. Tomorrow, she knew, she would surrender to it once again, seizing all she could of love and happiness. Perhaps the heartbreak would be worth it.

XXXIX

The Spy Lessons Resume

"$\mathcal{A}$RE YOU RESPONSIBLE FOR Miss Deschamps' unusual attire this morning?" Westfield asked, as they watched the hotel porter loading their trunks onto the carriage. Henry thought he sounded defeated, as if he had finally accepted he had no control over Elle.

"Absolutely. I forced her into the garments myself."

Westfield sighed. "I think I have said before that I do not appreciate your sarcasm."

"No one appreciates my sarcasm, sir. I won't hold it against you."

"Will you at least share your plans with me so I won't worry? It's clear the two of you are conspiring again."

Henry chuckled. "Nothing too extraordinary. I will be giving her a few more lessons, is all. She has chosen something comfortable and modest. You ought to be pleased by that."

"Truly, I don't know what to be pleased about, these days," he admitted. "I can only beg you to make an honest woman of her before long."

"There is nothing dishonest about her. In fact, she has scolded me often for lying."

"Henry…"

"Language is a funny thing, isn't it?"

Westfield shook his head. "I feel sorry for your father. The combination of your clever mind and stubborn eccentricity can be most trying." His expression grew thoughtful. "It is also a great asset, so I will refrain from telling you you ought to be ordinary."

"Thank you. You may consider saying something similar to Elle. I'm sure she thinks you would prefer her to be ordinary."

"No." The older man shook his head and then chuckled. "No, I would not love her half so much were she ordinary."

Elle stood some distance away, bouncing little Daisy in her arms, reciting the French words for everything the little girl pointed at. She caught Henry's eye and gave him an arch smile. She knew they were talking about her.

The outfit became her well. She wore her simple black dress, with her boy's trousers underneath instead of petticoats. Her sturdy boots peeped out from beneath the hem. She had added a jaunty black hat to the ensemble that Henry particularly liked. She was a woman ready to take on any challenge and she would look cute doing it.

Henry had opted for practical attire today as well, wearing his black work clothes, his bowler, and his most comfortable boots. He'd thrown a suit coat on, to look more as if he actually belonged in first class, but the outfit had already been met with skepticism. His sister had declared he looked "like a gambler."

Despite the criticism from family, no one paid any heed to their unconventional dress during the ride to port or during boarding. In fact, the passengers were all so busy with their own arrangements that Elle and Henry had been up on the deck for near an hour before more than a few people began to take notice of their sparring.

"We're gathering quite an audience," Henry said as Elle took another swing at him. "And you're still hesitating."

"Let them watch. I don't care."

She tried again, but he shook his head. "You need to really try to hit me. Don't pretend."

"I don't want to hurt you."

He threw a punch of his own, and she blocked it well. The defense, at least, she had taken to with ease. He needed to get her mad to put her in an offensive frame of mind. "You aren't strong enough to hurt me."

She was no weakling, and if she bothered to stop to think about it, she would realize he knew that. She reacted emotionally to the lie, however, as he had hoped. Her eyes narrowed and her stance widened.

"Hit me," he challenged. "I dare you."

Her fist flew at his shoulder—she was still trying not to hurt him—but with far better velocity and power. He put up a hand to take the blow, and her knuckles smashed against his palm. It stung more than he had expected.

"Much better. That was a proper punch."

"You angered me intentionally," she accused, realizing what he had done.

He grinned. "And now you are mad that I made you mad. It's perfect. Let's fight."

For the next several minutes he fended off her punches, all the while pestering her with jabs and kicks, testing the blocks and dodges they had drilled at the beginning of the lesson. She responded well, so he changed tactics, and moved in closer to try to grab her. She spun away from his first attempt, displaying her agility, but made the mistake of turning her back on him. He lunged at her from behind, pinning both her arms at her sides. She wriggled in his grasp, which he found uncomfortably arousing.

"Don't let your attacker get—" He yelped in pain as the solid heel of her boot collided with his shin. It threw him off balance just enough that she was able to twist her body around. Her knee came up toward his groin and he jumped backward so quickly that he stumbled and crashed to the ground.

"Damnation, woman, don't damage me!"

She walked over and held out a hand to help him up. "I wouldn't truly have struck you, Henry."

He clasped her hand and climbed to his feet. "Is that so?" he asked skeptically.

"It is." She stepped close to him. "I'm rather fond of that part of your body, you know."

He was aware of the heat rising in his cheeks and the crowd of people still watching them, and he tried to confine the conversation to the training. "You did well. I made the mistake of assuming I had won, and you took advantage of that, as the giant bruise on my shin will no doubt testify to. You made a mistake of your own, however, when you let me get behind you. We will work on that tomorrow. I think we've done quite enough for one session."

"I'm glad you think so," she admitted. "I have grown both tired and hungry from the exertion."

"If you ever need to rest while we are doing this, you need only ask."

"Thank you, but I had rather push myself here, in a safe environment, to gain strength and know my limits before I ever have to put any of this knowledge to use."

"I hope you shall never have to put any of this to use."

She looped her arm through his. "I hope so, too, but we must not kid ourselves. I think chances are high there are enemies aboard this very ship."

Henry winced, thinking about the last time an enemy had been aboard their ship. "At least now you are my lover in truth," he whispered. "I won't feel quite so bad if you need to provide me an alibi for murder."

"I will take more care on this voyage. Neither of us ought to go anywhere alone or unarmed." She nudged him. "Your sister is headed this way. I wonder if she has been watching us."

"Yes. I noticed her some time ago."

"You were scanning the crowd?"

"Always."

"I have found you your new profession, Henry," Emma declared, not bothering with any sort of greeting.

"I can't wait to hear about it."

"Don't be sarcastic. It's most unattractive."

Elle's eyes twinkled, and he decided that perhaps one person liked his impertinence after all.

"Elle doesn't think so."

"Elle is newly in love," his sister rationalized. "Some day she, too, will sigh and roll her eyes and wonder why she puts up with you."

"Oh, she does that plenty. Usually when I make some attempt to be chivalrous. She protests when I carry things for her."

Elle and Emma both frowned, for entirely different reasons.

"That's peculiar. But not on topic. Your new job." She placed her hand on his free arm. "I was watching you just now, and it occurred to me that you are very good at this business of teaching spy techniques. You could make a living with those skills. You wouldn't have to give up the career entirely, and you wouldn't make the rest of us worry for your safety."

Emma's idea had merit, and he did enjoy teaching Elle, but it could never be the permanent solution his family longed for. He knew himself. Knew just how much he craved action and adventure. A month or two of inaction and he'd be begging for a new assignment.

"I'll start teaching when I start getting too old for the work," he replied. "I learned from the men who had this job before me. It's expected I will do the same for the next generation, but it will be some time, yet, before that happens. I'm sorry to dash all your hopes."

"You don't sound sorry at all," she huffed.

"My apologies. I'm a habitual liar."

"It's a very good thing we aren't children anymore, or else I would slap you."

"I have missed out on a lot of arguments, it seems, by virtue of growing up without brothers or sisters," Elle mused.

"I am certain Emma will argue with you, if you desire," Henry told her. "It's her favorite amusement."

"That is entirely false, a fact which we can discuss over tea. Come down to the dining room with me. I'm sure the rest of the family has already arrived."

Henry slipped free of his sister's grasp. "No, thank you. Elle and I will be taking tea alone this afternoon."

Elle looked startled. "We will?"

"Yes. I've made arrangements similar to those during our previous ocean voyage."

A grin spread across her face. "Now I'm intrigued. Will we be stopping by the kitchen on the way to our customary meeting place?"

"Indeed."

"Do I want to know?" Emma asked.

"No. And yes. Either way, I won't tell you. We will see you again at dinner."

"Very well," she sighed. "I'd best get back to the children. Reggie is beginning to tire of them."

"I will mind them for you tomorrow morning, if you wish some time alone with your husband," Elle offered.

Emma's eyes lit up. "Would you? Elle, you are such a dear." She gave the other woman a kiss on the cheek. "I will see you at dinner."

"I think I will be kicked out of the family, and they will claim you in my stead," Henry observed, after Emma had departed.

Elle shook her head. "Your family loves you. They just don't understand you."

"You do, though."

She smiled. "I'm trying. You still baffle me on occasion."

He couldn't help but laugh. "I know the feeling."

$\cdots \mathbf{\hat{o}} \cdots$

Elle stretched out in the lifeboat, trying to decide which she was enjoying more: eating her food or watching Henry eat his. Today if he got any jam on his face, she would lick it off. Or perhaps he could lick some off of her, she considered, taking a bite of her jam-laden scone. His eyes were on her mouth. She wet her lips.

"Enjoying your meal, love?" he asked.

"Yes. You?"

His wide smile made deep dimples in his cheeks. "I'm enjoying watching you."

She laughed. "We seem to be very in tune with one another today." She took another bite. The scone was buttery, flaky, and sweet. "The food is something I will miss when I end my days as a fine lady," she sighed. "My pay is enough that I will have better fare than I did in the past, but it won't be so good as this, and there will be less meat and no fresh seafood unless I move to the seaside. I swear I must have gained twenty pounds since I left Paris."

"Unlikely. You don't look different from when we first met, and you are wearing many of the same clothes, unaltered."

"I exaggerate, of course, but I'm certain there is more weight around my hips than before."

"You have lovely hips. They are full and curvy and…" He adjusted his breeches. "…Very feminine."

"Thank you. I hope to keep them that way. It's not always easy when money is tight. There were times, before I acquired the job at the Folies, when we were forced to choose between food and rent. I intend to take care that doesn't happen in the future."

"It will certainly not happen on my watch." Henry poured himself another cup of tea and picked an olive off of his sandwich. "I wish they hadn't given us olives. I can't stand the thought of eating them." He peeled back the bread to check for any he may have missed.

"Henry, they aren't poisoned," Elle laughed.

"Even so, I don't want to eat them."

"If you can collect an assortment of beverages for us at dinner, we can begin your poison training. I think it best to do it in the evening in our cabin, as you will need to taste the ingredients in spirits as well as water and tea, so there is the possibility for some tipsiness."

"I don't think I entirely approve of this plan. Last time I was intoxicated you wouldn't make love to me."

"You were groping me in the library and your life was in danger."

"Was it the library? I don't recall. I only remember disappointment. I suppose I wasn't in my right mind that night."

"Not at all. Don't worry. I will stop long before you reach that sort of state. If you are a quick study, you may not feel even slightly off. Regardless, I have no desire to keep you from my bed."

"Good. It has been an age."

"You are always so theatrical. One would think you hadn't seen me in months. We were last together three nights ago."

"Ah! So you are counting the days."

She gave him a flirtatious smile. "Perhaps."

He set down his teacup and slid closer to her. "We have already completed your lesson for the day, and mine won't begin until after dinner. There is damn little to do on this ship, so we shall have to find some way to pass the time."

"We could play chess," she teased.

He covered her body with his own. His hot breath caressed her cheek. His lips brushed her earlobe. "Knight takes queen," he murmured, his voice low and husky.

The tickle of fingertips down the side of her neck made her breath catch. He slipped his fingers beneath her neckline, his light touch across the swell of her breasts making her tingle in anticipation.

"Isn't the queen the most powerful piece?" Her fingers tugged at the buttons of his shirt.

"Yes. Perhaps she sacrificed herself. It's necessary, sometimes, to win the game."

"Is it? I don't play well. I have never owned a chess set."

His kisses began to follow his hands, trailing down her throat to the top of her chest. Her skin burned.

"I assure you, it's a time-honored strategy."

Her fingers popped the last of the buttons on his shirt, and she pried it open and pulled it down off his shoulders, baring him to her touch and her sight. It was dark beneath the tarpaulin, but their potion-fueled lantern bathed them in a smooth, yellow glow. It felt to her like making love beneath a sunset, and she vowed to compare the two someday.

His skin was flushed already. She loved the feel of it, warm and smooth beneath her hands. She would never tire of his strong, solid flesh. She explored his chest, teasing his nipples, tracing the trail of fine, blond hairs down his flat belly to where it disappeared beneath his waistband. She admired the outline of his hard shaft beneath his snug breeches. She would divest him of those, as well.

Not to be outdone, Henry began to undress her, swiftly removing her boots and trousers. She had to pause in her own efforts to allow him to pull the dress over her head. He tossed it aside and grinned down at her. She wore nothing, now, save for her corset and stockings.

"I see you have chosen a limited selection of undergarments today." Henry finished pulling off his own clothing, and his hands settled on the hips he had praised earlier. "I approve. This look suits you."

"Now you sound a libertine," she laughed.

"Fortunately, I have a devoted woman who is willing to assuage my lustful desires."

He kissed her breasts where they bulged from the top of her corset. His hands, still on her hips, drew her tightly to him. Her pulse raced as the fullness of his erection rubbed along her inner thigh. She pressed against him, ready to take him inside of her, but he pulled away.

"As a libertine, I think it my duty to expand our repertoire. I'd like to try something different."

She frowned at him, puzzled, but curious. He slid down her body, easing her legs apart, and planted a kiss among the tangle of curls where they joined. Ah. So that was what he intended.

"You learned this from your book of naughty pictures, didn't you?"

"Mmmm," was his only reply, and then his mouth was on her, hot and wet against her sex. She closed her eyes and let the sensations wash over her. He kissed her, explored her, tasted her. When his tongue flicked at her clit, her lips parted in a gasp of pure delight.

"Oh, Henry," she moaned. "That is… it is… mon Dieu."

Frissons of pleasure coursed down her legs, up her spine, and out to the very tips of her fingers as he licked and sucked her exquisitely sensitive flesh. The ache of desire between her legs swelled with each tiny movement of his mouth. She stretched her arms above her head to brace herself against the wooden slats of the lifeboat, certain that any moment she would shatter into a million pieces.

She cried out when the climax took her, forgetting she wasn't in her own bedroom, and someone might overhear. Tremors racked her body as the agony of bliss washed over her. She put a hand to her temple and sighed. Her clenched muscles loosened and a soothing satisfaction spread across her body.

"That was magnificent," she breathed.

Henry crawled back up next to her, kissing her brow and letting her snuggle against him as she recovered from the shattering orgasm. Giving all she needed. Asking nothing in return. Loving her.

Forever, she thought to herself. *I want this forever.*

Her whole body ached with longing for him. She wanted to share his home and bear his children. She wanted to be his one and only for life. See the world with him. Grow old with him.

She would never manage as a high-class lady, but she could learn to be some approximation of a gentleman's wife. Good enough for a Captain Ainsworth, though perhaps a bit short of a Lord Henry. And while he couldn't marry a shopkeeper, the match might be acceptable if she abandoned the dream of her potion shop. She didn't know who she would be without it, what her purpose would become. Maybe she wouldn't have one. Maybe the idea was terrible and she would end up miserable. But for the first time she was giving it serious consideration.

Elle eased herself from his arms. The long journey would afford her plenty of time to think. For now she would simply love him.

She arched her eyebrows as she gazed into his deep blue eyes and gave him a wicked smile.

"Now it's your turn."

Henry blinked. He'd been admiring the look of happiness on her face when it had morphed in an instant into a predatory gleam.

"On your back, please," she instructed.

He didn't think he could have disobeyed if he'd wanted to. His body was so hungry for her touch he suspected it had a mind of its own. She wasn't really going to do what he thought she was, was she? Ladies didn't…

Her lips brushed the tip of his cock. "Oh, God," he moaned. "Elle. You don't have to… I don't…"

"Hush." Her warm breath on his skin made him tremble.

She kissed up and down the length of him, her tongue snaking out to caress him. Her hand cupped his bollocks and played with him as her mouth continued to explore. He groaned in ecstasy, certain he could die on the spot and consider it a life well-lived.

The sparkle in her eye as she pleasured him was almost enough on its own to kill him. She knew what she was doing to him and she was enjoying it.

She took him fully into her mouth, her fingers curling around the base of his shaft. Her strokes matched the movement of her lips, teasing him, tormenting him, until he could stand the slick heat of her no longer. His back arced. His fingers tangled in her hair. A strangled sound tore from his throat and he lost himself inside of her.

Elle lifted herself off of him and stretched out at his side, her fingers toying with the hairs on his chest.

"Excellent choice, Henry. I would be happy to repeat that particular exercise in the future."

"I enjoyed it fully as much as the times you have been up on top," he said, then blushed furiously. Only weeks ago he would never have thought himself capable of saying such things to a woman.

"You never answered me before. Were there pictures of what we did in your book?"

"Bloody hell, I'm going to have to scare up one of the damned things just to satisfy your curiosity."

"It could be useful. The instructions must be quite good, because you are an excellent lover."

"I should never have mentioned it. It's not fit for a lady's eyes. It's not even fit for a gentleman's eyes, I'm certain."

"Bah. I don't care. A lady doesn't look at naughty pictures? I imagine a lady doesn't have any fun in the bedroom, either. She lays like a board on the bed and waits for her husband to do his duty, oui?"

"I don't know, but I'm positive she doesn't suck on a man's cock," he blurted, still unable to get past the fact that she was not only willing, but eager to do such a thing for him.

"Then it's very good for you I'm not a lady," Elle declared. "I never have been, and I never will be, and that should please you, because you don't want a lady, do you?"

He stared at her for a long moment, gaping like a fool, the truth of her words sinking in.

"No. I don't," he replied at last. "I want a woman who isn't afraid to speak her mind." He had his family to thank for that particular desire. "I want a woman who knows what she is about. Who knows what she wants and is willing to work for it. A woman who values the same things I do, and society be damned." He grinned sheepishly. "And a woman who looks past my all-too-frequent cursing."

Elle's musical laugh warmed his heart. She snuggled against him and kissed his neck. "You love me for all my quirks. It's only fair I should love you for yours."

"You love me?" His whole body jerked, the movement causing him to realize something had been poking into his back this entire time. "Ow."

"Have I never said so before? And why are you wincing?"

"I think I was lying on a nail."

Elle sat up at once. "Let me see."

He turned his back and her delicate touch ran down his spine. As soft as her fingers were, he still flinched when she reached the injury.

"That is quite the scratch. Why didn't you say something?"

"I didn't notice," he admitted. A wicked smile spread across his features. "Regardless, it was worth the price."

She returned his grin. "Tomorrow you can steal a hammer so it won't happen again. When we return to our room this evening I will rub some ointment on it."

"Ointment, eh?"

"Yes. My favorite fully herbal balm. Not a drop of serum, but it smells of lavender and it is warm and soothing."

He examined his shin where she had kicked him earlier. "I'm afraid I have many scratches and bruises all over my body. You may have to do quite a lot of rubbing."

She wet her lips as her eyes raked over him. "As much as you need, mon coeur, but I expect you to return the favor."

"Of course." He drew her close and lay his head atop hers. "Do you really love me?"

"I do. More every day."

Marry me.

He couldn't ask it. He wouldn't steal her chance for independence. He would see her in that potion shop if it killed him.

He had nine days until they reached London. Nine days of love and laughter and secret trysts. Nine days to plot how to turn their time into forever.

XL

Sworn Duty

"Mother, why must we leave again so soon?" Georgey complained. "We arrived home only yesterday."

Emma sighed and restated what she had told him a few minutes earlier. "Your Uncle Henry thinks it may be dangerous here, and I'm inclined to agree. You father and I have decided it's best to go to Italy and spend some time with your grandparents and cousins. We haven't visited since Christmas. You will enjoy the summer there."

"I want to stay here and help. I'm old enough to be of use."

To prove his point, he walked about the room, distributing the day's mail to everyone in the household. Henry suspected he just wanted to see who was receiving letters from whom, and sneak a peek at the contents if he had the chance.

"You will do as your mother says, young man," Reggie scolded. "Now say goodbye so we can be on our way."

Georgey sighed. He handed Henry a stack of letters and then wrapped both arms around his waist.

"I will miss you, Uncle Henry. You must visit me again soon and give me more spying lessons."

Henry ruffled the boy's hair and ignored Emma's frown. "Goodbye, Georgey. Take good care of the family."

The boy released him and nodded fervently. "I promise."

Georgey rushed over to embrace Elle, who already had Lily in her arms and Daisy clinging to her skirts.

"I'll dig up more potions for you in Italy," Lily promised, pressing her dirty face against Elle's cheek. "Just like I found in our garden."

"I'm sure you will." Elle kissed her, set her down, and picked up her sister. *"Au revoir, ma petite fleur."*

"Au revoir," Daisy said, lifting her chin for a kiss of her own.

Somehow, Elle managed to squirm free from the Faraday children long enough to say farewell to their parents. Reggie gave her a peck on the cheek, and she and Emma exchanged a long hug and warm smiles.

"Thank you for your expertise as a seamstress," Elle said, smoothing down her dress. "I would never spy the new pockets if I didn't know of them."

"You're most welcome. It was the least I could do after you occupied the children so often onboard ship. Reggie and I had more time to relax than we have had in years!"

"You have a lovely family. Thank you for sharing them with me for a time."

There was a resignation in Elle's tone, a sense that she was waiting for some inevitable tragedy to tear them apart. Henry couldn't blame her. Her life had been hard. She'd seen her family stripped away from her, one after another. Well, no more. She deserved some happiness, and he was bloody well going to see she got it.

He joined the family, kissed his nieces, shook Reggie's hand, and hugged his sister.

"You had better marry her, Henry," Emma whispered, "or you shall break all our hearts."

"Yours are in far less danger than mine, I assure you. Put in a good word for me with Father."

"Ha! I shall tell him you have behaved abominably. You know he won't be happy unless he has a reason to scold you."

"Splendid."

"Do try to work on the sarcasm and the cursing before our next visit," she sighed.

"I shall practice both as often as possible."

"Oh, you!" She punched him in the shoulder. "I'm sorry. That wasn't very ladylike."

He laughed. "Safe travels, Emma. I love you all and will see you when I can."

She looked back and forth between him and Elle. "Take care of one another."

"We will," Henry promised, taking hold of Elle's hand. She nodded in agreement. They waved their goodbyes and watched until the Faraday carriage disappeared from sight.

He turned at last to the stack of telegrams in his hand. All save one were requests he meet promptly for debriefing and submit a full report in writing. The last, a frantic missive from Colonel Wilton-Bowles dated the night before, set him on edge. He read it aloud to Elle.

"Rachael arrived alone and in a panic. She fears for her life. What has happened? Come at once."

"Was she on the ship with us?"

"I don't know. I didn't read the passenger manifest. It doesn't matter. There are other, faster ships. Not as comfortable, perhaps, but anyone who truly wanted to could have left a day after us and arrived by now."

"So Fasching could be here as well. He could be at that very house, chasing his runaway wife."

"I'm working under the assumption all our enemies are in London. That's why I sent my family away." He tucked the letters into a pocket. "I'm going to gather my things and pay a visit to the Wilton-Bowles household. I no longer report to him since leaving the army, but my stopping in won't be so unusual as to draw suspicion. When I'm done there, I will have to make my official reports. I'll likely be gone until evening."

"*Non et non!*" She grabbed his arm. "It's too dangerous. I won't let you go alone."

"You can't come with me. The reports are confidential."

"I have read your reports. You had me edit them for accuracy!"

"The papers, yes. The face-to-face meetings are confidential. I can't reveal my contacts. You can't come. I'm sorry."

"Westfield has already gone out to finalize arrangements for our presentation," she argued. "You would leave me here, unprotected?"

He shook free from her grip, fighting a burst of irritation. "That may have worked on me once upon a time, but now I know better. You don't need my protection, especially while you are safe in the house. You don't even want my protection. You think to protect *me*, and while I appreciate your concern, it won't sway me. I have a job to complete. If it makes you feel better, I will be calling upon friends, and I intend to take my pistol."

She crossed her arms and glared at him. "It does not."

"I'm sorry to leave you alone to worry, but it's my duty and my responsibility to see this finished."

She gave him a curt nod, but he wasn't certain whether that meant she wouldn't protest further, or only that she understood his reasoning. He hated to cause her grief, but such was the natural consequence of being involved with a spy.

A knot twisted inside his gut. Days' worth of carefully crafted plans disintegrated. For the first time, he had to acknowledge she might be right to think they couldn't have a future together. He couldn't marry her, not even if he waited for her to establish herself as a shopkeeper. He couldn't even live with her. Doing so would condemn her to a lifetime of waiting and worrying.

A sensible man would break it off with a sum of money to provide for her and best wishes for her future happiness. The thought made him nauseous. His heart hammered in his chest.

Damned if he did, damned if he didn't.

Enough.

He couldn't dwell on this now. Not when they had

information to deliver that could bring a permanent end to this potions crisis. His report and Elle's testimony would help millions. The small sources would increase potion availability and drive down prices. The mission came first. He couldn't let it be otherwise. He would do his duty. He would be a man deserving of her.

He drew her into his arms dropped a soft kiss on her lips. She relaxed into the embrace, her body sagging against his. Frightened, exhausted—much as he was—but fighting it. So strong. So extraordinary.

A day, perhaps two. He had no guarantee of more. The end had already begun. He would cling to her, fight for her, love her, adore her, work beside her for all he was worth. He would give her everything he had, for whatever time they had remaining. They would see this through. Together.

Then, and only then, would he allow himself a moment to examine the pieces of his shattered heart.

He deepened the kiss, and she yanked him close, claiming his mouth with such hungry, possessive passion that he began to undress her, right there in the foyer.

She eased his hand off her breast and straightened her dress, with a gesture at the butler, who stood nearby at his post, politely looking the other direction. Henry was glad there was no mirror in the room, for he didn't wish to know how red his face was.

"I should go. You will be safe here. If you need anything at all, Carter will help you."

The butler turned and bowed. "I'm at your service, miss."

"Thank you," Elle replied. She turned back to Henry. "Be careful."

"You have my word."

"You are taking your gun and your knife, but you don't yet know all your poisons."

"I won't eat or drink anything."

"No cigars."

"I'm aware of your distaste for tobacco products."

"They could carry poison," she huffed.

"This isn't my first brush with danger, love."

"I know. I'm sorry. This is where you are the expert. I will see you soon." It sounded like a command.

She kissed him again, this time a quick, chaste peck, and disappeared into the house. Henry gathered his papers, his journal, and his pistol and stashed them all in various pockets in his coat.

"Take care of her," he instructed Carter. "Don't let anyone in the house except myself and Westfield. Do you know where Faraday keeps his hunting rifles?"

"I do, and I know which one is loaded."

"Good man."

"I will guard your lady as I would any of the family. She is an Ainsworth de facto, if not yet de jure."

"Did you study law, Carter?"

A smile cracked the butler's usually stoic face. "I have studied many things, my lord. That is why your father chose to employ me."

Henry nodded and started for the door. His hand was on the knob when he turned back.

"Would you be willing to tell me some stories from my father's spying days?"

"What makes you think your father was a spy?"

"Mother has always said I'm more like him than any of the other children. Father has always been very hard on himself. I think he is harder on me than on the others because he, too, sees a reflection of himself in me."

"You are a good lad, Henry. You do him proud."

"Thank you." Henry tipped his hat and departed.

Elle wandered the house in a vain attempt to combat the anxiety of idleness. The sprawling mansion was as cozy a home as she could imagine. Well-used, mismatched furnishings occupied every room. Warm draperies were spread wide to let in the sunlight, with no concern for whether it would fade the rugs and upholstery. Toys and books lay scattered about, evidence of the family who not only resided, but lived here.

The neighborhood, too, was beautiful, bursting with eclectic global decor and the perpetual smell of curry. A happy, vibrant place, full of nouveau riche and foreigners. A place where she could belong.

She missed the boisterous Faradays already. Her own family had been boisterous once. All she remembered of the time when her father and brother were alive was a sense of noise and happiness. Things had been more subdued without them, but her mother and grandmother had been lively and had kept busy. Elle felt their absence keenly today.

In the study, she ran her fingers across an old desk that generations of youngsters had carved their initials into. A recent marking read "GRF"—Georgey's handiwork. Elle had to search for some time to find the small "HCMA" that Henry had carved years ago. He'd scratched it on the underside, next to the rear leg, where no one would see it without a deliberate search. Emma's elegant script "EA" lay precisely in the center. Beside it, very small and clean, were the letters "RF". Spouses, too, were represented on this odd family heirloom. The whole family. A family Elle yearned for with all of her heart.

For days she had agonized over her situation, considering sacrifices, weighing the consequences.

Every solution seemed destined to end in misery. The thought of giving up her dream made her want to cry, and she had no guarantee it would even result in a future with Henry. Leaving him to pursue her potion shop alone was similarly unthinkable. Trying to get both looked impossible. She couldn't live as his mistress because respectability was key to a successful business. She couldn't marry him without either giving up the shop or damaging his relationships and his career.

While the Faradays accepted her, Henry's parents had

titles and reputations to protect. His brothers were—according to Emma—extremely proper. Elle couldn't let herself be the wedge between Henry and the people he loved.

Soon enough they would go their separate ways, and this would all fade. They would both move on, knowing it had never been meant to be. Wouldn't they?

She retrieved her penknife from her potions bag, crawled beneath the desk, and carved her initials beneath Henry's. It might be years before some youngster discovered the markings and wondered who had made them. Perhaps no one would ever know. But she would remember. She scratched a little heart, overlapping her E and his H. A physical reminder that he would always own some piece of her. And her of him. Even if she never saw him again.

"I see you have joined in the family tradition of defacing furniture."

Elle came within a hair's width of smashing her head on the desk. She needed more spy lessons, if someone could enter the room without her noticing. Or perhaps Carter the butler was as sneaky as the family he served.

He waited patiently as she wiggled her way out from under the desk, and then offered a hand to help her up.

"A message arrived for you, mademoiselle. I'm informed it is urgent."

Elle looked at the letter. There was no address or marking on the outside save for her name, written in an unfamiliar hand. She ripped it open and read the contents.

> *Your uncle has come to stay for a few days. He would like you to visit that we may discuss the speech you have been preparing. If we do not hear from you shortly, we will send someone to fetch you.*
>
> *CdW*

"*Merde!*"

"Is there anything I can do to help?" Carter asked.

"Do you know where Lady Charlotte de Winter lives?"

"I do not, though I can find out if you have need."

Elle crumpled the paper in her hand. She couldn't hope to go after Westfield alone. Henry's skills would be vital to any rescue attempt. Much as she hated it, she had no choice but to await his return.

She paced the room, wringing her hands. "I'm going to go mad." Her eyes darted all around, as if the room would somehow assist her. Much to her surprise, she found it did. "This is a study. There is pen and paper here?"

"Of course, miss."

"Good." She continued pacing, speaking aloud to gather her thoughts. "I shall write out a plan. Then I shall write out an alternative plan, a plan for what to do if we are captured, and a plan for what I might do on my own if Henry doesn't return. Then I will make a stock of useful potions. After that is done, if I still need something to do I will go back and review the plans."

"There are many supplies in the large desk," the butler informed her. "If you need assistance with anything, you may ask myself or any of the household. We will be happy to help you."

"I will need some lunch, and would be happy to have anyone at all to talk to. The choices are keep busy or go out of my mind with worry. I would much prefer the former."

Carter nodded. "I will let Cook know to have a tray made up for you. As for companionship, I can regale you with amusing family tales, if you need something lighthearted. Your Lord Henry has gotten himself in and out of many scrapes over the years, and even Lady Emma knew how to make trouble as a youngster. Her children come by it honestly."

Elle smiled at him. "I would love to hear your stories. Perhaps they will inspire me." Or perhaps they would do nothing but provide her some bittersweet beauty in the distant future. She would treasure them.

"I would say they're more apt to scare you off, but I suspect Henry has better sense than to fall for that sort of girl. You get to work on your plans, and I'll be back shortly with your luncheon and the story of the history of this old desk."

"Thank you."

She gathered pen and paper and at the top of the page wrote, "Plan A: Rescue." She would do this.

XLI

Enemies and Friends

A SICK DREAD SETTLED in Henry's stomach the moment he spotted the two soldiers standing outside of the Wilton-Bowles residence. What he had suspected since New York was a near certainty. He was walking into a trap, but he would do so willingly. He had to know the truth, and he had to know why.

The soldiers saluted as he approached, but he didn't return the gesture.

"I'm a civilian now, chaps. No need to stand on formality."

They didn't drop their rigid posture. "Captain Ainsworth," one greeted him. "The colonel has been waiting for you."

Henry ignored the critical tone and strode past the guards to knock at the front door. They were watching him, he was certain. He felt as if he had guns trained on his back. He itched to pull his pistol and turn around.

The butler didn't wait upon any greeting or announcement, but showed him directly to the study, where Wilton-Bowles sat behind a sturdy oak desk.

"Ainsworth. What has kept you?"

"Nothing, sir. I received your message this morning and came promptly."

"Ah. Of course." He motioned for Henry to sit.

"Thank you, sir, I prefer to stand." His own stance was as rigid as that of the soldiers outside. Military habits didn't change easily.

A brandy decanter sat at one end of the table, beside a box of cigars. Henry tried not to look at them, in the hopes the colonel wouldn't offer him anything. When Wilton-Bowles poured himself a glass of the liquor, Henry knew he would have no such luck.

"Brandy?"

"No, thank you, sir. I only drink with dinner."

"Ah, yes. I forgot you prefer tea. Shall I ring for some?"

"No, thank you. I'm not in need of any refreshments."

Wilton-Bowles nodded and opened the cigar box. Damn the man.

"Care for a smoke?"

"Not now, sir, but thank you again." The cigars were expensive imports. He was tempted to take one with him so he could have Elle verify it wasn't poisoned. Sadly, she was as likely to throw the cigar in a rubbish bin as to analyze it. She certainly wouldn't let him smoke it in the house, and she wouldn't want to kiss him afterward. It was a damned shame.

The colonel lit a cigar for himself. "Have you no vices, boy?"

"Only one, sir."

He cocked an eyebrow. "Gaming or women?"

"Just one woman."

"That's hardly a vice."

"It is if we are not married, sir."

The colonel chortled. "You always were the gentleman, Ainsworth. How did you ever manage to become my best spy?"

"I have a talent for lying and stealing, sir. But I consider those things less as vices and more as inherent character flaws."

"And useful flaws they are. Now, tell me, why is my daughter back in her childhood home, locked in her room and crying?"

"Because her husband is a murderer."

The colonel's eyes narrowed. He took a large swallow of brandy. "You have proof of this?"

"He poisoned me. I'm only alive because of Miss Deschamps and her potions skills. Another member of the household was less fortunate."

"You are certain it was Fasching who did it?"

"Yes. I confronted him the next morning. To say he was surprised to see me alive would be an understatement. He was livid. I'm certain he still wants to kill me, so I will have to be cautious. He is likely here in town already. I would advise Rachael not to go about unescorted, in case he is angry she has left him."

"How is this connected to your mission? Tell me everything."

Henry gave a brief summary of their findings, concentrating on the serum sources and the people controlling them. He watched Wilton-Bowles throughout the report, trying to gauge his reaction to the news. How much of this did he already know, and from what sources?

The colonel took notes as Henry spoke, and only interrupted a few times to ask for clarification. Henry went into greater detail about the happenings in New York, as they were relevant to Rachael's troubles. The note-taking stopped altogether, but he didn't comment on it.

"Thank you, Henry, that is most helpful," the colonel said at last. "I'm scheduled to meet with Gladstone and a few others this evening. Would you be willing to sign this document so I may present it to them?"

Henry flinched. It was no longer possible to ignore the wrongness of this meeting.

"No. I will not affix my name to anything I haven't read."

Wilton-Bowles laughed and pushed his notes across the table. "Read it. I haven't put down anything but what you told me."

Henry picked up the paper and scanned it. The basics were here: the serum sources they'd found, the troubles with accessing them. One phrase jumped out at him. "Military presence needed for protection of sources." He set the paper down and jabbed at it with his finger.

"This is your assumption. I said nothing about military action of any kind."

"It's true nonetheless. We have to protect our investments, keep criminals and others away. They need us, lad. We have to take care of what is ours."

Henry kept his face impassive, his voice calm, as he spoke, one liar to another. "I understand your point, sir. You have, however, left off the most important part. You didn't mention the abundance of small sources and the extraction of serum directly from the soil."

"Ah. That is yet so experimental. I would hate to get everyone's hopes up only to have them dashed when it doesn't work. You cover it in your full report, I assume? If you leave it with me, I can deliver it tonight."

Henry's jaw tightened. The betrayal hurt like a physical blow. This was the man who had recruited him, who had trained him. Henry had relied on his advice for years. Anger and pain swelled within him. He clamped it down with years of training.

"You forget yourself, sir. All sensitive information, both written and oral, is to be delivered in person. You were quite adamant on that point."

"I'm glad to see you still remember the things I taught you."

Enough. It was time to end this game. "How large of a stake do you hold in the Imperial Potions Company? Are you second to Lady de Winter, or only in the top five? I assume I have you to thank for the delay in relaying that list to me."

The colonel chuckled. "How long have you known?"

"Since I met Fasching. I wanted to believe you didn't know what sort of man he is, but that was no more than a fantasy. I ought not to have come today, but I needed to have this discussion. I needed to see for myself."

"If it makes you feel better, I had nothing to do with his attempt on your life."

"It does not."

"He will answer for that, to be sure. Are you certain you don't want a drink or a cigar? I assure you, they are not poisoned."

"No."

"Do you know, I considered you for Rachael once upon a time. You didn't have the money or connections I was looking for, of course, but your mind is sharp, and you are so very loyal. You were much too naive, however. You still are. You think you are a champion for some greater good. It's charming, but we all need to grow up sometime, my boy."

"At the very least, I'm a champion for more than my own pocketbook," Henry snarled.

"Ah, but you see, I won't be the only beneficiary of this effort. It has the potential to change the world, Henry, and I'd like you to be a part of that. Right now you are understandably hurt because I have deceived you, but when I explain—"

"Don't bother. The deception is the least of your sins. You used me. You are trying to use me still. You think you can convince me to lie to Parliament about our findings? That I would betray my whole country for a share of your filthy profits? That I would aid a man who shackles his only daughter to a monster for financial gain?"

"You don't understand. You can't see past the money. Yes, that is a part of it, but there is so much more. The empire is in decline, boy. She's slipping away from us, and someday soon Britain will be no more than this little island. Insignificant. We have the chance to build something in its place. With the sources in our control, we own the aristocracy, with their addictions to recreational potions. We own industry, which can't operate without lights and combustibles. Our American connections are just the beginning of our global expansion. We are not just a company anymore. We are a world power. And I will build the army to defend us."

"You are mad!"

"Don't turn your back on this, Henry. It is inevitable. If you fight this, you will be crushed, and I will have wasted one of my best operatives. Help us make something great."

"If I destroy your monopoly, if people can harvest serum from the dirt in their backyards, then everyone can have lights. Everyone can run a steam car. Everyone can afford medicines so they don't see their whole family die from curable diseases!" He pounded his fist on the desk, rattling the glassware. "*That* is something great, and that is the only thing I will fight for!"

The colonel leaned back in his chair, sighing. "You're an idealistic fool."

"I'd rather be an idealistic fool than a power-mad, mercenary bastard." He snatched up the cigar box. "I'll take that cigar, now."

"Take the whole box. I can afford more. You may want to smoke them quickly. There will be more men than just my son-in-law out for your blood."

Henry tucked the box under his arm. He'd share them with his family when Elle made him a father. Assuming they weren't all poisoned. He stalked from the room and slammed the door behind him. His hands shook. He needed to find a way out of the house. If he walked out the front door, the soldiers stationed there would arrest him, if he was lucky, or shoot him, if he wasn't.

He turned a corner, heading toward the back of the house, and nearly collided with Rachael. She was dressed more modestly than usual, in a high-necked day dress, though still in the crimson color she favored. Her hair was loose, her eyes rimmed with red, her face creased with worry. Still beautiful, but no longer a Greek goddess. She was flawed, human, and a small twinge of the affection he had once had for her resurfaced.

"Oh, Captain Ainsworth!" she exclaimed. "What is happening? I heard shouting." Her expression grew fearful. "My husband isn't here, is he?"

"No. But I'm sorry to tell you your father is involved as well."

She looked resigned rather than shocked. "I had suspected." She took hold of his arm and dragged him into a small sitting room, closing and locking the door behind them. "You must help me. What can I do?"

He matched her bleak expression. "Get thee to a nunnery."

She put her hands on her hips. "Thank you, Hamlet."

His lips twitched upward. He had forgotten how much he liked her sarcastic wit. Perhaps he could salvage something out of this mess. "Do you have a friend or a female relative you could stay with?"

She considered the question a moment. "Yes, a cousin. She is... not very well off."

Perfect. "Put as much money as you can in your own name, with a different banker. Go to your cousin and stay with her for as long as you are able. At least until this blows over. That should give you time to determine what you want to do with your life."

A look of puzzlement crossed her face. "What I want to do?"

"Start a business, make investments, run a finishing school, I don't know. Find a new husband. Have torrid affairs with foreign heads of state. Do whatever you like, just do something for yourself."

She blinked and stared at him for a long moment. "Thank you. You are a good man. I do remember you, now, from years ago. You were skinnier then, more awkward. You still looked a boy."

"I *was* a boy."

"You were a gentleman. You were not as aggressive as so many of the others, and I thought you weak. More fool I." Her laugh held no humor. "I'm sorry for slighting you. Look me up once you have made a widow out of me, and perhaps I can make it up to you."

"Thank you, but I'm spoken for."

"Ah, yes, your Miss Deschamps. You ought to marry her, before you ruin her completely."

He gritted his teeth. He was thoroughly sick of people telling him that.

"If you would truly like to make it up to me, help me get out of this house alive. Is there a back door I can use? A servants' entrance?"

Rachael shook her head. "There are soldiers out back, too. For my protection, Father said."

"A window then?"

She frowned and looked him up and down in an oddly contemplative manner before raising her gaze back to meet his. "You and I are of a size," she observed. "How attached are you to those clothes?"

He shook his head, scanning her large bosom and tightly corseted waist. "It will never work."

"We will make it work." She unlocked the door and peeked into the hall. "Come with me."

A short time later, he stood in her bedroom while she handed him article after article of clothing.

"We will have to pad the front and hide your shoulders, but something in that pile will suffice," she promised. "I will leave you so you don't have to tell your woman you were undressing in front of me."

He shrugged out of his suit coat. "You may as well stay here. There is no chance I can handle any of these ensembles on my own."

She laughed, just a short giggle, but it was an encouraging sign. "That is fine, but you must promise to tell Miss Deschamps this was your fault."

"She's going to kill me regardless," he muttered. "Or perhaps just ridicule me."

"No. She will be happy to have you home."

They both jumped at the sound of a fist hammering on the door.

"Open up in there!" a gruff voice ordered.

Henry stepped back against the wall, pistol in hand. Rachael yanked the door open, a pair of lacy drawers dangling from her fingers.

"What do you want?" she snapped.

"I, uh, so sorry, ma'am," the soldier sputtered. "Looking for a troublemaker."

"Well. Get on with it, then." She shooed him away and shut the door.

"Quickly," she mouthed.

After much scrambling, tugging, and swearing—on Henry's part at least—Rachael handed him the hatbox full of the things he refused to leave behind, and turned him about one last time, critiquing every angle of the costume. Satisfied with her work, she leaned in and kissed his cheek. "It will do. Good luck, Henry the spy."

He took her hand and gave it a squeeze. After six years of not caring, he loved her again, though in a different way, and for a different reason. This new affection ran deeper, and it wouldn't fade. "Good luck to you too, Rachael. Your mind is even prettier than your face. Don't be afraid to use it."

She pushed him out into the hall. "That is the worst come-on line I have ever heard," she mumbled, but he heard her laugh again as she closed the door behind him.

Henry headed straight for the front door, the bustle swaying awkwardly behind him and the skirts tangling around his legs. God, how did women stand these ridiculous costumes? He bit his lip, tugged the veil down from the enormous hat to hide his features, and pictured Rachael's confident, bold walk. He could do this. He'd watched her every move once for three months straight. He would get back to Elle. Any alternative was unthinkable.

Four armed soldiers waited in the front hall, talking

amongst themselves in low tones. Henry strode right past them, as if they were beneath his notice.

"Mrs. Fasching?" one of the men asked. "Where are you going?"

Henry didn't even glance back. He flicked his wrist in a gesture of dismissal that had broken the hearts of so many wide-eyed youths.

"Out," he snapped, mimicking her voice as best he could and thanking God she wasn't one of those high, trilly sopranos.

Not breaking stride, he marched out the door and down the street, hailing the first vehicle he saw. He scrambled into the carriage with all the grace of a drunken cow, falling over the skirts, smashing his knee, and tearing something that he hoped was the dress and not his breeches.

"Get me out of here without a tail and there's a shiny gold sovereign with your name on it."

"Righto, guv'nor."

The horses sprang into action.

XLII

Getting the Message

$\mathcal{E}$LLE SPOTTED HENRY before anyone else did. She had gone over her plans more times than she cared to mention, and resigned herself to sitting in the parlor, feigning reading while she watched out the window. She recognized him the moment he came into view. Even the absurd costume couldn't disguise his purposeful stride. She rushed to the front door and flung it open before he could even knock. He slammed it closed behind him, yanked off the wide-brimmed hat and veil and threw them to the floor.

"Someone help me out of this ridiculous get-up!"

She had never seen him in such a state, and couldn't entirely decipher the expression on his face. He was angry, yes, and frustrated, but there was something more. Some deeper pain that made her want to hold him and kiss him until it faded.

Carter picked up the hat and dusted it off, completely unfazed by the sight of Henry in a dress. Henry yanked off the wrap—which had hidden the fact that the buttons couldn't completely close across his broad shoulders—and the butler deftly caught it out of midair.

"Can I be of any service, sir?" he asked.

Elle was already working the remaining buttons.

"My hat is in that box. Could you hang it for me? Then, if you could arrange to donate these things to charity, I would appreciate it. Mrs. Fasching doesn't want them back."

Henry wriggled out of the dress, leaving him standing in the foyer in only his breeches and boots.

"These are Rachael Fasching's things? Goodness, Henry, what have you been doing?"

"Making enemies. Let's go into the parlor and I'll tell you about it."

They sat on the sofa, and Elle held his hand as he explained everything that had happened at the Wilton-Bowles residence. With the anger gone, the hurt in his eyes was unmistakable. She longed to take it away from him, but the best she could offer was her embrace and a handkerchief.

Carter came by shortly with a clean shirt and a tea tray. The tea buoyed Henry's spirits somewhat, and while he pulled the shirt on, he didn't button it, giving Elle the opportunity to keep a hand over his heart. They sat for some time in silence while she held him and he sipped at his drink.

"You resemble some sort of sophisticated barbarian, drinking tea while half undressed," she teased.

He smiled for the first time since arriving home. "Didn't you know? I'm heir to an ancient Viking kingdom. I've invaded British soil and adopted their customs. When they least expect, I will plunder their treasures, sling my desired bride over my shoulder, and carry my spoils home in triumph."

"And what if your desired bride doesn't wish to be carried off?"

"Of course she wishes to be carried off. She can't resist my barbarian allure."

Elle trailed her fingers across his warm skin. "True."

He turned and caught her mouth with his own. His tongue snaked across her lips, coaxing them apart. His kiss was her ambrosia, and she would never have enough. Separation left her aching, but they had no time to spare. He had work matters to consider. She needed to brief him on the situation with Westfield and review her plans.

"I would love to carry you off to my longboat and have my

way with you," Henry sighed, his wistful expression matching the longing in her heart, "but I still need to deliver my report. Wilton-Bowles with his private army complicates the issue. He knows who my contacts are and could have men placed to intercept me."

"Could you ask your contacts to come here instead?"

He grinned at her. "My thoughts were trending in that very direction. The trick will be to convince everyone I'm not merely paranoid."

"You think they will think that?"

"Most spies are paranoid. Deception is part of the job, and you learn to treat everyone with suspicion. I'm lucky to have a handful of people I can trust." Pain flashed in his eyes. "Though that number has decreased of late."

She squeezed his hand. "It wasn't so long ago the number increased."

"More than a fair trade." He kissed her again, hot and hungry, but quickly withdrew and rose from his seat. "I must draft messages to my contacts and send them out, but when that is finished this Viking lord intends to practice some pillaging. Since I have yet to find an opportunity to light anything on fire, I will settle for making you burn."

The passion in his eyes made her entire body quiver. She yearned to haul him upstairs to their bedroom. The anxiety of waiting all day had spiked her desire, and she wouldn't be satisfied until she had had all of him. If they were lucky, perhaps they could find time for a moment of fiery passion.

A sudden inspiration made her jump. "Oh! Burn! Of course!"

"What?"

"It's exactly what I need for my plans."

"Plans?"

She dug the note from Lady de Winter out of her pocket to show him. "Westfield has been captured."

Henry cursed and crumpled the note in his fist, just as she had done.

"I have written out plans for a potential rescue. I need your professional advice. Write your messages and then we can discuss the matter. We cannot storm Charlotte de Winter's townhouse in broad daylight, so we will have time to refine my ideas before we take any action."

He frowned down at her. "I don't suppose there's any chance that your plans involve letting me make the rescue attempt while you remain safely here with Carter and Faraday's hunting rifles?"

Elle stood and stepped towards him, once again placing her hand flat on his bare chest. "Not a chance in hell."

Henry paced back and forth across the study, his hands folded behind his back. He had said nothing since reading over her ideas for a rescue attempt. Elle waited at the desk, reviewing her notes while he mulled over her suggestions. After several minutes of silence, he finally stopped and spoke.

"Your plan calls for a distraction, but you didn't specify what that might entail."

"That was the idea I had before you left to write your messages. I have the necessary ingredients to make an explosive potion—akin to gunpowder, but even more volatile. Once exposed to air, it will flame up. It's dangerous, but we could use it to light a fire."

He wasn't entirely able to suppress his smile. "You have taken my urge to commit arson quite seriously, I see." He paced a bit more. "We could throw it into the kitchen. That is the most likely place for a fire, and ought to be well away from wherever they have chosen to hold Westfield captive."

Elle nodded. "They wouldn't keep him near the servants' areas. Lady de Winter and her co-conspirators will want privacy."

"If I were her, I would give most of the servants time off, and have only the hired guns about. She will still need a few people, however, particularly kitchen staff. She will need to feed her allies. Setting fire to the kitchen will cause a ruckus."

"Good." Elle stood and shoved her notes into a single stack. "That's what we will do, then."

Henry walked to the desk and stopped beside her. He placed his hands on her shoulders and looked her directly in the eye. He needed to be certain she understood the truth of the matter.

"It won't be enough. It will buy us a bit of time, is all. Even if we give ourselves every advantage possible—go late at night, plan an escape route ahead of time, create a serious distraction—our chance of success is near to zero. I wouldn't say it's impossible, but under ordinary circumstances, I wouldn't even attempt such a thing."

Elle turned away, shaking her head. "We can't leave him in the hands of criminals and murderers."

"No. Nor can we wait here for them to send men after us. If we delay too long they will try to force our hand."

"I will write a note to Lady de Winter telling her I plan to come first thing in the morning. Do you think that will help?" She looked back up at him, her expression hopeful.

The most encouragement he could offer her was a shrug.

"It can't hurt. It may keep them away a bit longer. The next note will threaten harm to Westfield, you can be certain of that."

"Which is why we must make some attempt to rescue him. If there is even a small chance to get him free, we should take it."

He took a deep breath, choosing one bad option over another. "I agree, but only on the condition that you will be willing to surrender should the plan go awry."

"Didn't you read the page where I wrote the plan for if we were captured?"

"I did. A few aspects need clarification. First of all, if we are caught out at any point during the rescue attempt, we are to surrender without a fight. Thereafter, we will make no attempts at escape. They need us alive and unharmed to testify before Westfield's committee. We will cooperate with their demands until that time."

They needed her alive, at least. Henry was expendable, except as a tool for manipulating her.

"And once that time comes?"

"There, I'm afraid, we will need to improvise. We don't as yet have enough information on what Lady de Winter and the other Company leaders intend for us. They will have to let us testify or it will be clear someone is interfering. They will try to control what we say—what you, in particular, say. You are the certified expert."

"They will threaten you and Westfield." Her eyes were hard. She understood all too well.

"Yes. It will be up to you to ignore those threats and see the truth is made known."

"What of your report?"

"I hope for a swift response to my messages. My papers are confidential, however. Your testimony will be public, and that will have a bigger and more immediate impact. Even if Gladstone—our Prime Minister—knows the truth, it will be difficult for him to take action against so large an entity as the Imperial Potions Company if they have the people on their side. You have the best chance to bring them down."

"And if they plan to lock me away and send their own 'expert' in my place?"

Henry shook his head. "Unlikely. Westfield is set to introduce you. They can't fake that, because too many people know him. If they've harmed you or kept you away, he wouldn't hesitate to put his own life at risk to expose them."

"They can't harm him, then, if he is necessary for my presentation."

"They can harm him. They can't kill him. At least, not until after he has spoken. But they may well threaten to do so afterward. They also may attempt to use Fasching's talent for potions to drug us all."

"That I know how to guard against. We can eat and drink as little as possible, and there are remedies we can take beforehand that will give us some amount of protection."

"Good. Give us whatever advantage you can."

He watched her think, her lips pursed, her forehead crinkled as she frowned. The situation was dire. He could see no good solution.

The enemy had the advantage of numbers. He could make a request for protection, except that he had no idea whom to trust. Wilton-Bowles had a lot of influence. Any soldier could be acting under his orders. Any general could be swayed by his lies.

If they did nothing, someone would come after them. They wouldn't make it to the testimony unmolested. Even if he and Elle snuck away and hid until then, enemies would be waiting when they arrived, and they would have Westfield as a hostage.

"If we make this rescue attempt," Elle mused, "there is a possibility, however small, to go into the meeting with all three of us free. If we fail and surrender, we will be hardly worse off than if we do nothing."

"Theoretically. We can't account for the unpredictability of known murderers crazed enough to think they can take over the world. We may both end up dead."

Henry didn't believe they had a chance in hell of succeeding, no matter which option they chose. Elle would go into her presentation under threat, and it would be up to her to denounce them, no matter the risk. All he could do was to stick by her, guard her to the best of his ability, and take as many precautions as possible. He would do everything in his power to see her come through unscathed.

"Two days," she sighed. "Only two days and this will be over."

She wrapped her arms around him, and he hugged her to his chest.

"Part of me wishes Westfield had never involved you in this," he lamented.

"If not me, then who?"

"There could have been no one better. I would never have met you, had anyone else been chosen, and I can't regret that. I hate to see you under such stress, though, and I hate that you may be in danger. You didn't choose this sort of life."

The truth of his words cut deep. She deserved better. He would give her anything. Even freedom from himself. He would sooner stab himself than walk away from her. But he could hand her the choice. If she wanted to, if she needed to, he would let her go.

"I swear, the moment this is over, I will make absolutely certain you will be free to pursue whatever you desire. To chase the happiness you deserve. To be away from lies and deception, worry and danger. That's my life. It needn't be yours."

She stared up into his eyes. "Henry..."

"I am what I am." His flat tone conveyed none of the emotions churning beneath. "Take it or leave it."

Elle's brow furrowed, her jaw set, and the soft amber of her eyes grew rock hard.

"I know what you are. A spy. A lover. An eccentric. So quiet, so unobtrusive, until something sparks your passions and they pour out in unquenchable flames. You may hide yourself from most of the world, but I have seen you, perhaps as no one has.

"I have seen you worry what others think of you. You believe there is something wrong with you, some inherent abnormality. Yet you make no attempt to change."

"I do change. You have changed me. But it is natural,

stemming from my experiences, not a forced perversion of my basic self."

"I think you like yourself the way you are."

"Yes." God help him, but he did. He liked his bizarre and unsavory skills. He liked to swear and make sarcastic comments. He liked the wicked thoughts that filled his mind every time he looked at her.

"And you won't be someone else."

"Never." He would loathe himself. He could *speak* lies, he couldn't *be* one.

"Not even for me."

He swallowed hard. "No."

She nodded, her expression still fierce. He would abide by her decision, even if it killed him.

"Good. If you did, you wouldn't be the man I fell in love with."

He exhaled in relief. She understood. It didn't say anything for their future, but she understood him. His chest constricted. Good God, he loved her.

"So." She drew the word out. "Take it or leave it?"

"Yes."

She placed a hand against his chest, seizing a fistful of his shirt. "You are too late. I already took you. Every last bit of you, exactly as you are. And I will never leave you, regardless of where you may go or what you may do. You could travel to the ends of the earth, and I would hunt you down. You are *mine*, Henry Ainsworth."

The tightness in his chest eased. A spattering of tears trickled down his cheek. He held her close, embracing this unparalleled gift, clinging to the most precious thing he had ever had the fortune to call his own.

"Always," he sighed. He took a moment more in her arms, then he pressed a heated kiss to her lips and stepped back. "No pillaging until we've finished our preparations. I will check my weapons and hammer out some of the details for implementing your plan."

"I will write a quick reply to Charlotte de Winter and then mix up the potions we need."

"Do you have serum enough for everything?"

She nodded. "With what I've managed to extract from the soil experiments, I should have plenty."

"Splendid. I have a request, then."

"Oh?"

"Make me a stamina potion." He didn't need to clarify which sort of stamina potion he meant. His pink cheeks would tell her plenty. "I'd like to make you forget your troubles, if only for a time."

XLIII

Search and Rescue

ELLE GROANED AND BUCKED against Henry, trying to pull him deeper inside of her. For the first time, she understood why the amatory stamina potions were so popular. She had climaxed twice so far, and the third promised to be beyond anything she'd experienced before. Her body was so taut, her senses so strained, she didn't know how she could withstand the onslaught. Each time she felt close to release, Henry drew back, picking up the pace little by little, keeping her writhing, edging her higher still. She longed for it to end. She ached for it to continue forever.

His every thrust was agony. Waves of pleasure assailed her body while she moved with him, desperate to reach that insurmountable plateau. She wrapped her arms and legs around him, pleading for more. Perspiration dampened his brow. His lips grazed her neck, and he rasped her name, his voice low and thick. His strokes grew faster and deeper, and she felt herself slipping, sliding, tumbling over the precipice, until at long last she convulsed beneath him. Henry shuddered atop her, and they clung to one another until the spasms of their passion subsided. They rolled apart and lay side-by-side, chests heaving, drained, but finally satiated.

"Christ almighty," Henry swore. "If I tried that every night, it would kill me."

Elle turned to nuzzle his neck. "You wouldn't be the first."

"You've killed other men this way, then?"

"No!" She laughed. "I mean that overuse of any potions can be dangerous. We must keep this for special occasions only."

"Every occasion is special with you, my love."

She smiled. "And the people in France say the English aren't romantic."

"Your countrymen don't know us very well. What could be more romantic than a man taking his lady out for a night of crime?"

"Very little, I'm certain," she laughed. "Remember, though, most men don't behave as you do, regardless of nationality."

"True, I'm rather odd. I aim to someday be written up as 'noted eccentric Henry Ainsworth.'"

"Do you prefer that epithet over 'notorious spy'?"

"I'm fond of both. I will use whichever proves most embarrassing to my offspring."

Our offspring.

Henry's ultimatum this afternoon had exposed the truth. A truth she hadn't comprehended until he had offered her the choice to walk away. Elle at the bar was no more. Elle at the bar would have left him, would have suffered sad-and-lonely for safe-and-familiar. New Elle would take the risk. She would speak her mind, she would bare her heart. She would fight against any odds. He was worth it. Just as he was.

Because he loved her as she was. Not as a lady, not as a barmaid. Just Elle. Elle with all her worries and fears, her hopes and dreams. Elle who was never more comfortable, never more herself, than when she was with him. Wife, mistress, spy partner—she didn't care. They would eke out a life together, whatever it took. Her children would join the ranks of the eccentric Ainsworths.

"More likely they will admire all your quirks and wish to emulate you."

"God forbid!"

Elle's chuckle was cut short by a yawn. Henry pulled up

the blanket and tucked it around her.

"Get some rest. Sunset is upon us and you had best grab a few hours of sleep. I will wake you when it's time for the rescue."

"You must rest, too. There's no need for you to stay up. I know I won't sleep the whole night through."

"Nor will I. You know I'm not a heavy sleeper."

She ran a finger down his chest. "You will sleep soundly tonight," she predicted.

· · · ◍ · · ·

Hours later, Elle woke and reached for Henry's pocket watch. Quarter to midnight. She eased out of bed, so as not to wake Henry, and turned up the lamp just enough to dress herself. She would have liked to wear her shirt and trousers, but she needed the new concealed pockets Emma had sewn into her petticoat, and she needed to look respectable for her talk. She didn't want to assume she would have an opportunity to return home or even to change clothes. The black dress and a minimum of cumbersome undergarments were the best she could manage.

She was plaiting her hair when Henry struggled out of bed.

"I don't think I've ever desired less to go out on a mission," he told her, his voice groggy. "Do you have anything in that array of potions to ease grumpiness?"

"No. Stamina to keep us awake and alert, a general antidote to protect us from poisons and other drugs, and a simple health potion to make our bodies as strong as possible before we set out. I don't know how much good any of these will do, but it's better than doing nothing. I will have the peppery spray potion and an extra healing potion concealed on my person."

"Did you create that sleeping draught to incapacitate any guards? We must assume there are men watching this house as well as Lady de Winter's residence."

"I did, but I have nothing we can use to inject them with it from any distance."

Henry frowned a moment, then his eyes lit up in childlike

glee. "I can use Reggie's darts from the billiard room. I'm a fair hand at throwing them."

"A small poke is all it takes. I hope Reggie won't mind you using his pub game as a weapon."

"He's less prudish than one might think."

"Good. That's settled then. We'll coat the darts before we set out. I will also be bringing my bag, though I don't expect to have time to mix anything up. It has a few additional potions and my penknife. I may need it during the presentation, as well, to show some of the samples we have collected. The rest I will leave here, in case the bag is lost or taken."

Henry nodded as he buttoned his shirt. "You are well prepared. I will bring my pistol, and I have my knife, as always." He had again opted for the breeches and tall boots that made the weapon more accessible than his fashionable trousers did. "I can carry the explosive potion in another pocket, if you don't have a convenient place for it. I ought to have plenty of room in my coat. All my papers will remain locked in the safe here. Carter is the only other person in the city who can open it. If any of my contacts should arrive to collect my report, he knows to verify their identities before giving them access."

They finished dressing, prepared their supplies, and drank the potions Elle had recommended. Dousing the lights, they joined hands and started together toward the back of the house, allowing their eyes to adjust to the darkness.

Henry navigated the silent halls at his usual brisk pace. He didn't once stumble or take a wrong turn, a testament to how well he knew this residence. Elle kept her fingers tightly entwined with his. While her adventures had taught her many new skills, a good sense of direction wasn't among them. She was happy to leave that responsibility to him.

It was an odd feeling, this camaraderie. She'd been self-reliant for so long that she was still awed by the prospect of being part of a team and having someone she could depend upon without fail. She'd never been a good delegator. When a task needed her attention, she took the full responsibility for it on her own shoulders. Sharing some of the work was such a relief it made her almost giddy.

Henry slowed when they reached the kitchen, guiding her in silence to the rear entrance. He stepped to one side of the door, and pulled her against the wall beside him. He released her hand and lifted something for her to see. She could just make out the shape of the drugged darts through the inky shadows. She palmed a potion and gave him a nod.

He unlatched the door and pushed it open, but remained against the wall. The door swung silently on well-oiled hinges. The household took pride in the maintenance and upkeep of their residence. A soft zip and a flutter of the air broke the stillness of the night. A second one followed only a moment later. Blowgun darts. She wasn't the only one using a sleeping potion tonight.

Elle remained frozen to the wall, her muscles tight, hardly daring to breathe. Henry put his booted foot against a sack of grain and shoved. It fell with a solid thud.

The shuffle of footsteps revealed an enemy even before his shape appeared in the doorway. Henry jabbed the man with a dart, caught him as he fell, and dragged him out of the way. More noise outside warned of additional danger, and Elle raised the spray bottle in her hand. A trio of thugs rushed into the house, and she caught them all together with a cloud of pepper potion. As they gagged and clawed at their eyes, Henry drugged each one with the sleeping draught.

Four darts used. They had but six in total. The potion bottle remained half-full, but to use it, the darts would need to be cleaned and re-dipped. Were there more than two enemies waiting outside? Would they have to surrender before their rescue even began? Several anxious seconds ticked by before Henry nudged her, and they ventured into the night.

Elle scanned the moonlit garden for signs of trouble, her potion clenched in her fist. She saw not the slightest movement and heard no sound. The neighborhood was all abed. If more foes awaited her, they were well concealed.

Henry hauled the four snoring bodies one-by-one into the garden and locked the door. In a matter of hours, the men would wake and vanish into the night. They wouldn't report their failure. Hired thugs didn't make loyal allies.

Henry motioned her toward the carriage house. She followed, puzzled. When he moved to unlock the door, she grasped his arm.

"Won't the carriage attract too much attention? Even the nicest of them still make noise."

"We aren't taking the steam car."

"What?"

He slid the door ajar and disappeared inside. A moment later, the large front wheel of a bicycle poked through the opening. Elle jumped back, startled. Henry wheeled the contraption past her and leaned it against the side of the building before closing and locking the door. He waved a hand at the vehicle.

"My bicycle," he announced, with unmistakable pride. "Much faster than walking and much simpler than trying to hail a cab at this time of night."

"You can't be serious," she blurted. "Those things are death traps, and I have no idea how to ride one."

"You need only sit. I'll do the rest."

He grasped her around the waist and hoisted her up onto the seat. Her skirts bunched beneath her, and she had to hike them up scandalously in order to sit astride. Henry put one hand on the handlebars, and the other on the seat, close enough to touching her that she shivered.

"Mounting will be a bit… backward with you on, so apologies if it's a bit wobbly. Jump off to your right if we tip."

Elle started to protest, but Henry pushed the bicycle into motion before she could say a word. He swung himself up into the seat, and the machine jerked and teetered for a few terrifying seconds before he brought it under control.

"Well, that was exciting. It should be smoother from now on."

Elle grasped him around the waist. "How many times have you crashed this thing?"

"I don't know. Dozens? It happened often when I first got it. I took a header and cracked a bone in my wrist about three years ago. Hurt like the devil."

"That's not reassuring. Have you ever ridden it in the dark before?"

"No."

"If we crash with that explosive in your pocket…"

"We will have one hell of a story."

"Henry!" she chided, unable to keep laughter from creeping into her voice. "You are terrible."

Safety concerns notwithstanding, she soon began to enjoy the ride. The bicycle was faster than she had expected, and it didn't jolt or jar her as it rolled over the cobblestones. The wind tugged strands of hair loose from her braids and only when she brushed them back from her face did she realize she was no longer clinging to Henry's shirt.

"I can see why you like this," she said. "It's exhilarating."

"Wait until you try riding down a large hill. You take your feet off the pedals and hook them over the handlebars. Then, if the wheel hits a rut, you'll fly off feet-first. You're usually going so fast you have to tuck and roll. Plenty of chaps race the big hills and jump off on purpose."

"I'm not mad enough to try that. Maybe I will learn to ride, though."

"I would love to teach you. You'll have to wear trousers. It will be scandalous." The glee in his voice warmed her heart.

"I love you," she blurted.

The bicycle slowed. "What prompted that?"

"I need you to know." She shook her head, trying to form her feelings into coherent words. "No. I need you to *understand*.

It doesn't matter if you are at home drinking tea and reading Shakespeare, or recklessly running headlong into danger. I love all of you."

"I love you, too. And I try not to be reckless."

"Good. Never forget you have someone to come home to."

"I promise."

The ride had taken them into the heart of fashionable London, tightly packed with towering terraced houses. Charlotte de Winter's territory. Elle's skin prickled with apprehension. Were they really going through with this mad plan? Did they have a choice?

Henry slowed the bicycle and jumped off in what she considered a foolhardy manner. It was apparent he had done so many times, because he landed and caught hold of the vehicle in one deft motion. He helped her down and rolled the bicycle into some shrubbery, leaning it against the wall behind.

"We will walk from here," he instructed. "It's but a few blocks."

"You will just leave the bicycle by a strange house?"

He shook his head. "I know the family in this house. I attended University with the eldest son. They are accustomed to my oddity. I chose our route accordingly."

"You plan for everything."

"Everything I can. Wasn't that your own intent when you wrote out five pages of notes?"

"I suppose it was."

They fell silent once more as they walked toward Lady de Winter's residence. Lights lit the windows in a number of houses. The people in this neighborhood could afford to use potions at all hours, even with the high prices.

"We will take a look at the back entrance," Henry whispered, "but it may be guarded better than the front. They will expect us to be sneaky."

Elle nodded her agreement. They turned down an alley leading to the gardens and carriage houses tucked behind the towering structures. They moved at a crawl, keeping to the shadows as much as possible. Elle's eyes swept across the area, looking for enemies, traps, or impediments. She thought she caught a bit of movement, and stilled. She scanned the area carefully and located a human-sized shadow. Henry stopped beside her. A moment later, he lifted his hand near to her face, showing three fingers. She nodded. She had found the locations of two of the guards, now, and had a good guess where the third was. Henry tugged on her sleeve and they backtracked out to the road.

They circled the block to come at the house from the front. The street was too well lit to provide good concealment, and they ducked behind bushes and stairs as they crept closer. Elle checked the address of the house beside them and gave Henry a questioning look. He held up two fingers on his right hand, five on the left. Number twenty-five. Their target was only a few houses down. She dared to poke her head out and spotted a single man, sitting with his chin in his hands. She couldn't tell from such a distance whether he was sleepy or only bored.

Henry pulled a dart from his pocket and motioned for her to stay put. She shook her head vigorously, but he ignored her and dashed around to the next house over, ducking down the stairs to the lower level servants' entrance. The guard turned his head in their direction, and Elle was forced to take cover. She counted to thirty before looking again.

She was just in time to see Henry run yet closer. He didn't conceal himself well this time, but he stopped in a shadow, and she couldn't get a good look at what he was doing. His arm jerked.

Something hit a house across the street with a clank. The guard on the steps sprang to his feet, then dropped like a stone as the dart found its target.

Elle raced down the street, meeting Henry at the basement door. He picked the lock and they stepped into the near-black kitchen.

Inch-by-inch, they felt their way through the room. Elle

held her breath. With each step they teetered on the edge of disaster. Her heart pounded, and her palm was sweaty against Henry's. When they found the stairs, she sagged in relief.

They tiptoed up to the ground floor and stole from room to room. Henry unlatched a window in the dining room, and another in the front hall to give them additional exits. They heard not a sound and saw no sign that any of the household was awake. Elle reviewed the plan in her head. Westfield would be upstairs, in a guest room, under guard. They needed to set the fire and wait until the servants woke Lady de Winter. When she and the others came down to investigate, Elle and Henry could dash upstairs, release her uncle, and run for the nearest exit, climbing out a window if necessary. Now that she was in the house, the plan seemed ludicrous. No wonder Henry had called it near-impossible.

They checked the first floor, which proved as empty as the one below, and had a few potential hiding places. Henry seemed satisfied. He led the way back down to the ground floor and chucked the potion down the basement stairs. Glass tinkled. Seconds later a concussion shook the floor, easily loud enough to wake every servant downstairs. She and Henry hurried back to the first floor and concealed themselves in a drawing room, listening for the inevitable chaos.

They didn't wait long. Shouts rose from the rooms below. Footsteps thundered up the stairs, followed by more shouting. Elle concentrated on the noises moving across the floors of the house. Voices both male and female, footsteps heavy and light echoed through the halls. It sounded at times as if dozens of people were running up and down the stairs at once.

When the chaos settled onto the lower floors, Henry and Elle rose as one and crept up the steps. They paused at the top of the stairs to survey the hall. A lone man stood guard outside a guest room. Henry used his final dart to bring him down.

Elle clutched her potions bag as Henry picked the lock, trying to quiet her trembling hands. She could smell smoke rising from below. They needed to grab Westfield and flee with all haste. She had formulated her explosive potion more for show than destruction, for the safety of the household staff, but couldn't entirely negate the possibility that they might all become trapped in a burning building.

The lock clicked. Henry paused with his hand on the knob, looking at her. He drew his gun. She lifted her spray potion. He gave her a silent nod and swung the door wide. A lamp flared. Henry Fasching, Ellison Blake, and two unfamiliar men stood in the center of the room, wicked grins on all of their faces. Each man held a pistol. Elle's heart skipped a beat, her entire body freezing in terror.

"Welcome," Blake chuckled. "The lady reckoned it was you who caused the mess down below."

Henry backed several steps down the hall, pulling Elle with him. "We surrender," he said, tossing his own gun to the floor.

"Now where's the fun in that?" Blake taunted. He glanced at the two men Elle didn't know. "Hollis, how about you and Wilson there escort our guests down to the drawing room. Missus de Winter wants to have a little chat."

The men started forward, but Elle's eyes were focused past them on Fasching. A grin of malevolent delight twisted his handsome features. He aimed his derringer straight at her heart. Her breath caught in her throat as she stared down the barrel of the tiny, terrifying weapon.

He can't shoot me, she told herself. *They need me.* She trembled anyway, not trusting him not to do something mad.

He walked towards her, laughing at her fear. "Why so worried, Miss Deschamps? Afraid I'll take revenge for those times you thwarted me?"

"Don't be a fool, Fasching," Blake chided. "We need her alive."

His grin broadened. "Yes, I know." He swung the pistol at Henry and pulled the trigger.

Elle screamed.

XLIV

Death Will Have His Day

$\mathcal{H}$ENRY COULDN'T SEE FOR THE PAIN. A haze of black dots and colored sparkles danced before his eyes. Noises sounded muted and indistinct. His whole world had contracted to the searing fire in his chest.

Something jarred him hard enough to catch his attention. He blinked, trying to bring the room into focus. A hand covered his own. Warm breath tickled his cheek. A wet droplet splashed against his skin.

"Henry," Elle wept. "Please, don't die. *Ne me quitte pas!*"

He would have doubled his pain to take the grief from her voice. He tried to speak her name, but even a shallow breath was agony. He wheezed and choked, tasting blood.

He wanted to look at her, but her face was pressed against his shoulder as she sobbed, and he could see only her arm stretched out against his own. Her potions bag lay at her fingertips, tipped on its side, the clasp unfastened. Was she reaching for something?

He blinked again, his vision clearing as the question distracted his mind from the pain. She was poking through the bag. He doubted even the best of her medicinal potions were strong enough to heal a gunshot wound, but he felt a glimmer of hope. He wouldn't leave her without a fight.

"Curse you, Fasching, look at the mess you've made," Blake

growled. "Hollis! Take that hysterical bitch downstairs before he shoots her, too."

Henry couldn't see the man grab Elle, but he knew when it happened, because she jerked and cried out. He heard the smack when her hard-heeled boot connected with flesh. Hollis yelped. Elle thrashed and screamed and fought. Potions and tools bounced across the floor.

Her body slid against his. Someone was dragging her toward the stairs. She clutched at Henry, still flailing, calling his name, shouting at her attackers to release her. She got a good grip on his left leg, and her hand slid down his boot.

His heart soared. She was going for the knife. Brilliant woman! The knife slipped free from the sheath, and a moment later her grip relaxed and she was pulled away from him. Her boots made muffled thuds as she stumbled down the stairs, still railing at the men who had captured her. She had a weapon. She would protect herself.

A boot prodded him. He didn't flinch, suspecting what was coming next. The kick to the ribs was so forceful it would have driven the wind from his lungs had he been breathing normally. The pain spiked with such intensity he nearly lost consciousness.

"Forget him," Blake ordered. "If he's not dead yet, he soon will be."

"Give me your gun," Fasching retorted. "I'll make sure of it."

"I won't give you anything, you damned Yank! Get the hell downstairs before I put a bullet in you!"

"Still sore you lost the war, Johnny Reb?"

The two men continued jawing as their footsteps pounded down the stairs.

Henry opened his eyes. The room was a blur again, but he could make out some of the potion vials that had fallen from Elle's bag. A rough, clay vessel caught his eye. The healing potion Elle had purchased from Nenet in Egypt.

A proper potion, made by an expert. Extremely potent.

He reached for the bottle. The movement tore the wound, causing a strangled half-cry to escape his lips. Tears of pain welled in his eyes. His feeble gasps of air weren't enough, and the world began to close in on him once again.

Henry fought for consciousness. He wouldn't give up. Never. Not while Elle was in the hands of the enemy. He tried again, stretching out with his opposite hand. The potion lay just out of reach. He gritted his teeth and lunged.

His hand closed around the vial and he dragged it closer. His body shook. His heart was pounding—too rapidly—pumping precious blood from the wound. Henry tugged at the cork stopper, but it stuck fast. He would have cursed had he enough air to form words. He was losing time. He dug his nails into the soft material and pried.

The bottle opened with an audible pop, and potion sloshed out onto his fingers. He pulled his hand beneath him, smearing the liquid directly onto the injury. An immediate cooling relief washed over him. He sucked in a deep breath. The lungful of fresh air felt like heaven. He spread more potion over the bullet hole, newly optimistic about his chances for survival.

Despite the improvement, his body remained weak, and the heavy breathing caused him to cough up blood. He couldn't reach the exit wound on his back, or spread the potion on the internal damage. He did the only thing he could think of. He brought the bottle to his lips and drank it down.

It took only seconds for the pain to dissipate. Henry almost tried to move, but thought better of it. He couldn't afford to undo the good the potion had done. He closed his eyes and rested, thankful he was breathing easily and no longer losing blood.

The relief lasted only seconds. His eyes flew open in shock as a sudden chill squeezed his heart. Cold crushed his chest, forcing the air from his lungs. Icy tendrils snaked down his limbs and crawled up his spine, freezing him from the inside out. He was paralyzed, helpless, unable to fight back.

"Elle," he murmured, her name a desperate prayer on his remaining breath.

He had failed her. He fixed an image of her in his mind, making her the last thing he remembered. His world crumbled into blackness.

· · · 👓 · · ·

"Sit down," the man named Hollis demanded. He shoved Elle onto the sofa beside a haggard-looking Lord Westfield without waiting to see if she would obey. He kept his pistol pointed in her direction. "Don't move."

Elle ignored him. He was no more than a hired thug, though better dressed and more intelligent than the men who had been assigned street duty. She assumed from his American-South accent that he worked directly for Ellison Blake. The other thug, Wilson, was British and wore Lady de Winter's livery, purporting to be a footman or some such.

The men waiting in the drawing room were of much greater import to her. She didn't recognize either of the gray-haired gentlemen flanking Charlotte, but she guessed them to be other leaders of the Imperial Potions Company. They both wore finely-cut suits and cufflinks of gold and diamonds that sparkled in the light. Men of wealth, if not also of rank. All three turned to Blake and Fasching as the two entered, still arguing.

"What's the trouble?" Lady de Winter demanded. "Why so much shouting? And did I hear gunfire?"

Fasching composed himself. "The spy attacked me. I was forced to defend myself."

Elle clenched her fists at her sides. It was all she could do not to pull out the knife and run at him. "You murdered him!" she raged.

She embraced the fury, let it hold sway over her, quashing the devastation that would otherwise incapacitate her.

One of the unknown men—the taller, more athletic of the

two—flinched as if someone had hit him. He stalked toward Fasching.

"What have you done?" he snarled.

Fasching shrugged. "He was useless to us."

The man grabbed Fasching by the lapels and slammed him against the wall. "That boy was like a son to me!"

Fasching shoved him off. "I *am* a son to you."

The older man was Rachael's father, Elle realized. Henry's former mentor.

"Not any longer. My daughter has left you. I would never have let you touch her had I known what a piece of filth you really are."

"Enough!" Charlotte yelled over them. "Sit down, all of you. We are here to see to it that Miss Deschamps understands her situation, not to squabble over unimportant matters. What's done is done. Wilson, go clean up the mess. Dump the body in the river. And do be discreet about it this time. I do not want any questions."

"Yes, my lady." He bowed and departed.

Elle glared at Lady de Winter and tried not to think about the orders she had just given. Her hands trembled. She wanted to run upstairs and throw herself at Henry. She wanted to hold him and kiss him and tell him she loved him until he opened his eyes and told her he was well. She fought back her tears and thought about the knife, deep in her concealed pocket, lying heavy against her thigh.

Beside her, Westfield wept, his head in his hands.

"You poor child," he moaned. "Oh, God, what have I done? George will never forgive me."

Elle covered her mouth to stifle a sob.

"You see, Miss Deschamps," Charlotte explained, "this is not some sort of game. This is not a grand adventure for a little girl from the slums. We are in deadly earnest, and if you do not cooperate with us, you can expect a great deal more unpleasantness in your future."

The threats meant nothing to Elle. It made no difference what her enemies said or did. She would never give in to their demands. She would make the truth known, whatever the cost. She was beyond them. Untouchable. Nothing they could do to her would hurt her more than she hurt now.

She let Charlotte ramble, going on about what Elle should and should not say, how she should present herself, how she might answer any questions. Most of the words flowed over Elle unabsorbed. They would make her rehearse tomorrow, and her mouth would learn their traitorous words. She would bide her time and then bring them down.

"Defiant little chit, isn't she?" Blake remarked, and Elle realized she had been asked a question and hadn't responded. Her jaw was set, her eyes free of tears, her spine straight. It was not a posture of defeat.

"Lock her up for the night," Lady de Winter sighed. "She will be more cooperative when she has had time to think upon her circumstances."

Elle rose from her seat. She wouldn't pass up the opportunity to rest. Blake used his large body to block the doorway, in case she tried to bolt. Fasching moved toward her.

"I will escort her upstairs," he leered.

"Don't damage her, Fasching," Wilton-Bowles rebuked him. "We need her for the testimony."

Fasching continued to approach until he was close enough for Elle to feel his breath. "Oh, I won't damage her," he laughed. "Whore that she is, she'll enjoy every second of it."

Elle spat in his face.

He slapped her, hard enough that she stumbled. Her hand plunged through the slit in her skirt. Her fingers found the wrapped leather hilt and curled around it.

Fasching grabbed her around the waist. It was his final mistake. She yanked the knife free and stabbed upward, thrusting it deep into his gut. He gasped and staggered, clutching at his bleeding midsection. She could see the others starting toward her, but they were too late. She lunged with the knife again, aiming higher. She forgot to turn the blade to slide between the ribs, but Henry's knife was tapered enough that it still plunged a full inch into Fasching's heart.

"Burn in hell," she snarled, and shoved him away from her.

Multiple pairs of hands grabbed hold of her, but they needn't have bothered. She would fight no more tonight.

They dragged her up the stairs, through the empty hall with the blood-soaked carpet where Henry had lain. Someone had cleared away the items she had spilled from her potions bag. Tears blinded her. She staggered up the steps to the next floor, where they pushed her into a guest room. The door slammed behind her. She crumpled to the ground and wept.

XLV

From the River

*H*ENRY JOLTED AWAKE. He had struck something, or something had struck him. He tumbled about. Was he floating? Falling? Sinking? He was disoriented, his senses slow to respond. He didn't know where he might be, or even if he was alive.

He tried to take a breath and choked on a mouthful of dirty water. The shock brought his mind fully alert. The river! He kicked and flailed, trying to find the surface. He had no notion which way was up. Under ordinary circumstances, he considered himself a strong swimmer, but his arms and legs were weak, and his clothes weighed him down.

One hand broke the surface, and he thrashed until he got his head above the water. He heaved and coughed, but pulled a few priceless breaths before the weight of his wet garments dragged him under once more.

Now that he had his bearings, Henry kicked with all his might, willing his muscles to function. What little strength he possessed had already begun to ebb. His chest felt tight, crushed in a tangle of ice and fire. His head swiveled back and forth in desperation, looking for anything he might cling to—a boat, the shore, a piece of floating jetsam. His eyesight failed him beneath the darkened water. He couldn't keep afloat for more than a few seconds at a time.

He heard a splash and spun to find the source. Above him, he could see the dim outline of something floating on the surface. He grabbed for it, his fingers closing on a thick length of rope. Whoever was on the other side began to reel him in. From beneath the water, he couldn't see the source of his salvation. His chest ached for lack of air, and his legs no longer possessed the strength to get him to the surface. He clung to the rope and prayed his grip would hold long enough to reach his rescuer.

The cold of the potion had seized control again, and it radiated throughout his body, easing the pain, but drawing him nearer to oblivion. He fought it with thoughts of Elle, captive of the enemy. He knew her mind. She would defy them at the testimony, and put her life in danger. He couldn't leave her to face that alone. He wouldn't. He would see her again, hold her again.

His shoulder smashed against something solid. He had reached the pier or the boat where the rope had originated. The cord scratched his palms as he was dragged upwards. He couldn't hold on. It tore his skin and slithered from his grasp. His limbs wouldn't respond. He began to sink again.

His shirt snagged on something, jerking him to a halt. He felt himself lifted until he cleared the water. His rescuer dumped him unceremoniously onto a wooden floor. Boat? Dock? He couldn't tell. His vision and his mind were both fogged. There were lights and voices—nearby, but growing ever distant.

"Damn. Too late."

"Poor blighter's been shot."

"Toss 'im back in?"

"Gimme them boots, first."

"No, he's breathing."

"Don't look like it to me."

"Bring him to shore. I'll take him..."

Henry blacked out.

He awoke hours later. The sun was high in the sky, providing ample light through the single window. He scanned the room, assessing his situation. He occupied what looked to be the primary living area of a small dwelling. A stone fireplace dominated the space, the fire providing additional light and making the room uncomfortably warm. A large pot hung over the flames. The smells that emanated from it made Henry's stomach rumble.

He lay atop a table—most probably the table where the family dined. It had been covered with a thick woolen blanket, and a similar blanket covered him. No wonder he felt overheated. Midday in June with the sun shining was too warm for the heavy coverings, even without the blazing fire. Had the people here feared he might be cold? He wondered what sort of state he had been in when he arrived. For that matter, what sort of state was he in now?

He tossed back the blanket and sat up. He had been stripped of all his clothes, and wiped clean of blood. The wound appeared closed, though still red and painful. His hands were raw from the rope, but would heal soon enough. He could find no other injuries from the previous night's misadventures. He was surprisingly well, given the circumstances.

His eyes roved across the room once more, hoping to locate his belongings. He felt uncomfortably naked, owing more to the lack of his knife than the lack of clothing. He had worn the sheath strapped to his leg for years, removing it only to bathe. Even then, it always remained in arm's reach. His gaze settled on the fireplace tools. Those would make good weapons if needed.

"Ha!" he muttered. Sitting up took effort. Wielding a weapon was out of the question. He was more apt to fall on his way to the hearth.

The door to the back of the house opened, and a girl's head poked through.

"Ooh! Mama! Mama, he's awake!"

A woman not much older than himself rushed into the room. She wore a modest dress covered by an apron, and had her hair pulled back with a single ribbon. She had a no-nonsense air about her that Henry liked. The girl followed behind, her eyes wide with curiosity.

Too late, Henry realized he ought to cover himself, and pulled the blanket to his chin, blushing furiously.

"Ye needn't be bashful, lad," the woman said, speaking as if she were much more than a few years his senior. "I know what a man looks like, and who d'ye think washed you up? Now, don't look like that. My husband handled removin' all your clothes."

"Could I possibly have them returned?" he asked, feeling a complete clod.

"You'll get yer things when they've dried. You'll be needin' a new shirt. Now, let me take a look at that wound."

Henry complied, laying back on the table while she poked and prodded his chest with cold fingers. The injured area was sensitive, but everything else felt normal. She frowned and mumbled and took a close look at the damage.

"How is your pain? High? Low?"

"It's still rather painful," he admitted. "It's nothing compared to last night, however."

She nodded. "And how d'ye feel? Cold? Warm?"

He shook his head. "Neither. I was too hot beneath the blanket, but I'm fine now."

"Interesting." She stepped back, shaking her head. "When my brother first brought ye in, ye looked dead. Cold as ice, you were. But there was some breath still about ye. Oughtn't have lived, shot through the chest like that. Now, here ye are, sittin' up and healin' unnatural fast. What did you drink?"

"A healing potion, but what sort I don't know. I didn't

have time to investigate the matter." He closed his eyes. "My apologies, I'm feeling tired again."

The woman tucked the blanket around him. It no longer felt warm, but comfortable. She touched his forehead.

"Colder than a moment ago," she marvelled. "Annie, make certain ye keep that fire stoked."

"It's the potion," Henry explained. "It comes and goes."

He no longer feared the cold, now that he knew he would wake from it. He allowed his body to relax and slept.

His nap was brief, and he woke hungry. The woman and the girl were gone, but a man sat near the fire. He silently looked Henry over and ladled him a bowlful of soup. Henry devoured it and followed it up with two more.

His clothes sat atop a chair, neatly folded. He dressed, disregarding the blood and bullet holes. It would do until he could return home and change. The man watched him check the condition of all his belongings, but said nothing until Henry strapped the empty sheath to his leg and pulled his boot over it.

"Lost your weapon?"

"I left it with a friend. I wouldn't wish her to be unprotected."

He took a seat. There was a lingering unsteadiness in his legs. At the rate he was improving, he believed his best course of action would be to spend the remainder of the day and night doing nothing but eating and sleeping. First, however, he had business to attend to.

"Allow me to thank you, sir, and your wife for your kind assistance. I'm most obliged. It's not a common man who would open his home to a complete stranger."

The man chuckled. "It's common enough in this home. Peg and I, y'see, we do all the doctoring hereabouts. You were in a bad way. Wouldn't've been too Christian of us not to take ye in."

Henry nodded. "If you let me know your usual fee for such

work, I will make certain you are properly compensated for your time and effort."

The amount the man quoted was much lower than Henry thought fair. Once he was well, he would send a man by with payment. He intended to investigate the matter before deciding on a price he believed this family actually deserved.

He feigned weariness, and lay back down upon the table, refusing offers of a more comfortable place to rest or even a pillow. He had already imposed upon them enough by taking over half their house. He dozed off briefly. The effect of the potion left him only a bit chilled now, rather than icy cold. The man remained in the room for a time, but left within the half hour to attend to other matters. The girl entered shortly thereafter to tend the fire.

"Thank you, Annie."

She jumped and whirled to face him. "Oh!" She bobbed an awkward curtsy. "My pleasure, sir."

Henry sat up. "How old are you, Annie?"

"Nine, sir."

"Perfect. I'm in need of a youngster to carry a message for me."

Her lips pinched into a frown. "There's a boy a few doors down…"

"No. I would like to hire you for the job."

"Me, sir?"

"You have two good legs, yes? And a good head on your shoulders?"

She nodded. "Yes, sir, but I haven't never been a messenger, sir."

"If that boy down the street can do it, you can do it," he told her. "Do you know your way to 10 Downing Street?"

Her eyes grew big and round. "Where the government lives?" She nodded again, with vigor.

"Excellent. This message has two parts. The first will get

you to the right people. The second is for their ears only. Don't breathe a word of it to anyone else. Do you understand?"

"Yes, sir."

Henry dumped a few coins from the small purse he carried tied inside his breeches and held up one silver sixpence. She gasped. He doubted she'd had more than a few farthings in all of her life.

"I will pay you this for learning the message. If you deliver it successfully, I will add this." He set a half-crown beside the first coin.

Annie let out a low whistle. "Who are you, mister?"

"I'm not at liberty to say. Now, have a seat. You need to learn to recite this message exactly as I tell you."

He formulated the words in his head. Short. Clear. Difficult to mistake.

Testimony compromised. Expert in danger. Send loyal men.

Annie sat and folded her hands in her lap, as serious as any child he'd seen. "I'm ready. I'm gonna work real hard. I promise." Her voice dropped to a whisper. "When I grow up, I want to be a spy like you."

Her words brought a smile to his lips. "Good girl. I knew you'd be right for this job."

XLVI

I Will Speak My Mind

$\mathcal{E}$LLE COULDN'T BELIEVE how many people had turned out to witness her presentation. At least two hundred men and a scattering of women packed the atrium. Some of the men were high-ranking military, and, like Colonel Wilton-Bowles, had turned out in uniform. Most looked like men of some importance, with shining shoes and hats and glittering watch fobs. Their speech and demeanor were painfully proper. Elle bowed and nodded to one gentleman after another, as Westfield guided her through the crush, stopping often to shake hands and make introductions.

Even freshly washed and wearing a suit as fine as any here, Westfield looked haggard. The last few days had been rough on him, and he didn't expect a good outcome today. True smiles touched his lips, however, as he greeted friends and acquaintances. He was in his element. Crowds made him happy. They made Elle want to shrink into the background, just the unnamed girl behind the bar. Today she was the center of attention and she would be uncomfortable until her speech began.

Her plans played over and over in her head. Basic plan, contingency plan, secondary contingency plan. What to say. When to say it. Her drive to defy her captors and end their stranglehold on the potions market was all-consuming. It was the only thing keeping her going. They thought her silence submission, her trembling hands fear. Only she knew the truth. It was purpose. It was rage.

"...My niece, Miss Elle Deschamps?"

"Ah, Miss Deschamps!" the half-bald, white-haired gentleman exclaimed. "I understand you have some interesting information to impart this afternoon. I did not as yet have time to read through all my papers, but the summary was intriguing. I look forward to your take on the situation."

She blinked at him. Was he speaking of Henry's report? What had Westfield said his name was? Gladstone? *Merde.* She had been brooding while being introduced to the Prime Minister.

"Thank you, sir," she murmured.

He nodded to them and moved on to greet someone else.

Elle gripped her uncle's arm. "He has received Henry's report," she whispered. "Those papers and my speech were intended to verify one another. I will speak the truth today. I must. Do you understand?"

He patted her hand. "I do, child. I do. Say what is in your heart, and don't give a thought to anything else. They cannot do you harm while all eyes are upon you. The rest is in God's hands. I pray he will be merciful. You have suffered quite enough."

A tremor of grief shuddered through her, and tears stung her eyes. She choked them back, clenching her fists, straightening her spine. The pain fueled her resolve. Henry would never have given up, and neither would she.

A soldier held open the door to the lecture hall so she and Westfield could enter. Additional soldiers were stationed at the other doors, and yet more lined the walls inside. They were acting as ushers, but Elle knew they were here as enforcers. She wished she knew for whom. She prayed there wouldn't be violence.

Elle had never been in a lecture hall before, or even in a

university building, and she slowed her pace to get a look at the room as she entered. Rows of seats formed a semicircle that faced a raised platform adorned only with a single lectern. She didn't think she would use it. She would speak better moving back and forth across the stage. She had hardly slept in two days, yet her body felt afire with nervous energy.

She maneuvered her way to the dais, squeezing through the lines of people flooding into the seats. Several soldiers nodded at her as she passed by. Friends? Enemies? Their unflinching posture and watchful eyes reminded her of Henry.

A tear drizzled down her cheek as she fought the urge to seek out every glimpse of blond hair. He wasn't here. She couldn't bring him back. She would take the only path left to her. Destroy their enemies. Finish the mission they had begun together.

"You appear distressed, Miss Deschamps."

Elle jumped at the sound of Lady de Winter's voice.

"Have no fear," Charlotte continued in her fake sweet tone. "You are well-rehearsed. You know exactly what to say, do you not?"

Elle's face settled into a mask of impassivity. "I do, indeed, Lady de Winter." Her voice was cold with disdain. "My memory is not lacking, as you seem to think."

"Do as you are told," she hissed. "We will be watching and listening attentively. We don't want another repeat of the 'unfortunate incident' that occurred the other night, do we?"

Elle let her hatred show on her face. "No, we don't."

Charlotte smiled. "Good. I'm glad we understand one another."

She left Elle without any further farewell and took a seat in the front row, beside Colonel Wilton-Bowles and their silent companion whose name Elle had never learned. She didn't see Ellison Blake or any hired muscle. They would be lurking somewhere nearby.

Westfield walked her onto the stage, then left her standing

to the side while he took the podium. Not everyone had yet found a seat, and he had to wait for the room to fall quiet. He thanked everyone for coming with the same genuine enthusiasm he had expressed when greeting them in the hall. He reiterated why they were gathered here, though it seemed unlikely anyone had wandered in without prior knowledge. Lastly, he looked at Elle and introduced her to the audience. He went on at some length about her abilities and her experience in the potions industry. He kept his comments vague, not telling any falsehoods, but giving the impression her schooling and her work had been far more glamorous than the humble reality.

When he finished, he waved Elle toward the podium. She nodded to acknowledge the polite applause. She could no longer remember the words Charlotte de Winter had crafted for her. So many other, more important things warred for attention in her mind. She watched Westfield step down from the stage. Lady de Winter's servant, Wilson, met him there, and they remained standing, very near to a side exit. Elle turned her gaze to the front row and saw Charlotte nod. One wrong word, and Westfield would disappear out that door.

"Good afternoon, Ladies and Gentlemen," Elle began. "Thank you all for coming. I'm humbled to see such a large turnout for this briefing."

She was off-script already, and she looked for a reaction from her enemies. Their tight smiles didn't change. That wouldn't last.

Elle spent a few moments reiterating the severity of the potions shortage and the reasons for undertaking her journey. She paced back and forth as she spoke, which eased her nerves and let her watch the entire room.

The rehearsed speech came back to her as she continued, and she emphasized the rumors of bandits hijacking supply lines. Colonel Wilton-Bowles nodded approvingly. Elle turned to Egypt and their discovery of a serum source beyond the cataracts. Again, she dwelt on the inaccessibility of the source due to criminal behavior. She used the sabotaged gangplank and her dunking in the river as an example of the dangers.

Faces around the room grew grim. She looked for smiles among them, and found a few. Were they also shareholders of the company, she wondered, or men who wanted to see the potions industry fail? She was glad to see that, apart from Wilton-Bowles, the military men appeared universally unhappy with the news. They didn't want to expend their troops and resources harvesting serum.

"Unable to reach the Egyptian source on our own, we made the decision to sail to America and investigate the potions situation in the New World. Aboard the ocean liner to Charleston, I was attacked. Myself and my colleagues believe it was an attempt to halt our investigation."

This was the first serious deviation from her instructions. Lady de Winter scowled. Elle glanced at Westfield and rushed ahead with her talk, returning to approved topics. Charlotte's face grew smug. She still believed Elle was afraid to push too far.

Elle let her expertise shine as she discussed Charleston. She went into great detail about Blake's source, covering its abundance and the ease of extracting the serum. Some of the tension in the room began to subside as she gushed.

"Unfortunately, the Charleston source is privately owned, by a man named Ellison Blake. He has an absolute monopoly on the potions in that area of the world, and we wouldn't be able to make use of the serum without negotiating a deal with him."

At this point, Elle had been coached to say that representatives of the Imperial Potions Company were already in the process of negotiations, and were looking forward to further international agreements. Lady de Winter had worded this portion in a most particular manner. Elle saw her enemies lean forward in anticipation, eager to hear themselves presented as the heroes who would end the crisis.

Elle took a deep breath. It was time. "I highly recommend *against* such a course of action," she declared. "Blake is an unprincipled man who treats his workers poorly and who uses addictive potions to exert control over the wealthy and influential people in his town."

Charlotte turned red with rage. She made a signal, and Wilson seized Westfield, dragging him from the room. Elle choked back a sob of pain and terror and forged ahead, inflecting her voice with a strength she didn't feel.

"Blake used his rather questionable authority to send the police after us." A number of men in the audience would know Westfield had been detained for a time and know her words for the truth. "I do owe him something of a debt of thanks, however, because when I changed course to avoid his people, I stumbled upon the solution to our troubles—a small source, out in the countryside, difficult for an untrained eye to see, and too little to be of commercial value."

Her enemies had begun to fidget. They couldn't speak out against her without giving themselves away, and they had nothing further with which to threaten her. Colonel Wilton-Bowles had a hand on his sidearm, but she didn't think him mad enough to shoot her in front of a crowd. It didn't matter. They had taken her heart and her hope. They could take her life. But nothing could take away the truth. The words flowed now, fueled with a purpose that had become her all.

"I reunited with my uncle in New York," Elle continued, glancing to where Westfield should have been. Eyes followed her gaze and noted his absence. "While he arranged a meeting with representatives of the Imperial Potions Company—who had been following our every move—I explored the area for more of these small sources. I found a new source in every location I searched. These sources are everywhere. My little niece even dug up a bit of serum-laced soil in her own garden, right here in London."

Faces that had worn frowns were now wide-eyed, and riveted. Those that had been smiling looked angry.

"I have extracted serum from such places myself, and if

we can put more research into the extraction techniques, I'm certain we can reduce or even eliminate our need for foreign sources for our potions. Any person with time and knowledge can harvest some small amount. Potions can be made low in cost and easily available for business, recreation, and medicinal uses."

"You lying whore!" thundered Wilton-Bowles, springing to his feet. His hand grasped the gun at his side, sending a surge of fear through her.

"Sit down," hissed the man beside him.

"She'll ruin us, Pierce! She's a lying bitch. We need my men to protect us, not some harebrained backyard gardening!" The hand with the gun twitched.

"The gentlemen up front are unhappy with my findings, naturally," Elle said, protecting herself in the only way she could devise. "They hold large stakes in the Imperial Potions Company and don't wish to lose control over the industry. The colonel's words here simply reinforce our discovery that they have been recruiting a private army to protect their monopoly. If we dig deeper, I don't doubt the supposed criminals choking our serum supplies are mercenaries doing it at their urging."

Angry words rose from the crowd. She couldn't tell whether they were directed at her, or whether the men were squabbling amongst themselves. She rushed to finish.

"It's a shame such unscrupulous people run the company." She almost shouted to keep her words above the clamor. "I would have been happy to work with them to adapt their business based on my discoveries, but for their repeated attempts to harm and thwart me. I have suffered through harassment, kidnappings, attempts on my life, and threats intended to alter my words to you here today. Notice my uncle's absence. They hold him hostage to assure my silence and they have already murdered my p-partner." Her composure broke. A rush of tears clouded her vision, and violent sobs racked her body. "You m-m-must excuse me. I f-fear for my uncle's life."

She fled the stage and ran for the side door. Behind her a gun fired. Someone screamed. Men and women everywhere sprang to their feet, shouting and shoving. Elle pushed through the crowd, fending off questions, trying to shield herself from enemies as she forced her way to the exit.

"I did it, Henry," she whispered to the air. "I did the right thing. For us."

XLVII

Checkmate

$\mathcal{L}$ADY DE WINTER'S MAN made enough noise for an amateur to tail him. Henry ducked behind pillars and into doorways, picking his way down the corridor away from the lecture hall. He used more caution than necessary. Wilson was too preoccupied to turn around. He stomped and muttered as he pushed Westfield along, complaining and repeatedly referring to Elle as a "stupid bitch." Henry looked forward to clobbering him.

He wished he could have stayed behind and listened to the end of her speech. She had been magnificent. He could have watched her for hours, in awe of her beautiful defiance. But he had a job to do. A life to save. And it wasn't hers. She didn't need him.

He loved her all the more for it. His Elle. Elle who was his by choice. Elle who had enough wit and determination to save the world. Elle who knew how to seduce a spy and steal the heart of a thief. Elle who deserved a goddamned happily ever after.

He wasn't much of a prince, but he'd do his best. Starting by saving a man who had become like family to her.

Westfield plodded along, feigning fatigue. It allowed Henry to shorten the gap between them, but frustrated Wilson, who jabbed Westfield with the revolver and growled at him.

Westfield picked up the pace, and the men disappeared down a side hall. Henry hurried his step to catch them up.

He peered around the corner. They had paused near the end of the hall, some twenty yards off. Henry drew his weapon—a wooden gun belonging to his nephew. Reggie's hunting rifles were far too bulky to conceal, and the household had no other firearms. The large kitchen knives had been equally useless. Henry had only a paring knife in his boot.

"They ought to be here, somewhere," Wilson grumbled.

Henry didn't wait to discover who "they" might be. He sprinted down the hall. The pounding of his boots on the tile reverberated through the empty chamber. Wilson started and whirled around, but before he could take aim, Henry slammed into him, jamming the toy into his back.

"Drop your gun or I pull the trigger," he ordered.

The thug flinched, and the hand holding the pistol wavered. The hesitation was good enough for Henry. He brought his free hand crashing down on Wilson's wrist, and the gun clattered to the floor. Henry scooped it up. It was a poor quality revolver, not one he would ever choose for himself, but it was better than no weapon at all.

"Hollis!" Wilson shouted. "Dammit, man, where are you?"

Henry slammed the butt of the pistol against the side of Wilson's head. He staggered. Henry hit him a second time and he collapsed.

"Quickly," Henry urged. His breaths came fast and labored. A few seconds of running and his legs felt like jelly. The trauma of the gunshot wound had left him weak. They needed to get away while they still could. He gave Westfield a nudge. "Back to the lecture hall."

Westfield's face was ashen. He stood frozen in place, staring at Henry as if he were seeing a ghost. Henry couldn't fault him for it. He felt a bit shocked to be alive, himself.

"Henry," the older man gasped. "How—how are you alive?"

"Healing potion. From Elle's bag. She spilled it where I could reach."

Westfield blinked, seeming to come to his senses. "Thank the Lord."

"I do," Henry replied, pushing the older man down the hall. "I thank Him for her every damn day. And this from a man who never sets foot inside a church if he can possibly avoid it."

A door behind them swung open. Henry jerked around, his finger on the trigger.

"I'd stop right there, if I were you," Blake drawled in his thick American accent. His hireling, Hollis, stood behind his left shoulder. They were both brandishing heavy American revolvers. "It appears the young lady has been misbehaving. We can't let that go unpunished, can we?"

Westfield jumped in front of Henry, shielding him with his larger frame and cutting off most of Henry's sightlines.

"I won't let her lose you again," he vowed.

Blake chuckled. "So noble."

Henry took a step back, looking over Westfield's shoulder to keep the revolver aimed at Blake's heart. They were in an odd sort of stalemate. He couldn't shoot either man, or the other would fire on Westfield. If either Blake or Hollis were to shoot first, Henry would likewise respond. He could certainly kill Blake before anyone had a chance to shoot directly at him. Would Blake risk firing anyway, hoping a single bullet could incapacitate them both? Fasching's derringer had shot him clean through, but that had been at closer range.

Hollis nudged Wilson's unconscious form with his toe. "Don't think he's dead," he remarked.

"Who cares?" Blake replied. "The man isn't competent enough to bring the prisoner to his execution. Or even to check that a body is dead before dumping it, it seems."

"Your friends are ruined, Blake," Henry called out. "You may as well return home. You won't be making any money off them."

"And why should I believe the likes of you?"

"Because the alternative is for us all to die, right here, right now. Let us go, and you'll be free to return home. I won't send anyone after you."

It would be no use to pursue Blake. Prosecuting a foreign citizen on vague charges of conspiracy and accessory to various crimes would be impossible, and much as Henry disliked the man, assassination was out of the question. He would ask Gladstone to send a report to the American government.

Blake's scowl didn't change. "I think not. I think I can get a good shot from here."

He was bluffing. If he believed he had a chance, he would have taken it already.

"Don't be a fool. There's nothing here for you. The last thing Elle told the crowd was what a terrible idea it would be to do business with you."

The American's pale face turned a furious crimson. Henry's heart pounded. If he had miscalculated, they would all be dead within seconds.

"Pull the trigger and kill us all," he continued, "or walk out the nearest door and go back to Charleston, no worse off than before. The choice is yours."

Blake began to back away. Henry did the same, pulling Westfield along.

"I'll see you hanged someday, spy," Blake snarled.

"Not bloody likely."

They edged down the hallway. Each step made the accuracy of any shots less certain. Henry had little confidence in the reliability of Wilson's pistol. He suspected Blake's gun was of much higher quality. He chanced a glance over his shoulder to see how far the corner was. Ten feet, at most.

He tugged on Westfield's coat, and was about to tell him to run for it, when Blake and Hollis opened fire. Henry shoved Westfield aside and fired back. The revolver jammed after the third shot, but by that time the two men had reached the corner and spun out of harm's way. They raced half-way down the hall before ducking into a side room to rest.

Henry gasped for air. His chest burned, and his head spun. He couldn't keep up this pace for much longer. Westfield's face had gone pale, and he clutched his arm, grimacing in pain.

"Are you… hit?" Henry panted.

"Grazed," Westfield replied. "It's not bad."

Henry examined the wound. It was bleeding profusely, but it wasn't deep.

"Give me your handkerchief and your necktie."

Westfield winced as he unknotted the tie, but he gritted his teeth and made no complaints while Henry bound the gash. When it was over, a hint of a smile even touched his lips.

"Thank you. That is better already."

"We need to get back to the lecture hall. We will be safer among the crowd, and I'm concerned for Elle." He paused, listening to the rumble of distant voices that told him her speech had ended, one way or another.

Westfield looked at the door and hesitated. "Do you think Blake and his man have followed us?"

"No. I think they will cut their losses and leave for America. I nicked one of them when I returned fire. I heard a yelp, but didn't get a good look. Lady de Winter and the others watching Elle may be armed, though, and I haven't spotted Fasching at all."

"He's dead."

Henry's eyebrows shot up. "Elle stabbed him?"

"Yes. He tried to put his hands on her and she had a knife hidden in her skirts. Truly, though, I think she did it more for you than for herself."

Henry couldn't hold back a smile at that thought. She had made good use of his knife, it seemed, and saved him the trouble of doing the deed himself. "Hell of a woman. I'd wager half her audience is in love with her by now. Let's find her before I have to fight off dozens of rival suitors. We will need to take care, though. This blasted pistol has seized up completely."

Westfield nodded and reached for the doorknob. He had turned it halfway when he froze. "Someone is coming," he whispered.

Henry listened to the approaching footsteps. They were lighter than Blake and Hollis's had been, and made by a different sort of shoe. "Those are a woman's steps."

"Elle!" Westfield exclaimed. He threw open the door and rushed into the hall.

Henry cursed and ran after him, coming within an inch of colliding with Lady Charlotte de Winter. She jumped away, startled. An instant later, a smile spread across her face. She drew a dainty gun from her purse.

"Captain Ainsworth. What an interesting turn of events. You look rather pallid. Has your health suffered of late?"

Henry backpedaled and trained the inoperative revolver on her. He would have to bluff his way through this.

Charlotte craned her neck, looking past him down the corridor. "I suggest you come out, Miss Deschamps," she called, "unless you would like to see your lover gunned down a second time."

She brought her gaze back to Henry and raised her pistol until he was staring directly down the barrel.

"And I promise I will do a better job of it."

· · · 🝳 · · ·

Elle dashed from behind the pillar, boots in hand, her bare feet nearly silent on the hard floor.

Henry.

He was there. Real. Alive. Joy burst through her. His name sprang to her lips, only to die there, unspoken, choked by a new fear that clenched around her heart like an icy claw. Charlotte de Winter had a gun leveled straight at his beautiful blue eyes.

No!

Her boots clattered to the floor and she ran toward him, her memory burning with the sight of that horrible, bloody wound in his chest. She wanted to rip his jacket open to reassure herself that he was healed, that he wasn't a mere apparition. She wanted to fling herself at him and kiss him senseless. She wanted to throw herself into the path of the gun to shield him from harm.

She skidded to a halt at his side. His skin was pale and his eyes lacked their usual brightness, but she could find no signs he was otherwise in distress.

"Presume not that I am the thing I was," he murmured, quoting his favorite Henry play.

Elle spared a glance at Westfield. He wasn't as white as Henry, but he didn't look well, either. His right arm was bloodied, and she hoped he wasn't in too much pain. Thank God that was the only injury from the gunfire she'd heard.

She could feel the rapid beat of her pulse throbbing in her neck. Her breath came in ragged little gasps. *Henry. Oh, God, my Henry.*

She could lose him. What cruel fate would restore him to her only to make her watch as he was torn from her once again? No. No. She would not let it happen. She would die first.

She turned her gaze to Lady de Winter. "I'm here. You may lower your weapon."

Charlotte laughed. "And let him shoot me? I think not."

"You know he won't. We don't all condone murder."

"An odd sentiment from a woman who knifed a man not two days ago."

"There are three of us, Lady de Winter," Henry said, "and you have but one shot. You can't kill us all, and if you try, you will surely die. Is a moment's revenge worth that price?"

"And whom would you choose to revenge yourself upon?" Elle added brazenly, desperate to draw her attention away from Henry. "It is I who have ruined your plans, after all."

"Leaving you broken-hearted has a certain appeal,"

Charlotte replied, "but you showed surprising resilience before. Perhaps you are right." Her hand moved toward Elle.

"Drop your weapon or I will shoot!" Henry commanded. His finger squeezed the trigger.

Charlotte's gun clattered to the floor. Henry's grip relaxed. "Kick it over here."

She kicked it, but in the opposite direction, sending it skittering down the hall, well out of reach.

"That will do. Elle, perhaps you could fetch it for us?"

He sounded calm enough, but there was something anxious in his request. He knew she was terrified of guns. And why even bother with the pistol? It was too far away to be of use to anyone. If Charlotte ran for it, or one of her men appeared and tried to pick it up, Henry would fire, wouldn't he? Her stomach heaved. Unless he was out of bullets.

Sweat dripped from Elle's temple. Her mouth had gone dry. Henry was using a worthless gun and needed Charlotte's weapon. It would be too suspicious to go after it himself. Sending Elle made perfect sense. No one would doubt he wanted her to have protection, whatever his situation.

She fought back the sickness rising in her throat. Lady de Winter had surrendered too easily. Elle suspected hidden weapons or allies lying in wait nearby. She eyed the other woman, looking for bulges beneath her skirts, or any place where the fabric didn't hang as it should.

Elle edged toward the gun, not letting her eyes stray from her enemy. She had no weapons of her own, no potions, no other way to help. She slid over the black and white tiles, a chess piece in a deadly game. Henry had called her his queen, but her moves were limited, and none of the options good. With every square she stepped she left her knight more vulnerable.

"Westfield, could you pop back inside that reading room and find a curtain tie or other bit of rope?" Henry requested. "I think it best if we bind Lady de Winter's hands before we take her to the authorities."

The sounds of pandemonium still rumbled from the direction of the lecture hall. The authorities would be otherwise occupied.

Elle came to a halt beside the tiny gun. It was a pretty thing, with a polished silver barrel and a carved ivory handle. No amount of beauty could disguise its ugly purpose. Could she bring herself to touch it? She considered kicking it to Henry, but any jolt risked a misfire. Instead, she fidgeted and waited, watching Charlotte. Lady de Winter stood tall, her body calm. Not the look of a conquered foe. Her hands poked out of big, lacy cuffs. They were clearly visible, flat against the front of her skirt, her arms crossed at the wrist. It was a non-threatening pose, but Elle didn't like how a purse still dangled from her wrist. She could have anything in there—a knife, an explosive potion, another gun.

Elle looked back down at the pistol, trying to work past her fear and pick it up. All she had to do was to point it at Charlotte while Henry tied her up. Her hands were shaking already, and she didn't know the proper way to aim. It might be safer on the floor.

The carving in the center of the ivory handle caught her eye. The mirror of Venus, just like on the potion cups in Charleston. Emboldened by her curiosity, Elle knelt down. With one finger, she flipped the gun over. The opposite side bore not the shield and spear of Ares, but the de Winter monogram.

Her heart skipped a beat. Was there a male version of the pistol? His and hers matching guns? Her head jerked back up.

Westfield returned with a twisted gold curtain tie with tassels dangling from either end. He held it out to Henry, who offered him the revolver in return.

No!

Elle nearly screamed the word aloud. It didn't matter that the gun was useless. The lie was his protection, and he was destroying it by handing the weapon over to a man with an injury to his dominant arm.

Henry took a step forward. Elle's palm covered the ivory handle. Charlotte's hands shifted. Something glittered beneath her lacy cuffs.

"A pair!" Elle screamed. "The gun has a pair!"

She seized the pistol and lifted it, but Charlotte and Henry were both faster. Henry dove for the ground, taking out Charlotte's legs. She flailed and her gun discharged as she fell. Henry grunted in pain. A smear of blood spread across his thigh.

"Fuck!" he shouted. He grabbed a fistful of Charlotte's skirts to prevent her from fleeing and tried to pin her arms with his other hand. "God. Damn. Fucking. Bitch!"

Elle clasped the pistol with two hands, trying to hold it steady. Her entire body shook. Sweat dripped into her eyes. She had no clear shot. Westfield fumbled with the revolver, swinging the cylinder open and closed in an attempt to make it function.

On the floor, Charlotte kicked Henry repeatedly with her wicked-looking heels, aiming for his groin and other sensitive areas. She landed a blow directly on the bullet wound, and he shouted more obscenities. She thrust her hand into the mass of feathers that decorated her hat.

"Knife!" Elle cried.

Henry rolled away as Charlotte slashed at him with the nastiest-looking hatpin Elle had ever seen. It was wide and double-edged, almost a blade. The tip gleamed wetly.

Poison.

A long tear ran across the front of Henry's jacket. Elle could hardly breathe. If he had gotten even the slightest scratch it could be deadly, and she had no remedies at hand. Charlotte de Winter smiled and swung again, this time going for his face. Elle's terror for Henry overpowered all her other feelings. She pulled the trigger.

The recoil of the gun knocked her back onto her bottom, and the weapon clattered to the floor.

Charlotte whimpered in pain, but didn't release the knife. Her left arm hung limp at her side. Blood gushed from her shoulder.

"I will not go down alone," she snarled, and flung the knife at Elle.

Henry dove in front of the tumbling blade. The point caught him squarely in the back.

"No!" Elle screamed.

She scrambled toward him as he calmly picked up the hat pin, wiped it clean on Charlotte's skirts, then tossed it aside. He pulled a small kitchen knife from his boot and sliced a length of cloth from his trousers. Elle snatched up the pin. If she had the poison, she could make an antidote. The tip was dry. Her heart hammered. She grabbed at Charlotte's hem, trying to find where he had wiped it. Nothing. She couldn't waste more time searching.

"Henry, you must get up," she begged. She clutched at his sleeve, trying to urge him to follow as she sprang to her feet. "We must find an apothecary before the poison sets in!"

He glanced at her, but continued winding the cloth around his leg. Dear Lord, he was so pale. Tears filled her eyes. She was going to lose him and this time it would be forever.

"Elle…" he began. He tied off the bandage and looked up into her eyes. A smile spread across his face, showing the dimples she adored. "Darling, I'm not poisoned."

"It only takes a scratch." Lady de Winter's voice was weak, but her sneer had lost none of its arrogance. "I give you five minutes. At least I will have some measure of revenge."

She groaned in pain and closed her eyes. She was bleeding profusely and no longer able to sit up. Westfield knelt beside her. He tried to press a cloth to the wound, but she swatted him away.

Elle clung to Henry's arm, tugging on him in desperation. He pried her fingers off and began to unbutton his jacket.

"I'm fine, love. Look. After the other night, I thought it best to take precautions."

He peeled off the jacket to reveal a vest stitched together from scraps of leather that covered his entire chest and back. Scratches from the knife were visible, but hadn't come close to penetrating.

"I intend to make a nicer one when I have the time. Perhaps with a metal plate to cover my heart."

"Body armor!" She gasped a few heaving sighs of relief, sinking to the floor beside him. "Oh, Henry." She wrapped her arms around his neck, clutching him as tightly as she ever had. "Don't you ever scare me like that again, Henry Ainsworth!"

"I told you I try not to be reckless." He cradled her against his chest. "I will never forget that I have someone to come home to."

Every emotion that she had endured over the last forty-eight hours seemed to collapse in on her at once, leaving her with an overwhelming need to hold him, to possess him, to reassure herself that he was alive and he was hers. She crushed his mouth with a kiss, pushing him down onto the tile floor and straddling him until their whole bodies were pressed one against the other. She would never let him go. Not for the rest of her life.

"Elle!"

Westfield's sharp tone brought her back to her senses, and she looked up. He was no longer attempting to attend to Charlotte's wound, but he had bound her hands with the curtain tie. She still wore a scowl on her face. Elle pitied her. Even in danger of losing her life, the only emotion she possessed was hatred.

"Let the boy up so we can tend to his injuries."

"I have injuries?" Henry murmured. "I had almost forgotten."

He let Elle help him to his feet, and he rechecked the makeshift bandage as she pulled her boots on.

"It's not terrible, but it hurts like hell, and I ought to drink a healing potion when I can. Let's check in on the situation in the lecture hall and let someone know about all this."

"I will stay with Lady de Winter," Westfield offered.

"Good. Take shelter in the reading room if anything looks suspicious."

Elle took hold of Henry's hand and they started down the hall, Henry limping along on his wounded leg. She didn't walk as briskly as usual, but he struggled to keep pace with her, even so.

"I'm damned sick of getting shot," he growled.

"I'm damned sick of you getting shot, also."

He stopped abruptly. "Do you want me to retire?"

She did. She wanted him home. She wanted him safe. But more than anything she wanted him happy. She looked straight into his eyes and took a deep breath, knowing he would do whatever she asked.

"Never for me. For yourself alone."

He squeezed her hand. He knew her words were at best a half-truth. She knew he would never call her out on it.

XLVIII

Such Sweet Sorrow

$\mathcal{T}$wo full days of one-on-one debriefings and potions demonstrations had left Elle exhausted. The words on the page began to blur. She was forced to put aside the book, but she didn't turn down the lamp. She wouldn't sleep until Henry was in bed beside her.

She lay her head back on the pillow and closed her eyes. There were so many things she would need to do now that this job was over; but her thoughts kept drifting to her dream house, where she would have a parlor with a pianoforte and a library for all her books. She couldn't afford such a place yet, but if she accepted Henry's loan and started a successful business, perhaps someday…

She hovered just at the edge of true sleep when the door creaked. Her eyelids fluttered open and she rolled on to her side. Henry locked the door behind him and slipped out of his coat, hanging it over the back of a chair.

"I thought you might be waiting up. I'm sorry to have taken so long. We spent a great deal of time negotiating."

She watched him unbutton his shirt, feeling much more alert than she had only a moment before.

"Negotiating?"

"Yes." He heaved a sigh. "I'm going to Egypt. I am to leave tomorrow noon."

Elle nodded. It wasn't unexpected, but she wished the assignment weren't so soon, or so far away.

"The army is tasked with tracking down and flushing out the mercenaries who took over the serum supply," Henry continued. "They liked my maps. They want someone who knows the area and has local connections." He kicked off his boots and began to unfasten his trousers. "It's considered part of our same mission. I can't turn it down. We need the money if we are to start a family someday."

He didn't bother to don the worn trousers he used as nightclothes, but instead climbed into bed naked. He gave a murmur of appreciation when he found Elle in the same state.

"I'm sorry to leave you."

Elle wrapped an arm around him. "I understand. How long will you be gone?"

"I can't say. I was told a month, not counting travel time, but I've learned never to trust those predictions. It could easily run two, three, more. I need to be there before I can fully assess the situation."

She trailed her fingers across his chest, pausing over the scar he would now bear for the rest of his life.

"Be careful."

He kissed her brow. "I promise. There is some good to come out of this. It falls outside the scope of the original assignment, and I was able to argue for a pay increase."

Her eyes widened. "A pay increase? Above the five thousand pounds?"

"All of the information we have provided them over these last few days left quite the impression. Your soil samples are creating a sensation. They were reluctant at first, but I insisted. They have agreed to increase your salary threefold."

"What?" Elle blurted. *Her* salary?

"It's still far less than you deserve, but it should provide you enough to start your new life in good financial standing."

"You negotiated a pay increase for me?" She still couldn't quite believe it. And three times the amount? She was stunned.

"I threatened to quit."

"But you just said that you needed to take the assignment. That we need the money if we are to start a family."

"They didn't know that."

She could imagine the conversation. They must have been as shocked as she was now. He had risked walking away with nothing over a perceived slight to her. Then again, she considered, they probably liked such audacity from their spy. She certainly did.

She nuzzled his neck. "You are beyond wonderful, *mon espion téméraire.*"

"I'm not reckless," he huffed.

Elle could only laugh. She trailed kisses along his jawline until she reached his mouth.

His lips parted beneath hers. His strong hands grasped her about the waist and pulled her atop him. She sank into his embrace, and for a time let herself forget everything except the taste of him, the scent of him, and the sensation of their two bodies moving together. Afterward, she didn't roll off as usual, but lay against his chest, listening to the beating of his heart.

"We can travel together as far as Paris," he murmured. His fingers ran in long, slow strokes through her hair.

"That's good." She would have him all to herself for a few days.

"Should I expect to find you there when I return?"

"No," she answered immediately. "No, I can't stay. I will gather my things and say adieu to Aunt Madeline before she sets off with her new husband. There are too many old memories in the city. I will make my new home elsewhere."

"How will I find you?"

"I will write to you when I'm settled."

"Send your letters to my father's house. He will forward them if possible. Otherwise, I will read them all on my way home." His arms tightened around her. "I will miss you terribly. God, it makes me think I ought to have quit for real."

She snorted. "You would be crashing your bicycle within a week. What would you do when even that became boring? Steam car racing?"

"Cards. Better mental stimulation, and if I cheated, there would be a chance of getting shot. I also fancy the idea of becoming a jewel thief. Plenty of midnight sneaking in that profession."

"I can't tell if you are serious, or if you are teasing me."

"Both."

"Then I must tell you, I much prefer you as a spy."

"Even though I must leave you?"

She pressed a fierce kiss to his lips. "You promised never to do that. Since I know you to be a man of your word, I trust you to return to me."

His grip on her was so tight it hurt. She didn't complain.

"Always," he vowed.

Epilogue

December, 1882

*H*ENRY FROZE, staring up at the sign in disbelief. Either he was in the wrong place or he had gone stark-raving mad. He had to glance down at the paper in his hand, though he had memorized the address days ago, along with her brief note.

I miss you. I love you. -E

His eyes traveled back up to the sign, swaying gently in the winter breeze. *Ainsworth & Gérard - Fine Potions and Remedies.* Bloody hell, she was using his name. A carriage rumbled past, splattering him with icy water, and shaking some sense into him. He was in the right place, and he wasn't dreaming.

The shop was closed for the evening, but the lock gave way easily to his picks, even with shaky hands. He would be speaking to the landlord about that.

Henry pushed the door wide and stepped through. Darkness shrouded the small shop, but his well-adjusted eyes quickly located the shelf that held lanterns and other potion-fueled items. He lit two lanterns and pointed them in opposite directions to illuminate the space.

Elle's pocket torch sat on the top shelf, listed at a hefty five pounds sterling. He swiped it and stashed it in his pocket. He hoped she'd applied for a patent.

The shop was clean, uncluttered, and pristinely organized. He could see her influence in the selection of goods, the labels, the items locked behind the counter—quality items, stored simply, nothing flashy. He felt comfortable here, as if he belonged. The only thing missing was Elle herself.

Along one wall, above the non-potion herbs and remedies, was a full shelf of teas and herbal tisanes. He grinned and scanned the selection, pleased with the variety. Jammed in the back was a tin marked "not for sale." Curious, he pushed the other tins aside and reached for it.

"Stop, thief!"

Henry turned toward the woman who had shouted. She was petite, but her stance suggested an underlying toughness, and she held a revolver as if she knew how to use it. This was Marie, he surmised, Elle's friend from the bar, and now her business partner.

"You must be Madame Gérard," he said in French. He turned back to the tea, pulling the tin from the shelf. "My favorite!" he declared. "A second flush Darjeeling. Darker and more full-bodied than the first harvest tea, with delightful muscatel notes."

She stared at him as if he were crazy. He couldn't blame her. He sounded like his wine-peddling relatives.

Henry popped the top off the tin to take a sniff. Something glinted atop the tea. A gold wedding band, sized for a man, sat on a small slip of paper. He fished them both out. The note, written in Elle's curvy hand, read, "If this doesn't fit, the jeweler down the street will exchange it."

Between this discovery and the sign, he couldn't doubt her intentions. It seemed he would be getting married soon. He slipped the ring onto his finger and pocketed the note.

"Someone ought to tell Mrs. Ainsworth not to leave valuables lying around in tea tins," he observed. A thrill ran through him at addressing her in such a manner. "Would you be so good as to tell me where I might find her?"

The revolver was no longer pointed directly at him, but Marie continued to regard him with suspicion.

"She has gone home for the day."

Henry blinked in surprise. "She doesn't live here? Does she have a room nearby?"

"She lives with family."

"With family? But…" His puzzled frown morphed into a look of surprise. "Do you mean my family? She is staying with Emma?"

Marie's expression softened into a smile. "Oui, Monsieur Henri Ainsworth."

"That's rather far to walk here and back every day."

"Oui. She travels by bicycle."

"Does she?" He laughed. "That's my girl for you. Excuse me, I must be going now."

He turned toward the door, but Marie cleared her throat loudly. He glanced back, and she waved the revolver at him.

"Are you going to put back those things you stole?"

"No." He bowed to her. "It's been a pleasure, madame. Good night to you."

She swore at his departing back.

Henry paid the cab driver double, and made the trip to Emma's house in record time, leaping down from the vehicle before it even came to a full stop. Carter met him at the door, ushering him inside and taking his coat and shoulder bag.

"Welcome home, Lord Henry. The family will be pleased to have you home in time for Christmas."

"Is Elle here? I was told she has been living here."

"She is out at the moment."

"What?" Despair washed over him. Did the world despise him? Would he never hold her in his arms again?

"At the dressmaker, I believe. Having her party dress altered."

That hardly seemed like a typical errand for Elle, but Henry didn't know what to make of anything just now. His brain was all in a muddle. He'd raced here from Egypt like a madman, snatching sleep here and there, living on biscuits and tea.

Dainty footsteps tripped down the hall, then turned to pounding, as his mother ran to embrace him. "Henry, darling, you are home at last!" She kissed him on both cheeks. "You look a fright, child. Have you been sleeping in your clothes? Oh, never mind. Come say hello to your father. He has been waiting to give you a good scolding."

"Mother, what are you doing here? Father never travels anymore."

"We came for Christmas, dear. You know the family likes to be together for the holidays, and we couldn't have the ladies traveling all the way to Italy in their delicate condition."

"What?"

"Don't say, 'what,' Henry. It's vulgar. 'Pardon,' or 'excuse me,' are much more genteel."

"Mother, what are you talking about?"

"Emma, dear, and your Elle."

His sleep-deprived brain took a moment to make the connections. "Bloody hell! Do you mean she's pregnant?"

"Really, Henry! Such language! How did you ever find yourself a woman talking like that?"

"But is she, Mother?"

"Yes, dear. I don't know why you seem so surprised about it." Her brow knitted as she frowned. "You do know how these things happen, don't you?"

His face flamed. "Yes! Of course!"

"Well, regardless, she seems willing to tromp all over, running around on that ridiculous bicycle of yours, scandalizing the whole town. Quite the headstrong girl. Your father adores her."

"Henry, dearest, you are home!" Emma raced to join them, hugging him over her rounded belly.

"Hello, Emma. Congratulations to you and Reggie."

She patted her belly. "Thank you. You and Elle were most helpful. All those times you entertained the children onboard the ship—I'm certain that contributed."

He grimaced. "I didn't need to know that."

"Oh, don't be a prude. I wasn't the one going about conceiving children in lifeboats."

"Emma!"

She frowned at him. "You do know how these things happen, don't you?"

"Yes! For God's sake!"

"Pardon the interruption," Carter said, "but a bicycle just passed by on the way to the carriage house."

Henry was out the door like lightning, racing to the back of the house just in time to see Elle hop dexterously from his bicycle. Light spilled from a potion-fueled lamp, falling in a pool at her feet, casting the rest of the world into dark shadows. His eyes locked on her. Her black dress was stretched tight over her growing curves, her cheeks were rosy, her eyes shining. He had never seen anything so beautiful in the whole of his life.

She slid the bicycle through the open door, and Henry slipped across the garden while her back was turned. He crept up behind her, his arm stealing about her, his hand settling on her belly.

"Henry," she breathed. The bicycle clattered against the wall.

He planted a kiss just beneath her ear. "*Mon amour.*"

"Oh, Henry."

She spun in his arms, her lips seeking his. He kissed her like the starving man he was, drowning in the sweet taste of her mouth, crushing her body against his. His fingers tangled in her hair, his tongue swept across hers. His cock was so hard it hurt. He needed more of her. All of her. The relief would be temporary. He could never get enough.

He pulled back just enough to gaze into her eyes. They

sparkled with desire as she smiled up at him. She brushed a finger over the hair on his upper lip.

"Your moustache tickles."

"Yes, but it's quite dashing, don't you think?"

She shook her head. "It's horrid."

He sighed. "I shall tire of it soon enough. It requires an unpleasant amount of trimming."

"Do as you like. I shall love you regardless."

He cradled her against him, his hands rubbing slow strokes down her back. "I'm sorry to have been away so long."

"It wasn't your fault a war broke out."

"Fortunately, I had only peripheral involvement in that. My months were chiefly comprised of working my way into the mercenary camp controlling the serum source to prove their connection to the Imperial Potions Company."

"And did you?"

"Of course. And we apprehended the lot of them without bloodshed."

"How did you achieve that?"

"I poisoned the coffee with salinide. No one suspected a thing, because I never touched the stuff. While they were clutching their bellies in agony, our friend Durere swept in with his band of locals and trussed them all up like pigs destined for slaughter."

Her laugh tinkled in the night air. "Brilliant. And the source? Did you see it?"

"It's enormous. I mapped the entire thing. There is a small spot where the serum literally wells up out of the ground. That's what the locals use. But there is a much larger area extending out into the desert. Your extraction techniques will be necessary to take full advantage."

"Remarkable!"

"And I may just possibly have passed on your ideas to Lady Tabiry, while neglecting to inform certain exploitative colleagues. Her people deserve to be paid for their serum. She is confident she can develop a sand extraction method. I will take you to visit her and the source next time they send me to Egypt."

Her eyes lit up. "You will?"

"I'm now the world's foremost cartographer of serum sources, and I can't make a truly accurate map without my potions expert."

One hand dropped to her belly. "We will have to take our children."

"Naturally. It will be very educational. I anticipate future trips to Egypt, India, and a large source rumored to be in the Caribbean. For now, however, I have an assignment closer to home."

"Oh?"

"I'm tasked with mapping every single serum source in Britain."

Elle's eyes grew wide. "That will take years! It could take your entire life!"

He grinned at her. "That's the idea. Whatever other jobs I'm offered, if we don't like them, I can turn them down, knowing I have work at home to complete. I will begin right here in London."

"There are two nice sources in Hyde Park I can show you. Oh, but Henry, are you certain this won't bore you to tears?"

"There are already multiple cantankerous dukes refusing to let anyone even think of looking for serum on their land. I will have plenty of midnight sneaking and other illegal doings to keep me occupied."

Her arms tightened around his neck. "It's perfect."

He nudged her toward the house. "You're shivering. Let's go inside so I can warm you up."

Her hot breath grazed his cheek. "It would be my pleasure."

Henry trembled.

"I have some gifts for you," he said, as they slipped through the back door. "Several potions and recipes from our young friend Nenet. Also, I met a friendly young officer with a rather salacious book in his possession."

"Did you steal it?" she asked eagerly.

"No. I bought it. I suggest we go up to our room and begin acting it out, page-by-page." He paused, frowning. "Or have they put you up in some other location?"

"No, your room is my room."

"Huh. Well, expect my family to bar us from leaving the neighborhood until we are well and truly married."

She looked thoughtful. "You don't sound as though you want to marry me, yet you are wearing my ring."

"I should love to marry you, but in my own time under my own terms. I don't wish to be bullied into it. Mother doesn't like quarreling over the holidays, so we may be left in peace for a time, but it will spur them to plot our wedding, no doubt."

"Let them plot. As far as I'm concerned we are as good as married already. When the time comes, if you don't approve of their arrangements, we will sneak away the night before. The city is full of hiding places we can use while we search for our own house with a pianoforte and a library."

"You can't be serious."

"About the house?"

"About sneaking away."

"Why not? You and I are so good at sneaking together."

A smile touched his lips. Running away together in order to *not* get married? It was absurd and brilliant. His family would never let him hear the end of it. The thrill of sharing such an adventure with her would be worth anything they could throw at him.

"That we are," he agreed. "Let's do it."

The End

About the Author

CATHERINE STEIN started reading at age two, when her mother noticed that she could tell the difference between words that started with the same letter. Ever since, she has wandered around with a book in her hand, her backpack, her purse, or even tucked down the back of her pants. A few years after she began to read, she also began to write, spending the majority of her school career writing non-school-related stories in her notebooks. Now she writes sassy, sexy stories set during the Victorian and Edwardian eras and full of action, adventure, magic, and fantastic technologies.

Catherine lives in Michigan with her husband and three rambunctious girls. She can often be found dressed in clothing that was purchased at a Renaissance Festival, drinking copious amounts of tea.

Visit Catherine online at
www.catsteinbooks.com
and join her VIP mailing list.

Follow her on Twitter @catsteinbooks,
or like her page on Facebook @catsteinbooks.